degradation

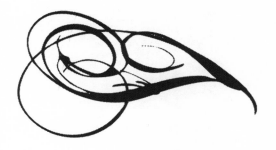

STYLO FANTÔME

Degradation
Published by BattleAxe Productions
Copyright © 2014
Stylo Fantôme

Cover Design:
Najla Qamber Designs
http://najlaqamberdesigns.com/
Copyright © 2014

Formating: Champagne Formats

ISBN-13: 978-1500605278
ISBN-10: 1500605271

Dedication

To The Book Blogs

I also want to dedicate this to the AMAZING people I have met. I thought when I sent out my ARCs, I might make a fan or two, or a connection here and there – I never counted on meeting a bunch of new friends. So even though I didn't know you when I wrote it, this book goes out to my friends/street team:

Rebeka – no one is a better HBIC. I would sincerely be lost without you.

Jolene – my sister from another mister

Ange, Beatriz, Betsy, Letty, ALL the girls at Cover To Cover – I have never laughed so much in my life. You guys are awesome, and everyone should be lucky enough to know people like you ladies.

Caryn – A new author, a new blogger, I think we have been a good team.

Shannon – thanks for sticking around for this crazy ride!

And I would like to particularly dedicate this book to a special kind of friend – Sue M.

You have a gift for pointing out simple things that always manage to escape my notice, but really make a huge difference to the story. This story is all it is directly because your help. A small part of Jameson Kane will always be yours.

Thank you so much, I couldn't have done this without you.

Seven Years Ago

SHE HAD COME OVER TO their apartment just to drop off some boxes of stuff for her sister, Eloise — *Ellie*. Tatum had just turned eighteen and was moving to her own apartment in downtown Boston. She had been in a dorm room for her first semester at Harvard, but her parents didn't "*approve*" of her roommate, so her father had rented her an apartment off campus. When Tate's father said jump, all she was ever allowed to say was "*how high?*", so, she was moving.

Her sister Ellie was four years older, and they had never gotten along very well. About two years ago, Ellie had started dating Jameson Kane – *Kane*, as just about everyone called him. The relationship was strange to Tate; Ellie and Jameson seemed more like acquaintances than people who slept with each other, but who was she to judge? She didn't even really like her own boyfriend.

Tate didn't really know what to make of Jameson. He was so good looking, it was probably illegal. She worried if she looked at him too long, she'd go blind. He was also *very* smart – he had graduated early from Yale with an MBA, and was taking some time off to review his job prospects. He came from old money, his father was some sort of big wig on Wall Street, and the talk was that Jameson would follow in his footsteps.

In the two years he had been dating her sister, Jameson hadn't seemed to take much notice of Tate. He ignored her, treated her with indifference. When he had to deal with her, it was almost like an after thought, like he had forgotten she existed. He was tall, and handsome, and experienced, and smart. Tate was a brainy, naive, clueless girl, fresh out of high school, no real experience with the world or worldly people. He intimidated her.

It felt weird, showing up at Ellie's apartment without her being there. Jameson had let Tate in, then pretty much ignored her. *Such a gentleman.* Tate had to haul several heavy boxes from the parking lot to the building, then down a long hall to their apartment, all by herself. When she got to the last box, she dropped it by their bed, huffing and puffing.

"Did you want me to help?" Jameson asked, appearing in the doorway. Tate whirled around, startled.

"No, that was the last box," she replied, straightening out her cardigan. He always made her feel nervous. His eyes wandered over her face.

"You look really red. Want something to drink?" he asked. She felt herself turn even redder than she apparently already was; she was never prepared for his blunt manners.

"If you have any tea, that would be great," she replied, then followed him to the kitchen. She thought he was going to pour it for her, but he just gestured to the fridge.

"I don't know what Ellie has in there, lots of health food shit. Dig around," he offered. She made a face at his back.

"Water is fine," she told him, then just filled a glass from the tap.

"So. New apartment, all alone in a big city. You ready?" he asked. She nodded and turned to face him. His piercing blue eyes were wandering over her face and she resisted the urge to wipe at her skin.

Was she dribbling water down her chin?

"As I'll ever be, I guess. I'm pretty self-reliant, so I think I'm ready," she replied, taking delicate sips of her drink. He chuckled.

"C'mon, you look like you're dying. Let's sit down, you can chug it," he offered, leading her to a table. He even shocked her by pulling out a chair for her.

"Thanks," Tate said, before following his instructions and downing the water in a few gulps. Without asking, he pulled the glass from her hands and refilled it before sitting down across from her.

"Don't you have like a boyfriend, or something? Is he in Boston?" Jameson asked, sliding her glass back across the table. She shook her head.

"No, Drew stayed in state," she replied.

"You guys have been going out for a while – how is it, being in a long distance relationship?" he asked. She was surprised at the question. Jameson never cared about anything she did.

"We've been together three years, but I don't know how long it's gonna last. He didn't want me to go to Harvard, wanted me to just follow him to Penn State. We argued about it a lot. He wants to try to work it out, but I think it's just time to get over it. Move on. We're in college now, I don't have time for that kind of crap," she let it all spill out. Jameson raised an eyebrow.

"Wow, very mature approach. How old are you again?" he asked. Tate rolled her eyes.

"You've known me for two years, Jameson, and you can't even remember my age?" she responded with a question. He shrugged.

"I don't think I even know Ellie's age. How old?" he pressed.

"I just turned eighteen, two weeks ago. How could you not know Ellie's age? You've been together for so long," Tate pointed out. He shrugged again.

"I don't pay attention to things like that. So what are you going to school for?" he asked. Tate had to stop herself from pointing out, *again*, that he should already know these things – it had been discussed, many times, in front of him. She had never realized it before, but he was kind of self centered. Arrogant.

"Political science," she said.

"We'll see how long that lasts. Go into economics, more money," he told her. She narrowed her eyes.

"I'm not doing it for money," she replied.

"Then you're stupid."

"You're kind of a dick," she blurted out, shocking herself. She wasn't prone to foul language most of the time, or being rude. She had just done both. He didn't seem bothered, though; he burst out laughing.

"You're just now realizing that?"

Tate smiled. He had a nice laugh, and a sexy smile. She could feel herself blushing. She could remember the first time Ellie had brought him home. Tate had developed a crush on him the instant she'd seen him – tall, dark hair, bright blue eyes, killer smile; what girl wouldn't fall head over heels in love with him at first sight? But it had never gone beyond that, she knew Jameson was so far out of her league, she wasn't even visible to him. She didn't waste too much time fantasizing about him.

But now, sitting across the table from him, she felt herself getting hot under her sweater.

"Well, yeah, you never talk to me," she pointed out.

"I talk to you."

"When?"

"Excuse me?"

"When do you talk to me? When was the last time you talked to me?" Tate asked. He thought for a second, looking up at the ceiling.

"I asked if you were okay, after your dog died," he replied, smiling at her.

"That was *last year*," she told him. Jameson started laughing again.

"Hey, at least I remembered," he pointed out. She found herself laughing as well.

"I guess that's something. Doesn't matter anyway, I'll be gone – no more awkward, silent family dinners to go to, thank god. You and Ellie will be on your own," she warned him.

"Well, you'll have to come back sometimes."

"No," she shook her head, "I won't. I've decided, I'm not coming back till I'm done with school, if then. I'm trying to get through a masters program in four years, or less."

"Wow. Hell of a challenge, baby girl. You think you're up for that?" he asked. She shivered at his use of "*baby girl*", he had never called her that before – never called her *anything*. She cleared her throat.

"I think I'm up for anything I set my mind to," she responded. He smiled.

"Good answer. Would you like a drink? Ellie should be home any minute, we could crack something open and have it ready for her," he suddenly asked, getting out of his chair. Tate held up her glass.

"I have water right here," she pointed out. He laughed as he pulled a bottle out of a cupboard.

"I meant a *real* drink, Tate. Seeing as how I've apparently '*never*' talked to you, I guess now is a good time to give you some congratulations. I'm assuming I never did that, right?" he asked, holding a bottle of champagne in his hand. She laughed.

"No, you weren't even at my graduation. And maybe just one glass," she replied, pushing the water she'd been drinking out of the way.

Having been too busy with school and all her extra classes, Tate had never been a party girl. No crazy parties and almost no experience with alcohol. Some champagne at Christmas with Granny

O'Shea at the O'Shea farm in the Hamptons was about it. But she didn't want Jameson to know that – she wanted to seem mature, like a girl who had champagne all the time. It was silly, but she couldn't help it.

They polished off the first bottle, discussing politics and the current economic situation in the country. He disagreed vehemently with most of her views, but he never got heated or upset. He managed to get under her skin, though, and she found herself arguing just to get a rise out of him, but he was impossible to rile up. The champagne loosened her up a little, and she was a lot bolder with her opinions; or at least, more so than usual.

"No more after this, baby girl needs to be presentable for her family tomorrow," Jameson said, taking out a second bottle. She made a face at him.

They drank and chatted some more. Ellie texted him that she would be late. She was a paralegal, and her hours were all over the place. Tate was fine with that, she never felt comfortable around her sister. Ellie was tall and beautiful, with dark blonde hair that was *always* done up in *just* the perfect style. She was *always* wearing *the most* stylish clothing.

Tate was average height, with dark hair, almost black, and she had never paid attention to what was stylish, just wore what her mother bought for her. She was intimidated by Ellie, plain and simple. That's why she was going into an accelerated program at Harvard – to beat Ellie. Ellie was the golden child, the favorite child. Tate had always had to work ten times harder, just to always fall slightly behind.

She wound up blabbering all that to Jameson. Then went onto tell him all about her boyfriend Drew, whom he couldn't remember ever having met, even though he had – *several times*. How boring Drew was, how he always wanted to tell her what to do, but he never wanted to do *anything*. Jameson nodded and listened to her prattle, sliding the champagne out of her reach.

"You're pretty funny, Tate. I never knew," he chuckled. She rolled her eyes, shrugging out of her cardigan.

"*Shocking.* No one ever notices me, not when Ellie's around," she snorted, pulling her hair into a ponytail. He raised an eyebrow.

"I wouldn't say that, Ellie's not as great as you make her out to be," he told her.

"*Pffft.* She looks like what would happen if Cindy Crawford and Christy Turlington had a baby," Tate pointed out.

"You're pretty, too."

"You have to say that, you're her boyfriend. You have to be nice to me."

"No I don't. I'm hardly ever nice, and I almost never lie. You're an attractive girl, you just have bad self esteem, and worse taste in men," he informed her. She shrugged.

"Maybe, but that doesn't change the fact that Ellie is still better in most peoples eyes," she replied, fiddling with the stem of her champagne glass. Jameson leaned back in his chair, folding his arms across his chest.

"I wouldn't say that. From a technical stand point, if we're being completely honest, I would have to say that you're *much* sexier than your sister," he told her.

She didn't breathe for a moment. Did Jameson Kane really just say that to her? Or was it the champagne? She glanced at him, and he was staring right back at her, a small smile playing on his lips. She shook her head and shook off her nerves. No. He was just being nice. That had to be it – what kind of a guy would tell his *girlfriend's sister* that she was the sexier of the two? Not a very good guy, that's for sure.

"Whatever. It'll all be behind me in a couple weeks. It'll be like a new Tate, that's what I'm going for; Ellie can suck it," Tate proclaimed, then abruptly hiccuped. Jameson burst out laughing.

"See, now *that's* funny. Your sister sucking something – would never happen," he joked. Tate could feel her cheeks turning bright red.

"Gross," she blurted out.

"Too much? I guess we're not that good of buddies yet," he sighed.

"You shouldn't talk that way about your girlfriend, it's not very nice," Tate told him. He shrugged.

"Sometimes she's not a very nice girlfriend," he replied. Tate's eyes got wide as she had a realization.

"Are you going to dump my sister?"

"Now, why would you ask that?" Jameson responded, his smile gone as his eyes stared into her own.

"I don't know. Your voice, your attitude. Are you?" she pressed. He sighed, rubbing a hand over his face.

"I shouldn't have given you champagne. I didn't know you'd turn into Nancy Drew," he commented.

"Oh my god. You're gonna dump Ellie. You've been together for two years. She thinks you're gonna propose. She's gonna die," Tate gushed, pressing a hand to her chest. His eyes narrowed.

"We haven't even talked about marriage, why would she think that? And I don't know what's going to happen with Ellie and I, we've got a lot to talk about; *do not* talk to her about this," Jameson commanded, pointing a finger at Tate. She raised her hands.

"I go out of my way to not talk to her, I won't breathe a word. But can I ask why?" she pressed, reaching out for the champagne. Jameson didn't even notice, he was so lost in thought, so she poured herself another glass.

"I don't know. It's … boring. Not exciting. Like you were saying about Drew. She wants this pre-programmed life, has everything decided for us. She knows what she's having for dinner next Tuesday, where we're going for the fourth of July, what we'll name our first child. She goes to bed at ten, gets up at six – I'm not allowed to touch her between those hours, I'm not even joking. I don't like being told what to do," his voice got quiet towards the end. Tate nodded, taking a large swig of her champagne.

"Sounds like Ellie. Did you know, one time when she was mad at me, to get back at me, she got into my room and organized my closet? That was her idea of revenge," she told him.

He burst out laughing, and that set Tate off. They both bent over, unable to breathe for how much they were laughing. It was hilarious, and it was totally true. Ellie was like OCD Barbie. Very pretty, and a little crazy.

"Oh my god, that sounds like her," he chuckled. Tate nodded.

"I know! I've got a hundred more, she —," Tate started, but she was gesturing with her glass, and champagne sloshed all over her front.

"Oh god, I knew this was going to happen," Jameson shook his head, but he was laughing. Tate snorted, holding her wet shirt away from her chest.

"Then you shouldn't have given it to me," she replied. He stood up.

"I tried to take it away. C'mon, I'm sure Ellie has something you can wear," he said, gesturing for her to follow him. She got out of her chair.

"Oh no, she'll kill me, I'm not allowed to wear her stuff," Tate told him, following him across the living room and back into the bedroom.

"Who cares? She owns so much shit, she'll never know. Just grab something, her stuff is in there," he explained, pointing to a section of the wardrobe before walking back out of the room.

Tate stared into the wardrobe for a while, letting her eyes wander over the clothes. Everything Ellie owned was expensive; from a designer. From a young age, Tate had been taught not to touch.

Jameson had just given her free reign. She snorted and dove in, yanking back the hangers. She laughed and pulled down a silk blouse – it looked *ridiculously* expensive.

Perfect.

She spun around and threw the shirt on the bed, stumbling as she did so. She didn't think she was drunk, but she was feeling a little light. *Spinny*. She laughed to herself, curling her fingers around the hem of her shirt and pulling the wet material up. She went to yank it over her head, but something happened. The shirt's tag got caught in a string of pearls she was wearing, which then got tangled in her hair, and she was stuck with her arms in the air, struggling to pull the shirt one way or the other.

"*Oh my god*," Tate laughed at herself, stepping back and forth.

She lost her footing and stumbled clear across the room. She rammed into something, a dresser, and moved so her butt was against it. She was really laughing now, struggling not to hyperventilate with the shirt covering her mouth. Her elbows were pinned above her head and she tried to reach the base of her neck with her fingers, arching her back. Her fingernails were just brushing the top of her spine when she heard something.

"What are you doing?"

She went stock still, her laughter dying. Jameson was in the room, and pretty close to her, judging by the sound of his voice. With her shirt up over her head, she was standing there in just her bra and khaki skirt.

Oh my god, oh my god, oh my god.

"Um, I got stuck," Tate offered in a small voice. He chuckled, and he was even closer than before – right in front of her.

"Obviously. Help?" he asked. She managed to shake her head.

"No, I think I —," she started, but then felt his fingers at the neck of the shirt. He pushed it up, exposing her mouth and nose, but then left it there. She took deep breaths.

"Are you drunk, Tate?" he asked, talking slowly. She shook her head again.

"No. I mean, I don't think so. I'm just stuck," she replied. He gave a small chuckle and she felt him pulling at the neck of the shirt again. A couple tugs, and the strand of pearls broke. She could feel them running down her body, some catching in her bra while the rest clattered to the floor. The shirt came free from her head and Jameson pulled it away, holding it in his right hand. He was staring down at her. She struggled to control her breathing.

"You're very different from Ellie," he told her in a quiet voice. She rubbed her lips together and nodded.

"I know," she replied.

Tate knew she should move, should grab her shirt, do something to cover herself. Run for the bathroom. She should not be standing in front of her sister's boyfriend, only wearing a black lace bra. He dropped her shirt as his eyes wandered down her body, and she found that she was frozen to the spot, unable to move a single muscle.

"Family heirloom?" he asked, then he reached out, tracing a finger down her chest. He ran it down her cleavage and she thought she might faint. But then he held his hand up, and he had a pearl pinched between his fingers.

"Present. From Drew," her voice was just above a whisper. He examined the pearl.

"He's cheap. It's not real," he commented. She almost laughed.

"What?"

Jameson let the pearl drop and his attention went back to her. Tate still couldn't move. Had even stopped breathing. He was looking at her like she was dinner. She couldn't believe it. Twenty-three year old Jameson Kane was looking at her, *really seeing her*, for the first time ever. It was wrong, so wrong. She tried to think of Ellie, but couldn't make herself. She could only see his eyes.

"You should leave this room," Jameson told her, his hands gliding onto her hips. Her skin jumped at his touch and she could feel an electrical current pass between them. She gave a full body shiver and nodded.

"I know," she breathed. His fingers spread as his hands moved to her back, up to her shoulder blades.

"Ellie's my girlfriend," he reminded her. As if she needed it.

"I know." Apparently her impressive vocabulary had deserted her. His hands slid back down, all the way to her butt. She put her hands on the dresser behind her, bracing herself.

"This isn't just me."

He'd said it as a statement, but she knew it was a question. She was feeling it, too.

"*I know*," she whispered.

"If you want to run, I suggest you do it now," he told her.

"Why?" she asked, and he leaned in close.

"*Because I eat girls like you for breakfast*," he hissed in her ear. She shivered again.

"Then stop holding onto me," she challenged, shocking herself.

Maybe it was the champagne, maybe it was him – Tate wasn't *ever* that bold, not in real life. Maybe that was it, she felt like she was in a dream. Jameson Kane, looking at *her*, not Ellie. Touching *her*, not Ellie. It couldn't be real. He was too … much. Everything. Too much for her. He couldn't want her, not in real life.

"Baby girl, this is nothing. If I didn't want you to get away, you wouldn't be able to," he chuckled. She took a deep breath, preparing to tell him off, to tell him to let her go.

"*Maybe I don't want to get away*," she whispered.

She hadn't meant to say that, hadn't even thought it. But it was out there, she coudn't take it back. Jameson groaned and his mouth dipped to her neck. She gasped when his lips touched her skin, and then moaned when his lips were followed by his teeth. She closed her eyes and let her head drop back.

This is wrong. WRONG. He belongs to your sister. You're the devil. Evil incarnate.

"Tatum, if you don't get the fuck out of here, I'm going to rip your clothes off, bend you over this dresser, and fuck you like you've never been fucked before," he growled at her, his voice angry and sharp. His words shocked her. She pushed him away.

"You act like this is my fault!" she snapped at him. His eyebrows went up, but he kept his hands on her hips.

"You're the one who was getting drunk in my kitchen, babbling on and on about hating her sister. You're the one who's half naked in my bedroom," he pointed out. She gasped.

"I never said I hated her! And *you* got *me* drunk! What does that say about you!?" she yelled. He laughed.

"I don't need to get girls drunk to fuck them, Tate," he told her, his voice low. She snorted.

"You are such an egotist, I wasn't going to … do … *that* with you," she replied, stuttering a little. Jameson threw his head back and laughed, taking a few steps away from her.

"'*That*'? God, I forget, you *are* just a little girl," he laughed at her. Flames raced across her face.

"And you're just a pathetic excuse for a man, trolling his girlfriend's *little sister*, cause he can't get anyone else to *fuck* him!" she yelled, shoving him in the chest before storming out of the room.

God, she was *so embarrassed*. What had she been thinking!? She had been playing with fire. Really, Tate was lucky. If he hadn't growled at her, she didn't know how far she would have let him go. Drew had never spoken to her, or touched her, the way Jameson had – it set her on fire. But the *things* he had said to her. She did feel like a little girl. She felt stupid. She swiped at the tears that were starting to fall down her cheeks. She grabbed her cardigan out of the kitchen and rushed back towards the front door. Jameson was strolling out of the bedroom.

"I wasn't trolling for you. I didn't even know you were coming over tonight. Like I said, you were the one bitching about how no one likes you, how everyone likes Ellie, asking about our relationship. Sounds like *you* were trolling for *me*," he commented, looking down at her. She sniffled, struggling to right the sleeves on her sweater.

"Then you're an awfully easy mark, I almost had you. Geez, what a great story that would've been to tell Ellie when she came home, *'hey, tricked your boyfriend into having sex with me – BTW, he's going to dump you.'* Sounds awesome, maybe I'll just call her and say it right now," Tate threatened. His eyes narrowed.

"Don't play with me, baby girl," he warned her. She glared right back at him.

"You're the one playing games, and you lost. *Move*," she ordered, waving her hand at him. He was blocking the door. He folded his arm across his chest and stood his ground.

"I don't lose," he replied. She rolled her eyes.

"God! Whatever! You tried to seduce me, it didn't work, get over yourself! I just want to —,"

She was shocked when he suddenly grabbed her by the back of the neck, yanking her forward so he could slam his mouth down onto hers. She gave a muffled shriek, pushing against his chest. He moved both of his hands to the back of her head, his tongue forcing its way into her mouth as he started walking them backwards.

She struggled at first, but it was half hearted at best. Tate knew he was an asshole. She knew it was just a game to him. Just sex. She knew she was doing something very wrong with her sister's boyfriend. She was doing something very wrong with a guy who was not her *own* boyfriend. She was going to burn in a special place in hell.

And she didn't care.

Tatum O'Shea was a good girl. She did the right things. Not because she wanted to, but because people were always telling her she had to, that she must. She dated Drew because her parents had set them up. She started having sex with Drew because he told her that's what couples do. She was going to an Ivy League school, because that's what O'Sheas did. They did not engage in illicit affairs with their relatives' significant others.

She still didn't care.

She moaned into his mouth, running her hands under his shirt, pushing it up. He broke away from her long enough for it to go over his head, then his mouth was back on her own. He was demanding, almost punishing, with his kiss. Rough and aggressive. Drew had never been that way with her.

She loved it.

"Doesn't feel like I'm losing now," Jameson growled against her mouth, his teeth biting into her bottom lip as they backed into the couch.

"Shut up, or I'll still leave," she threatened, then gasped when his hands covered her breasts. He chuckled.

"I don't think so," he replied, one of his hands sliding down her stomach and over skirt. His fingertips brushed against her thigh.

"I can do whatever I —," she ended in a gasp as his hand suddenly yanked her skirt up, diving into her underwear.

"You'll _do_ whatever _I say_," he amended her statement. Her eyes squeezed shut and she pressed her lips together, nodding.

"Yes, yes," she finally breathed, standing on her toes.

"You wanted this – from the moment you got here tonight, you wanted this," he said, his fingers plucking and playing with her like she was an instrument.

"No, I didn't. I didn't want this," Tate managed to pant, one of her hands moving to grab onto his wrist. Not to stop him, but to ground herself. To _feel_ him. He chuckled.

"You're awfully wet for someone who doesn't want to do this," he laughed at her.

"Oh god."

It was the truth, she knew. She was always like that around him, for as long as she could remember. She had touched herself to many fantasies about him. With Drew, it took a lot of foreplay to get her in the mood. But sometimes just thinking about Jameson was enough that she would have to change her panties.

"Turn around," he ordered, but he didn't even give her a chance to comply. He pulled his hands away and grabbed her by the arm, spinning her in a circle. She was still getting her bearings when he started yanking her skirt up over her hips.

"Are we really doing this?" she gasped, gripping onto the back of the couch.

"Unless you walk away right now, *yes*," he replied, yanking her underwear down her legs.

She didn't move.

He put a hand in the middle of her back and shoved her forward, forcing her to bend in half over the couch. She put her hands into the cushions, trying to gain a sense of balance. She felt his hands kneading the flesh on her butt, then he was shoving one, two fingers inside of her. She cried out.

"Oh my god!"

But before she could even adjust to that, she could feel his erection. She didn't even make a sound, just held her breath. He was *huge*, or at least a lot bigger than Drew. She bent completely in half, her face in the couch cushions, her ass in the air. It felt like everything was moving in slow motion, and when he was inside of her, pressed up against her, she sucked in a gasp of air, her whole body shaking. She had only ever had sex with Drew. Nobody else. Until now.

It occurred to her that she had been missing out.

"Goddamn, Tate," Jameson growled. "You're so fucking tight."

This was surreal. Having sex with Jameson. Jameson talking dirty to her. How had this happened?

Then he was pulling out of her. Then pounding into her. Pull. Pound. In. Out. She moaned, made noises in her throat, and managed to push herself upright. She couldn't even think straight. Everything felt so amazing. She'd never had sex like that before, with someone behind her. Drew was not adventurous. Only ever at night. Her laying down. Him on top. Lights always off.

All the lights were on in Jameson's trendy loft apartment. It wasn't daylight out, but all the shades were open. Anyone in the building across the way would be able to see her having sex. No wait, what had he said; what hadn't she been able to say earlier? *Fucking*. He was *fucking* her. She hadn't ever really been fucked before, but she could now see that there was a huge difference. This was much, *much* better. Jameson Kane could fuck her whenever he wanted, she thought to herself.

Oh my god, I am fucking my sister's boyfriend.

"This is wrong, Jameson. *So wrong*," she panted out. His hand suddenly came around her throat and pulled her towards him. She had to arch her back to meet him.

"Then tell me to stop," he dared her, pressing his face to the side of hers, his teeth bared against her skin. She shook her head.

"I can't, I can't," she cried out. He laughed and the hand on her throat went to her ponytail, pulling hard on it.

"You love this. You've probably fantasized about this. Did you ever? Ever touch yourself while you were thinking of me?" he asked, his fingers pulling at the roots of her hair. She shrieked.

"*God, yes!* Yes!" she answered. He laughed again and leaned away from her, but didn't relinquish his hold on her hair.

"Fuck, Tate, you are *so sexy*. You should see yourself," he groaned, his free hand running over her ass. "I knew I should've fucked you a long time ago."

She was shocked.

"You … wanted to do this … before?" she managed to get out

between thrusts.

"Are you fucking kidding? I don't know any guy who hasn't thought about trying to fuck his girlfriend's *hotter* sister, and baby girl, you are *definitely* a hotter fuck," Jameson informed her, pulling harder on her hair.

God, he's talking about fucking Ellie while he's fucking me. So wrong.

"Oh my god, we have to stop, this is wrong. You're Ellie's ... I'm her ... this is so wrong. *Oh my god!*" she cried out. He pulled out of her, and she moaned at the loss. But then he was spinning her around to face him, his fingers digging roughly into her arms.

"Don't fucking say her name again," he told her.

"But it's wrong, Ellie could be —,"

"If you say her name *one more time*, I'm warning you, I will *fuck your mouth*," he growled, and then he was kissing her again.

It was like getting slapped, when Jameson spoke to her that way. No one had *ever* spoken to Tate like that before – she couldn't believe it. She knew she should be offended. She *wanted* to be offended. But she wasn't. If anything, it made her hotter. Did he talk to Ellie that way? She couldn't imagine it. She moaned, wrapping her arms around his neck.

"I won't say it again," she whispered, kissing him back. They stumbled into the bedroom, lips attached, hands roaming everywhere. It hadn't escaped her attention that his kisses seemed just as desperate as hers, just as needy. As if he couldn't get enough of her taste. He wanted this just as much as she did – maybe even more.

"You're goddamn right you won't," he snapped, giving her a rough shove so that she fell onto the bed.

He was on top of her in an instant, his hands everywhere. He pulled the cups of her bra down and lavished attention on her breasts, teasing her nipples with his teeth. His hand was back between her legs, his fingers gliding through her wetness. She moaned and thrashed around beneath him, her fingernails raking across his shoulders, no thought about hurting him. He hissed and brought his mouth back to hers.

"*Jameson*," she breathed against his lips.

"What?" he snapped.

"Are we —," she started to ask, but then he was plunging inside of her. No hesitation, no accomodating her – just full, *hard,* length, driving as deep as he could go. She screamed his name, her legs moving to wrap around his waist.

"'*Are we*' what, Tate?" he asked, his voice breathless as he slammed his hips against hers.

"Are we going to do this again?" she managed to ask. He pulled himself up onto his knees and grabbed her by the hips, driving into her even harder. Her eyes rolled back in her head.

"You're going to let me do this *whenever I want,*" he informed her.

"*Yes, Jameson, yes, yes, yes,*" she chanted, scratching her nails down his arms. One of his hands came to rest flat against her chest, between her breasts, pushing her down against the bed. Anchoring her to his thrusts.

He's going to turn me inside out.

"You love this, *fucking me.* Your *sister's boyfriend. Winning,* right? Don't you think this kind of makes you a slut?" he asked, slowing his thrusts. She started panting again.

"Yes, I do," she answered, and the hand on her chest slowly slid upwards, creeping onto her neck.

"Tatum O'Shea. Perfect, princess, goody-two-shoes, Tate. Who would've thought, a *slut,*" he swore at her. She moaned, raking her hands across her own chest. His fingers gently wrapped around her throat.

This shouldn't be turning me on. Why is this turning me on!?

"Yes, for you, Jameson. Just for you," she moaned. His movements were so slow. He would almost pull all the way out of her, then he would plunge back inside, to the hilt, *so slow*. It made it hard to breathe.

"*Whenever I want,*" he repeated his earlier statement. She rubbed her lips together and nodded again.

"Of course," she sighed, and he let go of her throat.

It was almost like he was massaging her, on the inside. Only instead of relaxing her, it was causing her to tense up every muscle in her body. She was going to burst apart, completely explode, and no one would ever find Tatum again.

"Goddamn, you're so fucking sexy, Tate," Jameson groaned, dragging his fingers up the insides of her thighs. She took a deep breath.

"Are we together?" she blurted out.

He stopped moving.

Uh oh.

"What?" he asked, his voice like steel. She let her head roll to the side and she opened her eyes, staring at the wall across from her.

"You're dumping Ellie. Does this mean we'll be together?" she asked.

He barked out a cruel laugh and then he was slamming into her again. She cried out, her hands going to his chest, hooking her nails into his muscles. He leaned down close, forcing her legs as wide apart as they could go, his chest pressed against hers.

"I don't date *sluts*, Tatum," he told her.

"But I'm —,"

"*A good fuck*, yes. But Ellie *is* my girlfriend. I never said I was dumping her. And even if I did, I wouldn't date her sister. Wouldn't date some eighteen year old," Jameson laughed in her ear.

"We have to stop, we have to stop, we have to stop," she started moaning. Her brain was telling her one thing – *get out, now, you stupid bitch!* — but her body was going a completely different route

*– holy fuck, this is amazing, don't ever stop doing this, why didn't you do this sooner, if you stop him now, you will **never** feel this way again!*

"I don't think so," he whispered, then his hand was sliding between their bodies, his fingers pinching at the part of her that was aching the most.

She screamed. Her body felt like it was ripping up the middle. She had never had an orgasm like that before, not with Drew, not even with herself. She jerked forward off the bed and clamped her teeth onto his shoulder. He let out a roar and she could feel him coming as well. Every muscle he had tensed and pressed down onto her. Her orgasm intensified and she let out a sob. It took a moment for the tremors to subside, for both of their bodies to become still again.

"Holy shit," Tate breathed, collapsing back onto the bed.

"Fuck. *Fuck*," Jameson whispered, his breath hot against her skin as he rested his forehead on her chest.

They laid like that for a while, coming down from the high of good sex. Tate had never experienced it before – Drew wasn't good enough to induce it. Jameson had just blasted her into the stratosphere. She didn't think she'd ever come down. She took deep breaths, trying to find herself in space. She rested her hand against his back, feeling his steamy slick skin.

"Did you —," she started to ask in a thick voice, but he pulled away. He lurched off the bed, yanking his pants up as he went. She was a little shocked, and sat up, putting her bra to rights as she did so.

"Shut up. Don't say a fucking thing. Just get dressed," he ordered, picking up the silk blouse from the other side of the bed and throwing it at her. She caught it as it landed over her face.

"How can you –," she started when she was interrupted by a buzzing sound. They both froze for a second, then Jameson made his way into the living room. She heard him walk over to the door, assumed he was pressing the button for the intercom to the downstairs.

"What?" he asked, his voice rough and agitated sounding.

"I'm locked out down here, I forgot my keys. Buzz me in," Ellie's voice filled the apartment.

Tate dropped her face into her hands, the gravity of the situation falling down on her. She had just had sex with her sister's boyfriend. It was all fine and dandy to be caught up in the kink and sex of the moment – but the afterwards was *horrible*. She was a horrible person. Ellie was a mean sister, but Tatum was officially the worst.

"What are you doing? I suggest you get dressed," Jameson's voice floated to her. She lifted her head to watch him walk across the bedroom and into the bathroom.

"How can you be so calm!? After what we just did!?" she demanded. There was the sound of running water, then a toilet flushing, and then he reappeared, his pants done up.

"It's not a big deal unless you make it a big deal, Tate. Get dressed, or you're going to have a lot of explaining to do to your sister," he said, pulling a shirt out of his closet and yanking it on. Tate struggled to push herself to her feet and pushed her skirt back into place.

"I just had sex with you! *We* just had sex! We have to tell her!" she shouted at him.

Jameson finally looked at her, one eyebrow raised, and her breath caught in her throat. He was a massive asshole, but holy shit, he was good looking. And she now knew what he looked like while having sex. She would never be able to look at him the same way again. She swallowed and looked away.

"Alright. You want to start that conversation? Once I'm gone, it's over, I never have to see her again. But you, you're her sister. Much worse for you," he pointed out.

Tate struggled with her conscience, her bottom lip beginning to quiver. She was going to cry again. He was so cold. He had always been so cold, how could she have thought he'd be different? Sex didn't change things. But he was right. Telling Ellie would just upset the whole family, and he would escape unscathed. He had said he didn't want to date her, so it wasn't like she would gain anything by telling her sister.

"You're an absolutely horrible person," she hissed at him, blinking through her tears. He laughed, his voice loud in the large apartment.

"No shit, but you just fucked your sister's boyfriend, so what kind of a person does that make you? Now get your goddamn clothes on, and get out," he said, grabbing her by the arm and dragging her through the bedroom door.

They stopped just long enough for Tate to button up the silk shirt while he grabbed her cardigan off the floor. She refused to look at him while she tried to make herself look presentable, finger combing her hair as best she could, praying she looked semi-decent. Or at the very least not like someone who had just had a steamy affair with their sister's boyfriend.

Oh god.

"I'm going to forget tonight ever happened," she informed him as they strode towards the front door. Jameson laughed again.

"Baby girl, you couldn't forget if you tried," he told her in a low voice, pressing himself against her from behind. She shivered and had to force herself not to press back into him.

"You had better break up with her. If you stay with her, you're … you're *sick*," she informed him, her hand on the door knob. He shrugged, not moving his weight away from her. His body was so warm, like a furnace. She wanted to curl up in him.

"I can live with that. See you around, Tate," he said. She yanked open the door.

"No, you won't."

His laughter followed her into the hallway. It sounded demonic. Like Satan was laughing at her.

"I will if I want to."

She stomped down the hallway, tears streaming down her face. How could she have let that happen!? She *was* a goody-two-shoes. Tate never acted wild, never did anything bad, never did anything wrong. Sure, she had always secretly kind of wanted to – but maybe something more along the lines of sneaking her dad's brandy, or staying out past curfew. Not *fucking her sister's boyfriend*. That was a little beyond wild.

Speak of the devil – her sister was getting off the antiquated freight elevator at the end of the hall. Tate let out a deep breath, wiping at her face. She didn't know if she could handle this moment. Jameson had just ripped her in half. Ellie would mop the floor with her remains.

"Kane didn't tell me you were still here," Ellie clipped out in a brisk tone, striding down the hall in her expensive ballet flats.

I would never call him Kane, I hate that. He has a first name, I just screamed it about twenty times.

"I was just on my way out, I dropped off your stuff," Tate said, her voice low and her head ducked, hoping they could just pass each other. No such luck.

"Are you wearing my shirt!?" Ellie suddenly demanded, grabbing Tate by the arm.

"Yeah, uh, I spilled something on myself. Jameson told me to grab something, so I just grabbed something," Tate mumbled.

"Jesus, Tate, you're such a child. Kane doesn't know anything about clothing, do you have any idea how much this cost? Take it off, right now," Ellie demanded. Tate gasped.

Can this day get any worse?

"Ellie! I don't have anything else! You want me to drive home naked?" she asked. Ellie rolled her eyes.

"You're so over-dramatic. You have your sweater."

"It doesn't close! Ellie, c'mon, I can have your shirt sent back tomorrow. I'll even dry clean it," Tate offered.

"No. You'll ruin it. Take it off, *now*," Ellie ordered her.

Something snapped in Tate.

"*Fuck you*, Eloise. It's a *goddamn shirt*, and I'm going to wear this *goddamn shirt*, all the *goddamn way* home," she snarled, then stomped into the elevator.

She leaned against the wall as the old contraption clanked and rattled its way to the ground floor. She couldn't believe she had spoken like that to Ellie. She had never talked that way, *to anyone*. Jameson had loosened something in her, shaken her up. She now knew that he was Satan in a male model's body, but he had done something to her, there was no denying it.

She dragged her feet as she made her way outside. She didn't want to think of the repercussions of her actions. It was safe to assume that Ellie was already calling their father. That never ended well for Tate, under the best of circumstances, and *these* circumstances were complete shit.

Snow was coming down, adding to the layer that was already on the ground. She got to the back of her car, but then couldn't resist looking up. Jameson's apartment had huge floor-to-ceiling windows that faced out over the parking lot and street. Gorgeous on a sunny day.

She had a clear view of the inside of the loft. Ellie looked like she was throwing a temper tantrum, shaking her arms and head at a very still Jameson. He had his arms crossed, and almost looked bored. At first Tate couldn't figure it out – if Ellie was freaking out over the shirt, then she was totally overreacting. Usually, she was sugary-sweet to Jameson. *Fake*. But she looked like she was screaming. She was holding something in her hand, and it clicked into place in Tate's mind.

*She's shaking **my** panties in her boyfriend's face. Apparently, this night **can** get worse.*

Tate knew she should be scared. That she should feel bad, or guilty, or some kind of upset. But she didn't. Her sister was a bitch, and Tate just didn't care any more. About *anything*. She let out a shaky breath, and it was like she was breathing for the first time ever.

I really, truly, honestly, completely, just don't give a fuck.

Ellie's form turned to look out the window, and saw Tate standing down there. She fumbled with a latch, then a huge section of the window was swinging open. A black scrap of lace was thrown outside, and Tate watched her underwear float to the ground.

"You stupid whore! I'm telling Daddy! I'm telling him *everything!*" Ellie was shrieking, leaning halfway out the window.

Tate smiled.

"You know what, Ellie!?" she called back, her fingers working at the buttons on the front of the blouse. She slipped it off her shoulders. "*I don't give a shit!*" She let the shirt fall to the snow covered pavement, and then she stepped on it, grinding her heel into the fabric.

"*No!* You bitch! You stupid bitch!" Ellie screamed, then ran from the window. Tate could just picture her tearing down the hall. She laughed to herself.

"Good for you, baby girl!" Jameson laughed down at her.

Tate stared up at him, shivering as snow sprinkled down on her bare shoulders. She was standing in a parking lot, at eight o'clock at night, and it was freezing out, and she was only wearing her bra and a nerdy skirt. She had gone crazy.

And she absolutely loved it.

She raised her arm and gave Jameson the middle finger. He laughed again, then blew her a kiss before walking away from the window. Tate scowled and hustled into her car. As she pulled out of her spot, she saw Ellie running into the parking lot, waving her arms like a crazy person. She scooped up the shirt from the ground, screaming something at Tatum's car as it drove away.

I don't care. I don't think I ever did.

1

"ALRIGHT, WHO WANTS TO GET *fucked up tonight!?*"

Tate grabbed a guy by the back of the head and forced him to lean backwards over the bar. He smiled up at her and she winked at him, right before pouring straight tequila down his throat. She then clamped her hand over his mouth and shook his head back and forth. He stumbled when he stood up, but managed to turn around.

"That one's on me, honey," she said, her voice flirty while she spun the tequila bottle in her hand. He dug around in his pocket and pulled out some bills.

"You're the best bartender *ever!*" he shouted, slapping the money on the bar.

"That's what they all say!" she laughed, sweeping the money off the bar top. She eyeballed it quickly before shoving it into a jar behind her. Two twenties. Not a bad tip at all.

"You *are* the best, Tatey! We goin' out after this!?" her fellow bartender, and roommate, Rusty Dobber shouted at her. As loud as the music always was in their bar, a person had to shout to be heard at any given time.

"We'll see, Rus. I'm working on something," Tate replied, nodding her head. Rus glanced over her shoulder. A sexy guy sat at the end of the bar, eyeing Tatum up and down. Brad, one of Tate's regulars.

In more ways than one.

"Oh pooh, you're so boring!" Rusty laughed before dancing away, heading to a group of guys who were clamoring for a drink.

Tate loved being a bartender. She had never gone back to Harvard. After Eloise had tattle-taled on her, her "free ride" had been stopped. But Tate would have quit anyway. She knew that before she even got home that fateful night. She hated going to college. She had hated high school. She hated studying. Hated her pastel colored wardrobe. Her pastel colored *life*. She got home, packed her bags, and ran. Didn't stop till she got to Boston – a seven hour drive.

Once there, it wasn't long before she got the phone call from Daddy. Her parents were beyond strict. They had their daughters' lives all mapped out. Ellie was a paralegal, on her way to becoming a lawyer – someday a supreme court judge. Tatum was going to become a political adviser, and someday a senator, or a governor.

But Tate didn't want those things. She had loved to paint, but had never been allowed to. She loved to sing, and dance, and be silly. All against the rules in the O'Shea house. So was sleeping with a sister's boyfriend – even if said boyfriend didn't even like the sister. The Kane family was very wealthy, very well connected. The O'Sheas wanted that connection. In their minds, Tatum had ruined that, had ruined *everything*. Worst. Christmas. *Ever*.

She wasn't invited back for Easter.

Her apartment had been paid up till the summer, nothing Daddy could do about that, and Tate certainly wasn't lazy. Going against her own nature for years had been hard work. She went out and found a job. Found two jobs. Made friends. *Real* friends, for the first time ever. Had a social life. Dated. Screwed around. *Acted her age.*

She didn't talk to her family at all, but that was okay, because she didn't like them anymore than they liked her.

So now all these years later, life was better than ever – in her opinion. She realized that sure, maybe some of that was thanks to a certain blue eyed he-demon, but she didn't think about him too much. Jameson had awakened something in her, brought about her change, but *she* was responsible for her life. She had taken control. She had grown up. And he hadn't been there for that. He wasn't anything to her. Nothing at all. He didn't exist anymore.

And she was perfectly fine with that.

Tatum came to with a start the next morning, not quite sure where she was, at first. She squinted in the bright sunlight, held up a hand. There was an open window across from her. She moaned and almost pulled the covers up over her head, but a snort came from the pillow next to hers, and she stopped moving.

"Oh, jesus," she groaned, bringing a hand to her head. Brad was snoring next to her.

She kind of remembered now. She had gone to an after-hours club with Rus and Brad. More drinks had flowed between them. Shots were taken. Tate was a pretty solid party girl. Under normal circumstances, she could handle her liquor and controlled substances very well, but last night had gotten a little wild, even for her. She could sort of remember stumbling up to Brad's apartment. Doing something naughty in the hallway outside his door.

There was something about going down on a guy in public that just drove her wild.

But it hadn't gotten a whole lot better from there on – a couple drinks, and Brad was pretty much done for the night. He'd passed out on the bed, right in the middle of Tate's striptease. Not confidence inspiring. But since she was already half naked, she just crawled into the bed next to him and passed out, as well.

She was regretting that now. Brad tended to get clingy when she stayed the night. He wasn't her boyfriend. More of a stress reliever, really. She liked that, and wanted it to stay that way. But it had become more and more obvious that *he* didn't want it to stay that way.

Tate managed to slide out of the bed without waking him up. She tip toed around the room, collecting the clothing she'd tossed everywhere. She shimmied into her tight white t-shirt and then hopped around, struggling more with the tight leather leggings.

"Now that's a sight I could get used to," she heard Brad say from behind her. She glanced over her shoulder and laughed. She was bent over, struggling to get her foot through the pant leg. Her thong-clad ass was pointed straight at Brad.

"You could take a picture," she offered, then succeeded in getting her foot through. She got the other leg in no problem and yanked the leggings up over her hips.

"You'd really let me do that?" he asked. She shrugged, pulling on her boots.

"Maybe. Depends. Not with my face in the picture," she said, grabbing her jacket off a chair.

"Why are you always in such a rush? I could use some help here," he chuckled, gesturing to the tent that was happening in his sheets. Tate laughed out loud.

"Are you joking? You owe *me* one, after last night," she pointed out, searching around for her purse.

"What are you talking about? I thought we had a great time," he said. She gave him a Look.

"*You* had a great time, coming in my mouth after about two seconds, and then passing out. You have the the *worst* case of whiskey dick, of anyone I've ever met," she informed him, then spotted her purse, halfway under the bed. She crawled around, struggling to get to it.

"I could make up for it now," he offered, his hand stroking his erection. She snorted.

"No thanks, that train has left the station. See you around!" she sang, dashing out of the room.

She stood on the corner down the street, waiting for Rus to come pick her up. She sipped at a coffee she had bought, playing on her phone. After about fifteen minutes, a beat up looking VW Beetle pulled up to the curb. She slid into the passenger seat.

"So, was it amazing? Fireworks?" Rus asked. Tate chuckled, resting a booted foot against the dash.

"*Pshaw*, not hardly. I don't know why I keep trying with him. It used to be fun. Now it's just like … *eh*," she replied, pushing her aviators higher up on her nose.

"You say that about every guy you're with, you know. Even back when you used to date. Now you don't even do that – just screw 'em and lose 'em. What kind of man does it take to satisfy the insatiable Tatum O'Shea?" Rus asked.

"If I'm '*the insatiable Tatum O'Shea*', then by definition, I can't be satisfied," Tate joked.

"No, seriously. What would it take? Perfect man. What do you want?" Rus pressed.

"I don't want a boyfriend. I've tried that, don't like it, over it. I like playing around," Tate replied. Rus shrugged.

"Okay, so what would it take for a guy to be so good in bed, that you'd never want to leave it?" she changed the question.

Tate pressed her lips together and stared out the window, silent for a minute. It wasn't a line of questioning she liked too much. Made her think about the past, which she didn't like to do, *at all*.

"Someone a little domineering, someone who can handle my crazy, weird, personality. Someone who can make my eyes roll back in my head. Someone who can talk absolute *filth* to me, but still know where the line is, and even know when to step over it on occasion," Tate started. "Someone who … will just let me be *me*, and be cool with it. Let me come and go."

"Emphasis on the come?" Rus asked, and Tate burst out laughing.

"You have the maturity of a twelve year old. Let's get some tacos, I'm *starving*," she groaned.

They sat outside, on top of a picnic table. Tate threw excess lettuce to some birds while Rus chattered on about her own guy problems. She was always looking for Mr. Right, and her current boyfriend wasn't stacking up. She was explaining how Vinny wouldn't know his way around her body even if she printed him a map, when Tate's phone went off. She glanced at the screen and then groaned before answering it.

"Yeah?" she answered, her voice muffled by almost half a taco.

"Tate, sweetie, cover for me tonight? I'll make it up to you, I promise," a voice whined over the other end. Rachel. Another friend, who worked for a catering business. Tate temped with them on occasion, so Rachel would call her to cover every now and then.

"I don't know, I had kind of a late night last night," Tate grumbled.

"This'll be easy. Drinks and hors d'oeuvres at some swanky building downtown, seven to ten; get there at six, done by eleven. Please, please, *please*, I will owe you my life," Rachel begged. Tate rolled her eyes.

"Keep it, it's not worth anything anyway. I'll do it, I'll do it," she responded. She could always use more money.

"*Eeeeek!* You're the best, Tatey-Watey, the absolute best," Rachel gushed, then passed along the address and event info. Tate hung up the phone and sighed.

"Her voice is so hard to resist. Wha'd she rope you into, this time?" Rus asked, finishing off the last taco.

"Just some party, cocktails and stuff. Some new company that just opened downtown, kind of a welcome event thingy. Kraven and Dunn, brokerage firm or something. A bunch of suits, people that are rich out the ass," Tate explained.

"Oh, so your kind of people?"

"Shut up," Tate snapped, punching Rus in the arm when she started to laugh. "Not anymore. My mother would die if she saw the way I lived."

"We're not so bad," Rus piped up. Tate nodded.

"I know – it's more of a comment on them than us," she explained before jumping off the table. "Let's get out of here. I gotta go shower and find that uniform."

Tate showed up at the address at six o'clock sharp. The whole office building belonged to the firm, and the party was being held on the top floor. Ooohhh, big money. Could mean big tip. Or no tip. Rich people were funny that way, she had noticed.

She changed in a bathroom stall, then examined herself in a mirror. She hadn't really been sure how cleaned up she should get – when she catered, she always tried to score more low key events. She hoped her heavy eye makeup wasn't too much, she didn't want to go through the hassle of scrubbing it all off. She pulled her hair into a high ponytail and made her way into the kitchen.

All the servers were gathered together and walked through the event space, a large conference room that had been cleared of all its furniture and set up for the party with little tables everywhere. No guests were there yet, but some guys in suits were wandering around, looking things over. Tate sighed and picked at her nails, ignoring the run through; blah blah, serve the drinks, blah blah, don't talk to the guests, blah blah, drop a tray and instant death. It was always the same.

There wasn't a whole lot to do till guests got there, and Tate was a mover by nature. She didn't like standing around doing nothing. She began prepping drink trays, preloading some with champagne glasses that had been designed special for the occasion – there was supposed to be a toast at the end of the night, and all of the glasses had a large, cursive *K* etched into the glass. She set them up in the kitchen, then carried them to a table where the other trays were filled with food, ready to go. She was on her last tray when she turned around and rammed right into somebody.

"*What the shit!*" she exclaimed, dropping the tray and falling to her knees.

"Excuse me," a man's voice floated down to her. She grumbled and began grabbing at the broken glasses, slamming them onto the tray.

"Walk much!? Or is this your first time as a pedestrian?" she snapped. The guy squatted down next to her.

"Sorry, I didn't see you there," he repeated, though his voice sounded anything but sorry.

She flicked her eyes to his face, giving him her most severe glare before concentrating on the glass in front of her. She frowned. Light eyes. Dark hair. He had been staring at her. He was very good looking, and wearing an expensive looking suit. God, had she just told off one of the guests? What was a guest doing in the kitchen?

"Sorry, I shouldn't have snapped. You just startled me," Tate mumbled an apology. He laughed.

"That didn't exactly sound genuine," he chuckled.

"Just doing my job, sir," she managed a tight lipped response.

"You work here?"

"No, I just like to wear aprons and run around kitchens for fun," she said before she could stop herself. He laughed again.

"Ah, a caterer. C'mon, get up. Ignore those, I'll get someone to clean it up," he said, then grabbed her arm, forcing her to climb to her feet. She was a little shocked at the audacity of just grabbing her like that, but she didn't say anything. Couldn't. His fingers felt like they were burning holes through the oxford shirt she was wearing.

"But I can't just leave that, I —," she started, trying to bend back down. He kept his grip on her.

"Leave it," he ordered, and a shiver ran down her spine. She finally looked at him again.

"You can't just tell me to leave a mess there, and it's okay. Who are you?" she demanded. He smiled down at her, and something fluttered in her chest.

No. Not possible.

"See the *K* on those glasses?" he asked. She glanced down at the tray.

"Yeah?"

"That's me. I'm the Kraven in Kraven and Dunn," he explained. She managed a nod.

"Oh."

"You seem surprised."

"No. Just really wishing I hadn't yelled at you now," Tate replied. He laughed again, loudly. She frowned. Something wasn't right. Her universe felt like it was tilting to the left.

"It's fine. I wasn't paying attention, I shouldn't have just barged in here. I just thought … thought I saw something," he told her.

"I should probably get back to work," she said, staring into his eyes. His blue, blue eyes. He squeezed her elbow and then let it go. She took a couple steps away.

"You probably should. See you around," he said. She nodded and walked off.

See you around.

Tate stopped breathing. Almost stopped moving. She made it to the end of a short hall and then stepped to the side, pressing her back against a wall. She felt like she was going to hyperventilate. It was ridiculous. It couldn't be, that guy said his name was Kraven.

Not Kane.

She leaned to the side and peeked her head around the corner. He was still standing there, his hands in his pants pockets, looking down at the mess. She studied his profile. Dark hair. Strong features. Light eyes. Broad shouldered, and tall, probably like six-foot-two, or so. *Very* sexy. So good looking ... she felt like if she stared at him for too long, she'd go blind.

Oh my god.

She hurried off, pushing her way through the other waitstaff till she found one of the event coordinators. The poor girl looked like she was on the verge of a nervous break down, but Tate didn't care. She had to know something.

"Who is hosting this event?" she demanded.

"We went over this earlier, Kraven and Dunn," the girl responded.

"Yes, I know that – what are their names, Kraven and Dunn? Their full names?" Tate asked, struggling not to shake the girl.

"Never address the hosts by their first name, call them —,"

"Just tell me their goddamn names!" Tate snapped. The woman began flipping through pages on a clipboard.

"Wenseworth Dunn and ... hmmm, let me see," she kept flipping. It took *forever*. "Ah! Kraven. *Jameson* Kraven."

Jameson Kraven. Not Kane. Still, what are the chances!?

Tate didn't have time to ponder it – another coordinator rushed in and clapped them all to attention. They were handed trays and sent out into the fray. Tate balanced a platter of crab cakes on her palm and made her way into the crowd of suits and cocktail dresses.

She didn't want to see him, but her eyes kept searching for him. She hadn't thought about Jameson much during all the time that had passed since that crazy night; except for when she was alone in bed. Or the shower. Sometimes on the couch.

But other than that, he had been absent from her mind. He had scarred her to a certain extent. For a little while, right after, her silly heart had hoped and prayed he would get intouch with her. "*I will if I want to,*" he had said about seeing her. Very soon, it became apparent that he *didn't* want to – he never contacted her. Then her life had gotten so crazy, Tate hadn't had time to dwell on him, she was too concerned with figuring out where her next meal would come from, or how she was going to pay her rent, to care about Jameson Kane. He hadn't ever really been anything to her. Just a moment in time, that had happened to change her life forever.

She served crab cakes and shrimp balls, delivered drinks and took empty glasses. She smiled and flirted, encouraged everyone to drink more, and assured them that everything tasted *amazing*. She knew she didn't look as polished as most of the other waiters, but sometimes that worked to her advantage, especially with uptight suit types. They saw her nighttime makeup and mussy hair, and tended to think naughty thoughts. Naughty thoughts equalled bigger tips – and in this case, where the tips were pooled together, it meant more for everyone. So she worked it.

After the toast – which she made sure to miss – the place started to thin out. No one was eating anymore, and they were encouraged to not serve anymore alcohol. She had busied herself with clearing off tables, starting in the back corner, when she heard a noise behind her.

"It is you, right?" he asked. Tate sighed and stood upright.

"I was wondering that myself," she replied, slow to turn around. Jameson was smiling at her.

"God, you look so different, I didn't even recognize you at first. How long has it been? Six years?" he asked.

"More like seven. What's with the Kraven?" she asked, holding up a champagne glass with the etching facing him. He chuckled.

"Mother's maiden name – *Jameson Kraven Kane*. Has a nice ring," he explained.

"Makes sense."

"Are you a waitress?" he asked. Tate laughed.

"Like I said, I just wear aprons for fun," she responded. He made her uncomfortable. Tatum didn't get uncomfortable anymore, so it was a foreign feeling.

"Cute. So do you just work catering gigs?"

"Among other things."

"Like what?'

"I'm a bartender on the weekends. Temp a lot. Walk dogs. Taught yoga at a retirement home the other day. Do bicycle tours, walking tours, riverboat tours —," she started to list off when he held up a hand.

"Tours. I get it. I thought you were going to Harvard. You were gonna change the world, or something," he remembered. She laughed again.

"Once upon a time. But then I had this epiphany – I fucking hated school. I hated my life. I hated my parents. They pretty much hated me, so it worked out great. I left school and got a job," she re-capped her life.

"Why do they hate you?" he asked, his eyebrows raised.

"One guess, Mr. Kane."

"No shit," Jameson said in a low voice, looking down his nose at her.

"Yup. Eloise was never one to take things lying down. Though you would know more about that than me," Tate teased. His eye-brows went up even higher.

"You are so ... different," he told her, his voice soft.

"Well, you never really knew me," she pointed out.

"I think I got to know you pretty well."

She sucked in a quick breath and held it. It got about ten degrees hotter in the room. Tatum was no blushing girl, not anymore – she had broken up with Drew that same night, and since then she had slept with a lot of guys. Probably more than she'd like to admit. She wasn't shy about sex. But something about *him*, made her feel that way. She didn't like it. She had to regain the upper hand. She stepped up close to him, almost close enough for their chests to meet.

"It was one night, Jameson. You don't know *anything*," she whispered the last part, staring up at him.

Before he could respond, she turned and walked away. She halfway expected him to follow her, but he didn't. When she got back into the kitchen, she peered out the porthole in the door. He was still standing there, staring after her. She smiled to herself.

Upper hand, achieved.

She didn't know why she felt the need to "beat him"; she didn't matter to him. He didn't matter to her. One fucked up, incredibly hot night together didn't mean anything, in the grand scheme of things. He had done her a favor, if she was honest with herself, and he had seemed to enjoy himself in the process, so it all worked out.

Closure. It was closure, Tate figured, for a chapter in her life she hadn't even known needed closure. Jameson Kane was most definitely a thing of the past. For real, now.

2

"**H**OW COULD YOU NOT RECOGNIZE him!?"

Tate bent at the waist, swung her hips in a circle, clapped her hands, then stood upright.

"I don't know, I was caught off guard! I didn't recognize him."

Bend, circle, clap, stand.

"He must look really different."

Bend, circle, clap, stand.

"Not really. Older, for sure, but still the same. Sexy as fuck."

Bend, circle, clap, stand.

"Then how did you not recognize him!? I find it hard to believe you forgot the face of the guy who fucked you retarded and then treated you like shit."

"*Excuse me!*"

Both Tate and her best friend, Angier Hollingsworth, looked over their shoulders at the woman who had just interrupted them. Okay, so maybe a Zumba class wasn't the best place to be having that particular discussion, but Tate hadn't started it. Plus, she thought eavesdropping was a nasty trait – if people were going to do it, they should have the good graces to pretend not to be listening and keep their mouth shut.

"Oh, shut up, this is probably the hottest thing you've heard all week," Ang snapped at the woman before he turned back towards the instructor. They began hiking their knees up, skipping in place at the same time as pumping their fists in the air.

Zumba wasn't Tate's usual work out, but free was free, and she couldn't exactly afford a gym membership. Ang was a compulsive coupon hoarder, and always took her when he got a buy-one-get-one deal. She had been to many a jazzercise, step, Tae Bo, cycling class, courtesy of Ang. They also always knew where to go to score free smoothies, appetizers, cookies, whatever. When they really put their minds to it, the two of them could spend a whole day on the town and not spend a dime.

"I don't think about him that much. I guess I kinda forgot," Tate kept their conversation going, body rolling to the right.

"So he's still sexy, huh? Gonna hit that?" Ang asked, rolling right behind her. She laughed.

"Um, *no.* Don't think so. I think one time was plenty, thank you. The things he said to me …" she let her voice trail off as they sashayed to the left.

"Get you so hot, you're probably soaking wet right now," Ang finished for her, and she burst out laughing. The woman behind them huffed, but didn't say anything.

"You're so disgusting," Tate snorted at him, brushing sweaty hair away from her forehead. Stupid as she felt, Zumba was one hell of a workout.

"I'm not the one getting off in the middle of a gym full of middle-aged women. Oh my god, you really are, aren't you? I can tell, come here," Ang said, and broke out of the line to grab at her. She burst out laughing, slapping his hands away. They stumbled to the left, Ang digging his fingers into her waist and hips. She laughed uncontrollably, trying to skip away from him.

"*Excuse me!* We are in the middle of a lesson!" the instructor barked out over the microphone. Ang rolled his eyes.

"C'mon, we can do this at home with techno music and vodka, let's blow this place," he said in a loud voice, swinging an arm around Tate's shoulders and dragging her away from the floor.

"We probably won't be allowed back, you realize," she pointed out.

"Who cares? There's a ton of other places. Shower?" he asked, stopping in front of the locker rooms.

"Yeah, I feel disgusting. Meet you in fifteen," she said, but he started bustling after her through the women's door. She laughed and put a hand against his chest.

"What? If you're all randy from Mr. Angry-Fucker, I think I should get to benefit," Ang said with a serious face. She snorted.

"I am not randy, and I don't think so," she laughed, pushing at him.

"Oh c'mon, sweetie, it'll be quick. You always love it," he begged, pouting out his bottom lip. She put both hands on his chest.

"I'll take a rain check."

He let up when a disgruntled looking soccer-mom shoved her way out past them. Tate crossed her eyes at him and then danced off into the locker room. Gathering her shower stuff together, she headed under the spray.

She had met Angier at a frat party, five years ago. Her rebellious phase had been in full swing. Streaks of color in her hair, way too much eye makeup – she might have even had her eyebrow pierced. It was the first night Tate had ever tried coke, and she had felt like a live wire, running around the building. She wanted to talk to everyone, meet everyone. Ang had cornered her. A lanky six-foot-four topped with light brown hair and striking gray eyes, he was very good looking. She had thought he was going to hit on her, but he had something else in mind.

He had asked her if she would be interested in doing a porno with him.

Tate had thought it was a joke at first, but he had been very serious. She had a great body, he told her. Perfect smile, good teeth. Great for porn. She politely declined. He had shrugged it off, but then invited her to come to a taping, get a *"feel"* for it, maybe. It was one of the most surreal moments she'd ever had with another person.

They had been best friends ever since.

Tate never got into porn, but Ang swore by it. He did gay, straight, "selfie" porn – he would do pretty much anything. He explained that although he was straight, for the right price he could be just about anything someone wanted him to be; she knew that feeling, having been desperate for money in those days. Since she wouldn't do porn, he taught her the ways of coupon clipping.

After a drunken night at a wine tasting – free, of course – they slept together for the first time. Ang came the closest, of anyone she had ever been with, to making her feel the way Jameson had made her feel. And best of all, he didn't have any expectations of her. Sex was just sex to Ang. Almost like exercising. Something that had to be done to stay healthy, and it felt super good – bonus! But it didn't really mean anything to him beyond that, which made it easy to be with him. He was also a total freak, so she never felt bad about her own preferences, the way she sometimes did with other men. Ang was like a security blanket. A sexy, naughty, deviant, security blanket.

"What's taking you so long!?" Ang's voice boomed through the locker room while Tate held her head under a hand dryer. A couple ladies shrieked, but Tate just laughed. She righted herself, ran her fingers through her black locks, then grabbed her stuff, hurrying out to meet him.

"I'm a girl, I take longer to look presentable," she pointed out.

"What, exactly, looks presentable about you?" he asked, and she elbowed him in the stomach.

"Shut up."

"So," he began as they pushed their way outside. "Seriously. Are you going to see him again?"

"No. I mean, why would I? Unless he needs a waiter at his firm, I don't think I'll be hearing from him," Tate replied, bouncing her gym bag off her knees.

"So. You could call him, you know where he works," Ang pointed out. She scrunched up her nose.

"Why on earth would I want to call him?"

"Because you still think about him," Ang replied, and she barked out a laugh.

"I do not. I told you, I didn't even recognize him at first," she reminded him. Ang shook his head.

"But you compare every guy you're with to him. I've pulled some of my best moves on you – remember the swing!? – and I still don't stack up," he said. She stopped laughing.

"I do not. You're amazing, you know that."

"Well, duh, but I can tell. I'm good at these things – have to be, in my line of work. I'm pretty good, I can tell I'm one of your faves, but I'm not him," he finished. She frowned. She didn't like this subject. She did not compare every guy to Jameson Kane.

Did she?

How could she? She'd only slept with him once. Surely he hadn't left that big of an impression on her.

She had to change the channel.

"If you're so good at sizing sex up, how do I stack up against all the people *you've* slept with? It's not really fair, I have to compete with both sexes – twice the competition," Tate joked.

"Bitch, please. If I could find a woman who fucks like you, and would let me actually film it and sell it for money, I would *marry her*," Ang said with a straight face. She laughed.

"That's what I like to hear."

He walked her up to her apartment and stayed for a little while, making flirty comments at Rusty. It wasn't right, Rus had a huge crush on him. Tate had tried to explainto her that Ang didn't really date, wasn't looking for a relationship, but it didn't stop Rus from hoping. Tate was beginning to think she'd have to share some of her and Ang's dirtier stories, in hopes of scaring her roommate off from him. Rus was a sweetheart – sex swings and ball gags probably weren't her thing.

"Oh! I forgot, you left your cell phone here – it rang a whole bunch," Rus said, after Ang had danced out the door. Tate grabbed the phone off the table, squinting at the screen. It was the temp agency she worked for – a new job? Score. She called them back.

"Hi, Tatum, how are you?" the temp agency manager, Carla, breathed down the phone line.

"Super dooper. You called me, like eight times? What's up?" Tate asked, rifling through a bowl of of mixed nuts and goodies.

"I've got a job for you, if you're interested!" Carla breathed.

"Sure. What is it?" Tate said around a mouthful of food.

"A law firm downtown is having a conference. Their regular assistant is sick and they have an important meeting with a client tomorrow afternoon. You won't have to perform her normal duties, just show up for the meeting and serve water, muffins, that kind of stuff. Quick and easy," Carla's voice got even breathier.

How does she talk like that? Did she take lessons?

"Sounds like my kind of job. What should I wear?" Tate asked.

"Business attire. If you have a dress that works, that would be great, but a skirt, or trousers, and button down blouse would be fine. Be there at one o'clock sharp, okay?" Breathy McBreather breathed.

"Sure, sure. Where is it at?"

"Um …" Carla prattled off the address, her voice barely a whisper. "And make sure you're on time. They made a big deal out of that. They requested you especially, you know."

Tate choked on an almond.

"Me!? Why me?" she managed to cough out.

"I don't know. Said they'd seen your work. I guess you did a really great job! One o'clock, remember!" Carla's breathy voice almost sang.

"Remembered."

Tate stared down at her phone after she'd ended the call. She could kinda remember temping for a lawyer, but it wasn't like she'd done anything amazing. At least she didn't think so. She wasn't even sure if it was for the same law firm, but maybe it was; maybe her filing skills were super impressive. Legendary. Maybe she'd blown the guy. Who knows.

Oh well. A job was a job. She wandered into her room and spent the next hour digging through her closet, seeing if she had anything that fit the bill.

3

JAMESON KANE STOOD IN FRONT of his desk, staring down at a file folder. Tatum O'Shea's file from the temp agency stared back up at him. It had taken him forever to find which temp agency she even worked for – and then he had paid a hefty price for a copy of her file.

Over the years, he'd thought about her occasionally, but not enough to ask about her to anyone. The sex had been mind blowing. A young, twenty-three year old at the time, he had just been discovering the kind of man he was; he'd been dating Ellie for two years, and hadn't quite yet had the chance to fully explore his sexual appetites.

He had slept with other people, multiple times, but he never cheated – Ellie always knew, beforehand *and* afterwards. He had tried to break up with her, *several* times, but then the screaming would start. The crying. The begging. Then threatening. The Kanes and the O'Sheas were close friends. Did he really want to jeopardize that?

After two years together, Jameson had finally begun to realize he didn't care if he jeopardized anything. He was going to end things with Eloise O'Shea. Move away from Harrisburg, go back to school, something. Head to Manhattan. Just get away from everything. He was bored with everything, bored with his life. He needed something different. He just had to figure out what it was, and how to go about getting it.

Then Tatum had walked into his apartment. He had developed a sort of hard on for Tate. Eloise's younger sister had always been a sex bomb waiting to happen. Leggy and tone, with chocolate eyes and a sexy body, he'd had more than a couple fantasies about her. But she was off limits. Too young, and too naive; not to mention the whole dating-her-sister thing.

Yet in the end, none of that had stopped him.

She'd come apart under his hands. Like clay. He had felt like he could mold her. Do anything he wanted to her. *Say* anything he wanted to her. Every word that crossed his lips, no matter what she'd said in response, she'd just gotten hotter. Needier. Pretty incredible. If Ellie hadn't come home when she had, he was pretty sure Tate never would've made it out the door. Ellie would've walked in on them in action.

Sometimes Jameson wondered how different things would have turned out, if that had happened.

He moved away almost immediately after the break up, didn't bother to keep in contact with the O'Sheas. His father died not long after, and Jameson pretty much filled his role in the world. Stocks and bonds. Acquisitions. Silent partnerships in a lot of businesses. On top of that, he inherited the family fortune. Jameson had more money than he knew what to do with – but that didn't mean he slacked off. He went above and beyond his father, was bolder, made more money, more connections. Garnered worldwide attention for his knack for making a profit.

He owned homes in Manhattan, Copenhagen, Rio – and now Boston. He dated supermodels and went to red carpet premieres.

DEGRADATION

He had women falling at his feet. Life was pretty damn near perfect.

But then he had seen Tatum in that kitchen, and time had shifted. In the flash of an instant, he was back in his old apartment, talking so mean to her. Watching her cry. Watching her moan. He had to admit it, she had been a pretty powerful moment in his life. *Profound.*

She looked so different. Her curves had filled out a little more, but she still had the same tone frame he remembered. He would kill to see what her ass looked like now. Her dark hair had been pulled up into a messy ponytail, making him think of sex. Her eye makeup had been dark and smudged, making him think of more sex. Her sarcastic smile and smart mouth were a complete one-eighty from the girl he had known before; this woman was a new creature. And he wanted to find out exactly what kind.

4

TATUM PLUCKED AT HER SHIRT in a nervous manner. She had tucked it into a tight pencil skirt and even put on a pair of sling back stilettos. If someone had personally requested her, she wanted to make an effort to look nice. She had blown out her hair and put curls in the ends, and toned down her make up. Even she had to admit it, she looked presentable.

For once.

Men in expensive business suits began to file into the conference room and she stood still, giving a polite smile to everyone who entered. A team of lawyers was meeting with their client. Six chairs were lined up on one side of a long table, with just a single chair on the other side.

Tate had been positioned at the back of the room, next to a sideboard filled with goodies and coffee and water. She fussed about, straightening napkins and setting up the glasses. When all six chairs were filled on the one side, she stared at their backs, wondering who the big shot was that got to stare them all down. The person who would be facing her. A door at the back of the room swung open and her breath caught in her threat.

Holy. Shit.

Jameson Kane strode into the room, only offering a curt smile to his lawyers. His eyes flashed to her for just a second, then he looked back. His smile became genuine and he tipped his head towards her, almost like a bow.

She gaped back at him, positive that her mouth was hanging open. What was he doing there!? Had he known she would be there? Had he been the one to request her? Impossible, he didn't know what temp agency she worked for – but what would be the chances? She hadn't seen him in seven years, and now twice in two days.

Tate felt like swallowing her tongue.

"Gentlemen," Jameson began, seating himself across from the lawyers. "Thanks for meeting with me today. Would anyone care for any coffee? Water? The lovely Ms. O'Shea will be helping us today." He gestured towards Tate, but no one turned around. Several people asked for coffee. Jameson asked for water, his smile still in place. It was almost a smirk. Like he knew something she didn't.

She began to grind her teeth.

She delivered everyone's drinks, then carried around a tray of snacks. No one took anything. She moved to the back of the room, refilled the water pitcher. Tidied up. Felt Jameson staring at her.

This is ridiculous. You're Tatum O'Shea. You eat boys for breakfast.

But thinking that made her remember when he had said something very similar to her, and she felt a blush creep up her cheeks.

She was pretty much ignored the whole time. They all argued back and forth about what business decisions Jameson should, or shouldn't, make. He was very keen on dismantling struggling companies and selling them off. They tried to curb his desires. His tax lawyer explained how his tax shelter in Hong Kong was doing. Another lawyer gave him a run down on property law in Switzerland. Tate tried to hide her yawns.

They took a five minute break after an hour had passed. Tate had her back to the room, rearranging some muffins on a tray, when she felt the hair on the back of her neck start to stand up. She turned around in slow motion, taking in Jameson as he walked up to her.

"Surprised?" he asked, smiling down at her.

"Very. Did you ask for me?" she questioned. He nodded.

"Yes. You ran away so quickly the other night. I wanted to get reacquainted," he explained. She laughed.

"Maybe I didn't," she responded. He shrugged.

"That doesn't really matter to me. What are you doing tonight?" he asked. She was a little caught off guard.

"Are you asking me out, Kane?" she blurted out. He threw back his head and laughed.

"Oh god, still a little girl. *No.* I don't ask people out. I was asking what you were doing tonight," Jameson replied.

She willed away the blush she felt coming on. He still had the ability to make her feel so stupid. She had been through so much since him, come so far with her esteem and her life. It wasn't fair that he could still make her feel so small. She wanted to return the favor. She cleared her throat.

"I'm working."

"Where?"

"At a bar."

"What bar?"

"A bar you don't know."

"And tomorrow night?"

"Busy."

"And the night after that?"

"*Every* night after that," Tate informed him, crossing her arms. He narrowed his eyes, but continued smiling.

"Surely you can find some time to meet up with an old friend," he said. She shook her head.

DEGRADATION

"We were never friends, Kane," she pointed out. He laughed.

"Then what is it? Are you scared of me? Scared I'll eat you alive?" he asked. She stepped closer to him, refusing to be intimidated.

"I think *you're* the one who should be scared. You don't know me, Kane. You never did. *And you never will,*" she whispered. Jameson leaned down so his lips were almost against her ear.

"I know what you feel like from the inside. That's good enough for me," he whispered back. Tate stepped away. She felt like she couldn't breathe. He did something to her insides.

"You, and a lot of other people. You're not as big a deal as you think," she taunted. It was a complete lie, but she had to get the upper hand back. He smirked at her.

"That sounds like a challenge to me. I have to defend my honor," he warned her. She snorted.

"Whatever. Point to the challenger then, *me*. Defend away," she responded, rolling her eyes.

He didn't respond, just continued smirking down at her. The lawyers began filing back into the room and Jameson took his position on the other side of the table. She wasn't really sure what their little spar had been about, or what had come out of it. She was just going to try to get through the rest of the conference, and then she would scurry away before he could talk to her again. She didn't want anything to do with Jameson Kane, or his —,

"Ms. O'Shea," his sharp voice interrupted her thoughts. Tate lifted her head.

"Yes, sir?" she asked, making sure to keep her voice soft and polite.

"Could you bring me some water, and something to eat," he asked, not even bothering to look at her as he flipped through a contract.

She loaded up a tray with his requests and made her way around the table. No one even looked at her, they just threw legal jargon around at each other – a language she didn't know. She stood next to Jameson and leaned forward, setting his water down and then going about arranging cheese and crackers on a plate for him. She was about halfway done when she felt it.

Are those … his fingers!?

Tate froze for a second. His touch was light as he ran his fingers up and down between her legs. She glanced down at her knees and then glanced over at him. He was still looking down, but she could see him smirking. She tried to ignore him, tried to go back to setting up his food, but his hand went higher. Daring to brush up past her knees, well underneath her skirt. He couldn't get any farther, not unless he pushed up her skirt, or sunk down in his chair. She dumped the rest of the cheese on his plate and started to scoot away. She had just gotten back to her station when she heard a thunking noise, followed by groans.

"No worries. Ms. O'Shea! So sorry, could you get this?" Jameson's voice was bored sounding.

She turned around and saw that he had knocked over his water glass. He was blotting at the liquid as it spread across the table. The lawyers were all holding their papers aloft, grumbling back and forth.

Tate groaned and grabbed a towel before striding back to the table. She glared at him the whole way, but he still refused to look at her. She started as far away from him as she could get, mopping everything up, but eventually she had to almost lean across him to reach the mess. She stood on her toes, stretching across the table top.

As she had assumed it would, his hand found its way back to her legs. Only this time he wasn't shy, and her position allowed for a lot of access. His hand shot straight up the back of her skirt, his fingertips brushing against the lace of her panties.

She swallowed a squeak and glanced around. If any of the other gentlemen lifted their heads, they would have been able to see their client with half of his arm up his assistant's skirt, plain as day. He managed to run his finger under the hem of her underwear, down the left side of her butt cheek, before she pulled away. She stomped back to the food station, throwing the towel down with such violence, she knocked over a stack of sugar cubes.

When she turned around, Jameson was finally looking at her. She plunked her fists on her hips, staring straight back. His smirk was in place – as she had expected it would be – and he held up a finger, pointing it straight up. *One.* Then he pointed at himself. One point. *Tied.* He thought they were playing a game. She hadn't wanted to play games with him, but she hated to lose at *anything*, and she never wanted to lose to a man like Jameson Kane.

An idea flitted across her mind. Tate wanted to make him as uncomfortable as he had just made her feel. She coolly raised an eyebrow and then took her time looking around the room. The lawyers all still had their backs to her – not one of them had turned around the entire time she'd been there. Blinds had been drawn over every window, no one could see in the office, but she knew the door wasn't locked. Anyone could walk into the room. She took a deep breath. It didn't matter anyway, what was the worst that could happen? She would get fired? It was a temp job, that Jameson had requested her for – he didn't even work there. Did she really care what happened?

She dragged her stare back to meet his and then ran her hands down the sides of her skirt. He raised an eyebrow as well, his eyes following her hands. When she got to the hem of the skirt, she pressed her palms flat and began to slowly, *achingly*, slide the material up her legs. Now both his eyebrows were raised. He flicked his gaze to her face, then went right back to her skirt. Higher, up past her knees. To the middle of her thighs. Higher still. If anyone turned around, they would be very surprised at what they saw. One more inch, and her skirt would be moot. Jameson's stare was practically burning holes through her.

Taking short, quick, breaths through her nose, Tate slid her hands around to her butt. She wiggled the material up higher back there, careful to keep the front low enough to hide her whole business, and was able to hook her fingers into her underwear. She didn't even think about what she was doing, couldn't take her eyes off of Jameson, as she slid her underwear over her butt and down her hips. As the lace slid to her ankles, she pushed her skirt back into place. Then she stepped out of the panties and bent over, picking them up. When she stood upright, she let the lace dangle from her hand while she held up one finger. Point.

Winning.

Jameson nodded his head at her, obviously conceding to her victory, then returned his attention to the papers in front of him. Tate let out a breath that she hadn't even realized she was holding, and turned around, bracing her hands against the table. She leaned forward and took deep breaths. She had just started to gain some ground on slowing her heart rate, when a throat cleared.

"What is that, Ms. O'Shea?" Jameson called out from behind her. She spun around, balling up her underwear in her fist.

"Excuse me, sir?" she asked.

"That," he continued, gesturing with his pen at her. "In your hands. You have something for me. Bring it here."

Now everyone turned towards her. Tate held herself as still as possible, her hands clasped together in front of her legs, hiding the underwear between her fingers. All eyes were on her. Jameson smirked at her and leaned back in his chair. She took a shaky breath.

"I don't know what —,"

"Bring it here, Ms. O'Shea, *now*," he ordered, tapping the table top with his pen. She glared at him.

Fuck this.

She turned around and pulled one of the silver trays in front of her. She laid her panties out neatly on top, making sure the material was smooth and flat. She was very thankful that she had gone all out and worn her good, expensive, "*I'm-successful-and-career-oriented!*", underwear. She balanced the tray on top of her fingertips and spun around, striding towards their table, a big smile on her face.

"For you, Mr. Kane," she said in a breathy voice, then dropped the tray in front of him. It clattered loudly and spun around a little before coming to a rest, the panties sliding off to one side.

As she walked away, she could hear some gasps. A couple laughs. A very familiar chuckle. When she got to the door, she pulled it open before turning back to the room. A couple of the lawyers were gawking at her, and the rest were laughing, gesturing to the display she had just put on; Jameson was looking straight at her, his smirk in place. She blew him a kiss and then stomped out the door.

A couple hours later, Tate sat on the edge of her bed, staring at her closet. She should have been getting ready for work. She had promised to do a shift at the bar for one of the other girls, Tuesday was usually her day off. She had taken a shower, tried to motivate herself to get dressed, but after the afternoon she'd had, she really didn't want to get sexy-ed up and go sling drinks. She sighed.

Get over it. Rent is due.

She began yanking out clothing, not paying attention to what she picked out. Her mind kept wandering back to the conference room. Tate had grown pretty bold over the years, very confident in herself and her sexuality, but she had never done something like that before; had never stripped in a room full of people.

How was it possible that he still had that kind of power over her? One time. They had been together only *one time*, it wasn't fair. And weirder still – why did it seem like he was pursuing her? Jameson Kane didn't pursue anybody, not even seven years ago. Ellie had asked him out. He had certainly never pursued Tate. She had all but fallen on his dick that night, she'd been so eager for him. She shook her head back and forth, trying to clear her thoughts.

Never again. I am never going to think of Jameson Kane, never —,

"*Tate!*" Rusty's voice squealed through her door.

"What? It's open," Tate called out, dropping the towel she had been wearing and shimmying into a pair of sweat pants. Her door cracked open and Rus peeked her head around the corner.

"There is some guy here to see you," she said in an excited voice. Tate scrunched her eyebrows together. Some guy?

"Who? What does he want?" she asked, pulling on a t-shirt and then yanking her damp hair up into a ponytail.

"I don't know who he is, but he is so good looking, I can't believe he's real life. He's wearing some expensive looking suit," Rus described. Tate groaned, rubbing her hands over her face.

"Jesus! What, is he stalking me now!?" she moaned.

"No," a deep voice came from her doorway. She looked up.

Jameson Kane is in my piece of shit apartment.

"Make yourself at home," she sighed, gesturing for him to come into her room. Rus giggled and turned bright red, making room for him and then scurrying out the door.

"She's cute," Jameson commented as he wandered around the tiny room, inspecting things.

"Oh really? Want to eat her for breakfast, too?" Tate asked. Jameson laughed, leaning close to a photo.

"Hmmm, not really my tastes. I'm hungering for something a little darker," he replied. Tate narrowed her eyes.

"Well, that '*something*' isn't on the menu," she informed him. He stood upright and faced her.

"We'll see about that."

"Seriously. What the fuck do you want?" she snapped at him. He raised an eyebrow.

"Attitude. I like it. Where's all that shit you normally have around your eyes?" he asked, walking towards her. She started to back up but then stopped, holding her ground.

"I was just about to put *all that shit* back on when I was interrupted by a conceited asshole," she replied.

"Look. I want to talk to you. We haven't seen each other in a long time. You … intrigue me. Not much does anymore," he explained a little.

"Intrigue?"

"You're so different, but still kind of the same. It's interesting. I'm curious to see how deep both go," he added. She sighed.

"Look, Kane, you don't just get to decide —,"

"Jameson," he corrected her. She blinked at him.

"Excuse me?"

"*Jameson.* That's my name. Call me by my name," he instructed her.

"But everyone calls you Kane. All those lawyers today, my sister, *everyone*," Tate replied, a little lost in the conversation. He shook his head.

"I don't care. You always called me Jameson. Say it again," he ordered. She laughed.

"Okay, play time is over. Get out of my apartment. I'm very flattered that you think you want to know something about me, but I don't really give two fucks. I don't want anything to do with you. You are nothing to me. So thank you, and goodbye," she stated, gesturing towards her door.

Jameson watched her for a second and then walked towards her, his steps slow and deliberate. She refused to back away, so they wound up almost chest to chest. Not quite touching, but close enough that he sucked all the oxygen out of her. She stared up at him, rubbing her lips together so she wouldn't blurt out the thoughts in her head.

"It hasn't escaped my attention that you growing a massive set of balls seems to have happened right after I fucked you. I think I deserve some credit, and therefore, you owe me," he broke it down for her. She burst out laughing.

"You're an amazing piece of work! Just because we had sex, doesn't mean —,"

"*I* fucked *you*. There is a big difference."

"*It was seven years ago!*" Tate was suddenly shrieking. "Seven fucking years! Who gives a fuck!? I've fucked a lot of people since then! I'm sure you have, too! So big fucking deal!"

Nothing rattled him. He stood still, continuing to smirk down at her. It drove her insane. She wanted to slap him. Claw her nails across his face. Knock him to the ground. And then possibly fuck his brains out ...

"I think it was a *very* big deal, and we can discuss that another time. For now, let me take you to work. Let me see this shit hole bar you work at, then maybe we can set up a time to *chat*," Jameson offered.

Her mind was spinning. It had been a big deal to him? Not possible. *Not. Fucking. Possible.* He'd barely even looked at her after it had happened, and she had been a puddle on the floor. Jameson Kane wasn't that kind of guy, she couldn't imagine anything being that big of a deal to him. She had always assumed he had forgotten about it.

That's why she was so stunned.

"I ... you ... what?" she asked. He laughed.

"I'll be waiting downstairs. Your apartment scares me. Be down in fifteen minutes. Do not make me come back up here," he ordered, pointing a finger at her before walking towards the door.

"You can't tell me —,"

"Oh, and Tate, you forgot these," he said, digging in his pocket. He pulled her panties out and tossed them onto the floor. "You always seem to be dropping these around me."

DEGRADATION

Mother fucker.

Jameson was a little shocked that she came down within the fifteen minutes. She eyed him sideways for a minute, and it was obvious she was considering just walking off, but something made her think twice. She must have figured out that he would just follow after her. She sighed and stepped around him, letting herself into the passenger side of his car.

Tate didn't talk to him, other than to give directions. Her voice had gotten just a touch lower than it had been when she was eighteen. A huskiness had been added to it, or something. Something *sexy*. Everything about her was sexy. Seven years ago, she had been sexy as a clueless, naive, young woman. Now, as a confident, forward, twenty-five year old, she stopped his heart. Made it hard to think straight.

She had put makeup on. She seemed to favor a smudgy, smoky eye. It looked good on her. A little trashy, but in a *very* sexy way. Her pert mouth was coated in a pale, pink gloss, that really emphasized the fact that she most definitely had CSL - cock-sucking-lips. Seven years ago, he wouldn't have ever been able to imagine Tatum O'Shea sucking dick. Now he couldn't stop.

Jameson wouldn't let himself think about her body, or he'd have to pull over the car and ease the tension between them, right then and there.

She was fighting against him, and it just turned him on even more. When she had started pulling down her panties, in the middle of that room, with all those people ... it had taken every bit of restraint he had not to dismiss everyone and fuck her right then. The old Tatum had been fun to play with, cute. This Tatum, he wanted to *own*. He wanted to break her down, bend her to him. She seemed a worthy adversary, and Jameson loved a good fight.

"Do you always start work this late?" he questioned, pulling up in front of a kind of dive looking bar. She shook her head.

"No, I'm filling in for someone, I normally work weekends. Thanks for the ride," she said before leaping out of the car. He got out right behind her.

"Oh, I've gotta see this place. I'm fascinated by your life. Good girl goes bad. Is there piss on the floor?" he asked, holding the door to the bar open. She gave him a smile full of sweetness.

"You have such a sexy way with words."

Then she elbowed him and strode through the door.

She made a beeline to the bar, ducking under the partition and heading into a back room. Jameson planted himself on a bar stool and ordered a bourbon. Neat. The woman serving him was wearing a pair of tight leather pants and a string-bikini top, and wore them well. It made him curious as to what Tate would be wearing, wondered if it would be as slutty.

He wasn't disappointed. Fifteen minutes later, at ten o'clock on the dot, she reappeared. His tongue got stuck to the roof of his mouth. She was wearing a tiny pair of jean cut-offs. He had wanted to see her ass, and now his wish was pretty much granted. When she leaned over the back of the bar to grab something, he could see the bottom swell of her ass cheeks.

On top she was wearing a t-shirt with some sort of baseball logo on it, but she had ripped off the bottom half of it. It stopped just beneath her breasts, and when she lifted her arms, he could see a gray, lacy bra. The shirt also show-cased her stomach, with was tone and flat. The girl took care of her body. She had leather boots on her feet, almost combat like, but with the tops folded down. They should have looked at odds with her sexy outfit, but they worked some how.

"Is this how you normally dress for work?" Jameson asked when she made her way towards his end of the bar. She glanced down at herself.

"No. Sometimes I wear less," she replied, and he laughed.

"Less? So if I come in here on the weekend, you might be serving people in a bikini?" he had to shout to be heard over the music and the rowdy patrons. It had been pretty full when they'd walked in – now it was standing room only.

"Only if it's a game day."

"Hot. But those shorts, I think they have to go. Sometimes less is more, you know," he teased. Tate raised an eyebrow.

"You think they're too short?"

"Yes."

She whirled away from him and took long strides to the other end of the bar. She picked something up and then headed back towards him. It took him a second before he realized it was a blow horn. She smirked at him and then lifted it to her lips.

"Everybody! Hey!" she shouted. There was a roar of cheers and the music was turned down. "This man here thinks my shorts are too short! What do you all think!?" She pulled the blow horn away, lifting her arms up in a questioning gesture.

The place went nuts. The crowd had to be seventy-five percent male, and all of them were hooting and hollering at her. Tate smiled, and winked, biting the tip of her tongue between her teeth. It was clear that she knew what she was doing, knew how to work the crowd. She turned around and bent at the waist, shaking her ass a little. The roar grew to a deafening level. She finally stood up and turned back around, waving everyone away. Then she turned to Jameson.

"I didn't say you looked bad," he pointed out. She shook her head.

"You're ridiculous. If you don't like what I'm wearing, *leave*," she suggested before prancing back down the bar to wait on customers.

"Not until you agree to talk with me, Tatum!" Jameson shouted over the din. She glanced at him while she expertly twirled bottles in her hands, throwing liquor into glasses.

"I still don't know what it is we have to talk about!" she yelled back, twirling two shakers at once. She was very good at her job.

"The way you talk, the way you dress, your makeup, your ass!" he replied. At the word "*ass*", some idiot next to him cheered.

"Best I can tell, not one of those things is any of your business!" she pointed out, cracking open one of the shakers and letting a blue concoction pour into a martini glass.

"I'm making them my business. I want to get to know you," he said.

"But not date me," she clarified, pouring the second drink.

"Don't be fucking stupid," Jameson laughed.

Tate made her way back to him and then planted her hands on the bar, spreading her arms wide. She leaned close to him, very close, her breath hot against his lips. Her loose shirt hung forward and he had a perfect view down her cleavage.

"What do you *want*, Kane?" she asked in a low voice. He dragged his gaze away from her tits and stared her in the eye.

"Call me that name again, and I will punish your mouth," he warned her. She chuckled.

"Don't make promises you won't keep," she retorted.

Oh my, I may have met my match. This should be interesting.

"Who says I won't? I have big plans for that mouth," Jameson said, pinching her chin between his fingers. She rolled her eyes.

"Not gonna happen, Kane. Not any part of me, is going to touch any part of you, so you had better get used to that idea," she informed him before pulling away.

We'll see about that.

"Alright. But we are going to talk," he repeated himself. She heaved a sigh.

"Fine. *Fine*. How about we make an appointment? Say, tomorrow? One o'clock? Does that work for you, my lord and master?" she taunted. He took out his phone.

"I'm marking it down. Meet me at my office," he told her. She snorted.

"Fine, whatever," she grumbled at him. He glanced up at her.

"You had better show up. If I have to come get you, you won't like it," Jameson warned her.

"Talk, talk, talk. In my experience, men who talk as much as you, have very little action to back it up," she said. He cocked up an eyebrow.

"You've experienced me in action. And there wasn't very much talking."

She rolled her eyes and then grabbed his glass, drinking the rest of his bourbon in one shot.

"You put too much emphasis on the past, Kane. It was one time, *one time*. The great Jameson Kane is hung up on a one night stand? It was nothing, it's long gone. We'll talk about whatever you want tomorrow, then it's goodbye," she informed him before walking off. He smirked at her.

Twice. She called me by my last name twice. Now she really owes me.

5

TATE SAT IN A CHAIR in an anteroom outside of Jameson's office. She had thought about blowing him off, but she didn't want him showing up at her apartment again. How had he known where she lived, anyway? And he had said he was scared of it – Mr. Prissy Pants had probably never been in a low-rent building.

Asshole.

She had no clue what was going on between them. He challenged her, she played his games. She could have walked away from him – the moment he entered that conference room, she could've walked out. When he touched her leg, she could have slapped him. Could have screamed and acted like a scared girl.

But something about him still got under her skin. There was truth to what Ang had said, her night with Jameson had greatly affected her. It not only set about a major change in her life, but had helped her discover a new side to herself. Tate liked to be treated roughly. She liked to be talked dirty to, liked to be pushed around. Of course, only on her terms, and only by men she liked. She didn't like Jameson Kane, and nothing with him was ever on her terms. He made her nervous. He made her hot. He confused her.

"*Ms. O'Shea?*"

She snapped out of her daze. It was obvious that the secretary had been standing there for a while. Tate smiled and got up, following the woman into a large office. Jameson hadn't spared any expense – large windows with amazing views. Mahogany furniture. Impressive credentials in frames. Was that a real Mark Rothko on the wall!?

"I figured you would stand me up," Jameson got out of his chair as the secretary backed out of the room. Tate shrugged and walked forward, flopping into a chair across from his desk.

"As cute as stalking is, I figured I'd better nip this in the bud," she replied. His eyes traveled up and down her form.

"You look different today. Every time I see you, it's like a different person," he said. She glanced down at herself. She was wearing wide legged suit pants, ballet flats, and a blouse with puffed, cap sleeves. All black.

"I'm temping for an upscale salon today. What do you want?" Tate got to the point. He smiled at her.

"So impatient. How've you been? Did you finish school?" he inquired, taking his seat again.

She narrowed her eyes at him. He said he just wanted to talk, but then he would make comments about punishing her mouth, and other things. He said he didn't want to date her, but he seemed borderline obsessed with getting to know her. He made her mind spin in circles.

"I've been fan-fucking-tastic. I dropped out of school right after I left Harrisburg. Is that it?" she asked, surging to her feet.

"*Sit down,*" he commanded in a stern voice, and she immediately did so – shocking herself a little.

"What do you want, Kane? Let's not beat around the bush. You don't know me – you never cared to know me before, so what's the big deal now? If I disappeared off the face of the earth tomorrow, it wouldn't affect your life," Tate pointed out.

"Maybe not. But I'm kind of used to getting what I want, and like I said, you intrigue me," Jameson replied. She scooted to the edge of her chair.

"Okay, fine. My life story – I left home after the night I slept with you, didn't look back. My father called me, told me he wouldn't pay my tuition anymore. I told him to fuck off. My mother called me and told me I wasn't welcome in their home anymore. I told *her* to fuck off. Ellie called me and told me I was the biggest whore she'd ever met. I told her to go fuck herself. I dropped out of school. I got a job at a Chili's. I moved out my apartment. Got a second job cleaning motel rooms. Moved to a shittier apartment. Got my job at the bar – moved in with Rusty, to an *even shittier* apartment.

"But you know what's crazy? I was happy. I got to be me – I never got to be me, before I left. It was awesome. I drank a lot, I did a lot of drugs, I had a lot of sex, and it was all *awesome*. Now you're pretty much caught up to speed. Can I go?" she said it all rapid fire, speaking as fast as she could. Jameson leaned back in his chair.

"Do you still do drugs?" he asked. She rolled her eyes.

"Pot sometimes. I've tried ecstasy, and coke. Acid once, but not really into all that stuff anymore. Never did anything super hard core," she replied.

"Scandalous. How many guys have you slept with?"

"Too many to count," she responded. Now it was his turn to roll his eyes.

"Stop being cute. How many?" he asked again. She shrugged.

"I don't keep count. A lot, but not, like, astronomical."

"Any as good as me?"

"A couple."

"Doubtful."

Tate stared at him for a minute. Was he really insecure about how he stacked up? Seemed ridiculous. He'd probably been fucking his way through the Ford Modeling Agency. She knew there was no way she could compare to the women he must have slept with since their time together. She let out a deep sigh.

"Is that what you really want to know about? You can just ask," she told him. "I'd had sex with one other person, before you. What you and I did was ... intense. Probably not right on more levels than I like to acknowledge, but I liked it. It took me a while to admit that, you know. That I liked it. I thought something was wrong with me – you were a complete dick, but I couldn't stop thinking about it.

"Then a couple months after I moved back here, after I moved out of the apartment Daddy had rented, I went to this party. Got a little drunk. This guy was hitting on me, really laying it on, and it was like the old Tate kept whispering *'ew, you can't stand here and listen to this, it's inappropriate! You'll get in trouble!'*, but another side of me started going, *'who cares? He's hot, you're horny – just fuck him, you don't have to answer to anyone but yourself'* – and it was like something in me changed. I could do that, if I wanted to. No parents to worry about upsetting, no reputation to really care about, none of that stuff. Turned out the guy was horrible in bed, a total waste of time. But it helped me realize something – I like sex. I like having sex, I like being sexy. I like being single. I like being me, and fuck anyone who doesn't like it," she finished.

"So, you couldn't stop thinking about it, huh? Do you still think about it?" Jameson asked. Tate groaned.

"You are the most self-obsessed asshole I've ever met," she told him. He laughed.

"You may have done a one-eighty, but I'm still pretty much the same guy – just sharper claws," he warned her.

"*No*, I don't think about it," she answered his question. "I didn't even recognize you at first, in that kitchen. Took a while for it to click."

"What about what happened in that conference room? Are you okay with that?" he asked. She blinked in surprise. He shifted gears so fast, completely dominated the conversation. If it could even be called that – she felt like she was being interrogated.

"Which part? You tricking me into a job? Or feeling me up in front of a bunch of suits?" she asked for clarification. He smiled.

"I already know you liked it when I touched you, so how about when you took off your panties? I didn't make you do that – pretty bold move, I didn't expect it," he said.

"Probably because *you don't know me*. Maybe that's an every day thing for me, not bold at all," she pointed out.

"I don't think so. I challenged you. You didn't like it. You stepped up to the plate. I admire that," he commented.

"Yeah, and I knocked it out of the park. Game *over*. I win. You lose," Tate replied. His eyebrows shot up.

"You didn't win shit, the game isn't over yet. How far would you be willing to go?"

"I'm not playing games with you, Kane."

"You started them. If you can't handle it, just say so."

"I can handle anything you can dish out."

They stared at each other for a minute, the tension thick in the air. She didn't know what was going on between them – she should get up and walk away. But it was like that night in his apartment all over again. What Tate should do, and what she was going to do, were two very different things. He fascinated her. She usually intimidated men, or was just a good-time girl to them. Rarely did she banter or spar with them, and if she did, she had no trouble ripping them a new ass hole. Jameson, though, was unrippable.

"I want to hear about the best sex you've ever had," he switched the subject again. Tate laughed.

"Are you sure? It's not you," she teased. It was a complete lie, but she wasn't about to tell him that.

"I'll be the judge of that. Let's hear it," he said, leaning back in his chair. She thought for a second, leaning back as well.

"It was probably with my friend Ang, like two years ago or something. I had a boyfriend, but he found out that I had slept with his best friend. It was before we had started dating, but he didn't care. Totally freaked out in a club, started screaming that I was the biggest slut he'd ever met, just a huge whore. He kept shouting it to anyone who would listen," Tate started. Jameson sighed.

"So your friend Ang came to your aide after a nasty, embarrassing break up. Comforted you, wanted you to feel good about yourself," he tried to fill in the story. Tate threw her head back and laughed.

"Not so much. Ang dragged him outside and beat the shit out of him. Pretty hot. We fucked right there in the alley. Ang bent me over a staircase and explained to my boyfriend, in graphic detail, what a good fuck he was missing out on by dumping me," she finished.

"Wow. *That* was the best sex you ever had?" Jameson asked. She shrugged.

"Easily in the top five. Most of those are Ang," she supplied.

"Must be an animal in bed."

"Yeah – he also has a *huge* dick."

She was trying to shock him on purpose, now. Tate was very comfortable talking about sex, and in her experience, men tended to get nervous when confronted with a woman who talked the way she did. Not Jameson Kane, however. He nodded at her comment, showing all the interest of someone listening to a weather report.

"That does help. Are you two still together?" he asked.

"We were never together. We're just friends who happen to sleep together, when the mood strikes us," she explained.

"And how does one become a friend like that to you?" Jameson inquired. Tate snickered.

"Why, Mr. Kane, do you want to be fuck buddies with me?" she asked in a teasing voice.

"Leave out the buddy part," he responded. She leaned forward in her chair.

"*Not be you*. Is that what this is really about? You want to have sex with me?" she asked.

"Of course I do. You can lie to me all you want, but I have no problem admitting that you are still, to this day, probably the hottest pussy I've ever had," he said, his voice casual.

Tate inhaled sharply and choked a little. Ang was pretty blunt with her, but very few other men ever talked to her quite like that – it did something to her blood pressure. Hearing *Jameson* say it, did something to her. She rubbed her thighs together and took a deep breath.

"That's very flattering, Kane. Doesn't mean there will ever be a repeat," she replied.

"Why not?"

"Because. It's a bad idea. You were a massive dick. I'm a different person. It wouldn't be the same," she suggested. He nodded.

"You're right. It'll probably be much better, you were so inexperienced last time," he said bluntly. She let out a snort – she was offended.

"If I was so '*inexperienced*' and am *still* the best pussy you've ever had, then you have been sleeping with some very subpar women," Tate pointed out.

"I'm beginning to think I have. Why is it a bad idea? I mean, even if those things are true, what do they have to do with us sleeping together? You don't want a boyfriend, I don't want a girlfriend, so me being a dick and you being different has nothing to do with us screwing," Jameson pointed out.

Hmmm, he has a good point.

She shook her head.

"How about I just don't want to."

"*Liar.*"

"You're like this super sexy, tycoon, wolf, man, person, *thing* –

you can sleep with any girl you want. What's the big deal about me?" Tate asked, picking a paperweight up off his desk and tossing it between her hands.

"Most girls want something from me. A commitment, a connection, a trophy. Mostly I just want sex. Maybe someone I can treat badly from time to time," he said. "I think you're looking for similar things. I think we could help each other."

That caught her off guard. Despite their history, they didn't actually know each other very well; yet he had her all figured out. His words were like poetry to her, and at first, all she could think about was saying *yes*. Yes, to *anything* he wanted. And his words paired with the smoldering look on his face made him all that harder to resist. It was a look that said he knew *exactly* what she wanted, and he knew *exactly* how to give it to her. She took a deep breath and steeled her nerves.

"You know what," Tate began, standing up and putting the paperweight down. "I think we're done here. You wanted to talk to me, you did. You wanted to hear how I've been doing, I told you. You asked if I would sleep with you, I declined. Are we finished?"

He stared up at her, a smile spreading across his lips. Even though he looked at her like he was picturing her naked, he still managed to have a slight look of disdain about him. Like he knew something she didn't, and was gloating about it. Holding it over her head, out of her reach. She hated that feeling.

"Yes, I suppose so. When your curiosity gets the better of you, come back and see me," Jameson told her. She rolled her eyes and grabbed her purse.

"Goodbye, Kane," she said before walking out of the room at a brisk pace.

Tatum hadn't gotten to the point she was in life by lying to herself. He was right – she *was* curious. She did want to sleep with him, wanted to see if it would be the same. If it would be *better*. There really wasn't any reason why they couldn't, or shouldn't, other than that she didn't want to let him win. If withholding sex was the only weapon she had, then she would wield it with a vengeance.

Maybe …

When she got outside, she dug her phone out of her purse and called Ang. She was walking so fast, her hair was bouncing all over the place, but she couldn't slow down. If she hadn't been worried about looking completely crazy, she would've started running. She felt like she had been infused with energy, with electricity. Ang didn't pick up the first time and she swore at his voicemail, then called him again. He picked up after the second ring.

"What's up, chica?" he sounded a little breathless.

"Are you busy right now!?" Tate burst out, weaving through the afternoon lunch crowd.

"Yes. What's up? You sound like you're jogging," he told her.

"I almost am, I'm walking through downtown. How busy? Can I come over?" she asked.

"Not a good idea, sweetie. Is it an emergency?" Ang asked. She finally stopped walking and dragged herself out of the flow of people, over to a building. She leaned against the wall.

"Kind of."

"What type of emergency is a '*kind of*' emergency?" he asked.

"I met with Jameson today. He wanted to have a '*talk*' with me, at his office. I just left," she spoke softly into the phone. Ang started laughing.

"Ooohhh, it's *that* kind of emergency. I can't fuck you right now, kitten. Normally I jump at the opportunity to fulfill your needs, but I'm prepping for filming right now," he explained. Tate rolled her eyes.

"It's not like that, I pretty much argued with him the whole time," she snapped at him. Ang snorted.

"And you love to fight. Exactly how wet are you right now? On a scale – like, pleasantly aware? Or need to lose your underwear?" he asked. She chewed on her lip and looked down at herself.

Definitely the latter.

"Could your film use an extra today?" she managed to laugh in a quiet voice.

"Oh, babe, you've really got it bad. What's the big deal? You want him, go get him. I've never seen you hold back from any guy. Why this guy?" Ang asked. She shrugged.

"Because, he's Jameson Kane. He's like my worst nightmare and my biggest dream, all rolled into one. Because if he wants me, and I don't want him, I win – but if he wants me, and I sleep with him, *he* wins," she babbled.

"Baby, the only thing you're losing out on is good sex. Why does it have to be a competition? Play *together*, then everybody wins," Ang suggested.

Tate stared out into the street. She *had* been thinking of it as a competition – Jameson had used her once, and she wanted to get back at him. But Ang was right, once she wanted a man, she didn't hold back. And she *really* wanted Jameson. She had to reconcile that in her mind, or make the two opposing thoughts work together some how.

"Maybe you have a point," she mumbled.

"I'm almost always right, babe. Think of it as closure. Or make-up sex. Or *oh!* An anger-bang, getting back at him for making you feel bad! You do love angry sex," Ang reminded her.

"God. What if I sleep with him, though, and it's horrible? Or weird? Or he, like, falls in love with me?" Tate asked, chewing on her lip.

"Jesus, when did you turn into such a girl? The way you describe him, the man sounds incapable of having bad sex – or falling in love, for that matter. Just make sure you don't lose *your* heart. Big, bad, demons don't marry little girls," Ang warned her. She laughed.

"I'm not even sure I have a heart to lose anymore," she replied.

"It's there. Buried underneath piles of used condoms and Jack Daniel's bottles, it's in there somewhere," he assured her.

"You're gross."

"Look, I gotta go, sweets. Pedro's all lubed up and ready to shoot. Go have nasty, hot, sex with that man. Make him worship the ground Tatum O'Shea walks on. You know, be yourself. Then walk away like it ain't no thang. And then give me all the details. Take care," he instructed her. She groaned.

"You can't just leave me like this – what do I do? Do I go back there? Do I wait for him to call me? I don't know how to be like this," she whined. Ang started laughing.

"Oh jesus, you really are strung out for him. What I wouldn't give to be with you right now, you'd probably let me do all those things to you that you normally won't let me," he laughed.

"If you come get me and save me from the big, bad, demon, I just might," she told him in a breathy voice.

"Stop it, no teasing me. Seriously. Just do whatever feels natural. If you want to call him, call him. If you want him to call you, wait. If you want to show up at his office wearing nothing but a trench coat, send me pictures. Ciao for now," he prattled off and then the phone line went dead.

Tate huffed out a breath and stared down at the blank screen on her phone. She needed a plan, if she was going to do this – Jameson Kane got under her skin, ripped her apart. She needed some stitching in place, before she dealt with him. She wanted to sleep with him, wanted him to want her like he'd never wanted any woman ever before, wanted him *obsessed* with her. But she also wanted to be able to walk away whenever she wanted; which she would do, whenever she got bored. Just like he had been able to do with her.

It's still a game, and I am going to win.

Her phone suddenly rang in her hand, startling her. It was the temp agency calling.

"Hi Carla, I know about the spa, I was going to head there in a little bit," Tate assured the woman.

"This isn't about that – we've had another request for you! Pretty impressive, Tatum. Kraven and Dunn Brokerage called, they need a data entry clerk. Heard you were good. It would have the potential for long term work!" Carla was excited, her voice even breathier than normal.

"Thanks, Carla, I'll think about it," Tate responded through clenched teeth. She listened to the woman babble for a while, then made her goodbyes.

She squared her shoulders and headed back to Jameson's building. While she was in the elevator, she hurried to slick on some lip gloss and ruffle up her hair. Then she smudged her eyeliner a little, to give her eyes a darker, sexier look. She had looked polished earlier. She wanted to look a little messy now. She strode onto his floor and right past his secretary, who yelled at her as Tate burst into his office.

"My, that didn't take very long," Jameson laughed, hanging up a phone that had been pressed to his ear. Tate shut the office door on the squawking secretary.

"Why do you want me to be your data entry clerk?" she demanded.

"Because if you're busy with all those pathetic little side jobs, it'll make it harder for me to turn you to the dark side," he teased. She walked up to his desk.

"I'm not about to take a job just so you can try to have your way with me in some shitty cubicle," she informed him. He quirked up an eyebrow.

"You'll let your friend fuck you in an alley, but I can't sexually harass you in a cubicle?" he asked. Tate actually laughed – she couldn't help it.

"Look, if you want to see me or whatever, then come see me. You

77

know where I live, you know where I work. I don't need to work in your office. I've played the secretary that the boss is fucking – it isn't fun. Most office women have very sharp insecurities and don't take kindly to the slutty new girl," she told him. He shook his head.

"I don't want to have to track you down at every ridiculous job you have; *bicycle tours?* You've gotta be shitting me. I want your schedule clear, so I can see you whenever I want," he informed her. She crossed her arms.

"For someone who doesn't want a girlfriend, sounds like you plan on spending an awful lot of time with me," she pointed out. Jameson finally stood up.

"I just want to get to know you, mostly in the naked sense. You're the one who keeps bringing up relationship status. I'm telling you, right now, that *will not* happen, so don't get your hopes up," he said, his voice serious.

"So what, you just want me to work in your building, hiding in some dark corner, like a dirty secret? Not very enticing," Tate told him. He shook his head.

"Not at all. Like I said, I would just like you … *available to me*, whenever I want," Jameson tried to explain. She shook her head.

"Well that's impossible. I *have* to work. I live in the real world, Kane, I have to make money, I have to pay rent."

"And I'm offering you a job here," he responded.

"I *am not* going to work here. Besides, I love the bar, I would never leave it," she said.

"So quit all the temp bullshit, the tours, the dog walking, ice cream trucks, drug running, and whatever else you do," Jameson suggested.

"And live off three nights a week!? I make pretty good tips, but I'm not quite there yet," Tate laughed. His eyes were starting to get hard, she noticed. It was a look she hadn't seen in a long time, but she remembered it well.

"Then just work *here*," he said again. She shook her head.

"*No.* I'm not doing that," she replied. He rolled his eyes.

"You know what? Fine. *I'll* pay you. For every day you miss out on a job because of me, I'll fucking pay you for it," Jameson snapped out. Her eyebrows shot up.

"You'd pay me, to miss work, just so you could hang out with me and potentially have sex with me?" she clarified. He nodded.

"*Definitely* have sex, and yes, if that's what it takes."

"That is the stupidest thing I've ever heard. You're gorgeous and rich – you could probably find women who would pay *you* to have sex with them," Tate pointed out. He finally smiled again.

"Gorgeous, huh. Flattery will get you nowhere with me. And I make more than enough money, I don't want to get paid to have sex," he replied.

"But you don't mind paying for it?"

"Not at all."

"You don't find that strange? Paying someone for sex?"

"I find it *exciting*."

Her breath caught in her throat.

"But if I let you pay me, and we have sex, that would make me a whore," she laid out the points bluntly. He shrugged.

"Do you really have a problem with that?" Jameson asked.

Tate had walked some fine lines in her adult life, done some things she wasn't 100% proud of, but she had never turned tricks. She liked sex, liked to use it as a weapon sometimes, but never to get paid. One time, when she was around twenty-one, she and some friends had been hard up for a good time. She wound up blowing a guy for some coke, and she'd felt guilty about it for days.

Was it still a game, or was it just being a whore? Fine lines were so hard to see. She was scared of what would happen to her if she stepped over that line. How far down the rabbit hole was she willing to fall?

"I'm not sure. I think I do. I'm not some prostitute. You can't just pay me, and then I have to fuck you whenever you snap your fingers, or blow all your friends in a circle jerk," she told him. He laughed.

"Well, I don't normally attend circle jerks, so you should be fine on that point, and I wouldn't even have to pay you, and you'd still fuck me whenever I snapped my fingers," he countered.

One point, Jameson Kane.

"Two thousand dollars," she blurted out.

"Excuse me?"

"I quit all my other jobs – except for the bar. That means all my days will be free, I'll be '*available to you*' virtually every single day. My salary for that is two thousand dollars, a week," Tate informed him. He narrowed his eyes.

"Five hundred dollars," he counter offered. She shook her head.

"Don't insult me, Kane."

"One thousand."

"Call me when you want to play for real," she started to walk away. He grabbed her arm.

"One and a half," he offered, an evil smile tugging at the corner of his lips. She gave the sweetest smile she could manage back to him.

"*Two and a half,*" she amended her original price. His smile spread to the rest of his mouth.

"Deal."

"I'm not some street corner whore, either. I'm getting paid to be available to you – not spread my legs whenever *you're* in the mood. You had better respect that, or I'm gonna Taser you in the balls," Tate warned him.

"Kinky."

"I'm fucking serious."

"I would never force you to do something, if you really didn't want to do it. But, you can't be a tease. I think you're hot, Tate. I can remember how hot you were, and when I decide it's time for us to sleep together, you better not pull some bullshit and try to stop it from happening," Jameson told her.

He's going to decide when it's time?

She smirked at him. He really didn't know her at all. She stepped up close to him, pressing her entire body against his front. She ran her hands over his chest and was pleased to feel solid muscle underneath his shirt. Of course, his frame had looked good under his expensive suit, and she remembered him having a good body seven years ago, but it was nice to have it confirmed. She moved her hands under his jacket and around to his back. She purred low in her throat and rubbed herself against him, leaning into place a long lick against his throat.

"Do I seem like a tease?" she asked, her voice husky.

She felt his hand work its way into her hair, and then he was jerking back, *hard*, forcing her to look straight up at him. She didn't make a sound, refused to let him see any kind of surprise or fear or want on her face. Just looked at him with hooded eyes as he held her head in place. He looked almost angry. She had gotten to him, ruffled him a little.

Point to me.

"You look like a girl who doesn't know she's playing with fire."

"You're a sucker, you know," Tate laughed, shaking herself away from him. He let go of her hair. "I could be horrible in bed – I could just be blowing smoke up your ass. Or maybe I'm *too* kinky for you, who knows. How do you feel about inflatable sheep?"

"They pop too easily," Jameson responded. She burst out laughing.

"You know, Kane, we might just get along," she snickered.

"I was thinking that myself. Maybe buddies *is* the right word. We should have been friends a long time ago," he said. She nodded.

"Maybe. But if things hadn't happened the way they did, I wouldn't be this person. You wouldn't want to be my friend," Tate pointed out.

"This person was always inside of you, maybe I could've helped bring it out sooner," he replied. She shrugged.

"Pointless now. So, *buddy*, what would you like to do now? I do a good walking tour of the Harvard Yard," she offered.

"Is it better than your blowjobs?" he asked. She thought for a second.

"Probably not. I mean, it's a pretty good tour, but sucking dick is, like, my specialty," she replied in an overly-serious, sarcastic voice. Jameson laughed.

"God, I hope so. Call that salon, tell them you won't be coming intoday. Call your temp agency, too. What was the figure we agreed on? Two-thousand dollars?" he asked, making his way back behind his desk.

"Two thousand, *five hundred*," she corrected him.

"Clever girl. Now get out of here, you've wasted enough of my time and some of us have real jobs – not all of us can be whores. Be ready at eight," he instructed her.

"What's at eight?" she asked.

"You're coming over to my house."

Tate went for drinks with Ang first, to steady her nerves. She let him prattle on about his porn shoot, then she spilled all the details on her dirty banter with Jameson. Ang had her repeat the "*punish your mouth*" story – it was one of her favorite parts, too. They agreed that she should play it cool, just see what Jameson's deal was, what he was thinking. And then she could pounce. Blow his mind, see if he was able to blow hers, and then they would go from there. While drinking, she got a text from Jameson, giving her his address.

"You're so tense, it's hilarious," Ang laughed, massaging her shoulders while they waited outside for a taxi.

"He makes me nervous."

"Did I ever make you nervous?"

"Of course you did," Tate replied.

"Really? You never acted like it," Ang pointed out, moving around to stand in front of her. She guffawed.

"Ang – you're frickin' gorgeous, and the first thing you ever said to me was *'you've got the perfect look for facials, wanna do porn?'*; of course you made me nervous!" she chuckled. He shrugged.

"Well, you always seem so comfortable around me. You never get all stupid and brainless, like you are for him," he replied. She smiled and pressed her hand against his cheek.

"Oh my god, Ang, are you jealous?" she asked. He tried to pull away and she put both hands on his face, following him as he moved backwards.

"Shut up, you stupid cow. Go fuck your abusive billionaire, have a blast," he snorted, batting her hands away.

"You'll always be my fave, you know that. C'mon, we can go have a quickie, real fast," she laughed, backing him up against a wall. He grabbed her by her wrists.

"I'm not jealous, Tate," he said, staring down at her. She stopped laughing. Ang very rarely ever said her name. Baby, honey, sweetie, kitten, fuck-bunny, everything under the sun – when he said *'Tate'*, she knew it was time to listen.

"What's wrong?" she asked. He sighed, pulling her hands to his chest.

"Look, I'm very excited that you're going to be fulfilling a fantasy tonight," he said. She went to argue, but he squeezed her wrists. "I just want you to be *very careful*." Tate frowned.

"I'm always careful, you know that," she replied, but he shook his head.

"It's all fun and games with the two of us, but this guy is new – he can say whatever he wants, but he doesn't know you like I do. The way you've talked about him … sounds like running with scissors. Play with him, hurt him, let him hurt you a little, but *be careful*," Ang instructed her.

"You've been psyching me up for this for the last couple days, and now it sounds like you're trying to talk me out of it," she told him. He shook his head.

"No, I want you to have fun – but *only* fun. You've got this look in your eye, and it spells trouble. You think you're playing a game. *Don't lose to him.*"

The cab driver whistled at her, but Tate stayed were she was, blinking up at Ang. He was staring down at her, his eyebrows drawn together. Not a natural look for him. She smoothed her fingers across his forehead and down the side of his face. She felt so comfortable with his skin, like it was her own.

"I *never* lose," she said with a smile before giving him a quick kiss. Ang rolled his eyes.

"That's the worst part about you, you know. You think you're winning, when really you're always losing," he replied, then spun her around, smacking her on the ass.

She stumbled to the cab and got in the backseat, waving an arm out the window at him. He waved back before wandering back into the bar. She frowned after him. He had never shown concern like that before, and he had been present for many a pre-date-jitters drink. She hoped it wasn't jealousy. She couldn't handle that, not from Ang.

She gave the address to the driver and they took off. It was going to be a long drive. She tried not to think about the cost. She had been living on the fringe for so long, buying a vehicle was something she didn't even think about, it wasn't even on her radar. She had kinda assumed Jameson might send a car for her, but no offer had been made to do that – maybe he was more of a liberal kind of guy.

He lived all the way out in Weston, the wealthiest suburb in Boston. One of the richest towns in America. *Figures.* She lived in an apartment in North Dorcester, right *in* Boston. Kind of sketchy at times. She had been to Weston before, but with her parents, and since then, she'd never had a reason to go back.

When the taxi started pulling down a long, wooded driveway, Tate tried to not to gag at the sixty dollar tab and began rooting around in her purse. There went some rent money. She wondered if Jameson would actually give her any money, or if it had all been play. She was just starting to uncrumple some twenty dollars bills as the taxi parked, when the front passenger door swung open.

"Here you are, and thank you," a crisp, cultured sounding voice said, followed by a hand holding out two one-hundred dollar bills. Tate and the driver stared at the cash, both a little shocked. The money was exchanged and then her door was pulled open, a hand reaching in for her. Tate took it and was pulled to her feet.

A slender man stood in front of her, wearing an impeccable suit. *Very* expensive looking. He wasn't a very big man in general; she was around five-foot-six, and he wasn't that much taller than her. Maybe five-foot-ten, give or take an inch. His dark hair was gelled and styled, brushed to the side. He looked like something out of GQ magazine – very handsome, with fair skin and stormy blue eyes. He gave her a tight-lipped smile.

"Hello, Ms. O'Shea. I am Sanders, Mr. Kane's assistant," he said in a polite voice. There was a hint of an accent there, but she couldn't place it. Not Boston, but a distinct burr, something else East Coast-y, or maybe even European. His fricatives were sharp, his voice soft.

He should do books on tape.

"Hi, I'm Tatum," she greeted him, holding out a hand. He clasped it briefly, not really shaking it, just pressing his skin to hers and then letting go.

"Welcome. Please, follow me," he instructed, then turned to lead the way.

She hadn't gotten a good look at the house on the drive up. She gaped at it now. It was like something from a hundred years ago. Huge, and gorgeous. Lots of brick, with white pillars in the front. She wondered if Jameson had bought it when he moved to Boston, or if it had been in the family. It looked like something that would be on the National Historical Registry.

"Were you with him at the office, today?" Tate asked as they crunched across the pebble stone driveway.

"No."

"Do you go into Boston a lot?"

"No."

"I got the impression he travels a lot, do you go with him on those trips?"

"No."

She smirked at the assistant's back as he held open the front door for her.

"I'm going to assume that living with Kane is what has given you this anti-social personality disorder," she said in a sweet voice. The man didn't even blink at her statement.

"I had this disorder long before Mr. Kane. He's in the library, through that door," Sanders told her, gesturing along the wall.

She gasped, taking in the huge entry way. Vaulted ceilings, original hard wood floors, a chandelier that probably dated back to the civil war. A huge sitting room opened off to her right, and two large, sliding doors were shut on the room to her left. Farther down the wall, just past a grand staircase, was another door, standing slightly ajar. She could see a glow, like candle light, spilling out into the hall.

Tate had come from money, grown up in a gorgeous home, but it had been a long time since that life. It felt strange now, to be surrounded by such opulence. The rug she was standing on probably cost more than everything she owned.

"You know, Sandy," she started, reaching out and grabbing onto his shoulder. He frowned while she steadied herself and bent over, undoing the straps on her shoes. "I think we're gonna get along, *just fine.*"

With her shoes dangling from her hand, Tate tip toed down the entry way and pushed through the library door. There was a roaring fire in a huge fireplace on the far wall; it was providing the only light in the room. Built-in bookshelves surrounded her, and there were two huge, over stuffed, wing-backed chairs pulled up close to the fire. Off to the right of them stood a ridiculously huge, ornate, gold-inlaid desk. Jameson was standing behind it, holding some papers, and he looked up at her entrance.

"You made it. Quite a cab ride," he commented as she walked towards him. She nodded.

"Forty-five minutes. I won't be doing that often," she warned him.

"You'll do it often enough. Drink?" he asked, setting down his work and coming out from around the desk.

"God, yes. Your assistant gave me freezer burn," she laughed, watching Jameson as he walked over to a small bar.

She stayed near his desk and stared at him, letting her eyes wander over his form. Every time she had seen him, he had been wearing expensive suits – blazers, ties, trousers, shiny shoes, and shinier watches. Now, he was in jeans and a plain white t-shirt. No shoes. No socks.

Tate had never once seen him so dressed down, not even when he'd been dating her sister. She was a little shocked. It gave him a whole different look. He almost – though not quite – looked approachable. He was too good looking to ever truly look like a mere mortal. But still. She found herself wanting to peel his shirt off so she could lick every inch of his skin.

"Ah, Sanders. Yes. You'll grow to love him, almost everyone does.

What would you like?" Jameson asked. When she didn't answer, he turned towards her. "What? What are you staring at?"

"You're barefoot," she blurted out, staring down at his feet. He laughed, looking down as well.

"Yes. So are you," he replied. She wiggled her toes at him.

"Yeah, but I expect that from me. Mr. Kane doesn't walk around barefoot. He has people to walk around for him," she teased, looking back up at him. He snorted.

"*Mr. Kane's* feet hurt after a long day. You look nice," Jameson commented, his eyes wandering over her. She had put on a fitted black dress, for her cocktail hour with Ang – a little overdressed for an evening in the country.

"Thank you. I went out for drinks with a friend, before coming here," she told him.

"Pre-gaming? Scared of coming out here?" he asked, turning back to the bar and picking up crystal bottles.

"No. Just drinks with a friend," Tate replied, spinning in a slow circle and looking around the room.

"The redheaded roommate?" he asked. She felt something cool, and turned to see him running a glass full of ice and liquid down the side of her arm. She took it from him.

"No. Ang," she answered, taking a sip. She tried not to make a face. *Gin and tonic.*

"Ah, the half-man, half-donkey friend. How was the tripod?" Jameson asked, making himself a drink, as well. She laughed.

"Careful, almost sounds like jealousy, and I got enough of that from him," Tate joked, heading over and falling into one of the chairs. She let her shoes drop to the floor and she tucked her feet up underneath herself.

"Tripod-man is jealous? I'm flattered," he replied, taking the chair next to hers.

"Not really jealous, I guess. Just … cautious. On my behalf," she tried to explain.

"Understandable."

"So, how did you find this place, Kane? Daddy's will?" Tate asked. She knew Jameson and his father hadn't had the best relationship.

"Something like that. Had it almost completely remodeled a couple years ago," he replied.

"Oh wow. Were you here for that?"

"For a little while."

"So you came to Boston a couple years ago."

"As my answer would imply."

She stayed silent, sipping at her drink. He had been in Boston a couple years ago, but hadn't contacted her. She still thought it was strange. If he was so into her, so obsessed with that one time they'd been together, why hadn't he looked her up? He would've had to assume that she'd still be in Boston, still going to school. She let out a sigh, tried not to think about it.

"Did you —," she started, but then he cleared his throat.

"I didn't call you because I didn't think about it. I had just acquired a shit ton of property and money, I was a little busy. You weren't even on my radar. Women were the last thing on my mind," Jameson said, reading her mind.

"It's probably a good thing – a couple years ago, I was even crazier than I am now."

"Jesus."

"I had a rough patch there, from about twenty to twenty-three. Like I was making up for lost time, or something. I just did everything and anything I could think of," she told him.

"Hmmm, sounds interesting. Now I wish I had called you," he responded, and she laughed again.

"What about you? What have you been doing?" she asked. He took a deep breath.

"I started my own brokerage firm, not long after I left Harrisburg. Invested in a start up film company, made a bundle. Sold my firm, moved to Germany for a year to head a new firm there. My dad died, and I inherited all of his businesses. Moved back, lived in Los Angeles for a while. Then Manhattan. Made a lot of investments. I do a lot of consulting work, now," he summed everything up.

"Wow. I moved from one bad neighborhood to another, while you were moving across the globe," she chuckled. Jameson nodded.

"Your life story is much shittier than mine," he agreed. She glared at him.

"But probably a lot funner," Tate countered, finishing off her drink.

"I highly doubt that. Have you ever had sex with a supermodel while sailing through the Mediterranean on your 250 foot yacht?" he asked. Tate thought for a second.

"No. I gave a handjob in an Arby's bathroom once, though. Kinda like the same thing," she told him with a bright smile.

"I stand corrected. Your life leaves me in awe," he chuckled, rubbing a hand over his face.

"Tired?" she asked, leaning back in her chair and getting comfy.

She had expected to be a lot more nervous around him. For the two years he had dated her sister, Tate had always been a nervous mess around Jameson. She was surprised to find that she felt almost comfortable. Something about knowing she was with someone that she could say absolutely anything to, anything at all, and he most likely wouldn't be shocked or offended, comforted her.

"Very tired. It was a long day. I'm also involved in mergers and acquisitions. Sometimes people are not so eager to give up their stuff," Jameson said in a gruff voice.

"Poor baby," she cooed at him. He snorted.

"Shut up. How is Ellie?" he asked.

She went still. She hadn't expected him to ask about her family. Sure, Tate had asked about his house and life, but in a general, "*let's make conversation before I explode and rape you*", kind of way. She knew he didn't care about her, or her family.

"Fine, I guess. We don't speak. My mother gets nostalgic after a couple bottles of wine, calls me, keeps me updated on the family. Last I heard, Ellie's pregnant," Tate replied, turning to stare into the fireplace.

"First child?"

"Yup."

"Married, I assume."

"Within a year of you two splitting up."

"She was always ambitious."

Tate didn't respond, staring at the flames. She got lost in thought. She hadn't seen or spoken to her sister in seven years. Most of the time she didn't think about it, but once in a while, the realization slapped her in the face. She hadn't spoken to her father, either, and the only times she spoke with her mother was when the woman was drunk off her face. God, she hated thinking about them.

There was coldness against her arm again, and she looked up to see Jameson handing her a fresh drink. She hadn't even heard him move. She smiled up at him, taking the glass. He didn't move away, though; just kept staring down at her. She kept her eyes trained on his while she took a drink.

"Ambitious, but boring as fuck. I think I started hating her, long before you and I happened," he said. Tate chuckled.

"Same here," she agreed.

"But you. You were always something else," he continued.

"Me? You never even noticed me. You were *Jameson Kane*. My family practically worshiped you. I was always shoved into the background. You didn't even know my age, that night, and you had been with Ellie for two years," she pointed out. He shrugged.

"So. I knew you were sexy. That first time I ever saw you, when Ellie brought me home to meet your parents. You walked in the front door. I can remember it so clearly – you were in tight running shorts, arguing with someone on your phone. I can remember thinking that I wanted to peel your shorts off of you and wrap them around your neck," he told her.

Who knew?

"Huh. That would've been an interesting introduction," Tate joked.

"And then the night you and I slept together. Ellie and I'd had a big fight. She never told me you were coming over. You walked in, in those preppy sweaters you always wore, and your tight skirt. Long, black hair. So different from her. Sitting at the kitchen table, trying to be an adult with me. You had no idea, but I knew then that something was going to happen," Jameson said.

"No way, Kane. I was whining and complaining like a little girl. You were probably annoyed with me. You didn't even try anything, till you caught me with my shirt off," she reminded him. He shrugged.

"What can I say, I'm a gentleman at heart," he replied.

"*Bullshit.*"

"No, I guess I'm not, not even a little bit. You just … there was something about you, the way you would always look at me. So shy. I wanted to hurt you a little bit."

Now they were getting somewhere. Tate leaned over the side of her chair a little, setting her glass on the floor. Then she sat forward, arching her neck to look up at him. He stared straight back at her, the fire casting shadows on one side of his face and burning up the other side.

He looks like Satan.

"I never did anything to you, why did you want to hurt me?" she asked. He chuckled.

"Not like how you're thinking."

"Then like how?"

He reached a hand out. He was gentle as he wrapped his fingers around her throat, then he squeezed, just enough for her to feel the pressure. He began pulling and she was forced to follow. He pulled her to her feet, so she was standing right in front of him. Then he applied more pressure, his short, sharp, nails biting into her skin.

"*Like this*," Jameson said, still staring straight into her eyes. She took quick breaths through her nose.

"Maybe you should've just asked," Tate whispered. "Maybe I would've been okay with it." He shook his head.

"No. Not back then. You weren't ready, and I wasn't ready to be that person for you," he replied. She raised an eyebrow.

"And you think you can be that person now?" she asked.

His fingers loosened and his hand trailed down her neck, then continued down to her chest. He pressed his palm flat against her, right over her breasts, and she had a flashback to their night together. She shivered.

"Yes, I do. I remember you being very concerned about Ellie, last time. Wouldn't shut up about her. I've been in threesomes where the women talked less about each other than you did about Ellie. Is that going to be an issue this time?" he asked. Tate laughed.

"You're the one who keeps bringing her up. Maybe you're actually more interested in meeting up with her," she teased. Jameson rolled his eyes and stepped way from her, heading back towards his desk.

"God, what a horrible thought, Eloise O'Shea, seven years later. Some how, I assume she hasn't turned out quite as ... *grown up* as you," he said, raking his eyes over Tate's body.

"I couldn't give two shits about Ellie. Maybe I should look up all her ex boyfriends, sleep with all of them, really stick it to her," Tate snorted, picking her glass up off the floor and taking a drink.

"Please don't. I know for a fact I was the wildest person she ever slept with, and even then, I kept things on a very tight leash for her. I would hate for you to waste your time. Now, I've been thinking about our terms. Two-thousand dollars seems like an awful lot of money, when what you said is right – how do I know I'm not getting skunked? I think I need to sample the goods first," Jameson said, sitting behind his desk. She laughed.

"You've sampled my goods once already. And the salary was two-thousand, *five hundred*," she reminded him.

"Ah, yes. But those goods are out of date now, and I didn't get a nearly big enough sample. Like your mouth, for example. How can I guarantee you even know what to do with it?" he asked, steepling his hands in front of his chest. She raised an eyebrow at him and sat her drink back down on the floor.

Challenge accepted.

"You know, Kane," she started, taking slow strides to reach his desk. "You have the strangest way of trying to get things. If you'd just ask, half the time you'd receive, instead of playing these silly games."

"But where's the fun in that? And you started these games," he reminded her. Tate hiked up her dress a little and lifted her knee to his desk.

"I didn't realize they'd go on for this long," she replied, lifting her other knee. She bent forward and crawled across the desk towards him. He didn't move.

"They're going to go on for a lot longer," he warned her. She reached out, putting her hand on his knee.

"For how long?" she asked, her voice husky as she slid her hand up his thigh, moving as slowly as possible.

"However long it takes for you to realize who the winner will always be," Jameson replied.

Before she could respond, there was a loud knock at the door. She didn't move, kept her eyes locked to his, her hand an inch away from his crotch. He stared back, a smile spreading across his face. He looked like the devil. She suddenly got nervous.

Oh no.

"Who is that?" she asked, when there was another knock.

"I forgot, a business associate is stopping by, just to go over some stuff," Jameson explained. His voice was too soft, too easy going. Tate leaned back, sitting on her heels.

"Oh. Okay. Want me to leave?" she offered, confused. He shook his head.

"No, you can stay in here. In fact, I have a wonderful idea," he started.

Now she was really nervous.

"Oh god. What?" she asked, looking over her shoulder at the door.

"You want two-thousand, five hundred dollars. You have to prove to me that you're worth it," he said.

"I thought we were doing that," she pointed out. He laughed.

"Too easy! Now you've got me worried. A handjob in my library? Don't I even get Arby's?" he joked. She smacked him on the chest.

"Shut up," she growled. He lurched forward in his chair, his face a couple inches away from her own.

"Mr. Greene is going to walk in here, in about two minutes. We are going to go over some property info – he's buying my farm in Vermont. If you can make me come, before he leaves the room, I will agree to your salary," Jameson offered.

She stared at him. A little shocked. A little surprised. A lot intrigued. *Make him come?* While another man was in the room? How was she going to do that? How had they gone from drinks and light banter, to acts of sexual indecency in front of a virtual stranger?

"You want me to jack you off in front of some dude," Tate clarified. Jameson roared with laughter.

"God, no, I have long since out grown any sort of voyeuristic phase. You have about one minute," he warned her, as there was another knock at the door.

Her breathing picked up. She wasn't even thinking about the

money. The look on his face said he thought she couldn't do it. She wanted to wipe it off his face. She smirked at him and moved, swinging her legs towards him. He had to roll his chair away as she scooted to the edge of the desk and hopped off, standing in the V of his legs. Jameson raised an eyebrow, but didn't say anything as she lowered herself to her knees. She backed herself under the desk – it was huge, with enough space for her to almost fully kneel under it. She grabbed his knees, dug her fingernails in, and urged him forward. He rolled towards her.

"There has to be rules. You can't purposefully stop me, no hair pulling," she stated, staring up at him while she undid his belt buckle.

"You'd like it if I pulled your hair," he retorted. Tate rolled her eyes, wiggling her hand through the zipper of his pants.

"You know what I mean."

There was a loud knock, then she heard the door sweep open. Jameson rolled forward, and she was left in the dark, just a little glow from the fire making its way under the desk. She yanked and pulled at the waist of his jeans, listening as another man came in the room, greeted Jameson, and sat down across from the desk.

Their only time together, Tate hadn't gotten to see, or even really feel, his dick. It had just been inside of her. *So much* inside of her. He was larger than she remembered. She had slept with quite a few men since him, and he still managed to be the most impressive, in almost every way.

She ran her hand up and down his shaft, resting her other hand against his thigh. She was hoping to feel tense skin, maybe a muscle tick. Something to show he was struggling. But his legs were relaxed, and even though she was jerking him off, his voice sounded completely normal as he spoke. Almost bored sounding.

We can change that.

Tate hadn't been lying, blowjobs were a kind of specialty of hers. She loved the act. Having so much power over a man, but at the same time, being completely subjugated by him. An illusion of control. She loved it, and doing it in public? If Jameson didn't wanna have sex after she was done, she was going to take care of herself, right on his desk.

She licked him from top to bottom, taking her time at first. When she wrapped her lips around his head, she finally felt a muscle in his thigh tense. She almost smiled, bobbing her head up and down a little. Getting a feel for him. She removed her hand from his leg, wrapped it around the base of his dick, then worked it up and down to cover the distance. She didn't know how long his meeting would last. It almost sounded more like a social call, with a smattering of property talk. She would love to draw it out for him, have him panting and sweating, but she didn't want to lose the game.

Taking a deep breath through her nose, she went for gold and lowered her mouth all the way down on him. When his tip hit the back of her mouth and started to slide down her throat, she finally heard his voice hitch. *Victory*. She slowly worked her mouth off of him, then plunged right back again. He coughed to cover up a stutter. With him fully sheathed in her mouth, she ran one hand up between his legs, rolling her fingers around his sack. He coughed again and she backed off.

Finish this.

She began pumping away, working her hand and mouth up and down his dick. Every up sweep, she swirled her tongue around his head. Every down sweep, she squeezed his testicles. Then she would switch it up. Take a couple deep throats. Then back to bobbing and sucking.

Tate could hear it in his voice, he was having trouble. She felt a hand on the back of her head, and his fingers worked their way into her hair. Twisted and pulled. Not enough to pull her away, but enough for her to feel him. She let out a small, breathy moan, dug her fingernails into his thighs.

"Well, John, it's kinda late, and I have some work I need to do upstairs," she heard Jameson say in a loud voice.

Cheating! He can't ask him to leave! Cheater!

Tate redoubled her efforts, pulled all her tricks out of the bag. Unsheathed her teeth, skimmed them against his skin. She heard him hiss at that one. Took him on the inside of her cheek, running the sensitive tip against the sides of her molars. He gave a full body shudder then. Then she ran her tongue over every inch of his nuts.

His voice was getting strained, his muscles were all tensing. He wasn't going to last much longer. She could hear Jameson trying to get the guy to leave. She ran her free hand up his leg, over his waist, and started up his stomach. When her fingertips were visible over the desk, his hand let go of her hair and grabbed at her fingers. Pressed his hand flat over them, against his stomach. She dug her claws in and raked the hand back down. More tension in his legs. He was breathing heavy, and through his t-shirt, she could feel sweat.

I'm going to win. I'm going to win. I'm going to —,

"It's almost eleven o'clock at night, John. Go the fuck home so I can go to bed," Jameson suddenly barked out.

She was enraged. The cheating bastard. Tate went to pull away, but his hand was back in her hair, forcing her head down on him. She moaned, loudly this time, then both his hands were in her hair, holding her in place. She braced her hands against either side of the dresser, taking shaky breaths through her nose.

When the door to the library banged shut, he let go of her. She all but spit him out, pushing at his knees and forcing him backwards. She quickly climbed to her feet and glared down at him, but he just grinned up at her.

"Goddamn, Tate, you weren't fucking around. You do that like it's your job," Jameson laughed, sounding proud of her. She put her hands on her hips.

"You cheated!" she snapped at him. He ignored her and climbed to his feet, tucking his hard on back into his pants.

"It wasn't ever actually your job, was it? Walking tours with a happy ending?" he joked.

"You cheated. You made him leave. I had you, and you *cheated*," Tate repeated herself. He stepped up close to her.

"I said you had to do it before he left the room. I didn't say when or how that was going to happen. Should've worked harder for it," he told her.

"Are you *fucking kidding me?*" she growled. He ran a finger down her cheek.

"Think of how much better it will be when I'm an active participant," he said. She shook her head.

"You'll be lucky if there ever is a next time," she spat out.

"So let's see. How does … *one-thousand, five hundred* a week sound," Jameson said it out loud, but sounded more like he was talking to himself as he reached around her, sifting through some papers.

"Oh no. The price just went up to four thousand," Tate informed him. He laughed, long and loud.

"Now that's a fucking joke. I wouldn't give you four thousand dollars a week if you needed it for a kidney transplant. You suck cock like a champion, but no mouth is worth four thousand," he assured at her. Tate got so close, her chest was brushing against his own.

"*My mouth is.* You can agree, or I can walk out the door," she told him, her voice low and angry.

It wasn't about the money. Tate would be there even if he hadn't offered to pay. It was about winning. Beating him at his own game. Getting him to admit that she was an equal, that she could turn him inside out, the same way he did to her.

"You're not going anywhere, baby girl. We have unfinished business."

Baby girl.

"That's not my fault," she replied.

"Seems to me it is, if you were better at your job," Jameson said.

"Doesn't matter how good I am, if what I have to work with, *doesn't work right,*" she taunted.

His hand was in her hair in a second, pulling at the base of her skull. She was yanked forward and was completely flush against him, her chin almost resting on his clavicle. His other hand went to her waist, his fingers hooking into her dress and her flesh. Her hands flew to his chest, to brace herself.

"You better watch what you say to me," he warned her in a soft voice. She chuckled, her eyes watering a little from the sting of her hair being pulled.

"Or what, *Kane?*" she pushed him. His lips tilted up in a soft, sly smile.

"You're so fucking stupid, Tate. You still think we're playing a game. *Stupid bitch.* What did I say about calling me Kane? You've said it *thirteen times.* I said I would punish you," Jameson threatened.

This is what I've been waiting for.

"You keep saying that, but I've yet to see anything happen. I think you're all talk, *Kane.*"

He spun her around and bent her over, slamming her down on the desk. She let out a grunt – that might leave a bruise. She reached back, pulling at the hand he had in her hair. He let go, but only to grab her wrist. He pinned it down on her back, then grabbed her other wrist, joining it with the first. He held them together with one hand, pressing down on her so hard, it was uncomfortable to breathe. She tried to turn her head, and her chin dug into the wood of the desk.

"Such a fucking child, Tate. Fucking games. Do I look like the kind of guy who plays games?" he was hissing behind her, his free hand raking up her thigh and pushing her dress up over her ass.

"You're the one who keeps playing them. You're the one who —," she started when his hand crashed down across her ass. She gasped.

"*This* is not a game. You would do well to remember the difference," Jameson growled. She laughed again, and was almost amazed by her own bravado.

"Maybe you should write me out a *game plan*, so I can know when you are, and when you aren't, playing around and —,"

His hand was so heavy, she knew he was going to leave a mark. Six slaps. She was crying out by the end, writhing under his grip. She didn't want to play the game anymore. She wanted him inside of her.

He knew what she needed, just like before; just like always, probably. He let go of her wrists and she gripped onto the edge of the desk, next to her head. He was rough as he yanked her underwear down, not even bothering to push them past her knees. He kicked her feet wider apart and she could feel the material pull. Wondered if they'd rip.

Then he was pushing inside of her. She let out a long moan, raising up onto her tip toes, trying to accommodate all of him in one go. She wiggled her hips against him, then he was pressed completely against her. Solid, warm flesh, inside and out. She let out a deep breath, her whole body starting to shake. He leaned down against her.

"Still feel like a game?" Jameson whispered, his voice full of disdain. Tate laughed and laid her cheek against the desk.

I'm such a glutton ...

"I don't know. Can't really feel much of anything at all," she said back in a raspy voice.

He fucked her like she offended him. Like he was *angry* at her. Pulled her hair, forcing her to raise up off the desk. Slammed into her so hard from behind, she was pretty sure she was going to have bruises where her legs were pressed against the desk. His dick was brushing against something inside of her. She couldn't tell if it was her cervix, or maybe a G-spot she didn't know about – whatever it was, it made her see spots and little flashes of paradise.

He let go of her hair and while one hand gripped her hip, the other worked the zipper down on the back of her dress. He pushed the material off her shoulders and she managed to lift her arms enough to slide it off. His hand was instantly at her breast, twisting and scratching through the material of her bra. She propped herself up, locking her elbows.

"Holy fucking shit, Tate, you feel even better than I remembered," Jameson groaned, a hand sliding up to her neck, his fingers wrapping around it and squeezing tight. She managed a nod, her eyes fluttering closed.

"Yes, yes, better. Much better," she managed to whisper.

He suddenly pulled away and then he was yanking her back with him. She wasn't sure if she could stand on her own. Her panties slid off onto the floor. He turned her and forced her to sit on the desk, pushed her onto her back. He yanked her legs apart, then was plunging back inside her.

His hands were on her knees, forcing her legs apart. Her own hands were at her breasts, at his command. He told her where, and how, to touch herself. Called her filthy names. Told her that *this* was all she was good for, and that was why he had found her again. Because even if this was the only thing she was good for, she was *so* good, he was the only one worthy of sharing it with her.

For once, she didn't argue with him.

"C'mon, Tate," he growled, peeling his t-shirt off over his head. "I would've thought you'd be done by now, crying like a girl, coming all over my dick." She pushed herself upright, hooked an arm around his back to anchor herself in place.

"You'll find ... it's a little harder ... to make me cry now," she told him, running her tongue up the center of his chest. His hands slid down her legs, moved around to grip onto her ass, forcing her even harder against his thrusts. She shrieked, letting her head fall back.

"Hmmm, we'll have to try for it another day," Jameson groaned, dropping his head to her shoulder. She felt his teeth against her skin, fangs to her jugular, claws to her heart. He bit down, once. Twice. A third time, so hard, she thought he was going to take out a piece of her.

He already did that, a long time ago, baby girl.

She came, *hard*. She clenched her thighs against his waist, pressed her face to his chest, her hand to his jaw. Her fingers dug into his cheek. He held completely still while she shook and moaned, his heart beat the only thing keeping her grounded to earth. She felt like she had just been shot out of a cannon.

"*So easy,*" he murmured.

He shoved her away and Tate collapsed against the desk, taking deep breaths. He started pounding away again, lifting her legs high, resting her calves on his shoulders. Then his hands were on her breasts, covering them, pressing down on them. She completely let go, relaxed every muscle, just let him do whatever he wanted to her. The desk began to jolt around and move forward; she couldn't even imagine how much the oak monstrosity weighed, that's how hard he was pushing into her.

Jameson came so hard, she could feel it. Felt his shaft tighten, swell. Felt the muscles in his shoulders strain and cord up underneath her calves. She let her legs fall to the side and he collapsed on top of her. All of his weight. He obviously wasn't worried about crushing her.

Just like last time.

Tate wondered what else would be like last time. She loved her some dirty, rough, sex – but getting kicked out of bed was never a fun experience. She didn't even mind if a guy hustled her out, but that was really the only part of her experience with Jameson that she didn't recall with pleasure. The way he had treated her afterwards. Not so much his words, but his indifference. Like she hadn't just rocked his world off its axis, the way he had done to hers.

"Scared, baby girl?" he suddenly breathed against her chest. She laughed.

"Not the word I would use," she replied, rubbing the back of her hand across her forehead.

"And what word would Tatum O'Shea use?"

"*Fucked.*"

Jameson laughed and pushed himself off of her. She waited for it, the indifference, but it didn't come. He pulled his pants up, left them undone, then grabbed her arm, pulling her so she was sitting upright. She felt like her body was made of jell-o. He cocked up an eyebrow and fixed her bra for her, then slid her dress back over her arms. He looked at her for a second, traced his finger along her jaw, then wrapped an arm around her waist, pulling her off the desk.

"No tears," he mumbled, looking down into her eyes. She laughed.

"Nope."

He turned her around and zipped up her dress. While she slipped her underwear back on, he grabbed her forgotten drink and refilled it. She chugged it down in a couple gulps and he made her another. She did the same thing to it, watching him over the rim of the glass.

"If that's how you fuck sober, it'll be very interesting to see what you're like drunk," Jameson laughed, pulling his shirt back on.

"You couldn't handle it."

"I can handle anything you've got."

Tate thought maybe he would tell her to go home, order up a cab, or a car, or something. But he didn't. He made her another drink and then grabbed her hand, pulling her behind him. She followed him out of the library and into the entry way. A light was on in the sitting room. There hadn't been any on when she'd come into the house.

"Is somebody here?" she asked. He glanced back at the room as he led her up the stairs.

"Sanders. He works late in there sometimes," he explained. She laughed.

"That poor man, I probably scared him," she snickered. She had been screaming like it was a competition, cursing a blue streak. *Oops.*

"Please. He's walked in on a lot of scenes like that, I doubt he even notices it any more," Jameson snorted as they reached the second floor. He dragged her down a hall, past a bunch of doors.

"Fuck a lot of women in your library?" Tate asked. Jameson looked over his shoulder at her.

"Jealous?"

She laughed.

"No. You fuck women in libraries. I fuck men in odd, semi-public locations. Po-TATE-o, po-TOT-o," she replied. He laughed and finally stopped them in front of a large door at the end of the hallway.

"Well, I feel left out. A desk and a bed seem kinda boring in comparison," he chuckled, pushing open the door.

"I didn't want to say anything," she said with a straight face, and he laughed again before leading her into his bedroom.

It. Was. *Huge.* She dropped his hand and walked foward, taking it all in, while he kicked the door shut behind him. He had a huge king size bed. Walk in closet. Expensive, heirloom looking furniture. She walked over to a side table, running her fingers across expensive looking cuff links and watches. Everything was dark, every inch of the room screaming with masculinity. With *him.*

Tate downed the rest of her drink and slowly turned around to face him. He was still in front of the doorway, his arms crossed, watching her. She sat her glass down on the table and slipped the top of her dress back off her arms. Peeled it over hips. Dropped it to the floor and kicked it aside. Stood in front of him, a hand on her hip.

"So. Fuck a lot of women in *here?*"

6

TATE YAWNED AND STRETCHED, UNABLE to help the wince that followed. She felt sore just about everywhere. It was *delicious*. She opened her eyes, focused on high ceilings with ornate crown molding. She turned her head to the right – day light was streaming in a window next to her. She turned her head to the left – Jameson was on the other side of the king sized bed, sleeping on his stomach. She smiled and sat up.

It had been a pretty amazing night. She hadn't really known what to expect. Maybe rougher sex and less talking. The way it had all gone was better, though. Like he had said, they were getting reacquainted. Best not to get into the crazy shit the first time they slept together. He had been almost gentle with her in his bedroom, and she could tell he was holding back for her. Prepping her. His words still had bite, though; a promise of what was to come.

Tate rubbed at her neck, working the kinks out with her fingers. She let her fingertips dance along the tops of her shoulders, and on the right side, she could feel a raised welt. She let her fingers play over it for a minute, trying to figure out exactly what it was, when she remembered him biting her.

Glancing at him, she slid out of the bed and scampered across the room, into the bathroom. She closed the door and looked at herself in a full length mirror. Her eye makeup was everywhere, she looked like a panda. Or really, with the combination crazy bed head, a punk rocker that had escaped from the '80's.

She leaned in close, examining the bite mark. He hadn't broken the skin, but it looked ugly. It made her feel warm. She turned around, looking over her shoulder, trying to see her butt. There was no bruising, but one side was distinctly redder than the other. Her back also had red marks going down its length. Jameson had sharp claws. When she turned to the front again, she could see bruise lines forming at the tops of her thighs – she had known those would show up. She then got right up against the mirror, looking over her jaw. She had smacked the desk pretty good, but no marks. That was good. She liked it rough, but she didn't like walking around with a black eye. People asked too many questions.

She tip toed back into the bedroom, and saw that Jameson was still asleep. She watched him for a moment. His hair was rumpled and cute, his arms akimbo to his head, hands clasped under a cheek. His position made the muscles in his broad shoulders bunch and come together, and she chewed on her bottom lip, tempted to scratch him awake.

She didn't, opting to find her underwear instead. She found her bra hanging from the side of a mirror and quickly slipped it on; she decided her underwear was a lost cause and threw them away. She was shimmying back into her dress when she heard the covers rustle around.

"Sneaking out, baby girl?" Jameson spoke, his voice scratchy with sleep. Tate chuckled.

"No, I would've woken you up to say goodbye," she replied, struggling with the zipper on her back. Once she had it all the way up, she looked at him. He had pulled himself into a sitting position against the headboard, hands behind his head. His piercing blue eyes were traveling over every inch of her.

"Ah, but who told you that you could leave?" he asked. She laughed and walked over to the bed.

"I didn't realize I needed permission," she responded, kneeling on the mattress and making her way to his side.

"You need to ask permission for *everything*."

"Probably not gonna happen, Jameson," she laughed, sitting back on her heels. He sighed and dropped his hands.

"Well at least we broke you of one bad habit. I swear, your mouth must get you into so much trouble. Very defiant, baby girl. If I had to hear you say '*Kane*' one more time," he didn't finish the thought, just sucked air through his teeth.

"I don't see what the big deal is – pretty much everyone else calls you Kane," she pointed out. He leaned forward.

"You're not '*everyone else*', you're different. You get to see the real me," he told her.

Her heart leapt in her chest. She was different to him, she got to see the real him. Too much info. She didn't know whether to jump for joy, or head for the hills. Ang had told her to be careful, and she had laughed at him. She should have heeded his warning a little better.

"Well, I'll have to see the '*real you*' later – I have to go," Tate laughed. Jameson narrowed his eyes.

"Why?"

"Because, it's almost eleven o'clock. I have to go home, run some errands, shower, get ready for work. I work at the bar Thursday through Saturday," she explained. He nodded and yawned, rubbing a hand over his face.

"Right, right, the shit hole. I'll be in Manhattan this weekend, but I'll be back Sunday. I'll call you," he told her.

"*Ooohhh*, Manhattan weekend. Lifestyles of the rich and the famous," she teased. He rolled his eyes.

"There's that mouth. Hold on, I'll have Sanders get the car," he said, leaning over and grabbing a phone that was next to the bed.

While Jameson barked orders at poor Sanders, Tate did her best to wipe away the makeup that was under her eyes. She could go into the bathroom and wet a towel, but it was too much effort. She didn't want to move away from him until she had to go. She swept her hair up into a ponytail just as he was hanging up the phone.

"Poor Sanders, I don't think you're very nice to him," she commented, pouting out her bottom lip. Jameson reached out and pinched it.

"It works for us," he replied, running the edge of his thumb along her bottom teeth.

"Where did you find him?" she asked, when he let his fingers trace over her lip and down the side of her jaw.

"London," he answered, his fingers moving down to her throat.

"Is that the accent he has? Didn't seem British," she commented. Jameson nodded, his fingers moving around the edge of his bite mark, which was just barely peeking out the side of her collar.

"It's not originally where he's from, but it's where I found him. He was trying to steal from me," he continued, pushing the material to the side and leaning close so he could examine the wound.

"Steal from you!?"

"Yeah. He was thirteen, a pickpocket. A bad one. Probably about a week away from collapsing. I admired his tenacity. He's been with me ever since," Jameson finished the story, smoothing her dress back into place.

"How old is he now?"

"Twenty."

"Wow. That's crazy, I thought he —,"

"Tate," Jameson interrupted, his hand going to her neck and cupping the back of it. "You're obsessed with other people, I swear."

"Says the man who stalked me to get me here," she countered. He snorted.

"I didn't hear you complaining last night."

"You wouldn't have listened, even if I did."

"You're okay with all this? You're not running away to hide from me?" he asked, narrowing his eyes at her. Tate laughed.

"Jameson. If you knew some of my stories. One time Ang and I got kicked out of a fancy restaurant because he crawled under the table and went down on me during the whole first course – last night was nothing scary to a girl like me. I can handle *anything* you can dish out," she assured him.

"There is a big difference between me going down on you, and me calling you the '*dumbest cunt I've ever fucked*'. It has been my experience that most women will say they're okay with something, and after the fact not be okay with it at all," he said, his fingers massaging her skin. A shiver ran through her body at his words.

"I'm not most women," she reminded him. "It's all fun to me. A game. Sometimes, I'm the dumb cunt. Sometimes, you'll get to be."

"I very much fucking doubt that," he snorted. She started laughing.

"I don't have time for this, Jameson," she managed to say. "We can play some more on Sunday, I have to go home now."

Tate started to move to get off the bed when he yanked her forward. Suddenly, his mouth was over hers, and she was gasping into him. Both his hands went to the back of her head, drawing her forward. She followed, straddling his lap and pressing her own hands against his chest.

They hadn't kissed at all the night before – she hadn't even realized it till after she had woken up. Their lips had been all over each others bodies, but no kissing. She hadn't thought it a big deal at the time. Now it seemed like a *very* big deal.

Tate had forgotten what kissing him was like, like he was stealing all her breath away. Sucking it right out of her lungs. She moaned, scooting as close to him as she could get, rubbing herself against his chest while she coiled her arms around his neck. She could feel her heart palpitating, and if she hadn't been so lost in the moment, lost in the taste, and scent, and feel of him, she would've gotten nervous. Heart palpitations weren't a good thing, when it was only supposed to be games between them.

His hands dropped to her spread knees and he slid them up her thighs, under her dress. The palpitations got worse. Just as he was discovering she wasn't wearing any underwear, the bedroom door opened behind them. Jameson pulled away a little, but didn't take his eyes off of hers.

"The car is ready, sir," Sanders' clipped voice came from the doorway. Jameson stared at her for a second longer and then flicked his eyes over her shoulder, his hands continuing their journey under her dress.

"Twenty-minutes, Sanders," he replied, his gaze going back to Tate's. She smirked down at him.

"Very good, I'll wait downstairs." And the door clicked shut, just before Jameson started to slide her skirt up over her butt.

"You're very authoritative, Mr. Kane," Tate breathed, licking her lips.

"You have no idea."

Then he was pinning her to the bed, forcing his tongue between her lips and his knee between her legs.

Why did I bother getting dressed?

When Tate finally got home, she rushed around like a mad man. Stopped in at the temp agency to tell them she was off the market for a while. Called Ang and left him a voicemail that pretty much consisted of just squealing into the phone, then hopped in the shower.

She had stayed much longer than twenty minutes in Jameson's room. It was closer to a whole hour later when she finally got out of the bed. After taking a shower together, arguing over whether or not it was appropriate for her to wear his clothing instead of her *just-had-sex-in-it* dress, him punishing her for arguing, then finding clothing of his that worked for her, it was actually hours later when she finally left, closer to three. Her shift at the bar started at six.

She came out of her bathroom and walked straight into a body. Tate screamed, slapping Ang across the face, not realizing it was him. He grabbed her arm before she could swing again.

"Jesus, starting a little early," he said. She yanked her hand away.

"You scared the fuck out of me! What are you doing here!?" she demanded. Ang had a key to her apartment, but she hadn't been expecting him. They usually didn't see too much of each other on the weekends.

"I'm not fluent in stupid-girl-speak, I have no idea what your voicemail was about, and I had a shitty day, so I thought I'd stop by," he explained. She frowned up at him, her anger vanishing in an instant. He looked kind of upset, and it took a lot for something get under Ang's skin.

"You had a shitty day? I'm sorry," she said, then led him into her room. He stretched out on her bed while she rummaged through her closet.

"Yeah. Pedro backed out of the film, so they're pulling the whole shoot. Then my grandma stopped by. You know how joyous that can be; *'Angier, when are you going to become a respectable person!? You're going to burn in hell!'* — one of my all time favorite speeches of hers," he told her. Tate threw some clothing at the foot of the bed and then sat down next to him, rubbing her hand over his flat stomach.

"You know she's just an old bitch. Why do you let her get to you?" she asked. He shrugged.

"She just does. I can still remember when she used to bring me over to her house, bake me cookies and shit. Now I'm not even allowed to go over there," he grumbled.

"Well, fuck her, then. She's missing out on the most amazing person I've ever met," Tate replied. Ang rolled his eyes and looked at her.

"Like it's so easy for you to have your family hate you," he pointed out. She blinked in surprise.

"It is. I don't care that they hate me," she responded. He shook his head and propped himself up.

"Yes, you do. Whenever you get drunk and talk about them, that's when you get the nastiest. I know when you start babbling about your sister, I finally get to pull out the ropes and lube," Ang told her. She laughed.

"That is so not true," she chuckled, but then his hand was on her knee, his fingers sliding up her leg. A very similar gesture to Jameson's, just a couple hours ago. Her breath caught in her throat when Ang scooted closer.

"Doesn't matter. I feel like shit. She makes me feel like shit, I hate it," he grumbled, leaning into kiss her neck.

Tate swallowed thickly. She was in unfamiliar territory. While under normal circumstances she and Ang got it on whenever they felt like it, it usually wasn't when one of them had just slept with another person. And she didn't know all the rules to the game she was playing with Jameson. Would he be mad if she slept with Ang? He had made it very clear that their relationship would be a purely sexual one, but that didn't necessarily mean it wasn't exclusive. She pushed at Ang's shoulders, forcing him to look her in the eye.

"You shouldn't let her get to you. I know it's hard, and sad, and kinda depressing sometimes, but it's still so much better than life with them. We always have each other, so fuck everyone else," she said. He sighed, then he leaned into kiss her, his arms wrapping around her waist.

Hmmm, maybe went the wrong way with that speech.

"It was horrible. You know how she is, she stood in the hallway after I kicked her out. Banged on peoples doors, screaming about her *'faggot grandson'*, same old shit. I don't want to hate her … *but I hate her so much,"* he breathed against Tate's skin.

Ang had been a huge part of her life, for a very long time. Jameson may have peeled away the excess material, exposing the real Tatum – but Ang had helped mold her. She had sharpened her tongue and claws against him, amongst other things. He needed her, and while most friends hashed shit out over beers or ice cream or *whatever*, she and him had their own fucked up ways. It just worked for them.

So she went with it. She felt kind of guilty and wrong – feelings she wasn't used to experiencing anymore – but she also wanted to make Ang feel better. Make him forget a little bit of his pain. He pulled her over so she was straddling him, and he ran his hands up and down her back before settling them on her shoulders.

"I have to go to work soon, Ang, so maybe I can just give you a —," she started, when he suddenly bolted upright. She clung to his shoulders, almost getting catapulted off the bed.

"What the fuck is this?" he asked, running his fingers over the welt on her shoulder.

"Jesus, you startled me!" Tate snapped, then looked at where his fingers were touching.

"Did he do this to you?" Ang asked, leaning in close to the bite mark.

"No, I was trying to chew through my own shoulder, so I could escape," Tate laughed. Ang glared at her. He had gone from upset to angry, very quickly.

"Are those teeth? What the fuck, Tate? That looks painful," he snapped. She laughed.

"You're joking, right?"

"And your legs! What the fuck happened!?" he demanded, his hands gripping her thighs. Her towel had ridden up, exposing her bruises. They both stared down at her lap.

"What the fuck do you think happened? Ang, it's not like any of this is new to you. A couple weeks ago, you practically gave me a concussion, when you were practicing one of your *'moves'* for your movies," she used air quotes, making a face at him.

"That's a little different, Tate. I've been fucking you for five years. This guy just found you two days ago, and you're letting him tear chunks out of you!?" Ang's voice was getting loud. Tate scowled and climbed off his lap, holding the towel secure around her body.

"*That guy* found me seven years ago, and not one mark on my body is unwanted, or was unasked for. If you're gonna give me a bunch of shit, then maybe you should go," she growled, stomping over to her door. Ang stayed on her bed, running a hand through his hair.

"I'm sorry, I'm sorry. You're totally right. I'm just not … I'm not used to seeing that, so quickly, with you. I've probably left bigger and worse marks," he apologized. She nodded.

"No shit."

"Look, I said I'm sorry. I came over here with this great idea to leave marks of my own all over you, and then I find out some guy got there first. Kind of puts a damper on my plans," Ang laughed, and she had trouble containing her own smile. It sounded so ridiculous when said out loud.

*We **are** ridiculous.*

"Well, sorry, but you knew where I was last night," she replied. He groaned and fell back onto the bed.

"*Arrrrrrg*, I just wanted to get laid. Is your roomie here?" he asked, lifting his head and giving her a sideways smile.

"No way, buddy. You are never laying a finger on Rus," Tate

laughed, turning and digging some underwear out of her dresser.

"Why not? You said she's hot for me. I think she's hot. Sounds like a party," he said from behind her. She snorted and managed to pull on the underwear while still wearing the towel.

"As far as you're concerned, Rus is the Virgin fuckin' Mary. Off limits," Tate replied. She let the towel drop and put on her bra. She turned around and Ang's eyes raked over her body, but he didn't say anything.

"Rus is a virgin?" he asked. She shook her head, shaking a tiny skirt out of the pile of clothing and sliding it on.

"No, but as far as you're concerned, she might as well be. She's a beautiful, tiny, angel, sent from heaven to be sweet and strawberry blonde. You are not allowed to corrupt that. *You are not fucking her,*" Tate stated, staring him in the eye.

"You ruin all my fun."

"You have like a ton of people on speed dial who would jump on you if you so much as breathed in their direction. Call one of them," she suggested, squeezing herself into a tiny cropped top that had long sleeves and a scoop neck.

"But I wanted my honey-bunny, and you won't play with me," he said in a whiny voice. She rolled her eyes and turned to face her mirror, spreading out her makeup supplies.

"Stop being ridiculous," she told him. He leapt off the bed.

"I'll go be a normal person, drown my sorrows, find some whore to take home. Wanna crash a show this weekend? I've got a guy who will let us sneak in during the second act," Ang offered, leaning against her doorway.

"Totally. And see if you can find any more gym stuff – I actually kinda liked the Zumba class," she laughed. He nodded.

"I'll keep my eyes peeled. See you later, don't let Mr. Mean take too many bites out of you," he cautioned her. She laughed again.

"He's in Manhattan for the weekend, so I'll be bite free for a couple days," she assured Ang. He thumped on her door and then took off down the hallway.

"Later, kitty-cat," he called out.

"Bye!"

She did her makeup heavy, but left her hair to air dry – sometimes the unpolished look worked really well on her. She finished off her outfit with a pair of wedge boots that went to her knees and then grabbed a large jacket, covering everything up for the bus ride to work.

The bar she worked in was always popular, though Thursday wasn't as rowdy as the actual weekend. The next night was better, the Red Sox had won a home game, and the city went crazy. Tate wore a baseball jersey and Rus even got her to do a line dance on the bar top. They wound up getting wasted at a hotel party afterwards. Though she had a very tantalizing offer to join some guy for a sexual romp in the hotel's lobby bathroom, she declined. Even in a drunken haze, Tate held out. She would try to be a good girl till she heard from Jameson.

Her will power didn't hold out very long. Saturday night, she stood behind the bar, clapping and moving her body to the beat of the song that was playing. She was laughing at something one of the regulars was saying, when someone caught her eye.

Ang was walking through the room, a head taller than most people. It wasn't often that he came to see her at work, and she gave a broad smile in his direction. He was making his way towards the bar, but he wasn't looking at her. He was flirting and having eye-sex with some sexy Korean girl as he moved through the crowd.

Tate didn't think she was a nymphomaniac; she could go for long periods of time without sex, and had done so. But she did like it a lot and had a tendency to use it as a kind of therapy. Angry at someone? Have angry sex. Sad about something? Have fun sex. Just plain old bored? Have exciting sex.

And when she was in the mood, she had a lot of trouble resisting. It was like a switch that she couldn't turn off. She had been thinking about Jameson non-stop, remembering their night and morning together in vivid detail. Fantasizing about what she would do to him when he got home. What he would do to her. Her switch was halfway flipped already, and as Tate watched Ang work his magic on the girls in the bar, the switch completely flipped on.

He was wearing a long jacket, the kind with a stiff, stand up collar that buttoned all the way to the chin – he looked stylish and handsome. His hair was messy, as usual, and his gray eyes were smiling, as usual. He had an impish smile, one that some how managed to look innocent *and* naughty at the same time, and she knew it drove most women nuts. It was in full effect, and Tate wasn't immune to it – add that to the fact that his body was almost as familiar to her as her own, and it was hard to resist him. She took a deep breath through her nose, letting her eyes wander over his frame.

Sunday night is so far away ...

When she dragged her eyes back up to his face, he was looking right at her. Smirking. He said something to the girl in front of him and then continued on his journey. He jostled and moved people out of the way, until he was leaning against the bar across from her. She stayed in her spot, still moving a little to the music.

"Well, well, sweetie pea, how're things?" Ang asked in his sexy voice, his eyes traveling up and down her body before going back to staring her in the face.

"Good. Busy," Tate replied.

"You don't look very busy," he pointed out. She shrugged.

"Lull in orders. We still going to the theatre?" she asked. He squinted his eyes at her.

"Hmmm, I don't think so," he replied. She finally moved forward, leaning against the bar in front of him.

"Why not? I thought you wanted to hang out," she said.

"I do. But I think little Tater-tot has something other than dinner and a show in mind," he told her. She laughed.

"Oh, there will definitely be a show later."

They didn't even make it till "*later*". When Tate went on break twenty minutes later, Ang followed her into the back of the bar and then dragged her outside. Pressed her up against a wall, raked his hands over her body. He had borrowed his roommate's car, and when it started to rain, he pulled her into the backseat with him. As his tongue ran across Jameson's fading bite mark, she groaned and dragged her fingernails across his scalp.

I should really feel like a bad person most of the time.

"Do you always keep it this hot?"

Tatum was laying on the floor in Jameson's library, a little ways back from the wingback chairs. The fire was raging again and the room was almost stifling. Sweat was causing her hair to stick to her face, her shirt to stick to her skin. Jameson was in his chair, his feet stretched towards the fire. The heat didn't seem to bother him.

Why would fire affect the devil?

"I like it hot," was all he said in response. She snorted, almost upsetting the glass she had balanced on her stomach.

"You like it *too* hot," she corrected him.

"If it's too hot for you, take off some clothes," he suggested. She smirked at the ceiling and moved the glass off her stomach before shimmying out of her jeans. She lifted her head enough to be able to see where he was, then threw the pants at him. They caught him in the side of the face.

"Much better, thank you," she told him in a happy voice.

Tate hadn't heard from him Sunday, but then Monday afternoon, she got a text message telling her to be ready by six o'clock, and to pack some clothes for an "extended" stay. *Ooohhh*. She was ready to go hours before she needed to be, and was waiting on the stoop of her building when Sanders pulled up in their sleek Bentley.

Jameson hadn't been too chatty once she got to the house, just content to sit and work. His home was enormous, but as far as she could tell, he spent most of his time in the library. She asked him why he had sent for her, if he was just going to work the whole time, and was told that just because he was working, didn't mean he couldn't appreciate something nice to look at once in a while.

They ate dinner and talked about the benefits of socialized health care versus private industry. Tate was a smart girl, she had gotten into Harvard, after all – she kept current. She just usually didn't have anyone to talk to about that kind of stuff. Ang was more interested in talking about which porn star made the most money and what angle was best for backside shots. Rus just wanted to talk about boys.

She loved her friends, she really did, but sometimes Tate wanted to shoot herself.

Jameson was like a breath of fresh air. He was smart, he was cultured, and he knew how to have a conversation, when someone was deemed worthy enough for him to talk to them. And he always kept his cool, even when she purposefully tried to get a rise out of him. The Unshakable Jameson Kane.

After dinner, he led them back into the library. The fire had already been going when she got there, but he kept building it higher, adding more logs. That was why she had opted to lay on the floor. The chairs were too hot.

"Sexy socks, Tate," Jameson chuckled. She lifted her legs, pointing her feet at the ceiling. She was wearing a pair of purple-striped socks that went all the way to her knees. Her guilty pleasure in life. If she was stranded on a desert island, and could only have one thing, it would probably be a pair of knee length socks.

"Thank you, I think so," she laughed, kicking her legs up and down before dropping them back to the floor.

"Are you drunk yet?" he asked. She shook her head and reached out a hand, running her fingers up and down the bottle of Jack Daniel's that was sitting near her.

"No. Do you want me to be drunk?"

"Could be interesting."

"You're in a dark mood tonight. What's wrong?" she asked. Jameson chuckled.

"Am I ever in a light mood?" he responded. She nodded.

"Sure you are. Sometimes you're downright happy. I mean, you're always mean, and kind of a bastard, but at least you're happy about it," she told him, and he burst out laughing.

"Okay, okay, stop with the flattery," he joked.

"So what's wrong?"

"Had a run in over the weekend. With an … ex, of sorts," he said. Tate stilled her fingers. He was speaking slowly, choosing his words carefully. Protecting her? Or hiding from her? She couldn't be sure.

"Bad kind of ex?" she asked.

"Is there any other kind?"

"Some people end on good notes, Jameson. It is possible to have an amicable break up," she pointed out. He snorted.

"Bullshit. Do you have any good exes in your past?" he asked. She laughed.

"I'm not a very normal person. I told you about the one guy, we don't exactly speak anymore. Another guy cried when I ended it – which was weird, considering I hadn't even known we were dating. Funny how some people mistake sex for a relationship," she replied.

"Now that's the truth."

"So what happened? Big fight? Stalker? Oh my god, please tell me it wasn't Ellie!" she suddenly gasped, sitting upright. He had turned to face her, and his Satan's smile was in place.

"Wouldn't that have been hilarious. You know, it could be interesting. Maybe we should arrange a family reunion," Jameson suggested. Tate narrowed her eyes.

"I don't think so. Look, if you don't wanna talk about your ex, fine, not a big deal to me, but you need to get in a better mood, or I'm gonna go find something else to do," she informed him. His eyebrows raised up.

"Oh really. Ms. O'Shea, talking tough. You really want me to talk about her? Most women don't want to hear men talk about other women. Particularly women those men have slept with," he pointed out.

"I'm not most women. How many times are we going to have this conversation? Fine, *I'll* take the lead. Is she hot? Did she dump you, when it ended? Did you guys fight, this weekend? Did you get in one last closure-fuck? Did you fuck her this weekend?" Tate prattled off. He smiled, turning his head back towards the fire.

"See, this is why I keep you around. No bullshit; so straight forward. I just might consider being nice to you tonight," he offered. She snorted.

"How boring."

"She's very hot. I guess you could say I dumped her. Yes, we argued this weekend. I can still fuck her whenever I want, so a '*closure-fuck*' wasn't necessary. I did not fuck her this weekend," Jameson answered every question.

Tate had meant to be cheeky. Prove that she didn't mind. He could sleep with other people. But when he had said that he could still sleep with the woman whenever he wanted, something happened to Tate's insides. Fucking some random woman was one thing – sleeping with an ex, someone he'd had a relationship with, that was dangerous. It made Tate nervous. She hadn't expected to feel that way.

She suddenly felt very guilty about her weekend.

"Would you? If the opportunity presented itself?" Tate asked, laying back against the floor.

"Sounds like it would bother you if I did."

"I don't really know. It might."

"Why?"

Tate had to think about it for a minute or two.

"I might be a slut, but … okay, I'm most definitely a slut, and I like to sleep with guys, and have no qualms about who or when or where. But I am *not* a cheater. I never cheated on any of my boyfriends. I won't sleep with a guy if I know he has a girlfriend or wife. I will *not* be that girl. If you start sleeping with your ex, you might get back together with her. Or really, she might just think you're back together – women are stupid that way. And if that happens, I would immediately become the other woman. I won't do that," she explained, ignoring her glass and dragging the bottle of Jack to her lips, taking a sip.

"You cheated on your boyfriend, with me, when I had a girlfriend, who also happened to be your sister," Jameson reminded her. Tate chuckled, took another swig of whiskey.

"So you understand why I'm so scarred about the whole thing. I don't want to be that girl ever again. It was a stupid accident, and look what happened. No thank you," she replied.

"It was probably the best thing that could have happened to me at that time, so I have the opposite view of it," he laughed.

"Po-TATE-o, po-TOT-o."

"Maybe. Maybe you're just too hard on yourself. I mean, yeah, every time I've ever slept with someone outside of a relationship, my girlfriends always knew. I made sure they knew – lying is ridiculous. If someone doesn't like it, they can get the fuck out. But you and I, we were young, dating the wrong people. It's not like either of us planned it. And we didn't even get a chance to hide it. We weren't trying to hurt anyone," he pointed out. She nodded.

"True. Still. You asked. That's my answer. No, I probably wouldn't like it if you started sleeping with this ex girlfriend. But I'm also not gonna stop you," she wrapped up their conversation.

"Well, thank you for that, Tate. I'll be sure to tell you before I start plowing my way through my little black book."

Tate rubbed her lips together, staring at the ceiling. Now was definitely the time to say something. Part of her didn't want to upset him or make him mad. She drew her knees up and rubbed her thighs together. Another part of her *really* wanted to make him mad, and see what would happen.

"I slept with Ang."

God, I just blurted it out. Like a slutty-goat. Jesus.

"Excuse me?"

She cleared her throat.

"I slept with Ang. Had sex with him," she clarified.

"What, like this weekend?" Jameson asked. She winced.

"Yes. Saturday night," she replied.

"So I can't sleep with my ex because I might get back together with her, but you can sleep with your best friend-slash-tripod?" he questioned, but there was laughter in his voice. He didn't sound angry.

"I'm horrible. I didn't want to, at first. But I was lonely, and I was thinking about you all weekend, then he was right in front of me, and it just … happened."

Three times.

"Okay. Thank you for telling me," Jameson replied in a simple tone. She felt a little like throwing up.

"I wasn't sure what is and isn't allowed. Ang and I have known each other forever – sex is more like a pickup game of basketball to us. We just do it, for like sport. But then I kept thinking that maybe it wasn't okay. I didn't know if we were allowed to sleep with other people, or what exactly is going on here, and I … I felt kinda bad afterwards," Tate told him. It was the truth. She'd spent most of Sunday working out rehearsed speeches to beg for his forgiveness. Jameson chuckled.

"I don't care if you sleep with other people when I'm not around. We're the same animal, you and I, so I get it. But I gotta be honest, I have the same issue you have – you're a little too close to this Ang guy for my tastes. What if the same problem happens? I don't really care about being the other man, as long as I'm *the* man. Can't be that, if you go off and fall in love with your best friend. I'm not quite ready to stop playing with you yet," he tried to explain. She laughed.

Oh, you are most definitely ***the*** *man, Satan.*

"That won't happen, trust me. But there we go – you can't sleep with ex girlfriends. I can't sleep with Ang. Deal?" she asked.

"If that makes you happy."

There was a long pause after that, Tate drinking more from the bottle and Jameson just being quiet. She rubbed her legs together, lifted them back into the air and did slow high kicks. She was pretty flexible, she could almost bring her knee to her chest. She let go of the bottle and laced her fingers behind her knee, gently pulling down. Just another inch, and —,

"Did you think about me?" Jameson's voice cut through the room.

"Excuse me?" she asked, letting go of her leg and propping herself up with her hands. He wasn't facing her, his eyes on the flames.

"While you were fucking Ang, did you think of me. You said you were lonely, that you had been thinking about me all weekend. When he was fucking you, were you thinking of me?" Jameson asked, finally turning to look at her.

Tate stared back, taking a deep breath. She didn't want to tell him, because the answer made her feel bad. Made her feel like a traitor. The other reason she had felt so bad all weekend. But he just kept staring at her, his eyes boring into her soul.

"*Yes*," she whispered. He smiled and leaned foward, over his arm rest.

"So while this guy, *Angier*, was inside of you, you were imagining it was me, weren't you?" he asked her. Tortured her.

"Yes."

Usually, Ang was so amazing, he was able to obliterate any other person from her mind. She could barely think straight, let alone think of another man. But Jameson had her all messed up. He'd gotten under her skin and was running rampant through her system. It wasn't a matter of one being better in bed than the other – they were both spectacular. But only one of them captured her mind.

And it wasn't her best friend.

"*Good*. New rule. *Anytime* you fuck someone else, you picture me. Understood?" Jameson demanded.

"I don't think that even needs to be a rule; it'll just happen on its own," Tate laughed. He gave one more tight lipped smile and leaned back in his chair.

"Jesus christ, that we even need these kinds of rules, really says something about us," he mumbled.

"I think they're a good idea," she told him. He laughed, and it was an evil sound. It sent shivers down her spine.

"You would think that, Tate, because you're a *whore*," he stated.

Ah, now we're getting somewhere.

"Maybe. But at least I'm a responsible one," she teased.

"That's an oxymoron," he told her.

"*You're* an oxymoron," she taunted him, laughing.

"That makes no sense."

"*You* make no sense."

"Stop it, Tatum.

"*You* stop —,"

"Don't make me come over there. I'm not in a good mood," Jameson warned her.

126

"Maybe if you come over here, I could cheer you up," she offered.

"Maybe I don't want to cheer up. Maybe I want to be in a bad mood," he countered. She rolled her eyes.

"You sound like a little kid who wants to bitch just to bitch," she told him. His head snapped towards her.

"What the fuck did you just say?"

"I think you heard me," she said with a smile. He stood up.

"I think you want to get hurt," he replied, moving to stand over her. She leaned back on her elbows, smiling up at him.

"I live to make you happy," she told him, sighing melodramatically. He squatted down next to her.

"Are you ever scared of me?" he asked, his voice soft. Tate shook her head.

"No, not even a little," she assured him.

"Sometimes I wonder if maybe you should be," he added.

"And why is that?"

"Because, I have the strangest feelings about you. Like I want to take you everywhere and have you by my side, but I also want to hold you down. Make you beg and cry," he told her. She kept her eyes focused on his, didn't move a muscle.

"Sounds like a pretty good plan to me," she whispered. He reached out and traced a finger down her leg, from the hem of her underwear to her knee, then back up again. His eyes watched his finger.

"How did I find you?" It was obvious that he was thinking out loud.

"That's pretty easy – you *made* me," she responded. Jameson's eyes cut to hers, flashing blue in the shadowy room.

"I didn't know that's what I was doing, at the time," he told her, then started digging his nails into her thigh, dragging them up her skin. She hissed.

"Me, neither. Maybe we found each other," she breathed, letting out a sigh when he lifted his hand. He moved back down to the same spot and repeated the motion. She hummed and let her head drop back, closing her eyes.

"Sometimes I still can't believe you're here, Tate. That it's really you. *Tatum O'Shea.* Mathias O'Shea's daugher; Ellie's little sister," he said, moving his hand to her other leg.

"I haven't been any of those things in a long time, maybe that's why it still feels so weird to you," she suggested.

"If you aren't those things, then what are you?" he asked. She thought for a second.

"Just Tate. Bartender. Party girl. Ang's friend," she prattled off things that came to mind when she thought of herself.

"*Slut?*" Jameson whispered. She opened her eyes.

"Oh yes. Most definitely that," she sighed. His nails moved to her throat, so she kept her head back.

"Pain," he added through clenched teeth. She gave a small nod as he dragged a sharp nail from underneath her ear down to her collar bone.

"Maybe just sex, period. Kinda encompasses it all," she suggested.

"Very thoughtful of you."

"I like it. Tatum '*Sex*' O'Shea. Why not," she laughed. Suddenly his hand was tight around her throat, squeezing. She rolled her eyes to look at him. He was staring at her neck.

"Sounds good to me. We could —," he started, but he was interrupted. The library door swung open. Tate didn't have to look to know it was Sanders. It was strange — he walked in and out of rooms without knocking, all the time, but he never seemed intrusive. She hardly even noticed him. She kept staring at Jameson, who gripped her neck even tighter. She took shallow breaths through her nose.

"Tokyo, sir. The eight o'clock meetings," Sanders' even voice carried over the room. Jameson sighed and finally looked her in the eye.

She smiled at him.

"Gotta go, baby girl. No rest for the wicked," he told her, before letting her go. He leaned in quick and kissed her throat before getting to his feet.

"Gonna be a while?" she asked. He nodded.

"Probably. You know where the kitchen is, or you can go up to my room. If you need anything, just ask Sanders," Jameson instructed, looking back and forth between the two of them. Tate gave him the biggest smile she could manage. Sanders stared at the wall.

"Got it. Go make my money," she told Jameson. He snorted.

"That's not even funny."

He strode out of the room and Tate stayed as she was for a moment, looking after him. Then she sighed and sat all the way up. Sanders was still standing in the room, still staring at a wall. She looked him over.

"Got a hot date tonight, Sandy?" she asked. She loved to tease him. She would crack him some day.

"No, Ms. O'Shea," was all he said.

"You look awfully nice tonight. New suit?" she pressed. He cleared his throat.

"No, Ms. O'Shea."

"Are you ever going to call me Tate, like I asked you to?"

"Probably not, Ms. O'Shea."

She had an idea. She got the impression that Sanders and Jameson virtually never left the house, unless it was to go to Jameson's office. Not right. Jameson hadn't ever asked to go back to her place, or taken her anywhere fancy. Tate loved every second she spent alone with him, but she didn't want to be someone's dirty laundry, either.

"Do you have any newspapers, Sandy?" she asked, climbing to her feet.

"Several. Which would you prefer, New York Times? LA Times?" he listed them off.

"Just Boston papers, any you got. And any weekly periodicals you have," she added, running her hands over her legs to shake off any carpet dust. She was standing in front of Sanders only wearing knee high socks, boy-briefs style underwear, and a tight white tank top. She should probably feel bad, she didn't like to make people feel uncomfortable – but if Sanders was uncomfortable, he didn't show it. If anything, he looked bored.

"Is that it?" he asked.

"Just that. Hurry back, it gets lonely in here," she teased him. He rolled his eyes and headed out of the library. She laughed and then went over to the fireplace, determined to figure out how to turn it down.

Jameson strode back into his library just over two hours later, and was in for a little shock. The fire was much smaller, and the over head lights were turned on – he almost never used them, himself. Tate was sitting cross legged in the middle of his floor, surrounded by newspapers and clippings. She was cutting something out of one of the papers, the tip of her tongue visible at the corner of her mouth.

Almost cute.

"What are you doing?" he asked, striding through the mess of papers.

She looked up at him and broke into a big smile. He had to steel himself against it. If he wasn't careful, he was going to get too comfortable with her, and Jameson tried to make it a habit to never get too comfortable.

"Coupon clipping!" Tate responded in an excited voice.

"Excuse me?"

"When I first met Ang," she started. He had never met the man, but Jameson already kind of hated her best friend. "I was really desperate for money. My jobs sucked, I was a shitty waitress. Scraping the bottom of the barrel. Ang showed me how far coupons can get you. He goes on Groupon all the time, too. We get into places free, get all kinds of free food, and free swag. It's pretty awesome."

"'*Awesome.*' Why are you doing that here, now?" Jameson pressed. She smiled up at him again, only this time it was a devilish smile. That was the smile he liked, the one he wanted to slap off her face.

"Because I'm taking you out on the city, mister. You and Sanders. We're gonna go out, and you're gonna live like a real urban-ite for a day," she informed him. He laughed.

"There is no fucking way I am *ever* fucking doing that, so get that out of your fucking mind, right fucking now," he suggested. She shook her head.

"Oh, you're going to do it, and afterwards we're going to a dinner party. I had already agreed to go to dinner at a friend's house. You can come with me," she told him. He scowled.

"And if I don't go?" he asked. Tate shrugged.

"Not that big of a deal. We can just officially declare you the king of all pussies. And *not* in the good way. You don't have to go, I can go as Ang's date," she assured him.

"I guess I'm going to a fucking dinner on the bad side of Boston. You get two hours, no more," he told her. She laughed.

"You hear that Sandy, you're getting out of here!" she called out. Jameson hadn't even realized the other man was in the room – he was in for another shock. Sanders was behind the desk, snipping and cutting away at a newspaper, as well.

"Sounds exhilarating. If no one requires my services anymore, I'm going to get back to work," Sanders said, getting up from his seat. Jameson nodded.

"We're not doing early tomorrow, so sleep in as late as you want," he told him. Sanders nodded, and walked forwards. Tate held up her hand, palm facing backwards.

"Up top, Sandy," she said, her eyes never leaving the paper she was scanning. Sanders high fived her and then continued out of the room. Jameson stared after him.

What just happened?

"I think he likes you," he mumbled. Tate shrugged.

"Most people do. I'm pretty fuckin' awesome," she told him. He burst out laughing and walked over to her, grabbing her by the arm and pulling her to her feet.

"Yes, but usually, Sanders doesn't like anybody," Jameson said, pulling the scissors out of her hand and tugging her away from the sea of newspapers.

"But I wasn't done. What are you doing?" she asked.

"Oh, you're done. Time for good girls to go upstairs and show me how bad they can be," Jameson told her.

"I don't think there's very much that's good about me anymore," she laughed, following him out of the room.

"I think you have no idea what bad really is – you almost have *too much* good," he replied.

"I don't think —,"

"Stop arguing, or I'll make you crawl up the stairs."

Tate was silent for about two seconds, then turned into a prosecuting attorney, arguing all the points on how she couldn't possibly be good. Jameson stopped moving, smiling at her back as she started up the stairs. Then he reached forward and grabbed her ankle, pulling her leg out from underneath her. She went to her knees, hands flying out to catch herself.

"*Shit!*" she cursed. He moved a few steps ahead of her, then squatted down and fisted his hand in her hair.

"Why are you always set on defying me, baby girl?" he asked, his voice low as he pulled her hair, forcing her head up towards his own.

She looked up at him, a smile playing on the edge of her lips.

"Because it's always so much fun."

"You are such a mindfuck, Tate. Something is wrong with you, that you want to be treated like this, that you like being a *whore*," he hissed at her. She chuckled low in her throat.

"Hmmm, but really, what does all that say about *you*? That you want to treat someone like this? That you want to be with a whore?" she replied.

"I've made peace with my desires."

"Like you said, we're the same animal. You had a bad weekend. Let's go upstairs, and you can take it out on me," she whispered. He tugged harder on her hair and she raised up onto her knees.

"Sounds like that works out more in your favor, than mine," he pointed out. She laughed, reaching out to scratch her nails down his arm.

"Baby, all I do is give you favors. You should feel blessed, to have such an accomodating *whore*," she purred. He snorted and shoved her forward, forcing her back onto her hands.

"Burdened is more like it. *Now fucking crawl.*"

And she did, all the way to his bedroom.

Maybe I should keep this one ...

7

A WEEK LATER, TATE RUSHED AROUND her apartment, a toothbrush sticking out of her mouth. She grabbed various articles of clothing, shoving them into an oversized purse. She had stayed at Jameson's for most of the last week – even gone back to his place after her shifts at the bar – and she didn't know how this week was going to go, but she wanted enough clothing to cover all her bases. She snorted at that thought.

Not that I wear much clothing.

It was August in Boston, which meant hot and humid – but Jameson insisted on keeping the house at near boiling temperatures. She pretty much lived in her underwear, tank tops, and socks when she was there. If it bothered Sanders, he didn't show it, so she didn't think twice about doing it.

Tate also liked to think that she and Sanders were developing a friendship of sorts. The kind where only one friend talks, and the other just stares and says the bare minimum. Friendship-*ish*.

That morning, she had managed to drag them into downtown Boston to play at being poor with her. She got them free lunch, took them through a Sunday market, forced Sanders to try on ridiculous clothing. Jameson wasn't as easy, he simply refused to do anything.

But he went along with her, and even laughed when she held Sanders' hand and told a clerk that he had just proposed, so could they, please, join in on the champagne brunch the store was throwing for newly-engaged people? Jameson laughed even harder when she really sold the act by planting a big kiss on Sanders' mouth – tongue and everything. The really shocking part was Sanders kissing her back. Cheeky man.

But then Jameson got called into work; a client was having some sort of financial crisis. Tate let him go, but only after making him promise to pick her up at six o'clock. He had said he would go to her dinner, and she was holding him to it.

Tate tried not to think of it as a dinner date with friends – she thought of it as an elaborate form of torture, *a game;* seeing how far she could push him. Also, a tiny part of her had wanted to see if he'd actually go through with it. They spent so much time at his place, only venturing out on occasion for dinner, that she was beginning to think he *was* hiding her away. It was strange – she didn't really mind being someone's whore, but she hated the thought of being someone's dirty secret.

She dropped her toothbrush into the sink and spit out the excess toothpaste foam. Water, gargle, spit, and she was good to go. She threw on a jacket and headed for the front door, when there was suddenly a loud banging. She paused, but the banging didn't. A voice with a heavy Boston accent started shouting.

"I know yuh in there! Open the doo-or!"

Landlord.

Tate cursed under her breath and began backing away. She noticed a note stuck to the fridge — *"Avoid front door – I would be mad you haven't paid rent yet, but can't pay either. Love ya, bitch! Rus."* Tate swallowed a groan and headed for her bedroom.

"Tatum! I know yuh in there! You owe me money! I want it,

now!" the landlord yelled. She hurried to her window and was fighting with it to go up when her cell phone rang. With an aggravated sigh, she pulled it out and answered it.

"I'm at the curb, where are you?" Jameson's voice demanded.

"Uh, still in here," she answered in a hushed voice. "Look, pull around to the back alley. I'll meet you out there."

"*Back alley?* And why the fuck are you whispering?"

She rolled her eyes and climbed out onto the fire escape.

"Just fucking meet me back here!" she hissed at him and then hung up the phone.

By the time she was dropping to the ground, Sanders was pulling the car up next to her. Tate practically fell into the backseat, the strap of her jumbo-sized bag tangling around her legs. She laughed, breathless, as the car started rolling again.

"Okay, first of all, *never hang up on me again.* Second of all, what the fuck is going on?" Jameson asked. She stretched a leg over his lap, pulling at the strap.

"My landlord was at the door," she was still laughing, pulling her foot towards her chest, the strap pulling tight around her ankle.

"Do you often run from him?"

"Only when rent is late."

Jameson grabbed her leg, stilling her, and he pulled the strap free.

"You haven't paid your rent, Tatum?" he asked in a soft voice. Only she knew better now – Jameson was only soft before he did something sharp.

"Well, *someone* wasn't being very truthful about paying me – I've only worked six days in the last two weeks. Not exactly raking in the dough, so I couldn't pay. I have to start temping again; I have to pay my rent, Jameson. Rus depends on me," she told him. He snorted.

"I'm not just going to give you a thousand dollars —,"

"*Four thousand dollars.*"

136

"*Any amount of money*, in cash, to run around with – you're insane. You'd probably spend it all on hookers and cocaine." She didn't deny it. "I'm going to set you up an investment portfolio. As fun as sucking dick for money at eighty probably is, I don't think you want to be doing that."

"Doesn't change the fact that I need to make rent. I need to eat, I need to pay my bills. Three days a week just doesn't cut it, I told you that," Tate reminded him as she smoothed out her skirt. It had climbed up to her hips during her struggle with her purse.

"I'll feed you, and don't worry about the rest," was all he snapped before turning away, looking out his window. Subject apparently closed. She snorted.

"You're too extra. What's got you in such a sweet mood?" she asked.

"Your life is ridiculous. You were skipped ahead in school, graduated at the top of your private school, and you were accepted into an accelerated program at *Harvard*. Why are you fucking around? Such a fucking child," Jameson growled.

She stared at him for a second. He sounded angry. Like, *for real* angry. It didn't make sense. Why did he care what she did? Since asking about Ellie that first night, Jameson hadn't asked her one single other thing about her life or family. She was kinda shocked he even remembered that she had been moved ahead in school. Tate frowned at him.

"You call it being a child. I call it living my life the way I want to," she replied.

"But it's the *wrong* way," he informed her, his voice dripping with disdain.

Who the fuck was he to judge her life!? She wasn't good enough to be his girlfriend, but he still got to boss her around and pass judgement on her life? She didn't think so. Her anger started to boil.

"Says who? *The great Jameson Kane?*" Tate snapped at him, her voice loud. "What, I should live a life more like *yours?* Why on earth would I want to do that? I get to be who I am, the real me, *every single day*. I say what I want, and do what I want. You hide behind your money, and your business, and your suits, and your intellect. *Pretending* to be this suave guy, when we both know you're two steps away from being a complete sociopath who —,"

She didn't get to finish her sentence. He turned around on her in an instant, grabbing her by the throat. She didn't miss a beat – Jameson Kane had yet to learn that Tate was usually capable of giving as good as she got. She knocked his arm loose, but by then he was halfway laying on top of her. It was a blur of hands and arms, her trying to push him back, him batting her away. They wound up stretched across the back seat, one of her arms pinned under his knee as he knelt over her. Her free hand pulled at his wrist, trying to yank away the hand that was back around her throat.

"You think I *hide*, Tate? You think I *pretend?*" he hissed, his face close to hers. She glared up at him.

"I don't think, *I know,*" she snapped back.

"And what is it you're doing, baby girl? Ran away from home. Ran away from your family. Ran away from school. That's all you do, *run away*. I'm counting down the days till you do it to me," he told her. She sucked in air through her teeth.

"You call it running, I call it freeing myself."

"Bullshit. If that was true, you wouldn't be so upset over what I said," he pointed out.

"I'm not upset, I —,"

Suddenly he was shaking her. She dug her nails into his wrist and he let go of her, but only long enough to pin that arm between her body and his thigh. His hand immediately went back to the base of her neck and he lowered his face till he was directly above her.

"Don't ever fucking lie to me, Tate. Stupid fucking girl. Put your fucking hands on me like that again, and you'll see how mean I can really get," he warned her, his lips so close they were brushing against her own.

She felt her temperature soar through the roof. Jameson had an uncanny gift that made it impossible for her to be truly mad at him – the angrier she got, the more she just wanted to have sex with him. He was blessed that way; or rather, she was cursed.

"You keep promising to show me. *Still waiting,*" Tate whispered back. He chuckled, and the anger in his eyes cooled a little. There was a long pause while he stared at her, then there was a cough from in front of them.

"One block away, sir," Sanders' voice carried into the back seat. Jameson glanced at him and then returned his attention to Tate.

"You just want to piss me off, I swear to god. You have no idea, the things I want to do to you," he told her.

"The windows are tinted. Sandy would probably like the show," she offered, sliding around underneath him, rubbing her body against his legs. Jameson quirked up an eyebrow.

"I doubt that. We'll go home, and I'll put a happy end to this argument," he informed her. She narrowed her eyes.

"We can't go home – we're going to dinner," she reminded him. He shook his head.

"Bad girls get sent to bed without dinner," he stated. She began to struggle against his weight.

"No. You agreed to go, so you have to go. I told everyone we would be there," she said.

"Do you really think I give a fuck?" he asked with a laugh.

"That's not *fair*. You *agreed*," Tate stressed.

"Why is this so important? You want me to meet your friends? I don't care about your friends, Tate. If you think I care about your life, you're mistaken. Stupidity annoys me, whether it's you, or some guy down the street, or something on TV, doesn't matter. I think you're *stupid*, and that *annoys me*. Don't read into things. We *are*

139

going home, and we will finish this discussion there. The only reason I'm not fucking you right now, is because I have too much respect for Sanders," Jameson spat out at her.

But not for me.

The problem with playing her games, Tate had long ago learned, was the line between fun and bad was too blurry. For instance, Ang had called her just about every dirty name they could both think of, but one time, while just hanging out at his apartment, he made a sarcastic remark about her family hating her because she was a huge whore. She didn't speak to him for two weeks. Took him even longer to get back in her pants.

What was real, and what wasn't real? Calling her a "*dumb cunt*" was fine, as long as Jameson didn't really think she was one. Knowing and thinking she was a whore was fine, as long as she was treated with respect. Was he playing a game now? If he had said all those same words at another time, a different situation, she would have already been thinking of ways to get him naked in the car. But it didn't feel like he was playing. If he was, it wasn't fun anymore. Her feelings were hurt. She *hated* that.

"*Get off of me.*"

Surprisingly, he complied without hesitation. Tate pushed away from him, getting as much distance between the two of them as she could on the seats. Sanders was just pulling into a parking spot outside of her friend's apartment building. She refused to look at Jameson, just went about straightening her clothing.

"Oh my, I've struck a nerve. I didn't know Tatum O'Shea had those anymore," he said, his voice quiet. She looked over at him.

"Fuck you, *Kane,*" she spat out. He laughed.

"Strike one. Let's go inside, get this over with."

"*I'm* going inside. *You* can go fuck yourself."

"I see. I've hurt you. Interesting," his voice was quieter still, his eyes wandering over her face. She shook her head.

"No, just enlightened me. If I'm so fucking stupid, so fucking annoying, so not worthy of your fucking respect, maybe you should just find someone else to play with," she told him.

"Not yet. You may be stupid and annoying, but you're one hell of a lay," Jameson told her, his smile wide. She rolled her eyes and climbed out of the car.

Tate was mad, though she wasn't sure why. She knew that Jameson didn't care about her – why was she angry that he had said it out loud? *Because it made it real.* When they were alone together, lazing around his library, he made it easy to forget. He would just talk with her sometimes, laugh with her. Made it seem like he actually liked her, for more than just her abilities in bed.

Stupid girl.

"What are you doing!?" she demanded, when he got out of the car on the other side.

"You were right about one thing. I agreed to go, so I'm going. Can't have you holding it over my head later. Say a lot of things about me, but I'm not a quitter," Jameson told her as she came around to stand next to him.

"But I don't want you here anymore," she said. He shrugged.

"Don't really care. What's the apartment number?"

Her vision started turning a little red. Never had she dealt with such a stubborn man. If she wanted to go left, he went right. If she went right with him, he decided to go left. Sometimes it turned her on. Other times, it just made her want to kill him.

Her game had been a bad one, a bust. Jameson had spent the whole day doing her "normal" things, and he hadn't acted normal at all. Deep down, she had thought maybe it would all humanize him a bit. *Mistake.* Now she wanted to make him hurt. Make him bleed a little. She didn't know if it was possible, but when she looked over his shoulder, something gave her the idea to try.

"*Ang!*" she called out, waving her arm in the air. Jameson turned as she pushed past him.

"Kitty-cat, how're things? Haven't seen you in a while," Ang called back, still a couple buildings down from her. She jogged the distance to him.

"Too long of a while," Tate replied, throwing herself into his arms.

"Well, you could —,"

She covered his lips with her own, swirling her tongue through his mouth. He sat her on her feet, clearly a little shocked, slow in kissing her back. She put on a good show, running her hands along his shoulders and clawing down his chest. He finally managed to break the kiss, gently pushing her away. She winked up at him.

"You're my *best* friend," she teased. He glanced behind her.

"Oh, are we onto the '*make-him-jealous*' phase of the relation-ship?" Ang asked, eyeballing Jameson. She shook her head.

"No, we're onto the '*make-him-piss-blood*' part. He hurt my feel-ings. I want to hurt his pride," Tate explained.

"Glad to be of service."

They walked up to Jameson hand in hand. The reception be-tween the two men was cool, at best. Ang smiled his shit-eating grin, wrapping an arm around Tate's waist. He knew he was the more cherished between the two. Jameson smiled back in a lazy manner, letting his eyes wander over Ang's wiry frame and then over to Tate's smaller form. He knew he was the one she was going home with that night – and any other night. They *both* knew what she was like in bed. It was like being in the middle of a very loud silent-argument. She felt like her hair was going to stand on end from all the tension.

"Inside! Everybody inside, chop chop," she ordered, scooting both men up the stairs ahead of her.

Of course it was super fucking awkward. Her friend Rachel – the girl she had covered for to cater the Kraven and Dunn event, thus the person responsible for the fucked up relationship Tate now found herself in – was the one throwing the dinner party, and it was mostly a bunch of twenty-somethings; all people who worked the same kind of jobs, led the same kind of lives. Jameson stuck out like a sore thumb. Originally, Tate had thought that would be part of the fun. But it just made things weird. He was quiet and taciturn, didn't even try to pretend to be interested in anything or anyone.

It didn't help that Ang took her statement very seriously and took every opportunity to touch her inappropriately. Jameson watched, that cool, disdainful look in his eye, but he didn't say or do anything. Just smiled. It made her a little nervous. She escaped into the kitchen where most of the other girls were; Tate was normally a dude kind of lady, would rather hang out with the boys. Not that night. She chugged pinot grigio, wishing it was whiskey, and just hoped that Ang and Jameson would kill each other, curing all her frustrations.

Dinner was finally served. Jameson took a seat towards one end of a large table. They hadn't spoken a word directly to each other since she had kissed Ang, and Tate hesitated about which seat she should take. Jameson solved the dilemma when he yanked on her arm, forcing her into the chair next to him. She didn't argue. Just drank more. Ang sat across from them and tried his hardest to flirt, but when she stopped responding, he turned his attentions to Rus, who became all giggly and red. Tate glared at her.

Stupid, normal girl. Bet she could just go out and have normal, boring sex. Bet no one calls her a dumb cunt – and if they did, bet she wouldn't be such a weirdo that she'd like it.

Jameson lightened up over the food, actually laughing and talking with some of the guys next to him. It made Tate feel a little better, up until he took her glass of wine away. Didn't even look at her, just reached out and grabbed it, moving it to the other side of his plate. Apparently, she was done drinking.

Asshole.

She helped clean up, and while she and Rachel washed dishes, everyone gathered in the living room. Ang was telling one of his *"a day in the life of a wannabe porn star"* stories, and everyone was laughing. When she peeked her head out, even Jameson had a smile on his face. She smiled and ducked back into the kitchen. At least he was pretending to have a good time. Maybe that would gentle the blow that would come later.

"Hey, Rach," Tate said, pressing her wrist to her forehead. "Do you have any aspirin or anything? I have a killer headache."

"In my bedroom, I have some tylenol in the bathroom – maybe some stronger stuff, I don't know what's all in there. Help yourself. Go lay down, if you want," Rachel offered, rubbing her back. Tate smiled and wandered down the hall.

Rachel's room was small, but she had an en suite, which Tate would kill for in her own apartment – even a half bath. She found the tylenol, but on another shelf in the medicine cabinet, she found some vicodin. *Thank god.* She took one pill and washed it down with the glass of wine she had snuck out of the kitchen.

She had pushed the bedroom door mostly closed behind her, left all the lights off, but she didn't lay down. She wandered around Rachel's room, not prying, but peeking through the stuff that was out. Standard pajamas, no lace or leather. Her closest didn't show a hint of kink. There was a dresser along one wall, with a bunch of jewelry on top of it. Tate picked through it, holding up earrings and moving to a mirror that was on the wall at the foot of the dresser, looking herself over.

Tatum O'Shea, nice, normal girl. Pshaw, right.

The door creaked and opened, light from the hall spilling inside. Out of the corner of her eye, she watched Jameson walk towards her. She didn't say anything, just grabbed a necklace off the dresser and moved back to the mirror. She struggled with the clasp and he walked up behind her, taking the necklace from her fingers.

"Too cheap," he commented. Tate stared at his reflection while he clasped the necklace.

"You think?" she asked, pressing her hand against the jewelry. It was several strands of pearls, of varying lengths, all connected as one at the ends.

"Yes. They're fake. I remember you wearing another set of fake pearls, once. You need real ones," he told her. She smiled.

"I'll put that on my to-do list. Rent, utilities, pearls," she joked, reaching back and unhooking the necklace. As soon as she removed it, his hands took its place, his thumbs hooked around the back of her neck and his fingers splaying down to her collar bone.

"I hurt you," Jameson repeated his statement from the car. She threw the necklace onto the dresser.

"A little bit. I'm mostly over it," she replied.

"I don't think you're stupid, Tate," he started, and she held her breath, her eyes locked on his in the mirror. Jameson, apologizing? No way. "I think the way you live is stupid. Maybe I hide a little, but you're running away, too. You are better than all of this, smarter than all of them, *and you know it.*"

"Those are my friends," her voice was soft.

"Can you honestly tell me that sometimes you don't want something different?" he asked.

"Who doesn't?" she responded. "It's knowing the worth of what you have. Fake pearls are just as good as real pearls, if they're given with good intentions and love. If Ang gave me the gaudiest, ugliest, tackiest, strand of fake pearls ever, I would love them more than any set of real pearls my parents ever gave me. Ang *loves* me. So good or bad, stupid or smart, those people care about me. I care about them. I could go back to Harvard tomorrow, and I would still be friends with these people, Jameson."

He stared at her for a while, his grip getting harder. Almost like he was pushing down on her shoulders. He looked a little angry, and she wondered if maybe honest candor could get to Jameson more

145

than childish games.

"If *Angier* gave you pearls, huh. And what if *I* gave you pearls? What would they mean to you?" he asked. She scrunched up her nose. The metaphor was starting to get awfully convoluted.

"Depends."

"Oh what?"

"On how much they cost. You don't love me, so to be impressed, that price tag better be huge," she halfway joked. He smirked at her.

"So, if I got you a $50,000 strand of pearls, and *Angier* got you some shitty fake ones, his would mean more to you, because he '*loves*' *you?*" Jameson clarified.

"There are pearl necklaces that cost $50,000!?" Tate almost shouted her response.

"There are ones that cost a lot more than that. At least I know I can aim a little lower if I want to impress you," he smirked. She swatted at his leg.

"Shut up. And don't be jealous of Ang, he just likes to play with me," she told him.

"I'm not jealous. And it looks more like *you* like to play with *him.*"

"It's a mutual kind of thing."

"So I played your game. I came downtown. I came to your dinner. I watched you kiss *two* guys. Do I win?" Jameson asked, his fingers massaging her skin. She sighed.

"Do you ever lose?" she replied.

"I keep trying to tell you that, I *never* lose," he said.

"We'll see about that, I still have some —,"

"Do you trust me, Tate?" he interrupted.

"Yes," she answered without hesitation. He looked a little surprised.

"Really?"

"Yes. You've never done something to me I didn't ask for, or didn't want. As far as I can tell, you've never lied to me. You have been upfront about everything and anything. Sometimes I don't like you very much; sometimes, I think you're the biggest dick I've ever met. You're rude, and mean, and spiteful half the time. But you never said you weren't – you've always claimed to be those things. So yes, I trust you," she explained. He laughed.

"The things you say, Tate. Sometimes it's like talking to a man. I wonder if that's why you're so easy to talk to," Jameson wondered out loud. She raised her eyebrows.

"I'm easy to talk to because I'm like a man?" she asked. He nodded.

"A little bit," he told her.

"I have awfully nice tits for a dude," she laughed, putting her hands over her breasts. He leaned close, his mouth against her ear.

"Stop talking. I came to dinner. I win. I get to extract payment," he said.

With an abrupt shove, he pushed her to the side. She fell against the dresser, catching herself with her hands before she could face plant on the wood. She went to push herself up, but his hand pressed down on the center of her back, holding her in place.

"What are you doing?" she asked.

"Whatever I want. You said you trust me," he pointed out, and she felt his other hand brush against the fabric of her skirt.

"I do, but I don't want to have sex in my friend's bedroom," Tate told him with a laugh.

"Why not? And what makes you think we're going to fuck?"

"Um, I was in a similar position last week, and you fucked the hell out of me, *that* makes me think we're going to fuck. And I don't want to be disrespectful. This is her house, her party; she thinks I'm laying down with a migraine. The door is open, anyone can see us," she told him.

"You're shy, Tate?" Jameson laughed. She snorted.

"No, but as I've been saying, these are my friends. I don't want to —," she stopped talking as he lifted her skirt up. It was long and flowy, went to just past her knees. He draped the material over her back.

"I'm not going to fuck you. That would be giving you a treat. You've been very bad. I'm going to do *whatever I want,*" he informed her, and she could feel her underwear sliding off of her butt.

Her argument caught in her throat. Lifting her head up off the dresser, she was facing the door – she could see down the hall. The living room was just to the right, and she could see the edges of a couple peoples backs. It was dark in the bedroom, and she and Jameson were towards the back of it. If anyone turned around, they probably wouldn't be able to see anything. But if anyone came down the hallway … not good. She took a deep breath.

"Jameson, I don't think we should do this," she started, but then ended in a gasp as two of his fingers slid inside of her.

She wasn't sure how *this* wasn't giving her a treat. He wasn't getting anything out of it, he was standing just enough back from her that she couldn't even reach him. She swallowed a groan and bit into a table runner that covered the length of the dresser. He hooked his fingers a little, almost massaging her insides.

"Don't hear any arguing now," Jameson's voice was dark behind her. Tate shook her head.

"We shouldn't … do this," she whispered, though her words had no conviction.

"You want this. Say stop, and I'll stop."

She pressed her lips together and hummed softly. Bit her tongue. Anything to keep from crying out. His other hand grabbed onto her hip and pulled her back a couple inches, enough so he could work his arm between her and the dresser. She made a high pitched squeaking noise when that hand reached her front. Dipped into wetness. Spun her into outer space.

"*Jameson,*" she whispered his name, almost a moan.

"You're awfully ready to play for someone who says she doesn't want to do this," he pointed out, and she laughed.

"You started it, in the car. Mean man," she joked, then really did moan. She flicked her eyes to the door. No one seemed to have heard her.

"Always mean. Remember that. Jesus, Tate, how are you still so tight? All these years, and you're still the tightest pussy I've ever had," he groaned, working his fingers faster.

"Kegels. Every day," she replied, then had to bite down on the runner again. She clawed her nails down Rachel's dresser.

"God, talk about being disrespectul. What about you is respect-ful, Tate? Your slutty mouth? Or your wide open legs? I'd only been back in your life for two days, and you fucked me. Easy fucking girl. Did *Angier* get it that easy?" Jameson asked. She knew he wasn't, but he sounded like a jealous lover. It drove her wild.

"Easier," she lied. His fingers were working on her so fast, she felt like she was being cut in half. Two Tatums. Which one would he want? She was pushing back against him, pushing for the edge, for the orgasm. It was very close.

"*Fucking bitch,*" he swore.

"You shouldn't be surprised."

"What am I going to do with you? *Fucking slut.* Fucked him while I was gone. Couldn't last three days. How much does it take to satisfy you?" Jameson demanded.

Maybe he is jealous ...

"Maybe more than you've got," she taunted in a breathy voice, gasping for air.

He pulled away and yanked her back from the dresser. She wait-ed for the swearing, the crushing fingers, the angry mouth. But none of that happened. He backed her up, pressed her butt against the dresser and her front to his chest. She looked up at him, breathing heavy, rubbing her thighs together.

"If you are very good, when we get home, I will let you finish this," he told her, smoothing his hands over her hair.

"Huh?" she asked, dumbfounded. He smirked down at her.

"That's all you get, baby girl. You'll learn not to push me," he whispered, before leaning down and kissing her.

Tate moaned and wrapped her arms around his waist, held him to her. She *loved* the way Jameson kissed. For an aggressive guy, sometimes he could be very gentle with his mouth. His lips moved over hers, his tongue against hers, quiet and soft. It made her heart flutter. She sighed and ran her hands down to his pants, ran her fingers along his belt, began pulling at the buckle. But then he pulled away, so fast she actually stumbled. He patted her cheek and then strode out of the room.

What. The. Fuck.

She was so close to coming, it was uncomfortable to walk. Her underwear was still around her knees. She thought she might have spontaneously developed asthma, it was so difficult to breathe right, and her heart was pounding out of her chest. Worst of all, she still had a room full of friends to get through before she could leave. She probably had her "*well fucked whore*" look on her face; Ang would take one look at her and know exactly what had happened. *Fuck.*

Well played, Mr. Kane. Well played.

She went into Rachel's bathroom and cleaned herself up. Patted her cheeks with cold water to calm down the serious flush she had going on. Seriously considered just getting herself off right then and there. But Jameson's words came back to her, about letting her finish at home, and she was never one to spoil her appetite.

She finished up, humming to herself as she left the bedroom. Weston was so far away, she wondered if she could convince him to disrespect Sanders enough to get it on in the car. She didn't know why, but she loved trying to make Sanders uncomfortable – mostly because she was pretty sure it wasn't possible. She walked down the hall, smoothing her hands down her skirt, thinking of some other possibilities, when someone hissed at her.

"*What are you doing!?*"

She turned to see Ang standing in a bedroom doorway. She smiled and opened her mouth to respond, when he suddenly grabbed her by the arm and dragged her to him. She was wearing a pair of absurdly tall cork wedges – she was practically as tall as Jameson – and she stumbled in them, falling into Ang's chest. She tried to push herself away, but he had a death grip on her arm.

"What's going on? I told you, no more hanky panky for a while," Tate laughed, but when she looked up, he wasn't smiling.

"What is wrong with you? One second, you're all over me, the next, you're letting him talk to you like you're some sort of insect while he violates you," Ang growled. She winced.

"Oh god. You saw?" she groaned. He nodded.

"Yeah, I fucking saw. He had his hand so far up inside of you, I thought he was checking your tonsils. What the fuck, Tate? You're at a dinner party with your friends, and you didn't even have the god-damn decency to close the fucking door?" Ang snapped at her. She was a little blown away.

"Um, forgive me, but half an hour ago, didn't you grab my breasts and proclaim to everyone within hearing that I had the best tits you've ever seen?" she pointed out.

"It was a fucking joke, Tate, with people who know us and know how we are. If I'd known how okay you are with really being a slut, I wouldn't have bothered with your tits; I would've just fucked you on the dining room table," he spat out. She gasped.

"Ang! What is wrong with you!?" she demanded.

"What's the big deal? You let him do it. When is it my turn?" he asked.

"What the fuck! Where is this coming from!? You have never

151

had a problem with me sleeping with other guys," she pointed out, yanking her arm free from him. He ran a hand through his hair.

"Because. You let some guy you've only known for like two weeks give you a pap smear at your friend's dinner party, in an open room, with an open door. You don't even really know him," Ang told her. She shook her head.

"I knew him for two years, and everything else is *none of your goddamn business*," she hissed.

"Maybe if I treat you like a piece of shit, just fuck you whenever and wherever I want, you'd fucking listen to me once in a while," he hissed back. She slapped him.

"*Enough.*"

They both whipped their heads to the side. Jameson was standing in the doorway, his hands in his pockets, that perfect, bored, detached expression on his face. Tate was embarrassed to be caught fighting about him. Ang didn't look embarrassed – he looked *pissed*. When Jameson started to walk into the room, Ang surged forward. Tate was quick to get between them.

"He's right, enough! Just stop!" she said loudly, hoping no one in the living room would hear. How embarrassing.

And this is why we don't engage in sexual activity at our friends' polite social gatherings.

"You know," Jameson started, clearing his throat. "It seems that you really have something to say to *me*. I've been here, waiting all night for this – *I* knew it was coming. But instead, you took it out on the person that you knew wouldn't really fight back."

She watched the anger roll over Ang's face. Watched his whole body tense up, a flush creeping up his neck. Her reaction was automatic, she lifted a hand and pressed it to his chest, rubbing gently. It never failed to calm him down. Both men cut their eyes to her, and she winced.

"*No one is fighting.* Ang, you're being a dick. If you want to talk, we can talk, later. If you want to keep being a dick, well, then we can talk about that later, too. But for now, this is *over*," she stated. He looked down at her for a long while, then nodded, taking a step back. Jameson laughed.

"It may be over with her, but not with me. If you *ever* treat her like that again, *you and I* will be having a talk. *Understood?*" Jameson demanded, his eyes like icicles as he stared at Ang.

"*Are you fucking kidding me!?*" Ang all but yelled. Tate put her hands on Jameson's chest and began pushing him out of the room.

"We're leaving," she growled, forcing him into the hallway.

To her surprise, he didn't fight her. He grabbed her hand and pulled her behind him, making a beeline for the door. As they gathered their coats, Tate managed to smile and act halfway normal. Jameson didn't say a word, just walked out the door. Tate said goodbye, made up some excuse about him having a work emergency. As she stepped out onto the stoop, she saw Ang emerge from the bedroom. She glared at him and then turned away, hurrying down the steps.

"Well, that went better than expected," Jameson commented in a dry voice, once they were in the car. She let out a frustrated yell.

"I can't believe he did that!"

"He's jealous."

"But why!? I have *literally* fucked guys in front of him. He has been there during boyfriends and break ups and quickies and coyote-uglies ..." her voice trailed off.

"Because I'm the first guy that's actually *threatened him*," Jameson explained. She turned to face him.

"Is that why you're not more upset? He said you treated me like shit," she pointed out. Jameson laughed.

"I *do* treat you like shit, about half the time. I'm not upset because you're in the car with *me*, and *he's* in that apartment, *alone*. *Winning*," he said, running his fingers through her hair.

"You're winning all kinds of things tonight," Tate said. He pulled her close.

"I told you, I always win."

She pressed him back into the seat and straddled his lap. It was like she was suddenly starving for him. She kissed and licked at his mouth, made fast work of getting his jacket off. But when she started to undo his belt, he grabbed her wrists and pinned her hands behind her back. She mewled in protest.

"I don't want to wait till Weston," she breathed, leaning against him and running her teeth down his neck.

"Ms. O'Shea's apartment, Sanders," he said in a loud voice.

She was surprised. He never wanted to go to her apartment. He hated where she lived, hated that part of town. She almost thought he was going to just drop her off, prolong her punishment. When they got there, though, he climbed out of the car with her and followed her up the stairs.

"Are you staying the night?" she asked, feeling giddy as she undid all the locks on the door.

"For as long as I want," was all he replied, pushing the door open and brushing past her.

He moved ahead of her into the room. Her apartment was tiny, two bedrooms and one bathroom – no tub, even. The kitchen was big enough for maybe one person to comfortably cook in; a *small* person. But it was clean, and it was cute, and she could afford her share.

Sometimes.

"I don't usually bring people here," Tate said, running her tongue across her bottom lip as she shut the door. She felt like she had cotton mouth. Even after all the time they'd spent together, he still had the ability to make her nervous.

"No?" he asked, stopping in the middle of the living room. She shook her head, dropping her purse onto a chair.

"No. It's like ... my space. *Me.* I've never slept with a guy here. Not even Ang," she blurted out.

"That's a surprise."

"We did it in the hallway once, outside the door. He threw —,"

"Jesus, Tate, as often as you talk about this guy, I'm beginning to think maybe *I* should fuck him, see what the big goddamn deal is," Jameson snapped. She laughed.

"Maybe you should. He'd probably like it," she told him.

"Oh, I'm sure he would."

"Can I watch?"

"Tatum. Come here."

It was a command and she heeded it. When she got to his side, he ran his hand up her arm, past her neck, into her hair. When he got to the back of her head, he made a fist, bunching up her hair. But he didn't pull. She stared at him.

"What are you waiting for?" she asked.

"If I hear his name, one more time tonight, I swear to god, I will make you regret it," Jameson told her in a quiet voice.

Looks like someone else is jealous. New game?

"What if I don't say his name, and just refer to him?" Tate asked. The grip on her hair tightened, pulling a little.

"Tate."

"You said *'hear his name',* so technically, I could just —,"

He used the fist in her hair to shove her forward. She stumbled into the hall and didn't need anymore prompting. She pushed open her bedroom door, barely sliding her skirt off before he grabbed her from behind. They crashed into her dresser and she threw her arms out, catching their weight.

"Why do you like to push me?" he groaned, lifting her hair so he could bite at the back of her neck.

"Because I like it when you push back," she whispered.

He turned her around and yanked her tank top over her head.

It was all push and pull after that. She unbuckled his belt and shoved his pants to the floor. He shrugged out of his shirt and she pushed him back, onto the bed. She quickly slid her panties off and then straddled his lap, letting her shoes fall to the floor. She didn't waste any time, just grabbed the base of his dick and sat down on it. She let out a shriek, holding herself still on him.

"Sometimes I think you don't even need me to be mean to you – you do a good job all on your own," Jameson chuckled in her ear. She reached for the back of his head and grabbed a handful of hair, pulling.

"*Shut. Up.*"

"I get what you're doing, you know. I know when you're baiting me," he informed her. She rocked her hips against his, and was rewarded with a fluttering of his eyelids.

"Really? Then why do you usually take it?" she asked, her voice a little breathless as she moved her hips faster.

"Because this is all on my terms, and sometimes I like to indulge you," he replied.

She couldn't respond. When she was on top with him, he hit spots inside of her that might have actually been portals to other dimensions. She couldn't think, couldn't breathe. Just gasped and pushed and pulled. But after a couple minutes, something wasn't right. She was perilously close to coming, but he was still sitting very still. Hands on her hips, silent. Jameson was *never* silent.

"What are you waiting for?" she gasped against his mouth.

"You're upset. I'm angry. It's too easy," he replied, trailing his lips down her shoulder. She laughed.

"*You're* too easy, Mr. Kane."

He playfully glared at her.

"That fucking mouth. Sometimes, I swear, you're just seeing if I'll ever actually hit you," he chuckled.

"*Do it.*"

She didn't know who was more surprised, him or her. But she had said it. She stopped moving, looking into his eyes. He had said it as a joke. Did she really want him to hit her? It was like another challenge to her. He didn't think she could handle him, didn't think she could take it. She didn't think he'd ever actually go for it, ever stop restraining himself.

"Baby girl, I don't want to hit you," Jameson murmured.

Tate slapped him.

Once again, shock on both their faces. She hadn't hit him hard, it was more noise than anything else. But his eyes were like fire when they came back to hers. She would have laughed, if she hadn't been so nervous.

What is wrong with me?

"At least one of us isn't scared," she tried to cover up her nerves. He gave an evil, dark laugh. Satan was in the room.

"Now *that* is a fucking lie," he hissed.

She slapped him again.

I'm suicidal.

"It feels good to be the one in charge for once, *Kane*. At least one of us isn't a pussy," she snapped at him.

"Tatum, I'm not fucking around, don't —,"

She slapped him hard, and without hesitation he slapped her back. Before her head could even fully snap to the side, he had a hand cupping her jaw, pulling her back to stare at him. His eyes blazed into hers. He hadn't slapped her hard, not really. But still. Her heart rate doubled.

"Do not *ever* fucking hit me again, *got it?*" he said in a slow, even voice. She looked down at him, her eyes hooded. She felt high.

"I can't make any promises."

He swung her around, slamming her into her mattress. She cried out as he pushed into her, one of his hands immediately holding her down by the throat, the other grabbing onto her thigh. She gasped in time to his thrusts.

"Fucking Tatum. Goddamn. *Fuck you.* Fucking tried to hit me in the car. Fucking hit me in here. Who the fuck do you think you are? Who the fuck do you think you're dealing with?" Jameson demanded.

"You. Only you," she moaned, raking her nails across her breasts.

"*Stupid fucking bitch,* I can't believe you made me hit you," he hissed.

If she would have been able to comprehend what he was saying, she probably would have slapped him right then. Just for emphasis. But she couldn't comprehend *anything* – she was being pounded into one of those other dimensions she had thought about earlier.

"I think … you liked it," she breathed, arching her back away from the bed. His hand moved from her throat to her breast bone, pressing her down hard into the mattress.

"*No shit.* Fuck. Fucking kissed him. I couldn't fucking believe it. I almost dragged you into the car, fucked you right in front of him – you'd probably like that, wouldn't you? Fucking kissed him in front of me, what were you thinking? *Stupid fucking slut,*" he growled.

Ah. It all came back to Ang. She was angry at Ang and angry at herself – so she wanted to be treated badly. Jameson was angry at Ang and angry at her – he wanted to treat someone badly.

We are a match made in Hell. He may be Satan, but I'm Lillith.

He pulled away and spun her around, forcing her onto her stomach. She didn't have a chance to move before he hiked her hips into the air and slammed into her, his dick bottoming out on the first push. She screamed, pounding a hand against the wall across from her. It was pain. It was sexy. It was aggressive. *She loved it.* She tried to prop herself up, and he pushed her back down, a hand on the back of her head. She reached a hand back to touch him, and he grabbed it, pressing her hand against her face. She couldn't see anything. Could only feel.

All she felt was him.

"I want you to come, Tate. Are you going to come for me?" he snapped from behind her, letting go of her head and dragging his nails down the length of her back.

"Yes, yes," she cried out.

"You *always* come for me." He kept dragging his nails down the exact same path, over and over.

"Yes."

"It's more than you deserve, *whore*."

"Yes."

"*You're so good to me*," he murmured. She let out a sob.

"*Oh my god!*"

She came, all those Kegel exercises she had told him about kicking in and locking his dick into place. He went as deep as he could and then stopped, one hand holding onto her hip. She screamed and panted, pounding one hand on the mattress. The orgasm lasted forever, shredding her. Making her ache. The whole time, he raked his nails down that path on her back. Peeling away a layer of skin, exposing a piece of her soul. Stealing it from her. Or just taking it back.

Houston, we have a problem.

While she was still trembling and trying to figure out what the hell she was feeling, he pulled out of her. She didn't have the energy to ask what he was doing; she just collapsed, sucking in air. After about a minute, she felt a hand on her ankle and she was suddenly yanked off the bed. She clawed at her bedding, taking a sheet down with her. She landed in a heap on the floor, the blanket falling over her shoulder. By the time she got her bearings, she saw Jameson sitting down in a chair in the corner of her room.

"Now that *that's* done," he said in a calm, soft voice, planting his feet widely apart and putting his hands on his knees. His erection jutted straight up and she had trouble not staring at it.

"Um … what?" Tate managed, her voice hoarse.

"You are going to crawl over here, on your hands and knees. And you are going to suck my dick, like your life depends on it. *If I decide to come for you, you are going to swallow every last drop. You're not going to move. Understood?*" he told her.

She didn't answer. Instead, she just started crawling.

Tatum O'Shea, always such a nice, normal girl.

8

JAMESON SPENT MOST OF THE next week in Los Angeles. He needed space. He couldn't think straight, not when she was around.

Tate had followed his instructions that night, swallowed every last drop he had to give. Say what he wanted about her life, Tate *had* gotten some good things out of living on the fringe of society – she gave the absolute best blowjobs he had ever been privileged enough to receive.

She laid on the floor for a while afterwards, and eventually he crawled down next to her. And just chatted with her. She told him that part of the reason she had made him go out on the town, meet her friends, was because she was beginning to feel like his dirty secret, being hidden away in his house.

Stupid. It wasn't that Jameson was ashamed of her; he just didn't like to be around other people. Plain and simple. He hated to leave his house, regardless of whether or not she was there. She didn't even factor into it. He reminded her that if she thought something was about her, it probably wasn't. She had laughed at him.

She told "scary" stories about her first year living alone in Boston. He told "scary" stories about the first hostile takeover he had overseen. She asked if he'd had any run-ins with her family, and he admitted that he'd dealt with her father several times, but they had never spoken about Tatum, or any of the O'Sheas. It hadn't occurred to him to ask about her, but judging by the way she talked, her father wouldn't have known anything about her, anyway.

Halfway through a very hair raising tale about her getting lost in the worst neighborhood in Boston, they heard the front door crash open. They stared at each other while they listened to a drunk Rusty stumble through the living room. There was some giggling, then a man's voice. Footsteps down the hall, some light sexy banter. Jameson pressed a hand to Tate's mouth, to keep her from laughing out loud.

When the moaning started, he almost laughed himself. God, how did people have sex like that? "*You're so beautiful,*" "*You're so amazing,*" "*Oh my god, **you're** so amazing!*" "*Oh my god, **you're** so beautiful!*" Moan, moan. Pant, pant. Tate was almost convulsing under his hand, she was laughing so hard. It sounded ridiculous, and worse, it sounded fake. Jameson didn't understand bad sex – why not just stop doing it? But the bed springs kept squeaking, the headboard banging out a dull rhythm.

Jameson had laid himself on top of Tate and began mocking the noises from the next room. She snorted and choked to keep from laughing, tried to push him off of her, but when he pawed at her breast, it stopped being a game. He pushed her legs apart, dipped his fingers into her, pushed inside of her. She kept her lips together and moaned in her throat.

He whispered that *she* was beautiful, that *she* was amazing. But it was different from their neighbors — Jameson actually meant it. He didn't know what to make of it. He had never treated her like that before, like she was delicate, or special. But he was beginning to realize that she was both of those things to him.

162

DEGRADATION

The next morning, he woke up before her. They had moved to the bed at some point and fallen asleep. Tate had been right next to him – the bed wasn't very big, maybe a full. He was used to a king. She had been laying on her stomach, with one arm and one leg hanging off the side. He had watched her sleep for a while, his eyes wandering down the angry scratch marks on her back, over the bruises on the side of her neck. She let him do so many things to her. Eventually, she would want something in return, and *that* thought scared him.

He snuck out without waking her up. Stopped in at her landlord's office, took care of her rent situation. If she couldn't act like an adult, he could be one for her, he figured. He called Sanders and then called her cell phone, left her a voicemail. He didn't want her accusing him of running away. That wasn't what he was doing.

At least, he didn't think so.

So he flew to L.A., tried to forget about her for a couple days. He was getting a little too attached to her. When he had seen her at the meeting with his lawyers, when he had known that he was going to sleep with her again, he had pretty much started thinking of her as a possession. Something he had created, thus something that belonged to him. Pretty to play with, fun to banter with, but nothing more than that. Now, though, it was beginning to seem like a whole lot more.

He didn't think that was okay. Jameson didn't want to be attached to her, or to any woman. He didn't want to need anyone, least of all Tatum O'Shea. So he set out to distract himself. Checked on some businesses he was involved with, went to some events, attended a gala. Met lots of women. It didn't work too well. He still thought about her a lot. Her body, her laugh, her little games.

He was a little surprised that she hadn't called him, then he realized Tate had actually never once called him. Had he given the impression that she wasn't allowed to? Sometimes he wasn't entirely aware of how much of an asshole he was being, at any given point in time. After three days had passed, his curiosity got the better of him.

"Sanders," Jameson barked across his hotel suite. A moment later, the other man's head peeked around the door.

"Yes?" he asked.

"Have you spoken to Tate?" Jameson asked, looking over some newspapers.

"What? No. Should I have?" Sanders asked, sounding surprised. Jameson had thought maybe she would have called him – the two had a developed a weird sort of camaraderie, made weirder by the fact that Sanders hardly ever spoke. But it was obvious he liked her, enjoyed her company.

"No. Give me your phone," Jameson said, holding out his hand. Sanders marched into the room and handed over his cell phone. It was four o'clock in L.A., which meant evening in Boston.

"Is everything alright?" he asked. Jameson nodded, dialing Tate's phone number. She answered on the fourth ring.

"*Guten Abend, haben Sie die voicemail-box erreicht —,*" her voice started prattling in German.

"What the fuck are you doing?" he interrupted.

"Jameson?" her voice laughed.

"Yes. I didn't know you spoke German," he said.

"I don't, I only know that line. Did you get a new phone?"

"No, I'm using Sanders' phone. Why did you answer in German?"

"I always do that, when it's an unknown number," she told him.

"That's ridiculous," he snapped.

"Aw, you miss me, don't you? That's why you're whispering sweet-nothings in my ear," she teased.

I do miss her.

"Don't be stupid. What are you doing?" he asked, getting out of his chair and heading out onto the balcony.

"Watching a movie with Ang," she replied.

They made up fast.

Jameson wasn't as immune to Ang as he liked to pretend. She was right, he *was* jealous. When she had kissed Ang, Jameson had nearly lost it. Then when he had gone back into the apartment, heard the way Ang was talking to her, it had taken everything he had not to destroy the younger man. He had wanted to beat Ang into the ground. Jameson could talk to Tate that way, but no one else could. *Only him.*

Scary thought.

"Are you sure you're just watching a movie?" he asked, running his hand along the railing. She laughed.

"I don't know, let me check. Ang, are we watching a movie or having sex?" her voice went away from the phone.

"Definitely fucking," came a reply from far away. There was some muffled smacking noises and Tate laughed, back to the phone again.

"He's lying. We're watching 'The Emperor's New Groove," she explained.

"The Disney movie?" Jameson asked, his eyebrows scrunching together

"Mmm hmmm."

"Why are you watching cartoons?"

"Because I like them. And we're really stoned," she told him. He groaned.

"Jesus. This is why I can't leave you alone," he grumbled into the phone.

"Then maybe you shouldn't," was her husky reply. Jameson paused for a long time, and could hear her get up. Move around. Go to somewhere quiet.

"I can't take you everywhere with me," he told her in a low voice.

"No. But you don't have to leave so much, either," she replied. He smiled.

165

"I think *you* miss *me*, Tate," he teased back. She snorted.

"I miss parts of your anatomy. When are you coming home?" she demanded.

Liar.

"Two days. Think you can wait that long?" he asked. She laughed.

"Probably not. I'm about to start humping inanimate objects."

"God, you're crude. *Filthy*. I'm going to fuck you so hard when I get home," he laughed.

"Promises, promises," Tate sang.

"Two days. Be at my place, at one o'clock. Bring a bathing suit," he instructed.

"Seriously?"

"Why do you make me repeat myself?"

"Two days. One o'clock. Bathing suit. You got it, boss."

Jameson didn't say goodbye, just hung up the phone. Hearing her voice made him happy. Seven years ago, if anyone had asked him if he thought he'd ever see Tatum again, he would have said no. And now he was sleeping with her on a regular basis, and hanging on her words. Stupid, stupid man.

"Sanders," he snapped out, heading back into the room.

"Yes?" the other man responded, taking his phone back when Jameson held it out.

"Call Dunn. Call the other associates. Call my lawyers. We're going to be having a get together when I get home. Food and drinks around the pool, weather permitting," he said. Sanders looked surprised.

"I'm sorry. We're having … what?" he asked. Jameson laughed.

"Ms. O'Shea seems to think she's my dirty little secret. We're going to prove to her that she's not," Jameson explained. Sanders stared at him for a minute.

"You really like her, don't you?" he asked. Jameson's laugh died away.

"You know I hate those kinds of questions. Now get to work."

"Alright, I'll call everyone and find a place to take care of the details. What about your arrangement for this evening, the Harmon sisters?" Sanders asked, picking up an appointment book and opening it.

"What about it?" Jameson asked, striding over to his closet and rummaging through his clothing.

"Do you want to cancel?" Sanders continued.

"Why the fuck would I want to do that?" Jameson blurted out, turning around. Sanders shrugged.

"Your phone call just now, the party. I thought maybe —," he started.

"You thought *wrong*. Now go, you have a party to plan."

Two days later, at one-thirty, Jameson stood on his front porch. His arms were folded across his chest and he wore an expensive pair of wayfarer sunglasses. His back yard was filled with about twenty of his friends and colleagues, most with their significant others, but he was waiting for one specific person.

And she was late.

"Did she call you?" he asked. Sanders appeared in his line of vision.

"No. You keep asking me that. Why would Ms. O'Shea ever call me?" Sanders responded. Jameson shrugged.

"She likes you, you two are friends," he replied.

"She likes you, too."

Jameson frowned.

Finally, ten minutes later, a cab pulled into the driveway. Jameson knew he could always send Sanders to get her, but then the whole process would take twice the amount of time. Plus, she needed some accountability – it was up to her to call the cab and get in it and get there. Frankly, he was surprised she managed it at all.

"Sorry, it really wasn't my fault this time," Tate laughed as she climbed out of the back seat.

"Sure it isn't," he replied, scowling at her.

She was wearing the same shorts she had worn when he had gone to her bar, and a sheer black blouse with a black bikini top underneath it. She had flip flops on her feet, a ridiculously huge purse, and aviator glasses that were so shiny, he could see his reflection in them. While they talked, she pulled her hair up into a sloppy ponytail. She looked completely different from any other person in the house.

He wanted to *devour* her.

"It's really not her fault, sir," the cab driver started, actually stepping out of the cab. They all turned towards him. "I got a flat tire on the freeway. I have a pinched nerve in my back; the young lady actually changed the tire for me. No charge for the ride."

Jameson turned back to Tate, his eyebrows raised. She smiled broadly and flexed her arms like a body builder, kissing one of her biceps. He laughed and gestured for Sanders to pay the man anyway.

"You changed a tire, dressed like this?" he asked as he led her into the house. She threw back her head and laughed.

"No, I changed into coveralls first. *Yes*, like this, Jameson. I didn't have much of a choice. Do *you* even know how to change a tire?" she asked. He pulled on her ponytail.

"No playing with me this early, we've got to act respectable for a little while," he told her.

"Why?"

But he didn't have to answer. The back part of the house was a conservatory that over looked his pool and back yard. She gave a low whistle. There were a lot of people on his back lawn, all laughing and smiling. Clinking glasses and chatting, looking like they were all having the time of their lives. Jameson Kane rarely invited people to his private dwellings. Tate stood completely still, staring at everything.

"Scared, baby girl?" Jameson whispered. She shook her head.

"No, but why? Why are you doing this?" she asked.

"You said I treat you like a secret. This is everyone I know in Boston. Except for *Angier*. Forgot to invite him," Jameson said, his tone full of bite. She lowered her glasses and gave him a Look.

"But *why?*" she pressed.

"You're not a secret to me, Tate. I'm not ashamed of you or what we do. You're two steps above being an employee anyway," he pointed out. She snorted.

"Employees *get paid*, and I haven't seen a fucking dollar. I ate macaroni and cheese ALL weekend," she told him.

"Whatever. I'm being nice. This may be your only opportunity to see it in action," he warned her. She took a deep breath.

"I'm not like these people, Jameson. I won't fit in. I'm very flattered, and this means a lot, that you did this. It's very sweet. But ..." she let the sentence hang.

*She **is** scared.*

"Alright. I made my statement. You don't have to go out there. Since you're *scared*. And hey, now we really know who the bigger *pussy* is," he mocked her.

Tate turned to look at him, shoving her glasses onto her head. She slowly unbuttoned her shirt and let it fall to the floor, then shoved her shorts off her hips. She was wearing a black bikini, the bottoms breaking into two strings that curved around her hips. She had an amazing body, and the scorching summer had given her a killer tan. He drank in the sight of her.

"I'm not scared. By the end of the day, those people out there will like me more than they like you," she informed him. He laughed.

"I have no doubt of that. But you do realize that not one single other person out there is just strutting around in their bathing suit. I didn't realize you had to be half naked to feel comfortable," Jameson said, gesturing outside. He was right. There were some board shorts, and a lot of ladies were wearing bathing suits underneath fancy covers and long dresses, but no one was serious about getting in the pool. Tatum shook her head.

"You said wear a bathing suit, so I'm ready. Let's do this," she replied, and strode out the back door. Jameson caught up with her, and it was obvious he surprised her when he hooked an arm around her hips, guiding her to the closest group of people.

"Cecily. Livvy. Tad, this is my friend, Tatum. Our families were close, in Pennsylvania. I recently discovered her living right here in Boston. Tate, Tad's a junior broker at the firm, Livvy is his wife, and Cecily keeps the accounting department in order," he introduced her.

Tad stared at her tits the whole time, Livvy looked like she wanted to draw blood, and Cecily laughed, shaking Tate's hand. Tate, of course, was friendly and personable. She laughed easily and it was obvious that making friends came naturally to her. Jameson introduced her to a couple more groups of people, then left her to her own devices. He had done his part, shown her that she wasn't someone he wanted to hide away. She was a friend, he guessed, just like the rest of them.

Now he could go back to being an asshole.

Jameson hovered near the makeshift bar, chatting and laughing with some of the guys, but always keeping an eye on her. She floated around the party, mingling with everyone. Cecily took to her, as did a couple of the other girls, but most of the women watched her with venom in their eyes. It was obvious that Tate was aware of this, and she flirted shamelessly with every single guy. More so with the ones who had judgemental girlfriends or wives at their sides. She stretched out on a lounge chair at one point, and made a show of putting sun tan lotion on every visible inch of skin.

He was not immune to the pull she was having on the other men.

"Where did you find her?" Wenseworth Dunn walked up to Jameson's side, gesturing to Tate as she stretched her arms above her head.

"I told you, our families —," Jameson started.

"Bullshit. Most blue blood types don't breed daughters that hot," Dunn laughed. Jameson nodded.

"Agreed. But she *is* Mathias O'Shea's estranged daughter," Jameson supplied. Dunn whistled.

"Oh wow. Pretty powerful guy. Playing with fire, Kane," he warned.

"Not really. *Severely* estranged. Haven't spoken for seven years. I'm part of the reason why, though he still speaks to me," Jameson said. Dunn turned to look at him.

"What do you mean?"

"I was dating her sister, and Tate and I slept together. They disowned her," Jameson explained. Dunn laughed.

"Good old Kane. You know how to pick 'em. She looks like the type to sleep with her sister's boyfriend. *Fucking hot.* She yours?" Dunn asked.

Jameson didn't like this line of questioning, but he didn't want to come off as a jealous lover. Tate didn't have any claim on him, nor did he on her – they had been very clear about that from the beginning. Still.

Fucking Dunn.

"We're sleeping together, if that's what you're asking," Jameson gave an evasive answer.

"Kinda low brow for you, Kane. I thought you only dated Eastern European supermodels," Dunn joked. It wasn't funny.

"I don't date *anyone* anymore. Tate and I like to fuck, that's it,"

Jameson snapped. It was harsh, but he didn't care. He didn't care if people knew they were sleeping together; what he didn't want was people thinking he was in the market for a wife or anything.

"Good time girl, all right. Tell her to call me sometime," Dunn mumbled, his eyes raking over Tate's form as she climbed out of her chair, looping her arm through Sanders' and walking with him towards the house. Jameson laughed darkly.

"You couldn't handle her, Dunn," he said.

"Oh really?"

"To say she likes things a little wild, is an understatement. And you most definitely couldn't afford her," he snapped. Dunn's eyebrows shot up.

"You mean she's a —,"

"I mean, this conversation is *over*. Go mingle, eat, drink, hit on someone, *jesus*," Jameson growled before stomping away.

He was angry. "*... thought you only dated Eastern European supermodels,*" – Jameson didn't appreciate obscure references to his ex. Didn't appreciate references to her, *at all*. And he *especially* didn't appreciate the way Dunn had been looking at Tatum. It was all fine and dandy for them to sleep with other people, but he certainly didn't want to be trading stories at the water cooler about her gymnastic abilities in bed.

And, a tiny part of him whispered, he simply didn't like Dunn looking at her, *period*.

Several hours later, Tatum hopped down the stairs on one leg, pulling up her sock on the other leg. When she got to the bottom of the stairs, she put the other sock on, as well. She had opted for long red socks. Better for evening wear. It was just starting to get dark outside and people were moving into the conservatory. As she headed into the library, she pulled a loose tank top on over her head and walked right into something. She stumbled backwards, quickly pulling the shirt over her bikini top.

"I'm sorry, I didn't know anyone was in here," she laughed. There was a man standing in the library. She had met him before, but couldn't remember his first name. Last name was Dunn, he was Jameson's business partner. He smiled down at her.

"Just looking around. I've only been to Jameson's house one other time," he told her. She laughed again.

"Yeah, he never lets anyone come over, treats it like a fortress. I'm surprised there aren't TSA agents at the bottom of the driveway, screening people before they come in," Tate joked, but she felt a little uncomfortable. Dunn's eyes never met hers, just stayed trained on her body, and she was very aware of the fact that she was standing in front of him wearing only knee socks, a bikini, and a light tank top.

"He's strange that way, isn't he? So open about some things, so private about others," Dunn mumbled. She frowned. His words were loaded with tension and double meanings.

"Not sure what you mean. He's always been pretty open with me," she replied.

"*Always.* You've known each other a long time, huh? I didn't even know Mathias had any kids," Dunn commented. Tate was surprised. Jameson had talked about her family with this guy?

"Yeah, there's two of us, I have an older sister."

"He mentioned her, too. Sounds like you were very naughty in your younger years."

She narrowed her eyes. *Jameson had talked about that!?* And she was liking this Dunn guy less and less. His voice was lascivious, and while normally that wouldn't bother her, he was Jameson's partner. They were in Jameson's home. And she was not the least bit attracted to Dunn. He gave her the creeps on a seismic scale.

"We all have a past, don't we?" she brushed past him, heading to where her cell phone was plugged in and charging.

"Oh yeah. Your past just sounds more interesting," Dunn told her, following her across the room. She frowned, pretending to concentrate on her phone.

"I'll be sure to let you know when I write my life story," she responded.

"Or we could get together sometime and you could tell me yourself," he offered.

She snapped her head up, a little surprised. Though he hadn't spent a lot of time with her at the party, she thought Jameson had made it very clear to everyone that he had some sort of a relationship going on with her. When he would stand next to her, he always draped an arm around her waist. When she had been off by herself, at one end of the pool, he had come up behind her and wrapped his arms around her shoulders, kissed the side of her neck. Turned her to face him while he whispered very dirty things in her ear, his hands running down her body. No one was next to them, but they were well within sight of the other guests. So it was a little bit of a shock to her that his business partner, and friend, was hitting on her.

"I don't think that's a good idea," Tate laughed, moving to walk past him. He blocked her way.

"Why? Because of Jameson? He won't care, we've shared girls before," Dunn assured her. She snorted.

"*I* care, and I say no thank you," she snapped, trying to go the other way. He moved again.

"Just name your price, I'm sure I can match whatever Jameson offered."

Tate stood stock still, staring Dunn in the eye. Jameson had told him that? Was telling people he had paid her to sleep with him? It was more of a joke than anything, he had never actually given her any money. She didn't want his friends thinking they could just slip

174

him some cash and they could fuck her in a dark corner of his house. She didn't want *Jameson* thinking that.

How could he think that!?

"I don't know what you're talking about. *Move*," she ordered. Dunn laughed.

"It's okay, I'm okay with it. Jameson's okay with it," he assured her, stepping closer to her. She backed away.

"Is everything alright?" Sanders' clear voice carried across the room. Dunn whirled around and Tate scurried past him, hooking her arm through Sanders'.

"No, this guy is an asshole," she said. Dunn laughed.

"Oh, c'mon, I just —," he started, when Sanders cleared his throat.

"I believe you'll find Mr. Kane in the conservatory, with the rest of the guests," he interrupted.

"Oh, was he asking for me?" Dunn asked.

"No, but I assumed since you're soliciting services from a woman who has been staying in his home, you would want to discuss it with him first," Sanders told Dunn, his voice like icicles. Dunn's face got hard, and Tate smiled. Apparently Jameson was not *"okay with"* this little proposition – based on Dunn's face, she would guess that Jameson didn't know anything about it at all.

"We could go together," Tate offered. "Tell the whole story, do a reenactment. He'd love it. What do you guys think?"

"Whatever you say, Ms. O'Shea," Sanders replied. Dunn huffed and stomped out of the room. Tate laughed.

"God, did you see his face? What a dick," she chuckled. Sanders nodded, turning and leading her across the hall, into the kitchen.

"Clearly. Would you care for a drink, Ms. O'Shea?" he asked. She nodded, and without even having to tell him, he went and grabbed a bottle of Jack Daniel's from a cupboard.

"You treat me so good, Sandy," she sighed as he sat the bottle on the huge island in the center of the kitchen. He gestured towards the glasses but she shook her head.

"Are you alright, Ms. O'Shea?" he asked in his careful tone. She shrugged, moving around to the other side of the island so she could face him.

"I don't know. I will be," she replied.

"Did he touch you?"

She lifted her eyes to Sanders, and for once, he was looking back at her. He almost never made direct eye contact with anyone, except for Jameson. His question surprised her. His voice lacked any emotion, like normal, but there was something in his eyes. He was worried about her, concerned. Tate was shocked.

"No, he didn't," she assured him. He nodded.

"Would you like me to get Mr. Kane?" Sanders offered. She shook her head and twisted the cap off the bottle.

"No," she laughed, taking a drink.

"I think he should know about this. He would be very upset," he told her. Tate laughed some more.

"You really think he'd be upset? I don't," she replied, taking an even bigger swig.

"You're wrong. He cares about you, Ms. O'Shea," Sanders assured her. She almost spit the liquor out.

"Jameson Kane doesn't care about anyone but himself," she snorted. She had to say things like that; she had to remind herself.

"I have seen a lot of women come through his life," Sanders' voice was quiet, almost soft. She stared at him. "But he has never treated *anyone* the way he treats you. He used to talk about you, you know. A long time ago, when he would drink. He would mention your name, mention that he wondered what you were doing, where you were. *He cares.*"

He stressed the last words, and Tate almost felt like tearing up. Who knew Sanders could be so passionate? And about her, of all people. For him to tell her these things, these obvious secrets, it meant a lot, on so many different levels. He really wanted her to know, Jameson cared about her.

She had told herself so many times that it wasn't a possibility, Jameson Kane would never truly care about her. Would never feel anything for her beyond desire. Maybe there was hope … *no.* She didn't want to believe it. Satan didn't have feelings, and if she began to think he did, he would eat her soul – what little she had left to give.

"You're very sweet, Sandy," she chuckled in a low voice, "but I think we both know that's not true."

"What's not true?"

Jameson's voice boomed in the doorway. He strode into the room, not looking very happy. He glared at both of them, crossing his arms over his chest as he came to a stop at the front of the island. Tate toasted him with her bottle before taking another drink. Sanders stood up straighter.

"Did you need something?" he asked.

"No. You can leave," Jameson told him. Sanders nodded.

"I'll be in the guest house. Ms. O'Shea," he said, and both Jameson and Tate looked at Sanders. "Please think about what I said, very seriously."

"What the fuck is he going on about?" Jameson demanded while Sanders walked out of the room. Tate shrugged.

"Sandy is an old soul in a young body, his riddles are too deep for us to understand," she joked. Jameson glared at her.

"I've been looking everywhere for you. What were you two talking about in here?" he asked. She laughed.

"Your friend, Dunn," she replied.

"Dunn? What about Dunn?"

"He seems to have gotten the impression that I'm a prostitute," Tate said. Jameson got very still, his eyes turning to ice.

Sanders must have learned that trick from him.

"What are you talking about?" Jameson asked in a low voice.

"He cornered me in the library, was being a super creep, hitting on me, telling me he could afford whatever you were paying, blah blah blah. Sandy came in and saved me," Tate explained.

"Are you serious right now?"

"Yup. Great friends, Jameson. Maybe keep our little game more on the down low, though. Unless you *want* me to sleep with your friends, which in that case, we could set up —,"

Jameson slammed his hand down on the island, causing her to jump.

"*Fuck no,* I don't want you sleeping with my friends. I can't fucking believe he did that, in my own house. I'm going to go in there and rip his fucking head off," Jameson swore. She laid her hand on his arm, before he could move.

"It's over, it's done with, not a big deal. Sandy gave him some of that magical freezer burn treatment, and the guy nearly pissed himself when we told him we were gonna tell on him, so it's cool. We're good," she assured him.

"It is *not* cool, and we are *not* good," Jameson growled.

"If you don't want your friends treating me like a whore, maybe don't mention that you offered to pay me," she suggested.

"I didn't, I made a *joke,*" he said. She rolled her eyes.

"Yes, and men are retarded assholes. You make a joke like that and he looks at my tits, and it's one-plus-one equals whore," she explained, and Jameson finally laughed.

"I wish I had gone to *that* school," he chuckled, running his hand through his hair.

"It's really not a big deal, Jameson. Don't go freaking out. He's business. I'm pleasure. We'll keep it separate from now on," Tate suggested. He nodded.

"Looks like neither of our little games worked out. Our worlds don't seem to mesh so well," he pointed out. She nodded.

"We seem to have assholes for friends."

"God, what does that say about us?"

"We're asshole royalty."

"King and Queen of the Assholes?"

"Totally."

They both cracked up after that – it was too far into the realm of ridiculous for Jameson, and the fact that he had kept it going made her laugh, as well. He pulled the Jack Daniel's bottle close and took a drink as well. He made a face as he passed it back to her.

"How you drink that shit, I'll never know," he grumbled.

"When you're just poor, white, trash, you don't exactly go straight for the Johnny Walker Blue Label," Tate laughed.

"I have some, we could be drinking that instead," he offered.

"Nah, I like to stay true to my roots," she joked, taking a healthy swig of the whiskey. He was silent for a moment, staring across the room. Sounds from the party drifted into the kitchen. Jameson scowled.

"I can't fucking believe Dunn did that," he grumbled, staring out the kitchen door.

"He said you've shared girls before," she told him. He glanced at her.

"Not like that, not like what we are," he replied, gesturing between himself and Tate.

"Like how, then?"

"Like the same girl from an escort service. I've never let him sleep with a girl I was actively sleeping with on a regular basis. I don't do that. I would *never* be okay with you sleeping with him, or any of my other colleagues. Not now, or at *any* point in time in the future," Jameson told her. She nodded.

"I'll keep that in mind."

"You had fucking better."

"Hey, don't get mad at me – I'm the one who was solicited. I deserve like restitution, or something," she joked. Jameson laughed.

"Restitution? Like what?" he asked.

"A $50,000 pearl necklace," Tate replied without hesitation. He snorted.

"Just go ahead and start holding your breath, I'll get right on that," he told her. She made a face at him.

"I missed you, you know," she blurted out. His eyebrows shot up.

"Really? The succubus missed her lord and master, Lucifer?" he joked, and she almost choked. It was basically the same joke she made about them in her head.

He's psychic, I knew it.

"Maybe '*miss*' is too strong of a word," she corrected herself. He laughed.

"Shut up, you couldn't have missed me that much. You were too busy getting stoned with *Angier*," he taunted.

"One night. It was a peace offering, he came over to apologize. I would never turn down good weed," she told him. Jameson laughed again.

"Are you sure that's all that happened? I don't know if I trust you," he said. She rolled her eyes.

"I solemnly swear that I did not sleep with Angier while you were in Los Angeles," Tate held a hand over her heart while she promised. He nodded.

"Good. So, what did you miss about me, baby girl?" he asked, leaning his forearms on the island. She thought for a second.

"Your penis."

He barked out a laugh.

"I already knew that. What else?"

"I don't know. Sometimes you're almost funny. You let me run around in my underwear all the time – Rus hates it when I do that at home. And sometimes you're almost halfway sweet to me," she tried to explain.

"Jesus, I sound like if Stalin owned the Playboy Mansion," he pointed out. She nodded.

"Yes. Exactly like that," Tate agreed.

"*Shut up.* What else?" Jameson pressed. She was thoughtful again.

"The way you treat me. Sometimes, and don't get me wrong, I love him, but just sometimes ... Ang kind of babies me. Coddles me. Tries to take care of me too much. Like he's afraid I'm gonna fall on my face if I'm out of his sight. You, on the other hand, practically push me down the stairs and just tell me to move my feet," she laughed.

"You make me sound abusive," he remarked. She shrugged.

"I meant it as a compliment. And you kinda are, in a way. I just happen to like it," she told him. He glared at her playfully.

"I'm not abusive. I'm ... aggressively sexual," Jameson explained. She rolled her eyes.

"More like a sexual aggressor," she teased.

"You flatter me too much. And I might have missed you, too, just a little bit," he confessed. She pressed a hand to her chest.

"See? There it is – sweetness. Be still, my beating heart."

"Shut the fuck up."

Tate got up and wandered across the kitchen, grabbed some crackers and then leaned back against the cupboards. While she munched away, she watched him. He had turned to watch her, as well.

"On a scale of one to ten," she started, "how much did you miss me?"

"I don't have a basis for comparison."

"One — you didn't think about me once, ten – you cut your trip short because you couldn't live without me," she suggested. He thought for a second.

"A two?"

181

She threw a cracker at him.

"God, you're such a dick. Sweetness, *gone*. You probably didn't miss me because you were too busy plowing some starlet," she joked. Jameson was silent, just stared at her, and she gasped. "Oh my god. You did, didn't you?"

"I don't think you really want to have this conversation right now," he said, moving away from the island and heading towards the kitchen door.

"Was it your ex?" she called out, and he stopped. Turned back towards her.

"No. She's not an actress, and she doesn't live in L.A.," he assured her.

"Then who was it? Has she been on tv? Please tell me I've seen her in a show or something," Tate laughed. He leaned against the doorway, shoving his hands into his pockets.

"You're really okay with this?" he asked. She moved back to the island and pulled herself up so she was sitting on top of it, facing him.

"I want all the gory details. Was she prettier than me?" Tate asked.

"I don't know how to answer that question," he replied. She laughed.

"You're shy, Jameson?" she teased. He shook his head.

"I can't say if *she* was prettier than you because there were *two* women."

"You slept with two women, in L.A., in one week?" Tate tried to lay everything out. He shook his head again.

"In one night."

"Impressive. Smooth operator. Did they pass each other going through the front door?"

"They walked through it together, at the same time."

Her breath caught in her throat. Oh wow, Jameson had been a

naughty boy while he was gone. She was touched that he was worried it would bother her, but it didn't really. She wasn't threatened by some random chicks in Los Angeles.

"Hot. So, were *either of them* prettier than me?" Tate asked again.

"They were twins, and they were very sexy, but not as sexy as you," Jameson assured her. She smiled big.

"I'm choosing to believe you on that. Were they better in bed?" she continued. He thought for a second.

"Well, that's hard to answer. Twice the anatomy to play with, kind of gives them an advantage," he said. Tate pouted her lower lip out at him, trying to hide her laughter. "But they weren't better. No. No, definitely not. No one takes care of me quite like you."

"That's good to hear, seeing as how it's usually you doing all the taking care of – have you ever slept with them before?" she asked, munching on a cracker. He shook his head.

"No, I just met them that week. Kind of a spur of the moment thing. They asked me to dinner, one thing led to another," he nodded his head for emphasis. Tate laughed.

"The ol' *one-thing-led-to-another-suddenly-I'm-fucking-twins* kind of night. I have that same problem all the time. Bitches just be falling for you in pairs, man," she teased. He rolled his eyes.

"God, I shouldn't have said anything."

"No, I'm glad you did. I want to know *everything*," she urged, pushing the box of crackers away. His face became hard, serious. Almost angry.

"Really? You want to know *everything*? Like how I tied one girl down and had her watch while I fucked the other? Or how they took turns sucking my dick? Things like that?" Jameson's voice was serious as well. The temperature in the kitchen suddenly cranked up about a hundred degrees. She licked her lips and nodded.

"*Exactly* like that," Tate replied, her voice breathy. He stared at her for a second, then he pulled his cell phone out of his pocket, pushed a button.

"Sanders," he barked into the phone, still staring at her. "Party's over. I want everyone out of my house in five minutes."

"Ooohhh, finally, alone time," Tate chuckled.

He didn't say anything in response, and they watched each other in silence. When they heard the sound of feet clomping through the house, he winked at her and slid out the door, closing it behind him.

She let out a breath, bowing her head forward. The mental image of Jameson, having sex, with two women. She rubbed her legs together. When she was having sex with him, she was too caught up in the moment, most of the time, to really pay attention. The idea of sitting back and watching him, seeing him in all his perfect kind of action; it turned her on. With two women? *Wow.*

The goodbyes seemed to take forever. She could hear voices murmuring, picked out Jameson's voice among them. She laid back flat on the island, propped her feet up on the edge. *Two women.* Did he talk with other women the way he talked with her? She imagined him tying a woman's wrists to a bed post, calling her names. Tracing his tongue down her prone body. Tate's hand crept onto her stomach. Fiddled with the edge of her bikini bottoms. She took a deep breath through her nose, forcing her hand to stay still.

It had been a long week without him.

"Getting started without me? Bad girl," Jameson's voice was soft as he walked back into the kitchen.

"No, but I thought about it," she replied, not lifting her head but holding up her hands for him to see.

"That's bad enough. I've barely told you anything, and you're already turned on?" he asked, moving so he was standing in front of her. She sat up, letting her legs fall back down against the drawers beneath her. He grabbed her knees and spread her legs so he could stand between them.

"I've got a very good imagination, Mr. Kane," she assured him.

He placed a hand against the crotch of her bikini bottoms, gently tracing his middle finger up and down. She sucked air through her teeth, trying not to moan.

"Apparently. You're soaking wet, Tatum," he informed her. She nodded.

"You have that effect on me, if you haven't noticed."

"You sure it wasn't all those men you were flirting with? Laying it on pretty thick out there," he told her, his fingers from his other hand digging into her knee.

"I thought you liked it when I was slutty," she pointed out. He narrowed his eyes.

"Hmmm, sometimes," was all he said in response, the pressure from his fingers getting harder. She sucked in another gasp of air and grabbed onto his wrist.

"No fair. I want to hear your story," she told him, stopping his movements.

"You are an amazing woman, Tatum O'Shea," Jameson chuckled, stepping back away from her.

"You have no idea. Now make it juicy. Lie if you have to," she told him, and he laughed, going back to his position by the door, leaning against the wall.

"Alright. What do you want to know first?" he asked. She laid back down.

"How it all started, start there. What were you wearing. What were they wearing," she suggested.

"Awfully detailed."

"I'm a very visual person."

"Let's see. I met them for dinner. I was wearing clothing. One of them was wearing a ridiculous dress, you would have loved it – short, slutty, only covered one shoulder. The other one was more demure, some fancy shirt, and tight pants," he described. Tate laughed.

"You were 'wearing clothing', huh? You're a horrible story teller.

Do these girls have names?" she asked, propping her foot up on the island top.

"Probably," was all he said, and she laughed.

"Terrible. So okay, we'll say Thing One is Slutty One — right up your alley. Thing Two, Demure Temptress. How long did it take you to talk them into coming home with you?" she asked. He snorted.

"I didn't talk them into shit, Tate. We had appetizers, I told them I was going home, they asked to join me. Demure Temptress sucked my dick during the cab ride to my hotel," Jameson stated.

"Oh my. Lucky cab driver," Tate whispered.

"Once we got into my room, I sat on the balcony while they took turns blowing me. Slutty One couldn't wait any longer, and climbed on top of me right out there," he continued.

"What was Demure Temptress doing?" Tate asked, staring up at the ceiling.

"She went back into the room, got naked. Stretched out on the bed. Played with herself," his voice was soft. Tate could feel her breathing pick up.

"Did you like that?"

"Very much so."

"*What else?*"

"I carried the slutty sister into the room, laid down on the bed between them. You can touch yourself, Tate, it's okay," Jameson said when her finger began to trace lines above her bikini. She laughed.

"I don't need your permission," she pointed out.

"*Wrong.*"

Her hand dived underneath the bathing suit material and she closed her eyes. She brought her other leg up so both knees were in the air, the balls of her feet balanced on the edge of the island. Sometimes she wondered who was better at touching her – herself, or Jameson. Her fingers could thread her like a needle; precise, knew exactly how to touch. Jameson was more like silk; smooth, finessing

186

everything. She began to pant.

"What else?" she moaned.

"Fuck, Tate, what did I do to deserve you?" his voice sounded strained. She chuckled.

"Nothing, *yet*. Keep talking, please," she begged, her other hand joining the first as she gently eased a finger into her opening.

"The demure sister rode my cock for a while, while slutty girl let me see how many fingers I could fit inside of her. Then they traded places," he continued. Tate moaned, pushing her hips into the air. She dragged one hand away, brought it to her hair and pulled a little.

"Get to the part with the ropes," she gasped.

"Tatum, naughty girl, you want me to tie you up, don't you?" Jameson asked.

"*I want you to do whatever you fucking want,*" she said, then cried out, pushing two fingers inside.

"*Good answer.* I didn't have any rope, I had to use the slutty one's tights. I tied her down flat to the mattress, to the legs of the bed. Bent the demure one in half right beside the other girl and fucked her as hard as I could."

"Oh my god, did you talk? Did you talk to them the way you talk to me?" the words rushed out of Tate, her voice sounding like she was almost whining. His story, the picture he was painting, was getting her so hot, she almost didn't need her hand to help her get off.

"Oh no. No, I reserve that for people that I think can actually handle it. That's why sex has always been better with you – I can always be myself," he told her in a whisper. She moaned again, long and low, her fingers thrusting in and out of herself.

"I'm glad," she whispered, the hand in her hair going behind her head, gripping onto the edge of the island.

"Not to say that boring, old, regular sex doesn't help pass the time. After demure one came apart all around me, I moved onto slutty one. Left her tied up, so I could do anything I wanted to her,"

Jameson's voice was almost menacing sounding.

"What did you do?" Tate's voice was starting to shake. She didn't want to come, not without him inside her, but she couldn't stop her fingers.

"What do *you* think I did?" he asked.

"Did you go down on her?" she asked, then held her breath.

"No. I don't do that for just anybody," he informed her. It made her happy to hear it, he hadn't done that for her yet.

"I noticed."

"You want me to go down on you, Tate?" he asked.

"I don't care."

"I consider that a *very* big favor. It's quite a treat for me to give. You would owe me, *big time,*" he told her. She shook her head.

"Obviously, I don't need your favors," she managed to chuckle, but it turned into a gasp as a tremor ripped through her body, forcing her hips into the air again. She was so close ...

"What the the fuck did you just say to me?" Jameson snapped. She smiled, pressing her knees together.

"God, *yes,* talk to me like that," she moaned, her fingers moving fast, running a race against him.

"Shut the fuck up and stop moving," he ordered. She shook her head.

"Can't. *Sorry,*" she whispered, her breathing beginning to hitch.

She hadn't heard him move, but suddenly she felt his hand on her knee. She turned her head forward and opened her eyes to find him staring down at her. He slid his hand between her thighs, moving them apart. She finally pulled her hand free of her bottoms, but he grabbed her by the wrist and raised her hand to his face, wrapping his lips around two of her fingers. She moaned again, scratching the nails of her free hand down her thigh. His tongue swirled around her sticky sweet fingers, then he slowly pulled them free.

"You *always* need my favors, Tatum," he informed her, dropping her hand and then grabbing her by the hips, pushing her back along the counter. Her legs stretched out, till her calves were resting against the edge.

"Yes, yes, I do," she groaned.

"Beg me," he ordered.

"Anything. *Do anything.* Just please, touch me, something, *anything,*" she begged.

He hooked his hands under knees and yanked them up. She planted her feet flat while he wrenched her thighs wide apart. A shudder ran down her body while his fingers dug into her flesh. Her eyes fluttered shut, and she felt his teeth against her inner thigh. Biting his way down, his tongue softening the blows. His breath was hot against her damp bikini bottoms and she wiggled her hips in anticipation.

"A *very big* favor," he reminded her, his fingers creeping across her skin. She laughed.

"I didn't ask for any favors," she told him.

"You're about to get one."

He roughly pulled the crotch of her bottoms to the side and then his mouth was on her. She cried out, her hands instantly going to his hair. His tongue made one long sweep up her center, cutting her like a knife. Her thighs shook, and she felt like her holding onto him was the only thing keeping her from flying off the island top.

The man wasn't all talk; his tongue moved expertly around her – she may have met her match in the oral sex department. Her breathing cranked back up and she started making harsh sounds in the back of her throat. Whining. Moaning. Panting. All of the above.

"God, I don't think I've ever tasted a pussy as sweet as yours," he groaned against her, running his hands over her breasts and then clawing them back down her body. "I didn't think there could be anything better than fucking it, but this is pretty close."

"I aim to please," Tate whispered, pulling at his hair.

His tongue was back at it, this time joined by two of his fingers. Tracing up and down, swimming in and out. She shrieked and moaned, writhed around underneath him. His other arm came down across her hips, his fingers digging into her skin. Her cries got louder, her hips undulating against his face. In the back of her mind, she knew that the door was open, that anyone could walk in on them – Sanders, a guest coming back for something, anyone – but she didn't care. It just excited her more.

"You're very close, Tate," Jameson lifted his head enough to whisper, biting on her thigh while his fingers still moved inside of her.

"Yes, please, please, so close, please," she whined, her hips lifting off the island, straining towards his mouth.

"Do you want to come on my tongue, or my dick?"

"Can't I do both?"

"Maybe another time. My generosity has run out for right now," he told her.

She sat up abruptly, forcing him to lean away. She grabbed his neck and pulled herself forward, sliding across the island into him. She locked her lips onto his warm, damp ones, tasting herself against his tongue. Her legs went around his waist and she hooked her ankles together.

"Now, it has to be *now*," she groaned, her hands back in his hair and pulling.

"So greedy," he laughed, picking her up off the island and carrying her out of the room. She clawed and writhed against him, all the way up the stairs. He carried her into his bedroom and then laid them down on his bed, stretching out on top of her.

"So what am I going to owe you, for that huge favor?" Tate breathed, stretching while he peeled her clothing off of her.

"Something big," he warned. She smiled, working a hand into his pants.

"Oh, I know it is," she replied. He laughed.

"All you think about is sex."

"Nothing wrong with that. It's your fault, anyway."

"*I aim to please.*"

She had made it pretty clear that she wanted to come on his dick, and she did – but before he could come, he slid down her body and latched his lips back onto her pussy. For having gone on and on about doing her such a big favor by eating her out, how it wasn't something he "*ever really did*", he couldn't seem to stop. He was like a man possessed. It wasn't until she was so oversensitized that even the idea of another orgasm was uncomfortable, that he finally stopped. She laid on her back, trembling and shaking, her hands above her head.

"Please, too much, no more," she gasped for air, rubbing her thighs together. He worked his way up her body, pausing at her breasts, his fingers circling a nipple, pinching it. Her back arched up and she whimpered.

"I could do this all night," Jameson breathed, his teeth going to the nipple.

"If only I had a twin," she joked.

"Jesus christ, I would die."

"But very happy. You would die a *very* happy man," she pointed out. He lifted his face to hers, rubbed his nose against her cheek.

"You're better than any set of twins, *any threesome*, I've ever had. You better be careful, Tatum, or my claws will get intoo deep for you to ever get away," he warned her. His voice was soft, but his words carried weight. They settled on her chest, interfered with her heart beat. She opened her eyes and stared at his ceiling.

"I like it better when you say mean things," she whispered.

"Why?"

"They don't hurt as much."

Jameson was silent for a while and then he rolled her over, slapped her on the ass. Called her a stupid slut for listening to anything that came out of his mouth in bed. Held her down by her shoulders and fucked her hard.

That was her comfort zone. She felt like if he was nice to her, if he was sweet to her, she would forget what was really going on, forget her place in the grand scheme of things. And he was Satan, after all. He would make sure to put her back in her place. *That* would be real pain, and she couldn't handle that, not from him. Not again.

I'm losing this game.

9

"*WAKE UP.*"

Something smacked hard against Tatum's ass and she jumped a little, propping herself up. Jameson was leaning over the bed, a paddle brush in his hand. She yawned and raised an eyebrow at him.

"A little early, but okay, at least we're finally getting to the good stuff," she joked. He laughed and spanked her again before pulling away.

"*Everything* I give you is good stuff; you haven't earned the right to play with toys yet," he informed her. She snorted and rolled over in the bed.

"Why are you so chipper? It's too early," she groaned.

"We're going somewhere. Get up and get showered!" he barked, disappearing into his closet. She sat up.

He was taking her somewhere? Jameson never took her anywhere, except for maybe out to eat, once in a while. Never in the mornings. They almost only ever did stuff at his house. Was this going to be like a date? Sanders' words came back to her, as well as some of Jameson's own words. She felt giddy. He had been very sweet to her the night before, said things she never would have thought he'd say. Maybe the tide was turning. Maybe Satan was growing a heart.

Tate hustled into the shower, hurried through her routine. When she got back out of the bathroom, Jameson was nowhere to be found, though there was a dress laid out on the bed. A tight black number, very prim and proper. Probably very expensive. While she fingered the material, her cell phone started going off, so she crawled across the bed to grab it. Rusty's phone number flashed across the screen.

"Hey, I meant to call —," Tate answered, but a shrill scream stopped her.

"*OH MY GOD HOW COME YOU DIDN'T TELL ME!?!?*" Rus was yelling. Tate yanked the phone away from her ear.

"Jesus, I'm deaf now, thanks. Tell you what?" Tate asked.

"The rent! It's amazing! Thank you, thank you, thank you *so much*, this will totally help me with so many things!" Rus was gushing on and on.

Rent? What about the rent? After Ang had crawled to her place, begging for forgiveness on his hands and knees, Tate had spent most of the week at his apartment, avoiding her landlord. She would sneak in her window at night, then back out again in the morning. So she had no clue what Rus was talking about – as far as Tate knew, they were still two weeks late on their rent.

"*What's* amazing, Rusty!? I don't know what you're talking about!" Tate snapped. There was a melodramatic sigh.

"Oh my god, it was *him*, wasn't it? I bet it was. I ran into Mr. Malley in the hall, and I was all prepared to beg, and cry, and plead, or offer your body up for sacrifice, when he said to say thank you to you, for paying the next six months rent in advance," Rus said in one quick breath.

Six months!?

Tate fell back against the pillows. She was blown away. Jameson must have done it, no one else she knew had that kind of money.

Why would he do that? They joked about him paying her, but he never actually had. Was paying her rent considered payment? Or was he just being a nice guy? He'd gotten awfully upset when he'd found out that she owed money. Maybe he was just trying to rectify the problem.

"I didn't know that he'd done that, he didn't tell me," Tate mumbled into the phone.

"Aw, maybe it was a secret and I ruined it. I'm so sorry, I was just so excited! I can finally afford those vet tech classes! Tell him I said thank you? What a sweetheart," Rus sighed into the phone. Tate snorted and rolled onto her stomach, picking at the bedspread.

"He didn't do it to be nice, Rus. He'll want something in return. I call him 'Satan' for a reason," she laughed.

"Shut up and try not to ruin this one! For once, you found a guy who treats you the way you like *and* also does nice things for you. You better do whatever it takes to hold onto him, understand!? If you don't, tell him to call me, and I will!" Rus snapped, then the line went dead. Tate made a face and dropped the phone. Rusty sleeping with Jameson. There was a thought. He would eat her alive.

"I'm Satan, am I?" Jameson's voice was behind her. She pulled herself to her knees and turned to face him.

"Mostly in my head, that's how I refer to you," she told him. He laughed as he walked across the room, carrying a black, carry-on type of roller bag.

"How flattering. You've already heard everything I like to call you," he said. She cleared her throat.

"Did you pay my rent?" she asked. He glanced at her.

"Yes. Last week, when I left your apartment," he told her, sitting the bag at the foot of the bed and opening it.

"Why would you do that?" she asked, crawling down and kneeling behind the bag.

"Because your rent was late. That's horrible. And if you were

195

so far behind that you couldn't pay it, I knew that meant you would have to work more to make the money. I didn't want that, I like having access to you at any time. It seemed the only answer was paying your rent for you," Jameson explained, disappearing into his closet.

"That's very nice, but six months worth? Seems a little excessive," she called out. He came back out, carrying some shirts and pants on hangers.

"I'm an excessive kind of person. I have no doubt that one of us will run the other off before six months is up, but it was a nice, even number," he told her, folding up the clothing and dropping it into the bag. She grabbed his wrist, halting his movements, and stared him in the eye.

"Thank you," she said plainly. He gave her a tight lipped smile.

"Don't thank me yet. It wasn't for free," he warned her, pulling his arm out of her grasp.

"And that's why I call you Satan," she sighed. "I don't think it's very fair, to expect payment for something I didn't ask to buy." He laughed and walked over to the side table, grabbing some watches and loading them into a travel case, which also went into the luggage.

"Are you fucking with me? Do you think I actually care what you think is fair? C'mon, get up and get dressed. We're leaving in half an hour," he informed her, heading back into the closet.

"Where are we going? Are you going away somewhere? You just got back," she said, running her hands over the shirts in his bag. He walked back out and dumped some socks, underwear, and a pair of shoes into the bag.

"*We* are going away somewhere," he said, pushing her hands away and closing the bag.

"Excuse me?" Tate asked, shocked. He pulled her off the bed.

"I have to get back at you for that ridiculous dinner last week, and you owe me for the rent situation. You are coming with me, on a trip," he said, moving her to stand against the edge of the bed.

"I am!?" she exclaimed. Her heart was suddenly ridiculously happy. If this was a punishment, she would take it without any questions. He wanted to go away with her somewhere. Surely, it couldn't just be sex between them.

"Yes. We're going away for the weekend," Jameson said, holding the dress up against her. She grabbed it and he walked away, grabbing a box off his side table.

"Wait, for the whole weekend? I have to work," Tate told him as he came back to her. He sat the box on the end of the bed and opened it, pulling out a very fine, sheer, black stocking.

"No, you don't. I arranged for you to have this weekend off," he informed her, laying the stocking across her forearm. It was quickly followed by the second one.

"You did!?"

Heart. Bursting.

"I set this up while I was in Los Angeles."

A pair of very expensive looking red panties joined the stockings.

"Where are we going?" she asked. Jameson laughed, finally moving to stand in front of her.

"Now *that* is a secret. Go change into everything. Put your hair up, nicely, and subtle makeup. No slutty-eyes today," he told her, scooting her towards the bathroom.

Tate laughed. Normally she would argue with him, but she was so happy, she couldn't bear to – that day, he could make her do whatever he wanted. So she swept her up into an artfully messy French twist, then took her time putting on her makeup. Cat's-eye style eyeliner and nude eye shadow, with just powder foundation. She did, however, put on a heavy, matte, red lipstick. Hint-o-slut, like a naughty secretary. Perfect, Jameson would love it.

She didn't know when he got the clothing, or how he had known just what size she wore. The red panties fit perfectly, the stockings felt like they came straight from Paris, and the dress was like a second skin. Went from her collar bone to her knees, and was very tight, with a thin belt around the waist. At first glance, it was almost demure, but when she turned around, she could see that there was virtually no back. Just open skin from her shoulders to her waist. She felt like she was wearing a woman's version of a power suit. With her hair and makeup, she looked very professional. Very rich. She frowned. Almost like … how she might have looked had she never left home. She shook her head. No, still too sexy. She wasn't that girl. She would *never* be that girl.

"How did you know all the right sizes, Jameson?" Tate asked as she padded out of the bathroom.

But he wasn't in the bedroom. A shoe box was sitting on the bed, with a couple of jewelry boxes next to it. She pulled out diamond earrings – *those can't be real* – and a simple chain with a solitary diamond pendant. She put them all on, and when she opened the shoe box, her breath caught in her throat. *Red bottoms.* The most coveted of all shoes. She actually moaned out loud as she took the heels out, her eyes traveling over every inch of the leather. Sex with Jameson was pretty amazing, but even Louboutins had him beat. She slipped them onto her feet and moaned again.

"You like?" Jameson asked as he strode back into the room.

"I want to fuck you, like, so hard right now," she told him. He laughed.

"Maybe when we're in the air. C'mon, baby girl, we have to go," he said.

"How did you know all the right sizes to get?" she asked.

"I took one of your dresses and a pair of your ridiculous socks, gave them to a private shopper. The underwear was easy, I am very familiar with your ass," he assured her, his eyes sweeping over her body.

"Well, it all fits like it was made for me. How do I look?" she asked.

"Absolutely stunning."

Tate blushed. He had never said something like that before, she was always sexy, or filthy, or hot. Rarely ever beautiful. Never stunning.

"Was it expensive?" she asked in a soft voice. He raised an eyebrow.

"*Very*. Now stop questioning me. Let's go," he ordered, and marched out of the room.

Sanders was waiting at the front door, next to two black rolling bags. Tate could only assume that one was for her, probably already packed with similar clothing. Sanders' eyes wandered over her, and she thought she might have seen a hint of a smile on his lips. She winked at him and pinched his butt while they walked out the door.

They didn't talk as they drove to an airfield a little ways away. She was surprised they didn't just go all the way into Logan Airport. Jameson barely even looked up from his phone as they breezed through security and headed out onto the actual tarmac. Money talked. They approached a small, private plane, and her jaw dropped.

"Where exactly are we going?" she asked as Sanders climbed into the plane ahead of them, loading up their bags.

"I told you, it's a secret," Jameson said, pressing a hand against her bare back and leaning close to her ear.

"Yeah, but … a private plane? Do you own this plane?" she asked. He laughed.

"No, I chartered it for the weekend. I feel like if I ever buy a plane, I will have irreversibly slipped into the land of douchey-rich-guy," he told her. Tate laughed.

"I don't know about that, might be nice to always have a plane on standby," she said.

He kept his hand on her back while she climbed the stairs ahead of him. Sanders was already seated in the back of the plane, a laptop open in front of him. A flight attendant fiddled around in the back and a pilot smiled at them from the cockpit. Tate wasn't sure where to sit, so she just plunked down in a chair close to the door. Jameson sat in the seat across from her, his eyes wandering over her face.

"You look excited," he commented.

"I am. I'm holding out hope that we're going to the Bahamas," she told him. He threw his head back and laughed.

"Oh, Tatum. So optimistic. I'm going to tell you right now, it's not the Bahamas. You should be very, very afraid," he teased. She rolled her eyes.

"We'll see."

He told her the flight would take about two hours, but that's all he would say. When they took off, they headed over land, so she knew they weren't going East. Somewhere West – back to Los Angeles? No, that would be way longer than two hours. How long did it take to go to Chicago? Did Jameson even like Chicago? She had no clue where they were headed, and his words started to get to her. She got nervous.

She talked Sanders into playing a couple rounds of gin rummy with her. Jameson produced a chess board, and beat her so quickly, it was embarrassing. Then he got Sanders to play, and that was actually interesting. They were both *very* good. She wondered if either had competed, and realized she knew almost nothing about either of their pasts. Jameson won, but it was a hard fought battle. Sanders made a noise in the back of his throat, and it took her about five minutes to realize it was a laugh.

This is going to be a hell of a weekend.

"Time to clip your wings, baby girl," Jameson commented after the pilot announced their descent.

"Excuse me?" Tate asked as he dug something out of his bag. A long, black sash appeared in his hands.

"You said you trusted me," he reminded her as he sat down next to her. She edged away from him.

"Yeah, with both eyes open. Not so much in the dark," she joked, even though she was a little nervous.

"I'm not asking, Tatum," he said in a stern voice.

The blindfold wrapped around her eyes, and she was left in darkness.

Tate had never really been into the whole bondage scene. Sure, it was fun once in a while, but she liked to touch, and she liked to be touched, too much for it to be a real thing. And blindfolding was the worst. She had said it once, she was a very visual person. She wanted to see *everything*. Ang loved it and was forever trying wrap things around her head. It was usually a battle that he won only after copious amounts of liquor.

After the plane landed, she stayed sitting in her chair, as still as a statue, while people and the crew moved around her. At one point, someone leaned close, and she jerked away, but then there was a hand covering her own. Sanders' voice assured her that everything would be just fine. She managed a smile and tried to grab onto his arm, her fingers trailing down his sleeve as he pulled away. Then Jameson was next to her, she recognized his cologne, and he pulled her out of her seat, led her down the aisle.

Her nerves abated a little when they had to figure out how to get down the stairs. She stumbled on the first step and refused to go down anymore while wearing the blindfold. Jameson simply picked her up and threw her over his shoulder, carried her all the way to a car. By the time she was ensconced in a back seat, she was laughing hysterically.

She made a mental checklist as they drove. They were somewhere that wasn't any warmer or cooler than Boston, really. Wherever they had landed, Tate could smell foliage, a heavy forest. Something familiar. She figured they were still in the Northeast. Maybe he was taking her to some getaway in Maine. Or Vermont – she remembered Jameson saying he owned a farm in Vermont. Her outfit wasn't very conducive to a weekend in a cabin, though. She hoped for a five-star hotel.

"I am going to take your blindfold off in a moment," his voice was soft, after they had been driving for about an hour.

"Thank god," she laughed.

"I want you to remember something, though," Jameson said, at the same time the car took a slow, but sharp, right turn. Gravel crunched under the wheels.

"What?" she asked.

"You started these games," he told her. Her nerves went through the roof at that statement.

This is not a romantic get away. This is something very, very bad.

The blindfold fell away and she blinked, trying to adjust to the light. The car they were in had tinted windows, making it hard to see outside. Jameson was sitting next to her, carefully folding the sash up and putting it in his jacket pocket. She scooted closer to her door, peering out the window. She didn't get it. All she could see were trees. A narrow, gravel road. She pressed her forehead to the glass, tried to see ahead of the car. Glimpsed a house in the distance.

Oh. My. God.

"You didn't," Tate breathed, her heart stopping in her chest. She turned to look at Jameson, and he smirked at her.

"I told you, I always win," he said, stretching an arm out along the seat behind her.

I am so. Fucking. Stupid. Goddamn Satan wins again.

She lost her damn mind. Screamed and slapped him across the face. He ducked the next blow and grabbed her wrist, but she was already throwing herself at him, grabbing his hair with her other hand and trying to kick at him. Her dress was too tight, she couldn't really reach, and had to settle for kicking him in the shin.

They wrestled around for about a minute. Jameson could stop

202

her whenever he wanted, she knew he was just letting her work out her frustrations – so she made the most of it, pulling his hair, pounding on his shoulders. When she scratched at his face, though, she apparently went too far. They were driving in an extended-back town car, and he slammed her onto the floor.

"*This isn't a fucking game!*" she screamed at him. He pinned her wrists by her head.

"Calm the fuck down!" he shouted at her. She used every muscle she had, swung her weight around underneath him. He didn't budge.

"How could you!? *How could you!?* You must really fucking hate me, Kane!" she shouted at him. His hand came down over her mouth, clamping it shut.

"*Calm. Down.* Take a deep breath. It's not that bad. This was going to happen some day, I just sped up the process," he said. She shook her head and cursed at him from behind his hand. He pressed down harder. "Shut the fuck up and calm down. You made me go to that ridiculous dinner. You kissed Sanders in front of me. You kissed *Angier* in front of me. *You owe me.*"

She forced herself to go still, and he finally removed his hand. She breathed heavily, staring up at him. He was very close to her, his hair messy and hanging over his forehead. One, long, red, scratch mark went from under his ear to just under his jaw. Not too noticeable. *Pity*. She took a deep breath.

"This wasn't about you, you had no right to do this. I'm nothing to you, why would you do this?" she whispered. He frowned at her.

"You are not nothing to me," Jameson replied. She shook her head.

"You're always telling me I'm nothing. Reminding me, over and over again. Nothing, nothing, nothing. You're the devil," she said, moving her eyes away from his to stare at the roof of the car. She could feel tears at the back of her throat and she didn't want him to have the satisfaction of seeing her cry.

"I will fully admit to being the devil, but I have never said you're nothing. Look, if you can't do this, if you can't handle this, we will go right back to the airport and I will take you home. You never have to talk to me again. Just say the words. Admit you can't handle this," he told her. She took a deep, shuddering breath.

"*Move,*" she snapped, and he got off of her. Pulled her onto the seat next to him.

She fixed her hair. Dug out a mirror and fixed her lipstick, which had smeared all over her chin. She straightened out her dress, pulled the stockings back into place, fidgeted with the jewelry. Jameson reached out and tried to place a hand over her own, but she pulled away from his touch as if he burned her, refusing to even look at him.

"Tate, we —," he started, but she shook her head. The car was pulling up in front of a large, colonial style home. Not unlike Jameson's home in Weston, though this one was on a much grander scale. More pillars, more bricks, more rooms. She knew it had more rooms, because she had been in it many times. She took a deep breath.

"You'll never win, Kane. So how are we doing this? Is there an explanation, a back story? Are you my boyfriend? Am I your paid whore?" Tate asked.

"We ran into each other in Boston. We're friends," he said in a slow voice. She cackled.

"*Friends*. We have *never* been friends, Jameson," she snapped, listening as Sanders got out of the driver's seat. Talked with someone who had come out the front door. Jameson put a finger under her chin and pulled her gaze to him. He looked angry.

"Baby girl, I might just be the best friend you've ever had," he told her. She smiled sweetly at him at the same time Sanders pulled her door open.

"You better start smiling, Jameson. You know how my family loves a happy face," she whispered, then took Sanders' hand, allowing him to pull her out of the car.

Her mother, sister, and some guy she didn't recognize, all stood on the porch of the house she had grown up in, the house she had been living in when she had first met Jameson; the house she hadn't been back to in seven years. She took a deep breath.

Show time.

Her mother actually cried. Like real tears, not drunk ones. Hugged her. Gushed over how beautiful Tatum was, how amazing she looked. Tate managed a smile, but she had a feeling that it looked more like a smirk, as that long ago phone call played through her mind. Her own mother, calling her a worthless whore, a good for nothing, a home wrecker. Telling her own daughter that she wasn't allowed to come home, ever again.

"Ever again" apparently only lasts seven years.

The mystery man turned out to be Ellie's husband. He was tall, dirty-blonde, and handsome. He smiled a lot and stared at Tate's chest the whole time, even though there wasn't even a hint of cleavage showing. Asshole rolled off of him and Tate moved away quickly.

She had often wondered what meeting up with her sister would be like; would she be forgiving? Would she be angry? She wasn't necessarily either, she was just the same, old, hateful Ellie. Like no time had passed. Scowling at Tate like she was a nuisance, an interruption. Like she was *lesser than*. And when Jameson came down the line, shook Ellie's hand while standing what could probably be considered too-close to Tatum, Ellie's eyes looked downright murderous. Tate could read her thoughts, *"you stole this from me, he was mine, and you ripped it all away."*

Funny that everyone had gotten so angry at her, but no one had seemed to care about Jameson's part in it all.

They all went inside and she was told that her father was out of town, but he would be back the next day. Her mother claimed that he was "looking forward" to seeing Tate, but the woman could barely get the words out through her painted on smile. Tate just nodded, following everyone into the kitchen.

Wine was poured and stories told. Jameson had called Mrs. Blanche O'Shea a couple days ago, explained how he had run into Tate, how they had developed a friendship of sorts. He just wanted to help, could he bring Tatum down for a visit? Tate's mom had been all over that idea, and got even more excited when he had invited himself along, as well. They were placed in rooms across from each other, neither of them Tate's old bedroom. That room had long ago been broken down and turned into a spare office.

Ellie's husband, Robert, talked non-stop. How he had heard so much about Tate, but he had no idea that she was so good look-ing. Mrs. O'Shea only made beautiful children, it seemed. Most of his speeches were made to her chest, and at one point she caught Jameson scowling at them, so she indulged Robert. Arched her back, stretched her arms, leaned into him. Made a big show of letting her hair down, shaking it out so it was wild and messy – a personal fave of Jameson's, she knew.

Ha, choke on it, Satan.

Ellie didn't even notice, she was so busy kissing Jameson's ass – Tate was just waiting for her to get down on her knees and make an offer to suck him off, right in front of everyone. It was ridiculous. In between flirting with Jameson, Ellie threw poison darts with her eyes at Tatum, who just rolled her own eyes and drank a little more. Finally, as if awkward small talk wasn't bad enough, they all sat down to dinner.

"So where do you live in Boston, honey?" her mother asked.

"North Dorchester," Tate answered.

"Oh wow, you must be a tough little thing," Robert laughed. Tate laughed as well, winking at him.

"You have no idea," she teased.

"Tate's never had a problem getting down and dirty, have you?" Ellie snapped, sipping at her water. She was two months pregnant, and it was obvious by the way she eye balled the wine that sobriety was difficult for her.

"Oh never. In fact, I absolutely *love it*," Tate drew out the words. Jameson cleared his throat.

"Tate has been working for me," he offered up. The whole table went silent and stared at him. Tate wondered how truthful he would be.

"Oh? Doing what?" Ellie asked in a cool voice.

"Oh, just some work here and there, around my house. Making the place brighter, you could say. In exchange, I have been setting her up with a retirement account," he explained, his eyes locked onto Tate's. She laughed at him.

"Making the place brighter - it's what I live to do, Mr. Kane," she replied in a husky voice.

"Well, you are very good at it."

Her mother interrupted then, not drunk enough – *yet* – to let the innuendos go over her head. Dessert was brought out and they ate mostly in silence, then retired to a drawing room. Mrs. O'Shea didn't last much longer before heading off to bed. Tate followed her to the stairs and gave her a hug goodnight. When she turned around, Ellie was behind her.

"I know what you're doing," she snapped. Tate sighed. She was so tired.

"What am I doing, Ellie?" Tate asked.

"You stole Jameson from me. He was going to propose, and you ruined it all. Now that Robert and I are about to have a baby, you want to steal him from me, too," Ellie replied, rubbing her hand over her belly. Tate laughed.

"I didn't steal Jameson – in seven years, I never even saw him, not until a couple weeks ago. He was *never* going to propose to you, he told me *that night* that he was going to dump you, so I didn't ruin shit. I just made it easier for him to end it. And trust me, in no way, shape, or form, do I want your husband, so you two can have all the babies you want," Tate assured her. Ellie narrowed her eyes.

"You're just a slut, Tate. It's so digusting. I can see what's going on between you two, '*doing work around the house*'. Is that what you call screwing? And he *pays you?* Now you really are a whore. He doesn't care about you. *Jameson Kane* would *never* be with a slut like you. Some day sex won't be enough, and he'll need a real woman, and that's when he'll marry a girl like me. Not one like *you*," Ellie hissed.

Her words were true, and they hurt because they were true, but before the cut could split open and bleed, Jameson walked into the room. Tate didn't even look at him, just kept her eyes locked on her sister. Tate was a little shocked, though, when he stopped next to her and coiled his arm around her waist.

"Clearly you underestimate good sex, Ellie. I could never have '*enough*' sex with Tate, and I can guarantee that I will *never* get tired of her, and I would most certaily *never* marry a girl like you. She didn't ruin anything – what happened between us that night was just a happy accident; I *was* going to end things with you. I wasn't going to marry someone like you seven years ago, and I am definitely not going to now," Jameson said in a cold, hard voice. Ellie took a step back.

"So you admit it, you're paying her for sex?" she demanded. Jameson lifted an eyebrow.

"Glad to hear you paid attention to the important part of that speech. Have I ever once given you cash for sex, Tatum?" he asked, looking down at Tate. She pretended to think for a minute.

"Does that time you made me bite down on a roll of money, to shut me up, count?" she asked. Ellie looked like she was going to be sick. Jameson smiled.

"No, I made sure to get that back when we were finished. I had to pay the taxi, after all," he reminded her.

"Then no. I have never received cash for sex," Tate agreed.

"You see, Ellie, some people don't need to get paid for sex. If anything, you expect more in return for sex than Tate ever has – all she wants is to get off, which I can provide for very easily. You, though, you require a husband, a name, children, acceptance, the right car, the right house. And you're not worth that price, not at all," Jameson explained.

If she had been the richest person in the world, Tate would have given every cent she had to have recorded that moment. Ellie's eyes bulging open, her jaw dropping down. Skin turning red. And hearing Jameson say that he would never get tired of Tate, even if it was an act, was priceless. She suddenly burst out laughing. Like hysterically. Like it was all the funniest thing she had ever heard, in her whole life. She bent over in half, stumbling forward.

"What's going on in here? Partying without me?" Robert laughed, joining them.

"I'm going to bed!" Ellie all but shrieked before stomping up the stairs.

"Life is always a party with the O'Sheas," Jameson said in a dry voice before heading upstairs as well.

"Looks like it's just you and me, Tatum," Robert's voice purred. She felt his fingers on her exposed back and she shuddered, stepping away from him.

"What are you doing?" she asked. He stepped closer to her again.

"Ellie's told me all about Jameson, about you and him. You got a thing for big sister's lovers? I'm cool with that," Robert told her in a low voice.

Might have laid on the flirting a little too thick. God, rich people are way creepier than poor people.

"Well, I'm not, so no thank you," Tate snapped.

"C'mon. She told me about Jameson, the crazy things he used to ask her to do for him. You must be a hell of a fuck, to keep a guy like him chasing after you," Robert pointed out. Tate was a little shocked. This needed to end, *now*.

"Look, I do not have a '*thing*' for Ellie's lovers – I didn't even have a thing for him, it just happened. It was an accident. I am not now, *nor ever*, going to fuck you, so you can fuck right off with that idea," she told him, crossing her arms. He glared at her.

"You're a fucking tease. You and your sister. Fucking teases," he snapped at her before pushing past her, checking her hard on the shoulder. She stumbled backwards and had to grab onto the banister, to keep from falling.

Mother fucker.

Tatum had been called a lot of things, but she was pretty sure that was the first time "*tease*" had ever been used.

She went upstairs as well, went into Jameson's room. He was in the shower and she didn't feel like joining him, so she wandered back into her own room. She was an odd combination of mad at him and grateful for him. He should not have ambushed her with her family, it was going too far – but it had felt better than words could describe to watch him put Ellie in her place, after all these years. To have someone back her up, when she said it hadn't been planned, that it hadn't been done on purpose. She was very thankful for him. It all made it hard to stay mad at him.

As she worked her way out of her dress, her mind went over Ellie's words. Robert's words. *Slut. Tease.* Tate was angry. She wanted to get back at them. They weren't so great. Six years, and one child – Tatum would put money on the fact that they never had sex. Ellie just wasn't a sexual person, and Robert was way too pervy; he had to be getting it elsewhere. Tate saw his type all the time in her bar, hitting on her when their wives went to the bathroom. It made her *so angry.* A thought crossed her mind. When she got angry, there was one thing that always made her feel better …

In just her heels, underwear, and stockings, she dashed across the hall, back into Jameson's room. He was still in his bathroom, so she stretched across his bed. He took a long time in the shower, so she knew it could be a while. She rolled onto her back and closed her eyes. Imagined him under the water. Naked. Her annoyance at him was slipping farther and farther away.

When his bathroom door finally opened, she was laying with her legs sticking straight up in the air, crossed at the ankles. The room was dark and he didn't seem to notice her at first. He walked across the room, securing a towel around his waist as he headed for his luggage. He was about halfway there when he saw her.

"What's this?" Jameson asked, stopping. Keeping her knees locked and her legs straight, Tate let them fall open, while her head hung over the side of the bed so she could look at him from upside down.

"You sound surprised," she commented, bringing her legs back together and then slowly fanning them apart again. His eyes followed the motion; he loved her legs.

"Three hours ago you were telling me you hated me. I was prepared to sleep alone tonight," Jameson explained.

"Tsk tsk, silly man. Just because I hate you doesn't mean I don't want to fuck you," Tate replied. He smirked at her.

"Someone is *very* angry," he said. She nodded and rolled onto her stomach, driving her knees into the mattress and using her legs to pull her body back so she was sitting upright – classic stripper move. He wasn't immune to it, she could tell interesting things were starting to happen underneath his towel.

"Yes. I won your little game, I stayed. I want my payment," she informed him, sliding her legs out from underneath her and moving to the edge of the bed.

"And what exactly do you want? Maybe I don't feel like paying," was his retort. Tate laughed and stood up.

"Oh, you'll pay," she chuckled, walking over to the wall to her right. She pressed her back against it, stretched her arms out to her sides.

"What's going through your head, baby girl?" Jameson asked in a quiet voice, walking towards her.

"I want you to fuck me, right here. Against this wall. As hard as you can," she told him.

"Seems like I'm winning on this deal."

Tate lifted a leg, stretching it out, touching his washboard stomach with the heel of the expensive shoe he had bought for her. Dug into his skin a little, hoping for blood. He grabbed her ankle, held it against his hip.

"I want you to call me every filthy name you can think of. I want you to fuck me like you *absolutely hate me*," Tate whispered. His eyes narrowed.

"Sounds like my kind of game What's the catch?" he asked.

"We can't move from this spot. This wall. I want you to pound me through this wall," she explained. He dropped her leg.

"Who is on the other side of that wall? Ellie and Robert? Very clever, baby girl. Very obscene," his voice was low as well.

"That's what I was going for. I won't be quiet," she warned him.

"Is this really what you want to do?" he double checked. His hesitancy annoyed her. She arched her back, pushing her hips away from the wall, and sighed. She let her eyes slide away from his, as if she were tired of their conversation.

"If you don't want to, it's fine. I'm sure I can find someone else to play with; Robert was very keen a moment ago," she said in a bored voice. Jameson's eyebrows shot up. Now she had his attention.

"Oh really? I saw the way he was looking at you. What did he say?" Jameson asked, stepping closer to her. She shrugged.

"Stuff. Things. Since I have a thing for Ellie's sloppy seconds, basically, why not give him a try. What a good fuck I must be. What a tease I am for not showing him," Tate replied nonchalantly. Jameson was now pressed against her.

"Would you show him?" he asked, his hands pressing against her ribs and then sliding around to her back. She chuckled.

"If I could tie Ellie down and make her watch, maybe," she replied.

"Kinky. Can I watch, too?" he asked, unhooking her bra and sliding it down her arms.

"I don't think so. You haven't been very good to me lately," she pointed out. He laughed, pulling the towel away from his hips.

"Baby girl, I am *always* good to you," Jameson countered.

"That's a matter of opinion."

"And *your* opinion doesn't matter."

It was like a switch. He ripped her panties away – the expensive ones he had bought for her – and grabbed her ass, forcing her legs around his waist, forcing his way inside of her. She cried out and slapped her hands against the wall above her head. She was going to put on a performance that Robert and Ellie would never forget.

It was almost comical at first – it was like being in one of Ang's pornos. She said things she normally never said, things she laughed at when other people said them – "*You fuck me so good, oh my god, your dick's so big, oh yeah, harder, slower, right there, you're amazing.*" And of course his name, over and over again. Couldn't let them forget who she was doing this with, after all. She even heard Jameson laugh at one point.

But as his thrusts got harder, the game melted away. She groaned and screamed for real, pounding one hand against the wall. Picture frames fell down. Books came off a shelf. There was a mirror across from them, and seeing their reflection, watching his muscled back and strong legs tense up, his hips moving against her so hard, it was practically her undoing. They hadn't even been standing there that long, and she was already coming like a freight train.

He didn't slow down at all. If anything, he pounded even harder. All his weight was pressing her into the wall, one hand digging into her ass and the other gripping her breast painfully. He pressed his face against the side of hers, growling at her through clenched teeth. Called her every filthy name she'd ever heard of, and a couple new ones. She was surprised, though, that he stuck to just names. Usually he liked to really degrade her, say horrible, horrible things about her, but not that night.

After what seemed like forever and two more orgasms for her, he literally dropped her to the floor and loudly told her to suck his cock. While she did so, he braced himself against the wall, beating his fist against it when she nipped at particularly tender areas. When he finally came, he announced it to the whole house, holding her head in place by her hair, pulling at the roots.

More of our games should be like this one.

"How was that? Good enough?" he whispered, breathing heavy as he leaned his forearms on the wall above her. She leaned away from him.

"It'll do for now," she joked, gasping for air as well while she wiped at her mouth. He groaned and grabbed a handful of her hair.

"I can't wait to take you home and really treat you bad," he grumbled, pulling her to her feet and leading her to the bed.

Me, neither.

10

TATUM WOKE UP THE NEXT morning to Jameson chewing on her butt, literally. She laughed and slapped him away. He informed her that her father would be home in a couple hours, so she should probably get ready and brace herself. He offered for her to join him in the shower, but she knew that never led to getting ready, so she passed and sent him in on his own.

Grumbling, she pulled on her trademark socks, some booty shorts, and a long tank top before heading downstairs. Jameson had bought her an entire wardrobe for the weekend, all miss-priss clothing, but he had been thoughtful enough to include her usual sleep wear. It made her feel more comfortable, and she felt like she was more herself as she wandered into the kitchen. Her mother was by a coffee pot, watching the coffee fill up.

"Good morning, honey," her mother yawned. Tate managed a smile.

"Morning," she replied, laying her top half across the counter and staring at the pot as well.

"I stopped and peeked in on you around five this morning, but you weren't in your room. Where were you?" her mom asked. Tate glanced at her. Was this for real?

"I was in Jameson's room," she answered truthfully. Had the lady not heard anything?

"Oh my! I thought you were just friends!" Mother exclaimed. Tate stood up.

"We are. We are very, *very* good friends," she emphasized. Her mother worried her hands.

"Do you think that's such a good idea, honey? I mean, what with Ellie and all, maybe it would be better to … you know, *not*," her mother suggested.

Is she fucking kidding me?

"Mother. I don't give *two fucks* about Ellie, or how she feels," Tate said in a hard voice. Her mother gasped.

"There is no need to talk like that! You should show some respect for your sister and her feelings!" she urged. Tate threw her head back and laughed.

"Is this a fucking joke? Why should I respect her? Or any of you? She hasn't spoken to me in seven years, she still treats me like the whore of Babylon, and her husband hit on me last night, *after* she complained about me ruining things between her and Jameson. Daddy doesn't even acknowledge my existence, and you only call me when you're drunk and feeling guilty," she spat out.

Her mother stared at her for a second, eyes swimming with tears, then she rushed out of the kitchen, letting out a sob. Ellie came in at the same time, jumping out of the way. She watched after her for a second and then turned her glare on Tate.

"See. You ruin everything. Your little show last night was *disgusting*. Something is wrong with you," Ellie hissed. Tate smiled sweetly.

"That show was the best sex you'll never have, so you're welcome," she replied, blowing a kiss at her sister. Ellie bristled up.

"I've had good sex. I slept with him first, you know," she snapped. Tate laughed.

"Not the same thing at all, Ellie. And it's not a competition, who got him first, who got him last. I didn't want him then, and I don't have him now. You shouldn't even care about who he is, or isn't, fucking; you're married," Tate pointed out.

"But I should have been married to him!" Ellie suddenly shrieked.

"What did you say?"

They both turned to see Robert standing in a separate entrance way. Ellie groaned.

"It was nothing, I didn't —," she started.

"We need to talk, *now*," he snapped before turning and walking out of the room. Ellie sighed and then glared at Tatum one last time.

"See!? Everything. You ruin *everything*," she repeated before hurrying after her husband.

Force myself on estranged family, Check. Jameson put sister in her place, Check. Have amazing loud sex that makes everyone uncomfortable, Check. Make mother cry, Check. Ruin a marriage, Check. Awesome family reunion!

Tate puttered around the kitchen, making herself a bowl of cereal and eating it. Then she filled two coffee mugs, knowing Jameson would want one once he was out of the bathroom. She carefully carried them up the stairs, listening for the sound of the shower. It had already been half an hour, but he was still in there. She shook her head. He preened more than a girl sometimes.

She was about to push her way into his room, when a noise caught her attention. Arguing. The door to Ellie's room hadn't been fully closed, and the sounds of a fight were reaching into the hallway. Giving an evil little chuckle, Tate tip toed closer, listening to what was being said.

"You stupid fucking bitch!"

Tate was surprised. Robert hadn't seemed like the kind of guy to talk to his wife that way.

"I'm sorry, I'm sorry," Ellie was saying over and over again. Tate frowned. Ellie didn't sound upset. She sounded ... *scared*.

"Fucking embarrass me!? In front of that *whore* sister!?" Robert was really yelling now. Tate touched a finger to the doorknob, just barely pressed against it enough to push the door open a smidge. She had a tiny view into the room. She could see Robert standing, his hands in his hair. Ellie was sitting on the edge of the bed, wringing her hands.

"No! I didn't mean to! I was ... upset! I'm sorry!"

"You know his New York offices have a contract with my firm! If she bitches to him about her *cunt sister*, I could lose everything!"

"*Cunt*" was a special kind of word to Tate. It was the dirtiest of all words, very taboo. Probably got her the most excited. But on the flip side, it was taboo for a reason. It was *very* bad; an angry, evil word. In her experience, people who used it comfortably in anger were not very nice people. For most people, it took a lot to whip out the C-word in a fight, and Robert had just dropped it like he was saying "*good morning*" or something.

"I'll talk to her, I promise. I'll make her promise not to tell him," Ellie assured him.

"Why would she listen to you!? You're the goddamn devil, as far she is concerned," Robert replied.

"I'll make her, I promise —,"

His hand crashed across Ellie's face, and Tate gasped, dropping the coffee cups. Her sister was not her friend. If anything, Ellie was an enemy. But she was also a woman. And she was pregnant. And her husband had just backhanded her. He grabbed Ellie's arm and lifted her off the bed, lifting his hand to hit her again.

"*HEY!*" Tate shouted, bursting through the door. They both turned and stared at her.

"Tatum!" Robert called out jovially, letting go of Ellie. "How was the coffee? Did you —,"

"Get the fuck away from my sister, you piece of shit!" Tate stated, marching to stand at the foot of the bed.

"Tate, just go away, you don't under—," Ellie started, holding up a hand.

"*Shut up*," Tate and Robert both snapped in unison.

"You are not really a part of this family. Please leave," Robert asked in a frosty voice. Tate crossed her arms.

"*You* leave. I'm not going anywhere," she informed him.

"I am not going to ask you again."

"You've never hit someone who hits back, have you?"

"Don't push me."

"Please!" Ellie interrupted, surging to her feet. "Please, just stop! Leave her alone!"

"Excuse me!?" Robert looked shocked, staring down at his wife. Tate was shocked, too.

"Leave her alone! Get out, let me talk to my sister!" Ellie demanded.

He slapped her again, and Tate was on him in a second, arms wheeling through the air. He tried to grab her, and she shrieked, throwing a punch. She was pretty sure it landed near his ear. She wasn't exactly a street brawler. He turned away and she climbed onto his back, pulling at his hair and hitting him on the top of the head. Ellie started screaming. Robert spun in a circle, yelling at Tate to get off of him. When it was obvious that she had no intention of doing that, he rammed them back up against a wall. Pain shimmied down Tate's spine and she let him go, falling to her feet. He spun around and slapped her so hard, she was knocked to the ground. She scrambled to get away, backing into a corner.

He hadn't made it two steps towards her when Jameson was on him, pinning him to the wall. Tate hadn't even noticed Jameson entering the room. He was by far the bigger man, with a much stronger physique – Robert couldn't move. Tate leapt to her feet, breathing hard, a hand pressed to her cheek. Jameson glanced at her.

"Are you okay?" he asked. She nodded.

"I'm fine. He hit her. *Hard,*" she replied, gesturing to Ellie, who had her face in her hands again.

"What kind of piece of shit hits a woman? A *pregnant* woman?" Jameson asked in a soft voice, his eyes very cold. He had his forearm pressed against Robert's windpipe and the smaller man squirmed around.

"It's none of your business, she's my wife," he choked out.

"And Tatum is *my* business," Jameson growled, nodding his head at Tate.

"Please, we heard the way you talked to her last night – the slut probably probably liked getting slapped."

There was no hesitation; Jameson's fist instantly slammed across Robert's jaw, and Robert slumped to the ground. Tate hurried forward, staring down at the unconscious man. She winced; his jaw was probably broken. She finally glanced up at Jameson. He was breathing hard, his hands balled into fists, and he was staring down at Robert with wild eyes. Tate stepped up close to him and pressed a hand to his chest, sliding it back and forth. The same move she used to calm Ang down. Jameson's eyes moved to hers. Stared at her.

This is not a game anymore.

Jameson left to go find Sanders, who was staying in a guest house. Tatum walked a practically sobbing Ellie back to her own room. They sat on the bed and she rubbed her sister's back, waited for her to calm down.

"How long has it been like this?" Tate whispered.

"Forever. Since we got married. During the honeymoon, he got mad at me, hit me. He had never done that before," Ellie sniffled.

Six years. Ellie had taken the abuse for six years. For the last six years, Tate had been begging men to push her around and call her dirty names. But never like that, not against her will. She sighed and wrapped her arms around her sister's shoulders – something she never thought she'd do.

"Leave him," she breathed. Ellie shook her head.

"I can't. I'm pregnant."

"There are lots of single moms out there."

"Daddy would be so angry. He picked him out for me."

"Fuck what Daddy says. Does he know he hits you?"

Silence.

Tate couldn't fucking believe it. Of course. *Of course* her father knew. Robert was a good old boy, from a good old family, so however he treated women was okay. While her father had never hit her mother, Tate had never seen him treat her with any kind of respect, either. Mrs. O'Shea was better seen, not heard. Its own kind of abuse. She handled it by popping pills and getting drunk. Ellie had married an abusive husband. Tate was fucking a sociopath.

We are all so fucked up.

"I can't leave him, Tatum," Ellie repeated, pulling away.

"Why? Why can't you?" Tate demanded.

"You don't know anything about us, about me. I have responsibilities. Where would I go, anyway?" she demanded. Her armor was suiting back up. Pretty soon, Tate would be shut out.

"Anywhere. Come with us, you can stay with me," Tate urged her. Ellie laughed.

"Thanks, but no thanks. I'm scarred for life by the things I heard last night from you two. I couldn't handle being in the same house while you pour hot candle wax on each other, or whatever," she joked. Tate almost laughed – it did sound like them.

"Please, Ellie," Tate whispered. There were footsteps up the stairs, two people going past the door.

"No. It'll be fine. He'll see the baby, and it'll be fine," Ellie said quickly and leapt to her feet, running for the door. Tate followed her out into the hall, just in time to see Sanders and Jameson carrying Robert's moaning body down the hall.

"Where are you taking him?" Tate asked.

"The hospital. After they help him regain consciousness, I'm going kill him," Jameson said matter-o-factly. Ellie started crying again.

"I'm coming with you," Tate said before dashing into her room and pulling on a pair of pants. They were suit pants, and looked at odds with her tank top, but she didn't care. She bustled Ellie out to her car and then drove them to the hospital, following Sanders the whole way.

Robert's jaw was, in fact, broken. Jameson didn't pull his punches, apparently. Ellie said he fell down the stairs. The hospital staff looked very unbelieving, probably due to the fact that Jameson stood behind everyone, staring everything down like a demon. He didn't even talk, had just dumped Robert in a wheel chair and then walked away. Sanders took care of everything, hustled off with Ellie and the nurses, leaving Tate alone with Satan.

"Are you okay?" he asked in a gruff voice. She glanced over at him. He was staring straight ahead, trying to burn a hole in the wall with his glare.

"I'm fine. Are you?" she replied.

"I'm not the one who got hit. Are you *okay?*" his voice was angry sounding.

"It wasn't even that hard, *I'm fine,*" she insisted. He suddenly turned and grabbed her face, turning her left side towards him. She stumbled and pressed her hands against his waist.

"He hit you. I saw you go down. Don't tell me it wasn't hard," Jameson growled at her, his eyes raking over her face.

"It wasn't, really, I promise. It doesn't even hurt," she assured him.

"He's lucky he didn't leave a mark. God, I want to kill him," he breathed against her, his grip on her jaw almost painful. She pushed at him.

"*You're* about to leave a mark. Calm down," she tried to laugh.

222

"I'm allowed to. If any mother fucker ever touches you like that again ..." his voice trailed off. She lifted her eyes to him.

He's really upset about this.

"Jameson," she stated his name loudly. His eyes went to hers. "I'm okay. I'm a tough girl from the bad side of Boston, who also happens to be sleeping with a psychotic stock broker who has an amazing right hook. I'm not worried."

He chuckled and finally let her go, but didn't take his eyes away from her.

"I didn't exactly think the weekend would go this way. I wanted to see you squirm. Make you uncomfortable," he explained. She laughed.

"Mission accomplished, Mr. Kane."

"Did your father ever hit you?" he asked. She shook her head.

"No. He was strict and he was mean, but he never hit anybody," she answered.

"Is Ellie going to be okay?" Jameson continued. Tate shrugged.

"I'm beginning to think she never was; she's like obsessed with this thing between us," Tate replied, gesturing between the two of them. "You should have heard her in the kitchen this morning. And then she told me he's been doing this to her since they got married. She thinks the baby will stop him."

"Jesus," Jameson mumbled, letting his head drop.

Ellie came back out right then, and they all headed home. Ellie went straight to her room, wouldn't talk to anyone. Tate walked Sanders to his guest house, and he stared at her for a long while at his door. He didn't say anything, so she squeezed his arm and then walked away. Jameson brooded in her father's office. Her mother drank, pretended everything was fine.

I'm not going to survive this weekend.

When she heard her father's car pulling up the drive, she went upstairs to change. She understood now why Jameson had bought her clothing for the weekend. Tate didn't own anything that was appropriate for her father, not anymore. After brushing her hair up into a nice, neat ponytail, she pulled on another dress, one with a knee-length flared skirt. It wasn't until she was trying to work the zipper up in the back that she realized her hands were shaking. She was pacing around, trying to get the feeling back in her fingers, when Jameson walked into the room.

"Stop," he murmured, grabbing her by the shoulders and turning her around. He zipped up the dress and then turned her back around, smoothing his hands over the material.

"Do I pass code?" she joked. He rested his hands on her hips and stared down the length of his nose at her.

"More than I ever could have thought."

The sentiment made her feel ill and she pushed past him, heading down the stairs. When she reached the bottom, her father was just walking out of the kitchen. They both stopped. Stared at each other. He was older, heavier. More gray in his hair. Tate knew she was different, had grown into herself over the years. She wondered what he thought when he looked at her. What he had ever thought.

"Tatum. I didn't believe Kane, when he said he would bring you," her father stated. Tate let out a breath.

"Here I am," she said softly.

"You look well," was all he said before brushing past her and going into the study. Jameson came to stand next to her and she looked up at him.

"Is your game still funny?" she whispered. He shook his head.

"Not even a little," he replied, lifting his hands and rubbing her shoulders. A moment later, though, Ellie shuffled around the corner and Tate automatically backed away from him.

Because he's not mine.

Dinner was awkward, to say the least. Her father asked where Robert was, and everyone looked at Ellie, who just laughed nervously. He asked Jameson how business was, asked his wife how her day had gone. Didn't say one word to Tatum. She drank. *Heavily*. Jameson took her glass away at one point, but she just started filling her water glass with wine.

Why can't rich people just be normal and drink whiskey!?

They "retired" to the drawing room. Jameson lit up a cigar, which she'd never seen him do before; it got her hot. She'd had a lot of wine, and she imagined the different things he could do with a large Macanudo.

She wondered what was wrong with her.

Tate finally escaped to bed around nine o'clock. She hadn't said a word in over an hour, no one had spoken to her, so she figured no one would miss her. She went into her room and peeled off all her clothing before climbing under the covers. Trying to hide her sniffles, she texted Ang.

What are you doing?

It took him a while to reply.

Three guesses.

She almost laughed.

Sex. Hang gliding. Battlestar Galactica marathon.

Got two of them right. What's up, chickadee?

I'm at home.

Thought you were locked away in the country! I'll kick this bitch to the curb and bring Battlestar to your house.

No. I'm at home. HOME home. Like where I was born. Pennsylvania.

Holy fuckballs.

She really did laugh at that one. He captured her feelings so well.

Still in shock myself.

Did Satan make you do it?

Who else? To say it hasn't gone well would be an understatement.

Bad?

Worse.

Details.

Mom is a pill popping alcoholic. Daddy still refuses to admit I exist. Ellie still thinks I'm the biggest slut in the world. Her husband is an abusive pervert. Got hit in the face. Got drunk.

There was another long pause.

If Satan hit you, I'm going to fucking kill him.

No. Ellie's husband.

Was Satan upset, or turned on?

He broke the dude's jaw.

Okay, even I'm a little turned on by that.

Tate burst out laughing and just then, her door started to creak open.

"You sound like a crazy person," Jameson's voice was soft. He was outlined in a burst of light and then the door closed, leaving them in darkness.

"Probably because I am one," she replied. She felt him sit on the edge of the bed and then his hand came to rest on her stomach.

"What were you laughing at?" he asked.

"Ang. We were texting each other," she explained.

"Ah, of course. *Angier.* Are you okay?"

"Do you really care?"

"Feisty."

"No. Tired," she ended in a sigh. His fingertips brushed across her forehead, moving her hair out of the way.

"I'll leave you alone. One more day, baby girl, then you win the whole thing," Jameson whispered, then got up. He walked out the door, closing it behind him without another word. Not even a backwards glance.

She stared after him. Her phone was clenched in her hand, resting against her chest. She could feel it vibrating with more incoming text messages from Ang. But she didn't read them. She stared at the door, willing Satan to come back.

I hate to be alone.

Another day, another dress. Jameson had only packed her one pair of pants, and she had worn them to the hospital – they were a wrinkled up mess in the corner of her room. So she slipped on a tweed dress.

Possibly Chanel. She felt horrible. She wanted her own clothing, a pair of cut-offs and a loose t-shirt. Her knee socks. Anything else. She was careful with her hair and makeup, then walked downstairs.

Jameson was already in the living room, talking to Sanders. They both turned at her entrance, but she only managed a smile for Sanders. She felt drained. Hollow. Her family sucked the life out of her. She hadn't realized it, but maybe that was why she'd been such a robot in her past life. They had sucked out her will to live. She had to get away. If Jameson didn't take them home that evening, she was going to hitchhike. Kidnap Sanders. Steal the car. Something.

"Alright?" Jameson asked with a curt nod of his head. She shrugged.

"As I'll ever be. Is it too early to start drinking?" she asked. He nodded.

"Yes."

"Sandy, got any xanax?" she asked, meaning it to be a joke.

"In my luggage, ma'am," Sanders responded. She was shocked for a second, then she laughed.

"Better be careful, Sandy, or I'll fall in love with you," she teased, heading into the kitchen.

Apparently it wasn't too early for some people, as she caught her mother spiking her coffee with brandy. Ellie wandered in a couple minutes later, not making eye contact with anyone. Robert had come home late the night before, and though his jaw was wired shut, he'd had plenty to say. His mumbled rants could be heard all over the house. He had gone crying to Tate's father. She could just imagine what she was in for that day.

She didn't have to wait long.

"Tatum! My office, now, please," her father's voice barked out. She took a deep breath and followed him into the dark room.

"Yes?" she asked, standing in front of his desk.

"What are you doing with your life?" he demanded. She blinked a couple times.

"Working."

"What do you do?"

"I'm a bartender, downtown."

"Disgraceful."

She started to get angry.

"Well, I had to do something, Daddy. No college degree, no money, no references. Pickings were slim. I'm very good at it, everyone knows that Tatum *O'Shea* is the best bartender in all of Boston," she said in a sweet voice, sarcasm dripping from her words.

"Don't blame any of that on me. You did it to yourself. Shameless girl," he grumbled.

"No. I was a *young* girl, stupid, confused, thoughtless; you never even asked me what happened. You just went by Ellie's word, like always," Tate pointed out.

"So you didn't have an affair with him!?" he shouted. She almost backed away, but then she remembered – he wasn't a part of her life. He had no power over her.

"No, I didn't have an affair with him. It was just one night, just sex," she replied bluntly.

"How dare you talk to me like that!"

"*You* asked."

"You don't feel any regret, do you!?" her father demanded. "Not a single goddamn regret. You ruined Ellie's chance for a decent marriage, and you don't even care."

"Is this over? I have things I could be doing," Tate snapped back.

"Don't you take that tone of voice with me, young lady," he warned her.

"I'll use whatever tone I fucking want," she said back. He jumped up from his chair.

"I knew this was a bad idea. I told that man that no good could come of you, that he should just turn his back on you. You are a waste

229

of time, Tatum. I don't know why I ever bothered with you," he told her. She sucked in a gasp.

"The feeling is entirely mutual," she replied, and before her father could respond, she swept from the room.

She was actually trembling as she stomped up the stairs. She stood in her room for a while, but she didn't want anything in there. Didn't care about her new clothing. She walked down to Ellie's room and didn't even bother to knock, just burst inside. Robert was laying on the bed and Ellie was standing next to him. Both gasped at her entrance.

"What are you doing!?" Ellie asked, startled by the brash entrance.

"I'm getting the fuck out of here. Come with me," Tate said quickly. Robert sat up, shaking his head and mumbling something.

"Tate, I know you don't —," Ellie started, but Tate shook her head.

"Last chance. Come with me," she offered again.

There was silence, then Ellie's eyes flicked to her husband. He shook his head again and Ellie sighed, turning back towards her sister. Tate nodded and walked out of the room. At least the going would be a lot quicker now. She breezed through the house, ignoring Jameson when he called out to her. She was halfway to the guest house when Sanders caught up to her.

"Can I help you with anything, Ms. O'Shea?" he asked quickly, jogging up to her side.

"Nope, Sandy, I'm good," she replied, walking through the guest house front door.

"Alright. Are you looking for something?" he asked again while she stood there, her eyes roaming over the entry way.

"Keys."

"Keys to what, may I ask?"

"The car."

"Our car?"

"That's the one."

"I'm sorry," Sanders tried again. "Did you want to go somewhere? I'd be happy to drive you."

"That's okay. I actually do know how to drive, you know, and where I want to go takes a while," she told him, walking up to a small desk and pulling the drawers open, rummaging around in them.

"I don't mind a long drive. I would be very happy to take you anywhere," he assured her. She glanced at him.

"Boston. I would like you to drive me to Boston," she said plainly. He hesitated, then nodded.

"Alright, ma'am. If you'll wait right here, I'll bring the car around," Sanders said, then took off back out the door.

Tate was a little stunned for a minute, and wondered if he was joking. But Sanders never joked, so she sat down on a decorative stool. She was too tired to stand anymore. It was taking every muscle she had to keep herself upright. She wanted to fold in on herself.

Waste of time.

"So we're leaving?" Jameson's voice was soft in the doorway. She laughed, not bothering to lift her head.

"Tattle-tale," she whispered.

"He's my assistant. He's not going to drive to Boston without at least telling me he's going to be busy for a couple hours, *or seven,*" Jameson pointed out. She nodded.

"Yup. Should've thought of that."

"I understand running away from your family. But trying to skip out on me, *that* surprises me," he said, moving so he was standing in front of her.

"I wasn't in the mood to hear you gloat. Not today, not right now," she explained. He sighed and put his hands on her knees. She still refused to look at him.

"How about, if you let me come with you, I promise to keep my gloating to myself until we get home," he offered. She laughed.

"I don't trust you to honor that promise," she joked. He tilted her head up to face him.

"You said you trusted me," Jameson reminded her.

"I trust that you'll be consistent. You're consistently mean," Tate pointed out. He laughed.

"Yes, but I also consistently keep my promises. Move your ass, we're out of here," he said before turning and walking out the door.

Tate went and waited on the front porch. She saw Ellie peeking out a window, but she moved away before Tate could make any sort of motion. Then Sanders pulled the car up and he hopped out, running around to open her door for her. Before she could climb in, though, he held out a fist. She raised her eyebrows.

"For you, ma'am. I assumed you were serious," was all he said. She held out her hand and he dropped two pills into it. She stared into her palm, almost laughing. Xanax.

"Sandy, I think you treat me better than anyone I've ever known," she chuckled, leaning in and kissing him on the cheek.

"I have no doubt of that, Ms. O'Shea," he replied before helping her into the car.

She dry swallowed the pills and waited for Jameson to appear. It took about fifteen minutes, then he was striding out the door, carrying both their bags. Her mother trailed after him, saying something that Tate couldn't hear. Jameson just ignored her, climbed into the back seat next to Tate. He didn't say anything, just nodded his head towards the rear view mirror. Sanders started up the car and pulled away.

"Did you talk to any of them?" Tate asked, staring out her window.

"Yes. I told your father that the only good thing he ever did in his life was produce a very fuckable daughter," Jameson replied. She burst out laughing.

"You're not serious."

"Dead serious. I also added that you're a very good person, sometimes. I told your mother that I would gladly pay for her rehab, and I warned Robert that if I came across Ellie anytime soon with another bruise, I wouldn't bother breaking his jaw again, I would just rip it clean off," he told her.

They weren't his family. As far as she knew, Jameson didn't really have much of a family. Mother died when he was young, father died a couple years ago. No siblings. No close cousins. Only Sanders. And he seemed to like it that way. So Tate couldn't figure out why he was bothering with her family, when she didn't even bother with them. It had started out as a game, a dare for her to undertake, but he had gone above and beyond that – he had made a mess, and he had done his best to clean it up. She was impressed. She felt a little like crying.

And when he reached over and clasped her hand – something he had never done before – Tate couldn't hold back the tears from streaming down her face. She would have been embarrassed, but the xanax made her not care. All she could focus on was his hand. His strong fingers, linked through hers. She squeezed his hand, so hard it hurt. So hard, she wouldn't be able to let go, not ever again.

Why did everything feel so different?

*Because **everything** is different.*

11

"TATUM."

"Yes, my liege?"

"Shut up."

"How can I answer you and —,"

"Why do you let me treat you the way I do?"

"I told you, I like it."

"I would kill another man for talking to you the way I talk to you."

"That's very sweet."

"Do you think there's something wrong with me, treating you the way I do?"

"Not necessarily. It's consensual. Empowering."

"Empowering?"

"Yes. You have the power to hold me down, say things, call me names. Slut. Bitch. But I have the power to say stop. End it all. Your power is an illusion. Mine is real."

"Sounds kind of backwards. I could just make you do whatever I want, regardless of whether or not you say stop."

"That's why I don't do all of that with just anybody. I trust you.

You wouldn't do that."

"You're very trusting of me."

"Look, I like it. You like doing it. That's why we fit so well together most of the time."

"Too well."

"You want this to end? Just say the word."

"It's not that easy anymore."

"Why not?"

"You accomodate me too much."

"How so?"

"The things ... the things I want to do to you."

"What do you want to do?"

"So many things."

"So do them."

"That's part of the problem."

"Jameson. I keep waiting for you to let go, to just do whatever it is you want to do."

"People say that, then later change their mind."

"Ooohhh, the mysterious ex. What did she go back on?"

"She said she wanted me to do something. I did it. It got thrown in my face. I don't want that to happen again."

"I, Tatum O'Shea, solemnly swear not to —,"

"When Robert hit you, you were angry. You didn't like it."

"There is a big difference between an abusive asshole knocking me to the ground, and you slapping me. You know me, I ask you to do it, we have sex. You don't want to hurt me, you want to fulfill me."

"Mmmm, fulfill you. I like that."

"Is this a game?"

"No games, Tatum."

"What are we, if we don't have games?"

"Something else."

12

JAMESON CONVINCED HER TO STAY with him for the next two weeks. That first night back, she had fallen asleep in the car, so he carried her up to his room. He stayed awake, watching her sleep. It was easy to forget while they played their little games, but she really was a very beautiful girl. Soft. Delicate.

Tatum woke up around three in the morning to catch him staring at her, and they started talking. They talked for a long time. It was the first time they had ever spent the night together and not had sex. Before, it would have seemed pointless.

It didn't seem so pointless anymore.

She didn't talk about her family, didn't really acknowledge that weekend at all. Though the next day, she did lock herself away in a guest room for about an hour, on the phone to Ang. When she emerged, she was smiling, but her eyes were puffy and red. Apparently she could discuss things with Ang, but not with Jameson. He tried not to let it bother him. They had gone to some different stage in their relationship, but they weren't quite ready to start sharing their feelings with each other.

It took her a while to get comfortable in her own skin again, but after a couple days, Tate was back to her old self. Running around in her underwear. Clipping coupons. Teasing Sanders. Begging James-on to do unspeakable things to her. He spent most of his days in Boston, and she would go into town with him, spend her days doing only god knew what with Ang and Rusty. But on the days she didn't work at the bar, she would always show up outside his office building at six o'clock. She *always* went home with him.

He wasn't sure exactly what was going on between them. James-on hadn't been lying in the beginning, he didn't want a girlfriend – a girlfriend usually meant exclusivity, and he liked to have sex with other people. Though sometimes, knowing Tatum was at home and that she not only liked hearing about his one-night stands, but they actually got her hot, made it even more enticing for him to go out and have sex with random women.

So point for her.

But he also wasn't in the market to get married, and say what she wanted, Tate was a chick, at her core. Sooner or later, she would want some sort of a commitment that he just wouldn't, and couldn't really, give her. Jameson liked his life exactly the way it was; every relation-ship he'd ever had, had ended on a sour note. If they tried to make their relationship into something more, it would just end badly, too.

It was just fun and games between them, and it had to stay that way.

She and Sanders had also gotten ridiculously close, ever since the weekend get-away to the O'Shea compound. They would stay up till all hours, just sitting in the kitchen, Tate babbling on and on to him – as far as Jameson could tell, Sanders virtually never said any-thing back. But it seemed to work for them.

Sometimes, Jameson would come out of work to discover his car sitting alone at the curb, and the two of them would be at a restau-rant somewhere. Or in a cafe. Milling around a shop. One time he couldn't find them at all, and it took forty-five minutes and eight phone calls to finally get ahold of Sanders – something that had never happened in the past. Sanders and Tate had gotten distracted by some live show in a park. When they came walking towards him down the street, arm in arm, he had a flash of anger and was shocked to realize something – he was *jealous*. Jealous of her easy going relationship with Sanders.

Jameson knew it was a ridiculous sentiment, especially since he knew he didn't make it easy for her to talk to him, or just be with him. And really, he knew he was the one she seemed to want to be with – he was the one who got tackled in the conservatory, he was the one who got violated in the pool, he was the one who woke up to blowjobs at two in the morning. Nobody else, she hadn't even talked about sleeping with other men. Hadn't even really mentioned Ang to him.

Winning.

"You never have time for me anymore," Ang was whining. Tate rolled her eyes.

"I see you almost every day. If anything, I see you more now than I did before I started sleeping with him," she pointed out. He pouted.

"You never have naked time for me anymore," Ang amended his whine. She laughed.

"Hush. We talked about this."

"But you're the only one who knows what I like, what I want, what I need."

"Teach somebody else."

"*Bitch.*"

She launched a pillow at him and he caught it, laughing. They were hanging out in his room on a Saturday night. She had to go to the bar in a little while, and she had swung by Ang's to use his laptop. She didn't have one of her own and they hadn't hung out, just the two of them, in a while. Two birds with one stone.

"Shut up, there are plenty of people out there wanting to ride the Angier train," she assured him, sitting on the end of his bed and folding her legs up lotus style. He stretched out on the mattress behind her, kneading his toes into her lower back.

"I am very train like, and you know, Rus has been lookin' mighty fine lately," he commented, and she laughed again.

"You better not look twice, Ang. I'm serious, I don't want you to break her," Tate said.

"I wouldn't break her. Just bend her a little. Fold her in half," he replied. She looked over her shoulder.

"I'm dead serious, Ang. If you fuck her, she'll, like, fall in love with you. And it'll break her heart. I would be pissed," she warned him.

"God, you're so boring anymore. I don't understand. You and Satan aren't boyfriend and girlfriend, but you spend all your time together, practically live together, and you aren't allowed to sleep with anyone else. Ummm ... I'm pretty sure that's the basic definition of boyfriend-and-girlfriend," Ang pointed out.

Tate already knew this, had already thought about it, *a lot*. Her relationship with Jameson was a strange one. It didn't have a label, but she kinda liked that – labels were boring. Labels could ruin things, made a person feel like they always had to be living up to it. She and Jameson, they just *existed*. It was easier. She tried not to think about it too much.

"We're allowed to sleep with other people," she corrected Ang.

"Oh, that's right – just not *me*," he grumbled, making a face. She laughed.

"Technically, it's just me who isn't allowed to sleep with you, so you could —,"

"Don't make me sick. You said he sleeps with other women all the time, but how many guys have *you* slept with?" Ang asked.

And that's where the *"open relationship"* aspect fell apart. Jameson had told her she could sleep with other men, and the independent-slutty-woman inside of her told her she could sleep with other people, but the desire wasn't there. She only wanted him.

And it was just her own thinking, just something inside of her, but Tate had the distinct feeling that though Jameson said it was okay, it was actually *not* okay. Not at all. Jameson Kane didn't like to share his toys, and Tate figured she was one of his better ones.

"Just because I haven't slept with anyone doesn't mean I can't, or won't. Besides, why go out for hamburger when I've got steak at home?" she offered as an explanation, trying to lighten the mood. Ang snorted.

"Sounds like bullshit. If your relationship didn't disgust me so much, I'd bug you more about it. Let's do something fun!" he proclaimed. She turned her attention back to the computer.

"Like what?"

"I don't know. What is Satan up to, anyway?"

"He's at home, going over some paperwork for some big to-do that's coming up in Europe," she replied.

"Some big to-do? In Europe? Like what? Where?" Ang pressed. She shrugged.

"I don't know, I don't really ask. He has a house in Denmark," she told him.

"Denmark? Odd, I would have figured him for a London man, or Berlin, or something. Why Denmark?" he asked. She shrugged again.

"I don't know. I told you, I don't ask," she replied.

"Jesus, Tate," Ang laughed, sitting upright. "He could be a serial killer, or a human trafficker, or a pedophile hiding from the law, or

..." he kept listing stuff off. She turned to face him, smacking him in the leg.

"Shut up!" she laughed.

"... or a drug smuggler, or a thief of rare art work, or secretly married with a family, or —,"

They both stopped at that idea. Tate stared at Ang. It was a secret fear of hers. Jameson went away a lot. New York for a weekend. L.A. For a week. Back to New York for a day. Miami for a day. Back to New York. The ex girlfriend lived in New York, Tate was pretty sure. Though she wasn't sure at all about the "ex" status.

"He's always been honest with me. He would have told me," Tate said in a soft voice. Ang snorted.

"Apparently you guys have more of a *'don't ask, don't tell'* relationship. Some people don't consider a lie by omission really a lie. Look him up," he suggested, nodding at the laptop. She glanced down.

"What do you mean?" she asked. He groaned and took the laptop from her hands.

"What's Satan's last name?" he grumbled. She chewed on her bottom lip.

"This isn't right, Ang. He doesn't pry into my stuff," she mumbled. He guffawed.

"Are fucking serious? Tate, he blindfolded you and made you spend the weekend with your family from hell. You're right, he doesn't pry – he rips shit open and makes a mess. Full name," he demanded.

Tate gave it to him.

After Ang typed it into the Google search bar, he handed the computer back to her. She was shocked at how many things came up right away. Jameson was a lot more "famous" than she would have ever guessed. She clicked on the images tab, and there were tons of him, in paparazzi photos. Him two years ago, at an L.A. movie premiere, some actress on his arm. Him at New York Fashion Week, just last February, a famous singer standing next to him. Him standing next to a pool in swim shorts, soaking wet, talking on a cell phone while some ridiculously beautiful girl floated in the pool underneath him – some model whose name she didn't recognize. Most of the photos were because he was with famous people. They were getting photographed, and he was just caught in the cross-hairs.

But there were some of just him. He was very wealthy, which made him an attraction in his own right. A lot of the photographs were from European tabloids, talking about his playboy lifestyle over the past couple years. Nothing too bad, nothing she hadn't already known about or assumed. None of it bothered her, and she could look at Jameson all day, so the pictures were fun.

She skimmed through the years, catching up on his past. Wondered if she'd ever been secretly photographed with him – and then she found one. She and Ang giggled over it, a grainy photo of her, Sanders, and Jameson, standing outside of some restaurant they had gone to on its opening day. A pretty swanky place, with some local celebrities making appearances. She hadn't thought much of that night, but there she was, on Google. It was from a local newspaper, and they didn't list her or Sanders' names, didn't even mention them at all, just that Jameson Kane had been in attendance, but still. She felt giddy.

But then she began to notice a cluster of other pictures, all of Jameson with the same girl. Them walking down a street together in Paris. Them entering a tube station in London. Lots of them eating in restaurants. Posing, with their arms around each other, at fashion events and movie premieres and award shows. Leaving nightclubs together, Jameson pulling her by the hand. *Holding her hand.* It made Tate feel a little nauseous.

"Who is she?" Ang finally asked. Tate sighed.

"I think she's his ex."

"What ex?"

"*The* ex."

She was absolutely. *Drop. Dead. Gorgeous.* Some super-doop-er-model, half Ukranian, half Danish. *Danish.* Tate's heart stopped a little. That must be why he owned a home in Copenhagen – he had bought it to be close to her. Shocking. The model was internationally famous and stupidly beautiful. Jameson was so rich, it was obscene. A match made in heaven. There were pictures of them all over the globe together.

He barely leaves the house with me.

"She hasn't got anything on you. Look at those skinny hips, I would rip her in half," Ang said quickly. Tate chuckled.

"She's gorgeous, Ang. I can admit when someone is better look-ing than me," she replied. Tate wasn't shy about her looks, she knew she was hot, knew she was downright sexy. But this woman, she was beautiful. *Stunning.*

"No, you're just as pretty as she is," Ang assured her. Tate snort-ed.

"No, I'm not. But I would put money on the fact that I'm better in bed," she said back, and Ang laughed.

"That's my girl. How long did they go out for?"

They did some digging. The earliest mention of them togeth-er was two years before – it had been on and off, apparently pretty rocky. Rumors of crazy fights and wild sex. The model's name was Petrushka Ivanovic. They went to her website, but it wasn't very help-ful. Just depressing. Then they went to her Wikipedia page, and the words on the screen slapped Tate across the face. And not in the good way.

Partner(s): Jameson Kane, American financier. Status: Engaged.

"*No, no, no, no, no,*" Tate whispered, and went back to Google.

She typed in their names together. A lot of the same pictures came up, but also ones she hadn't seen. A couple were pretty recent. She pulled the websites they were from – they were *very* recent. Like three weeks ago. Three weeks ago, he had gone to New York for the weekend – she remembered him mentioning it to her. They looked like they were arguing in the photographs, standing on a sidewalk. Another set of photographs were from two weeks ago, them walking down a street. One was from yesterday. He had just gotten back from New York, last night. They were sitting down across from each other in some sort of lobby, the picture taken through the windows.

Tate turned away from Ang, back towards the foot of the bed, and put her head in her hands. She wasn't going to cry, but she kind of wanted to hyperventilate. She kept reminding herself, over and over, that Jameson wasn't her boyfriend. Technically, he could do whatever he wanted. *She* could do whatever she wanted.

But we had a deal. He couldn't be with her. We had a deal.

She felt Ang move, slide down the bed behind her. His long legs went around either side of her and then his arms were around her, hugging her from behind, pulling her into his chest. She took deep breaths and leaned against him, let him rock her back and forth. She felt horrible. She felt *angry.*

"It's okay, Tate. It's just pictures, we don't know what they mean," Ang said softly.

"I know. I know that. It's just … hard," she replied, dropping her hands into her lap.

"You really like him, don't you?" Ang asked. She sighed.

"Yeah, I think I kinda do," she told him. He chuckled.

"Good girl Tate falls for Satan, who would've thought," he teased. She rolled her eyes.

"I'm not a good girl," she pointed out.

"Yes, you are. You've just gotten very good at hiding it," he replied.

"I don't want to see him tonight," she whispered. Ang's laugh was dark.

"Stay with me," he whispered back, his lips against her ear. She shivered.

"No. He may be an asshole, but I'm not. When I confront him about this, it will be with a clear conscience. If it turns out he's a massive, lying, dickhole, with some secret supermodel wife, then I'll come fuck your brains out to get back at him," Tate explained. Ang laughed.

"Cheers, thanks for that. Glad I have a say in this, that I'm good for something to you," he snickered. She laughed as well.

"Shut up, you love it," she told him.

"More than you know. I will happily be your revenge fuck, darling," he assured her. She took a deep breath.

"You're too good to me. I have to go, thanks for letting me come over, and for horrifically depressing me," she laughed, untangling herself from him and climbing off the bed.

"Where are you going?" he asked, standing up behind her. She bent over, pulling on her shoes.

"Home. Gotta get changed, head to work," she replied. She felt his hands slide over her hips, pulling her back against him, and she glanced over her shoulder.

"Just getting reacquainted," Ang told her. She stared at him for a moment, watched him as he looked down at her back, at her hips, his hands sliding back and forth. His voice was soft, but nothing else about him was.

Uh-oh.

"Save it for your porno, Ang. I'll talk to you later," she said, managing a laugh as she pulled away from him. He gave her a tight lipped smile, but didn't say anything as she walked out of his room.

At home, she put on some tiny black shorts, and a cropped Red Sox jersey. Her knee high black wedge boots. Did her eye makeup extra heavy, pulled her hair up into a *"just fucked"* looking ponytail.

She wanted to look bad. Slutty. *Angry.*

The Sox had played the day before, and her jersey got a lot of compliments – as did her stomach and ass. She slung drinks and flirted a lot more than she usually did, all while watching the front door. Sometimes, on a Saturday, Jameson would come to town early, sit at the end of the bar. Watch her in a way that usually had her squirming to get him alone.

He didn't show up, but while she had her eye on the door, another good looking man walked through it. Warm brown eyes. Shaggy hair. Open smile. Broad shoulders, thick arms. She recognized him, and suddenly a thought burst into her head.

She couldn't sleep with Ang, and since she and Jameson had started sleeping together, she hadn't felt the urge to be with anyone else. Well, right then, the urge was upon her. The man was sexy as sin, and he was a baseball player. The first baseman for the Boston Red Sox, Nick Castille, to be exact. Wealthy. Semi-famous. A challenge.

A threat.

She laid it on thick with him. Leaned over the bar to deliver his drinks, winked at him, touched Rusty inappropriately in front of him. He watched her with hooded eyes, obviously liking what he was seeing. He finally called her over.

"I like your jersey," he commented. She spun around, showing him the back while shaking her hips.

"Good, I'm glad," she laughed.

"But it's the wrong number," he informed her. She turned back, sauntered up and leaned against her side of the bar.

"And what number should I be wearing?" she asked, cocking an eyebrow up.

"*Mine,*" he replied.

"*Ooohhh,* and how would I go about getting one of your jerseys?" she asked, lowering her voice.

"You could have it tomorrow, when you wake up wearing it," he suggested. She laughed.

"Sounds like a plan."

They chatted on and off for a while. He was actually pretty funny, and very nice. He left after about two hours, but came back when the bar was closing. She chased everyone out, locked up. Didn't even ask to go back to his fancy hotel room, or penthouse condo, or *whatever*. Just straddled him right on his bar stool. Gave him a lap dance. Let him carry her to a booth and spread her out on the table, like she was Sunday dinner.

It wasn't the most exciting sex she'd ever had, but it wasn't bad, either. He was different than what she'd been dining on lately, and that made it fun. He was more than capable and she really put on a show for him, coming loudly and hard. Then she backed him into a chair, sat down on him, made him say her name like it was a swear. Slid under the table, wrapped her lips around him, and made him whisper her name like it was prayer.

I still got it.

Afterwards, he asked for her phone number. She laughed and said she didn't really plan on seeing him again. He shrugged and gave her his phone number, then really did give her a jersey. She thought it was cute and put it on, gave him a lingering kiss goodbye at the door.

"You're a pretty amazing girl," he mumbled, clasping his hands around the back of her neck. She laughed.

"No, just a huge Sox fan," she teased. He rolled his eyes.

"You didn't even know any of my stats, or what my number was," he pointed out.

"Well, I'm a huge fan *now*. And I will *definitely* remember your number," she assured him.

"Most girls *want* to give me their phone numbers, you know. I usually have trouble getting away. You seem like you're pushing me out the door," he told her with a laugh.

"I guess tonight's your lucky night. No strings attached, one night only, totally awesome sex," she said, laughing as well. He raised an eyebrow.

"One night only, huh. So if I come back, I won't get a repeat?" he asked.

Now that was surprising. This guy really seemed to like her. She didn't know why. She was a succubus. Couldn't he tell when he was being used? That they were using each other? But as she let her eyes wander over him, she bit into her bottom lip. He was very good looking, and it hadn't been a bad time at all. He was very nice to her. She wondered if he'd ever call her a waste of time.

"Not an *exact* repeat," she started, pressing herself against him as her voice fell into a breathy whisper. "I like to change things up, keep things exciting. There's a pool table in the back that is just the right height for —,"

He pushed back into the bar and it was another hour before they said goodbye for real.

She could have gone to her apartment, but she took a cab to Jameson's. She wanted to get it over with, end her suspense. Confess her sins. Find out if they even really were sins. It was after four-thirty in the morning, and she didn't expect anyone to be awake, but as the taxi rolled up to the porch, Sanders came outside.

"I can get it, Sandy," Tate assured him, hurrying to dig money out of her bag. But he already had bills in his hand and she hadn't even fished out one twenty dollar bill before the cab was rolling away. Sanders turned towards her.

"I was worried," he said very simply. She blinked in surprise.

DEGRADATION

"Really? I'm sorry. I should have called," she replied quickly. She never wanted to hurt Sanders. Jameson was fair game, but Sanders was special.

"May I ask where you were?" he questioned. She turned and started making her way into the house.

"At the bar, I got stuck behind," she gave an evasive answer.

"A call would have been appreciated, ma'am," he said in a terse voice, holding open the door for her.

"I'm really sorry. I will call you next time, I promise," she assured him, leaning against him as she pulled off her boots.

"He's in the kitchen," Sanders informed her. She stood upright.

"Really? You've both just been awake?" she asked.

"I waited up for you," Sanders replied. She smiled.

"Ah, and he didn't," she finished his statement.

"He has been ... concerned," was all Sanders would say.

Oooohhh, translation: pissed off.

As Sanders headed upstairs, Tate made her way into the kitchen. Jameson was sitting at the island, a coffee mug in front of him. He glanced up at her entrance but didn't say anything, just went back to looking at his phone. She looked around the kitchen. A bunch of dishes and cups and bowls were stacked up next to the sink, sparkling clean. She frowned.

"Have you been cleaning!?" she exclaimed. There was a dishwasher that she and Sanders usually took turns working. Jameson never touched anything.

"Yes," he replied.

"You cleaned them all, *by hand!?* I've never seen you wash *anything*," she laughed, heading over to look at them. All white, porcelain dishes, so clean, they looked polished.

"It calms me down. Where have you been?" Jameson asked, and she turned around to see him setting his phone down.

"At the bar," she replied, grabbing a mug and filling it with water.

"A call would have been nice."

Tate was surprised.

"Aw, Kane, I didn't know you cared," she teased.

"Fuck you, *O'Shea*," he said back. "Now. The truth, please. Why are you late?"

"I was fucking the first baseman for the Boston Red Sox," she told him bluntly. His eyebrows shot up.

"Really. Wasn't expecting that," his voice was soft.

"Does that bother you?" she asked. He shrugged.

"Hmmm, not sure. Have you ever slept with him before?" Jameson questioned, standing up and leaning against the fridge behind him.

"Never met him before tonight," she answered, sipping at her water.

"I see. Must have left quite a mark on him – that's his jersey, I presume?" Jameson asked, his eyes wandering over her clothing. She nodded.

"Yes. He gave me his phone number, too," she told him.

"Are you going to call him?" Jameson continued. Tate smiled. He was cool, calm, and collected – but she could tell, he was actually a little nervous. Deep down.

Good.

"I told him I probably wouldn't. I don't plan on it," she replied. Jameson nodded.

"Good."

Tate laughed.

"You fuck other girls all the time. You came home the other day from Miami, with that crazy story about that ribbon dancer," she pointed out.

"You love hearing those stories," he reminded her. She nodded.

"Yeah, but I was under the impression I was allowed to do the same," she said. He nodded as well.

"And so you are. So how was he? I want to hear all the details. Better than me?" Jameson asked, folding his arms across his chest. She shook her head.

"I don't want to talk about it right now."

"Well, I want to know about it right now, so —,"

"I want to know about Petrushka Ivanovic," Tate stated. Blunt was apparently the soup du jour that night.

There was a violent kind of silence. The rage that washed over his face; she was almost a little scared. Definitely a little turned on. Nick had been a lovely appetizer, but she wanted dinner now. She wondered if Jameson could get mad enough to actually be turned off.

"How the fuck do you know about her?" he demanded.

"Google is an amazing tool."

"You *Googled* me!?"

"Ang did."

"*Fucker.*"

"I would have found out sooner or later, Jameson," she pointed out. "You were with her yesterday. People take your picture. Did you know there's even a picture of us online?"

He looked surprised.

"No. Where, when?" he asked.

"Don't worry, no one can tell you're with a *whore*," she assured him. He frowned.

"I wouldn't care if they did. So that's why you slept with the baseball player? Because you saw pictures of me with Pet?" Jameson asked. She glared at him.

Pet. Of course that's her nickname. Goddammit.

"No, I fucked him because he was hot and he was there, same reason I fuck anybody," she snapped. Jameson laughed.

"*Liar.* You're very angry, baby girl. Tonight should be extra fun," he chuckled. Her anger went through the roof.

"Tonight should be *extra boring*. I'm all full up on good times," she told him. He laughed.

"A baseball player couldn't possibly satisfy you," he said.

"Funny, cause I feel that same way about '*financiers*'," she snapped back.

"Watch your mouth, baby girl," Jameson's voice was like ice.

"It said you were engaged," she blurted out. More silence.

"Stupid girl, reading the tabloids. I knew you were fucking stupid, Tate, I just didn't realize how much," his voice was quiet.

Tate shrieked and launched her coffee mug at him. She played on the bar's softball team, she was an athletic girl and knew how to throw a ball. The mug missed him by an inch, crashing into the cupboard next to him. He didn't even blink. Didn't even move.

"Don't call me stupid," she hissed.

"Those cups are expensive," he warned her. She turned, picked up a plate from the stack, and threw it to the ground. It exploded.

"How about that? Was that one expensive?" she asked.

"About fifty bucks a plate. More than you can afford," he assured her. She grabbed three more plates, slammed them to the ground, one right after the other.

"Just take it out of my salary," she replied.

"I don't think I'm going to be paying you for tonight," Jameson laughed in a dark manner. She grabbed one of the stacks, flung all the plates across the kitchen in one toss.

"You promised! Remember!? Nothing to do with her! I wouldn't give a shit if you fucked her, if I had known from the get go – but this whole time, you told me there would be nothing! There are pictures of you two together, *every time* you went to New York!" Tate shouted at him, grabbing plates and flinging them at his feet. He didn't move, not once.

"Careful, jealousy is not an attractive trait," he pointed out.

"*Lying* isn't an attractive trait," she snapped back.

"Are you done?" he asked, glancing down at the shattered

chunks of porcelain covering the kitchen floor. She looked down as well, then glanced at the remaining dishes. Only a dinner plate and two cups remained. Enough for her and Sanders to enjoy a late night meal together. Good enough.

"I think so," she replied.

He slowly started walking towards her. He wasn't wearing any shoes or socks, and she could hear the porcelain scratching and crunching under his feet. She winced. One wrong step, and he would cut himself. But silly, Jameson Kane never made a wrong step. He didn't stop moving till he was right in front of her.

"I am *not* a liar," he said, his cold, blue eyes staring very hard at her.

"Not according to what I read. *Engaged?* That would most definitely make me the other woman, *liar*," she snapped.

His hand was instantly at her neck, squeezing hard. She reached behind her and gripped the counter, squirming under his grasp. He pulled her up a little and she was forced onto her toes. Forced to drag miniscule gasps of air through her nose. She relaxed her throat, let her tongue go flat in her mouth. She knew this game.

"*I am not a liar*. We *were* engaged," Jameson hissed through clenched teeth.

"Then why have you been seeing her?" Tate croaked out.

"Because I can see whoever the fuck I want. Because we were involved in a lot of the same businesses and it takes time to dissolve all of that shit," he told her.

"Then why didn't you just tell me?" she asked. His hand squeezed harder and she grabbed onto his wrist.

"Because I don't have to tell you shit, Tate. I told you I wouldn't sleep with her, and I haven't. End of story. You said you trusted me – apparently you don't. Sounds like *you're* the liar," Jameson growled, dragging her face close to his own.

"You still … should've told me," she gasped, her voice a thready whisper.

"*You should've just asked*, instead of going out and finding the first available person to fuck, just so you could rub it in my face. Did you actually think that would work? *Stupid fucking whore*," he chuckled in a menacing tone.

Ah, there's my Satan.

"I guess I'll have to try harder," she managed to squeak. "Next time I fuck him, I'll make it really spectacular."

"There won't be a next time with him," Jameson informed her. She brought both hands to his wrist, attempted to laugh. No sound came out.

"You can't tell me what to do, *Kane*," she replied.

He slammed her down onto the ground, then hovered over her. Shards of porcelain dug into her back, and she hissed through clenched teeth. His hand was sill tight around her neck, his other hand on the floor by her head. She squirmed and moved underneath him.

"I tell you *everything* you're allowed to do," he growled.

"And there's that illusion of power," she breathed. She was starting to feel dizzy. How much was too much? When should she stop him? Did she want to?

"Let's get something straight about this power situation, Tate. I fuck you when I want, where I want, how I want. You come when I call. If I want to see my ex girlfriend, or *any* ex girlfriend, I will. I'm with *you* right now, this moment. That's all you get from me," he told her. Her eyes rolled back, her lids fluttering shut.

What if I want more?

"I can't ... I can't ..." she gasped for air, digging her nails into his skin.

His grip loosened considerably, but didn't let go. She gasped in air, her body going limp underneath him. She had been very close to passing out. She heard a clanging noise and opened her eyes. His free hand was rooting around in a drawer above them, searching for something. After a moment, a large pair of solid silver scissors appeared in his hand. Her eyes got wide.

"Stupid bitch. *Stupid fucking bitch.* Doesn't even know when to say enough. *Fuck,*" Jameson swore, bringing the scissors down to her stomach.

He glanced at her, but she didn't say anything, didn't make a move to stop him, so he continued on with whatever it was he was planning. It was rough going, using only his left hand, but he managed to make a jagged cut up the center of the jersey she was wearing. When he finally sawed through the thick lining at her collar, he rested the point of the scissors under her chin. Dug them in a little.

"Go ahead," she whispered, her voice hoarse. "Just another mark, right? Not like I'll even notice."

"I will say this only once, Tatum. I am *not* engaged. I wll continue to fuck other women. But I am with *you*," he said in a very serious voice.

Since that night, seven years ago, he hadn't ever made her cry again. Not with his harsh tone and degrading words. Not with any of his sadistic games. Not with his punishing hands. He had choked her to the point blood vessels broke in her face, squeezed her to the point there were whole hand prints around her thighs, held her down for so long that she didn't think she'd be able to find her way back up again.

But speaking nice to her, that was too much. Saying sweet things, even in the fucked up way they had, was more than she could handle. Tears filled her eyes, spilled over her temples. Ran into her hair. She hadn't wanted to care about this man. Not at all. She had wanted to play with him. Turned out, he was much better at the game.

"*Liar,*" she whispered.

He moved off of her then. Pulled her away from the floor enough to yank the remnants of her jersey off, then let her fall back down, only wearing her bra and shorts. She watched as he shoved the jersey into the garbage disposal, ran the machine till it clogged and stopped moving, smoke coming out from underneath the sink.

"I never lie, Tatum," was all he said as he strode out of the kitchen.

She started to laugh. *Really* laugh; a sort of body heaving laughter, lifting her shoulders off the floor and causing her to shake. She could feel the porcelain cutting into her, but she didn't care. She laughed, and the tears streamed down her face.

"Let me help you, Ms. O'Shea," Sanders' soft voice was above her. She opened her eyes.

"Oh, Sandy. Sandy, why didn't you tell me?" she gasped for air, pressing a hand to her chest.

"Tell you what, ma'am?" he asked, grabbing her arm and pulling her into a sitting position.

"That none of this is a game," she breathed. He grimaced as he looked over her back.

"Because I knew you'd figure it out sooner or later, ma'am," he replied, then pulled her to her feet.

"I didn't want to like him, Sandy. I really, really didn't. I thought, if we just played. If we slept with other people, and just played around, I would finally beat him. I would win," Tate babbled while Sanders wrapped an arm around her waist.

"If it's any consolation, ma'am, I think you have won," Sanders told her, helping her walk up the stairs. She shook her head and leaned into his shoulder.

"It's not fun anymore. It's scary. I don't know this game," she whispered. He nodded.

"I know, ma'am. I know."

Jameson was woken up a couple hours later to the sound of footsteps in his room.

Tate?

He had stayed up for a while, waiting for her to crawl into bed, or to hear her sneaking out of the house. He had maybe gone a little too far with her, but she had made him *so mad*. How dare she Google him. How dare she look into Petrushka. How dare she not trust him. How dare she fuck some guy just to get back at Jameson. Wear that guy's clothing home, to *Jameson's home*. He wanted to put her in her place. Remind her exactly *what* she was to him – even if he, himself, wasn't exactly sure.

But her eyes had looked so detached. Telling him to mark her with the scissors. Daring him. She wasn't present. She *wanted* the pain – not to remind her that she was with him, *but to make her forget*. He *never* wanted her to forget.

It broke his heart a little.

"Jameson."

Sanders was in his room. He couldn't remember the last time Sanders had fully entered his room. Jameson sat up, rubbed his face, then climbed out of bed. There was morning light shining through the windows, and the clock said it was six-twenty. He looked around him. Tatum wasn't in the room.

"Where is she?" he sighed. Sanders turned and left. Jameson followed close behind him.

She was asleep in Sanders' bed. Jameson was a little shocked – he was pretty sure no one else had ever been in Sanders' room. Jameson hadn't been in there since the remodel. She was laying on her stomach, and she didn't have anything on her top half. He winced when he saw the nicks and cuts on her back. They had been cleaned, there was no blood, but they still looked evil.

"I tried to take her to your room, but she wanted to get cleaned up first. She fell asleep. She was going to join you," Sanders explained in his soft voice. Jameson sat on the edge of the bed, traced his fingers down her spine. She shivered in her sleep.

"No. She wanted to be with you. She feels safe with you," Jameson replied.

"No. She wants *you*. She has been waiting for *you*."

Jameson scowled. He wasn't in the mood for Sanders' little riddles. He stood up and pulled Tate to the edge of the bed, picked her up in his arms, curled her into his chest. He nodded at Sanders and then strode from the room.

Once he had her laid down, he stripped the rest of her clothing off. She slept through the whole process, breathing heavily through her nose. She rolled back onto her stomach and he let his eyes wander over her body. He stretched out next to her, massaged his fingers against her skin. There were no signs on her body that another man had been there. She must have been a lot gentler with strangers.

"*Jameson*," she suddenly mumbled, her face still turned away from him.

"You sure it's not Sanders?" he teased. She managed a laugh.

"Oh, I'd know his fingers anywhere," she joked back.

"Are you okay?" he whispered, smoothing his hand over her skin. She shrugged.

"Yeah. Nothing a tough chick like me can't handle," she replied.

"Sometimes I wonder."

"I was just so angry. You had promised, and there were all these pictures of the two of you, and I just ... I got upset. I didn't have any right to, I'm sorry," she said softly. He sighed. He liked to pretend he didn't, but he knew he owed her something.

"I got upset when I realized you were wearing his shirt," he replied.

"You sleep with girls all the time," she pointed out.

"I still got upset."

"So I can't sleep with other guys?" she asked. He thought for a

258

second.

"I just don't want you using it against me, trying to upset me with the fact. I've never done that to you – if anything, I sleep with other women because I know it turns you on. I've never done it to hurt you. You wearing his shirt, in my house, though, trying to upset me; *it worked*," Jameson growled at her.

"I'm sorry," she whispered.

He rubbed a hand across his face. How far did he really want to go for this girl? He looked down at her, stretched out beside him. When he had first seen Tatum, at that party, he hadn't believed his eyes. A dark haired sex kitten engaging in dangerous banter with him. Then again at the meeting with his lawyers. Pulling her panties off in a room full of people; she had blown him away. He had wanted to play with her some more, maybe finish what they had started seven years ago. Only now, there wasn't an end in sight. He'd already gone too far.

"I met Petrushka at a party, a couple years ago. She's a huge bitch, so we hit it off. She's a freak in the sack, you'd love it," he said.

"Sounds like a keeper," Tate chuckled. He put his hand back on her back and her skin jumped at his touch. Just like the first time they had ever touched. Just like every time.

"She's fucking crazy. We fucked, we fought, we broke up. Got back together. She wants everything her way, very demanding. We stayed together mostly because of our positions, I think. Supermodel, rich guy, I don't know. I was doing a lot of work in Europe at the time, it was easy," he tried to explain.

"You have a home in Copenhagen. She's Danish," Tate commented. He laughed.

"Seriously, Tate, sometimes I forget what a girl you are. I owned my home before I even knew her. We met in Germany," he told her. She sighed.

"I'm so stupid."

He moved his hand up and down her back, touched his fingers to her scratches.

"Sometimes," he agreed. "I was unhappy. Pet dug her claws in, distracted me from that fact. I was angry a lot of the time, and sometimes she would let me treat her badly," he continued.

"Like me?" Tate asked. He laid down on his side and leaned close to her.

"No one is like you, Tate. You're the real deal, she was an act. She likes to play my part, she wants to be the one holding someone down. She faked everything for me. I don't think she ever really liked me, or that I even ever really liked her. We just liked how each other looked, liked how we fucked."

"You spun two years away on liking how someone fucks?" Tate asked.

"You've been doing the same thing for seven years," Jameson pointed out.

"Yeah, but with different people, different flavors. Not just one person that I don't even like. And if you didn't like her, how did you wind up engaged?" she pressed. He groaned and rolled onto his back

"It was an accident, I was kind of tricked into it. I was picking up a ring from Harry Winston, in New York. It was my grandmother's ring. Huge, gorgeous. Pet and I had just had a very public fight, it was all over the tabloids. Some fucking paparazzi piece of shit took a bunch of pictures of me in the store with the ring, talking to the jeweler, taking it out of the store. It was everywhere. She freaked out, got all excited. When I told her what had really happened, she freaked out even more, pointed out that it would be everywhere, if I took it back. How could I take it back, when I'd never put it out there?" he asked.

"What a prize bitch," Tate mumbled.

"I don't know, it was easier to go with the flow. There I was, almost thirty, and utterly alone; aside from Sanders. Who hated her, by the way. A very good judge of character, Sanders," he pointed out.

"*Duh*. I would trust anything Sanders said. I would trust him with my life," she was quick to comment.

"Goddamn, Tate, maybe you should be sleeping with him," Jameson laughed.

"Who says I'm not?"

He smacked her on the ass, and some of the awkward tension between them eased as they laughed.

"Shut up, don't make me kill him. He's my favorite person – *you* can be replaced, Sanders can't," he teased. She chuckled. "Anyway, I figured why not. She was one of the hottest fucks I'd ever had, she was gorgeous, and I had gotten pretty good at tuning out her bitching. I went with it. Gave her the ring. Big mistake. I never got it back."

"What made you finally end it for real?" Tate asked.

"I had tried to break it off a couple times; once when she flipped out after she caught me fucking this tennis player – she was not as free a thinker as you. She never wanted to have sex anymore, and when we did, it was always kind of weird. Well, you know, weirder than usual. I finally told her it was over, *for real* over. That I had *never* wanted to marry her, and *would* never marry her. She begged and pleaded. Cried. I could never resist tears, you know.

"We wound up fucking, and she asked me to hit her. She never let me do that before, never asked me to – she would let me do other things. Hot candle wax, cat-o-nine-tails, paddles; things she had the option of doing back to me. But hitting … it's kind of a one way street. You'll never be able to hit me as hard as I can hit you," Jameson said softly. Tate laughed.

"We'll see about that."

"Very few women will let you do that to them, I've discovered. Lot's of other crazy shit, but not that, so it was kind of like dangling forbidden fruit in front of me. I was gentle, I didn't do anything crazy. Slapped her once, maybe twice. She went fucking nuts. Fucked my goddamn brains out – almost comparative to you," he told her.

"Flattery will get you nowhere," Tate snorted.

"I mean, it was crazy. Even for me. We were all over the place, every surface in the apartment. But then she started hitting herself. *Hard.* It got a little strange. I tried to stop her. She gave herself a bloody lip, pulled out a hank of hair, and when she came, she gave herself a black eye. I like some freaky shit, but that was too much. I got off of her, made her stop. She laughed at me, said that I was the freak, that there was something wrong with me for liking the things I like, said she was gonna tell everyone, sell pictures of her face to the press. Fucked up. I packed a bag and left. I've never gone back to that apartment, though I'm pretty sure I'm still paying rent on it," Jameson said.

"Fuck the apartment! What happened to crazy bitch!?" Tate exclaimed, propping herself up on her elbows so she could look at him. He smiled and traced a finger down the side of her face. Her hair was a mess and her eye makeup was smeared down her cheeks, but she was looking at him. Really looking at him, all of the detachment from earlier gone.

She is so beautiful.

"I should've looked you up," he blurted out. Her eyes got wide.

"Excuse me?"

"Seven years. I should've looked you up. I thought about you. Wondered what you were doing. That night was a pretty big deal. I never imagined that you would turn out like you did," he told her.

"What, like you?" she asked. He nodded.

"Yeah."

"I wouldn't have imagined it, either, back then. You unleashed something in me. Thank you," she told him. He laughed and pushed himself so he was sitting up, resting back against the headboard.

"Don't thank me yet. You were ready to kill me earlier," he reminded her.

"I was hurt. I was stupid. I'll get over it," she assured him. He shook his head.

"It wasn't stupid. I could've told you. I would've wanted you to tell me, I guess. Dealing with her isn't always the most pleasant experience. We broke up last year, but besides having some investment plans together, we just run into each other a lot. Sex happens sometimes. Old feelings get stirred up. It's fucked up, but I'm kind of a fucked up guy," he told her. She laid back down, facing away from him, and there was silence for a few moments.

"Old feelings, huh," she said softly.

"Tatum."

"Hmmm?"

"If I tell you something, will you please, *please*, not be a girl about it? Not read too much into it?"

Tate propped herself back up. Pushed her messy hair out of her face. She scooted closer and rested her chin against his knee. He smiled down at her, reached out and ran a hand over her hair.

She deserves better than me.

"I make no promises, but I'll try. I'm usually pretty good about it. Just not today," she replied.

"I didn't want to like you," he stated bluntly. She held her breath, but kept staring at him. "When I first saw you, got them to hire you as a temp. I had no intention of knowing you. I just wanted to sleep with you again. You looked so amazing, and god, your mouth. That was my plan the whole time. I wanted to see if you were like how I remembered, if anything could ever be that good again. It was *better*. You weren't scared of me, you stuck around. Were willing to take more than I was even prepared to dish out," he told her. She laughed, leaned to the side and nibbled on his thigh.

"I told you, flattery will —,"

"I like you, Tatum. *A lot*. I don't want you to leave. When you didn't come home tonight, didn't answer your cell phone, that was my first thought. That it was over, you were bored, didn't care. I always thought it would be me first. I was upset. I don't want to let you go, not yet. *I like you,*" he stressed.

She frowned at him, her brows creasing together.

"That's very sweet, Jameson, but I'm not sure I understand. Why am I not supposed to be a girl about that?" she asked. He sighed, running his fingers through her hair.

"Because it won't ever be more than that. You're a friend, a very good friend. But that's it. There will never be a ring from Harry Winston. I will never ask you to marry me. I don't want those things, I never did. Not with Pet, not with anybody. I like to have fun, I like to fuck. I don't want to put stars in your eyes, I'm not that guy. I'm the devil, and I don't have any plans to change. But I like you, and I would like you to stay with me, for a little while longer," he said.

There. He didn't know how else he could say it. How did he explainto a woman that he only ever wanted to be ... how had she put it? *"Fuck buddies"*? He liked Tatum, probably a lot more than he was admitting to himself, or to her. But he didn't want to get her hopes up. Things had gone so badly between him and Pet; he didn't want that happening with Tate. She was someone he always wanted to call a friend. He wanted to hold her down, and bend her to his will, and make her do degrading, horrible things with him.

And I want her to be my friend.

"I'll stay, Jameson. I'll stay," she murmured, moving away from him to lay back on her stomach.

"You're okay with all that?" he asked. More silence.

"I have to be. It's all you have to offer," she finally replied.

"You don't want more?" he pressed.

"Do you want me to lie?"

"No."

"Of course I want more. I *am* a girl, you're right. I want Prince Charming to ride up on a white horse and carry me off to his castle.

DEGRADATION

The only difference between me and other girls is once I get there, I want him to bend me over the throne and pull my hair while he fucks me hard and calls me names. But I know that'll never happen with you. I'm not sure I'd even want it to be you – you *are* the devil," Tate agreed with him.

"Prince Charming could never treat you as good as the devil," he teased. She shrugged.

"Maybe not. But maybe so. What'll happen to you, if I'm ever so blessed to find this magical S&M Prince Charming?" she asked. He looked at the ceiling. He didn't want to think about that moment.

"Go back to hell. Find another succubus," Jameson replied.

"Whoever she is, I hope she's as good as me," she whispered.

"No one will ever be as good as you, Tatum."

13

JAMESON WATCHED TATE GO HOME later that afternoon. She didn't come back for three days. Three hair raising, teeth grinding, skin clawing days. She had said she wanted to be with him. He was halfway tempted to go find her and drag her home by her hair, force her to keep her word. But for the first time since they'd started sleeping together, Jameson didn't know if that would be welcome.

She turned up on her own, on a Wednesday night. Just strolled into his library, like no time had passed. She kissed him on the cheek, then went upstairs to change her clothes. He didn't see her again for about an hour, and when he went to look for her, she was in Sanders' room, playing chess. He felt left out, but he didn't want to intrude. He wound up laying in bed, staring at his ceiling, thinking about her.

"I looked for you downstairs," her voice came from his doorway.

"I'm not there."

"Ooohhh, there's a tone. Satan feeling especially devilish tonight?" Tate asked with a laugh, shutting the door behind her.

"No more than usual. How was the chess game?" he asked.

"Is that it? Sanders? I don't have to spend time with him," she told him. Jameson hadn't looked away from the ceiling and she hadn't come into his field of vision.

"I don't care. What have you been doing all week?" he questioned her. He felt the bed dip. She was sitting near his feet.

"Stuff. Just kinda moped around my apartment," she answered.

"No more baseball players?" he asked with a smirk.

"No. Truth? He was *nothing* compared to you," her voice was low and husky. She had come to play.

Am I game?

"Nice words. The question is whether or not I believe you," he said. She laughed again.

"I don't really care whether or not you believe me. If you don't want me sleeping with other people, just say so," she told him. He paused.

"Was he any good at all?" he asked.

"Yes."

"How good?"

"Not as good as you. Not as good as Ang. But pretty good. I wouldn't say no to seconds," she replied.

"Did you come?"

"Twice."

"Where did you fuck him?"

"The bar."

"In the bar? Wow, Tate. I'm missing out."

"I know. And in the back bar, on a pool table."

"Hot."

"I think I scared him a little, but he liked it."

"I know the feeling," Jameson laughed. Her hand rested on his leg.

"I could never scare you," she whispered.

"You scare me right now," he replied.

Suddenly she was crawling up his body. Her knees came to a rest on either side of his hips and he rested his hands on her thighs. Her hands were flat against his chest, pushing herself upright.

"Don't be ridiculous, it doesn't suit you. He wasn't exactly a take charge kind of guy, I had to lead the way," Tate continued with her story.

"Sounds like a pussy," Jameson commented, laughing. She shrugged.

"Just different. Sometimes it's fun to be in charge," she told him. He stopped laughing.

"Do you want to tell me what to do? Take the lead here?" he asked. She chuckled, a dark sound, and suddenly she was leaning close, her teeth against his neck.

"No. You're so good at it," she breathed. He clenched his fingers, digging them into her thighs.

"This isn't very interesting. Little man, so scared of the big bad wolf that you had to hold his hand to help you get off. We should just stick to my stories," Jameson taunted.

"Hmmm, maybe it wasn't about all that. It was a change up. Someone treating me nicely, like I was a nice, normal girl," she tried to explain.

"Nice, normal girls don't fuck baseball players in the backs of bars," he pointed out.

"Maybe they do. *He* thought one did," she whispered.

Well this is new.

"If that's what you want, then you better call your baseball player. I don't want a nice, normal girl. I want a girl who likes to be knocked down and dragged around. A girl who wants to be smacked around and called a whore. I want a girl who will let me fuck *other girls*, and then get so turned on by that fact, that she'll blow me while we're driving down a highway doing seventy-five," Jameson snapped.

True story.

"Sounds like a pretty hot girl," Tate commented.

"Hottest girl I know."

She was kissing him, suddenly, her tongue pressing against his lips. He grabbed her by the head and leaned forward, kissing her back. It felt like it had been a long time since he had tasted her mouth. He'd missed it. She gasped against him and her fingers flew to his shirt. She got about half of his buttons undone, then she just ripped the shirt open before moving onto his belt buckle.

Three days was a long time.

"Fuck anyone else while you were gone? Engineers? Fast food workers? Doctors?" he asked while she yanked his pants down his legs.

"Not that I can think of, but ask me later, something might come back while you're nailing me to the mattress," she replied casually. He grabbed her hair and dragged her back up his length.

"You better not think of *anyone else* but me," he growled. He could practically feel her eye roll.

"Shut up and fuck me."

He thought maybe she'd want to go slow. Not that Tate had ever been a slow kind of girl, but she'd been really upset the last time he'd seen her. They hadn't had sex in four days. Three days ago he'd told her he would never want her as anything more than a fuck buddy. She hadn't spoken to him again until that night, and even then, she'd spent most of the night with Sanders.

But if her actions were anything to go by, she was fired up and ready to go, even more so than normal. She was either making up for lost time, or punishing herself. Or him. Somebody was getting hurt.

She yanked off all of their clothes, her nails scratching sensitive skin. She went down on him, no-holds-barred, just immediately deep throated him. He thought she was going to make him come that way, but then she was moving again. Crawling on top of him, pulling him forward, wrapping her legs around his waist. They moved together, hips pushing at each other, and she got louder, pressing her forehead to his while her nails dug into the back of his neck.

"I want you to do it," Tate panted. He was gripping her hips so hard, he knew there would be bruises.

"I think I am," Jameson managed to chuckle.

"*Hit me,*" she breathed. He glared at her.

"No," he replied.

"You're denying me?" she asked.

"Cause I don't think you really want it."

"Oh, *I want it.*"

"You're punishing yourself. I don't want to hurt you," he told her. She shook her head.

"You can't hurt me. I *want* to be punished. *Please,*" she begged.

"You're upset with me. I'm not doing something just so you can hold it against me later," he snapped.

"*I'm not her.*"

He was suddenly very angry.

"Don't fucking talk about her," he swore, halting his movements, leaving her impaled on his length.

"Oh, *that* makes you angry? You talk about every other girl you fuck. Why don't you talk about her? She must have been pretty special to you, Kane," she said in an evil voice, rotating her hips against his. "*Pretty special.* An amazing fuck, you said. Was she *tight* like me? Did she get *wet* like me?"

"Shut your fucking mouth, Tate," he warned.

"Two years, she *must* have been pretty amazing. Do you want to pour hot candle wax on me? Whip me? Paddle me?" Tate asked, letting her head drop back.

God, this woman. If my dick gets any harder, it's gonna kill one of us.

"*I want to scar you,*" he groaned.

"Hit me."

"No."

"This is what I want, Jameson. I want you to do whatever you want. I want to be able to do whatever I want. *I'm not her.* Just let go," she urged.

"I can't," he whispered. She smirked down at him, her hips slowing their movements.

"Fine. If you won't do it, I'll find someone who will," she snapped. He glared again.

"Watch your fucking mouth," he snapped back. She shook her head.

"*Make me.* Ang likes to play, and I trust him. Maybe he'll do it," she taunted.

"*Stupid bitch,* you better shut the fuck up," Jameson growled.

"I'm sure there are lots of guys out there who would do it for me. Some random guy, in a hotel room somewhere. I'll pretend to be that nice, normal girl. Let some guy think he picked up a sweet girl, then I'll let him fuck me. Fuck me *hard;* harder than this, *harder than you.*"

He slapped her across the face, and the response was instantaneous. She cried out and her pussy clamped down so hard on his dick, he almost came right then and there. *Holy shit.* He moved fast, slammed her down onto the mattress and then got up onto his knees, holding her hips up while he pumped into her.

"Goddammit, Tate. Not every fucking thing is about you. I didn't want to fucking do that, *you stupid fucking whore. Fucking bitch,*" he swore, slamming against her hips as hard as he could. She was shrieking.

"God, it was so good, please say it was so good, it was so good, *so good,*" she panted. He slapped her again and it drove her wild, caused her to thrash and buck underneath him.

It drives **me** *wild.*

"Fucking hell, Tate. I'm going to fuck you every night from now on, for as long as I can. *Cunt. Whore.* Fuck. *Why are you so fuck-*

ing good to me?" he moaned, grabbing one of her legs and resting it against his shoulder. He grabbed her hand, placed it at her wet core, forced her fingers in and around herself. She was like his marionette, his own personal fuck doll.

"Because … you're the devil. You need someone to be with. I want to be that person," she gasped.

"Goddamn, do you let everyone treat you like such a slut?" he said, feeling the sweat pour down his body. He grabbed her ankle, held her leg out away from her body so he could get even deeper inside of her. He wanted to reach places no one had ever been before; places no one else would ever reach again. She suddenly laughed, a low, dark sound.

"You like to think you're the only one, don't you? That you're the only one who fucks me good," she replied.

"I *know* I am."

"Then why am I thinking about a baseball player right now?"

He slapped her across the face, hard, then grabbed her neck. She started coming, crying out and dragging her nails down his chest. He wasn't far behind her, pumping everything he had into her before collapsing on top of her chest.

It was a couple minutes before his brain could function again, wrap around what they had just done. He knew he should check on her, make sure she was okay, that what they had just done was actually okay. He pushed himself up over her, but instead of saying kind words, he grabbed her wrists instead, pinned them above her head. Her eyelids fluttered open and she stared up at him. She almost looked stoned. Satisfied. Glowing. *Happy.*

"Were you really thinking of him?" he demanded. She chuckled.

"Jameson, when you fuck me … *nothing else exists but you,*" she breathed. He leaned down, baring his fangs against her neck.

"Good," he whispered. She let out a groan.

"That was so good, Jameson. That is officially, without a doubt, *the best sex I've ever had,"* she said with a laugh.

"Better than *Angier* fucking you in a filthy alley?" he asked. She laughed harder.

"Stupid man. I lied. You were always the best sex I ever had, I just didn't want to admit it."

"I knew it."

He kissed her then. A long, slow kiss. He stretched out on top of her, inside of her. Ran his hands from her head to her thighs, and back up again. She breathed into his mouth, moaned his name, scratched her nails down his back. He started to get hard again, and he backed away. Rolled her onto her stomach, pulled her hips up. A couple minutes later, he laid down flat, pulled her on top of him. Then pushed her off, made her fuck herself for a little while before diving back inside of her.

It was slow, and it was almost sweet, but he liked it. Just being secure in the knowledge that it would be okay to let go and do *whatever* he wanted, made it easily the second best sex either of them had ever had.

Angier Hollingsworth was not in love with Tatum O'Shea, but he did feel a certain kind of possessiveness; he had always thought it was just friendship. Even when she started fucking Satan and stopped fucking Ang, he hadn't thought much about it. Men had come and gone from Tate's life, but Ang had always been a constant.

But then something changed, and he could feel the tide begin to turn. He had been there for the ex girlfriend discovery. Knew about the baseball player. The fight in the kitchen. He had cuddled with her for two of the three days that she had spent hiding in her room. She refused to talk about Jameson, but Ang knew she was thinking about him.

Then Tate went back to Jameson, and Ang didn't see her for a whole week. She texted a lot – apparently she and Satan had reached some new plateau in the interesting sex department, and she was living in orgasm-city. Coming into town to see her best friend was asking too much, and Ang wasn't exactly welcome in the devil's house. He hadn't asked, but he just knew that was true.

He was angry. He felt like he couldn't talk to her about it. He took it out on his coworkers, on the cast and crew of the porno he was working on, on his other friends. It was ridiculous, to be mad at his best friend for being happy, but Ang *was* mad. He knew it was fleeting. Jameson Kane *was* the devil. Tate claimed that she knew what she getting into, that she knew he would never love her or want to be with her. She tried to pretend that she felt the same way. But Ang knew better. He *always* knew better.

He was angry when he went over to her apartment. Tate had borrowed one of the movies he had starred in — *"I want Jameson to see you in action, so he can understand why I'm so infatuated with you"* — but Ang didn't want Jameson to see his movie. Didn't want Jameson knowing anything about him, *at all*. Tate was his friend, she understood where he was coming from – Jameson was a stuck up, rich boy, silver spoon sucking, *asshole*.

Ang was *very* angry.

So when he let himself into Tate's apartment, he wasn't in a very good frame of mind. Being in Tate's room, amongst all her things, smelling her scent, made it worse. He felt it should be him leaving marks on her body, not Satan. He got angrier. And then he walked into the hallway and nearly ran over Rusty, Tate's roommate. Looking down at the short girl, Ang suddenly understood where Tate was coming from, when she said sometimes she wanted to be treated badly during sex, and other times *she* wanted to be the one treating someone badly.

Rus smiled her sweet smile up at him. She was fresh out of the shower, wearing nothing but a towel, her strawberry blonde curls wet. She had a huge crush on him, he knew. He felt nothing for her. Tate had told him that under *no circumstances* was he *ever* allowed to mess with Rus. But he was *angry* at Tate. He wanted to treat her badly, and she wasn't there.

Strawberry shortcake would have to do.

Tate was in the library when her phone rang. She was laying on the floor, on her stomach, skimming through a magazine. Jameson was behind his desk, working on something. Sanders was somewhere in the depths of the house. She was about to go find him when her phone lit up. Rusty's number scrolled across the screen and Tate smiled, lifting her phone to her ear.

"Hey, chickee, I was about to call you," Tate answered.

"*EEEEEEK!* It happened! It finally happened!" Rus started gushing in a voice so loud even Jameson could hear it from across the room. Tate laughed and moved so she was sitting on her butt.

"What happened?" she asked. Jameson rolled his eyes, went back to his papers.

"I finally slept with him! It was amazing, oh my god, Tate. I saw the back of my own eyeballs. His hands, his tongue, I couldn't believe it!" Rus squealed. Tate snickered.

"Who is this sex god, and why haven't I slept with him?" she teased. Jameson snorted.

"That's kinda the weird part – you *have* slept with him," Rus said. Tate stopped smiling.

"Excuse me?" she asked, her voice serious.

"You always said he was so freaky, but Ang was so sweet! He

really took care of me, told me I was so beautiful, that I was so amazing. It *was* amazing. I really think we had a connection!" Rus blurted out in a breathy voice. Tate climbed to her feet.

"You didn't," she breathed.

"Oh, we did. Twice. Once in the bed, and once in the shower. Can you believe it!? *The shower.* I'm trying to become more adventurous," Rus was almost giggling. Tate groaned.

"No, no, no, please tell me you're joking," she begged, but Rus ignored her.

"Look, the reason I'm calling is because I haven't heard from him in a week, not since it happened. I was getting kinda nervous, but then I figured maybe he doesn't have my phone number. I mean, it was really good sex. He said we had something, said he felt it, too. He has to call, right? Could you give him my phone number?" Rus asked, the happiness fading out of her voice. Tate swallowed thickly.

"You know what, I'm going to call him. Right now," she managed to say.

That piece of shit mother fucker. He knew better.

"Thank you, thank you so much. I mean, I don't want to seem clingy. Am I being clingy? It's only been a week, I guess. A *whole* week," Rus' voice began to falter at the end, and the insecurity that she was obviously trying to hide broke through – she sounded close to tears.

"No, you're not clingy. I gotta go, chickee, I'll call you later," Tate assured her. Rus managed a small laugh, then the line went dead.

Tate let out a long shriek. Startled, Jameson leapt to his feet. As she called Ang's phone number, Sanders came running into the room. Both asked her what was wrong, but she ignored them. She pressed the phone to her ear and paced down the room.

"Hey, honey pot, I was just thinking about —," Ang answered.

"*YOU MOTHER FUCKER!*" she screamed into the phone.

"Whoa! Nice greeting! What the fuck is your problem!?" he demanded.

"You! *You* are my problem! How could you do that!? And not say anything to me!? I've talked to you *EVERY DAY THIS WEEK!*" Tate shouted at him. Jameson was now pacing along side her, demanding to know what was wrong. There was a sigh on the other end of the phone.

"It wasn't any of your business, Tate. And it wasn't a big deal," Ang told her.

"Not a big deal!? She's practically picking out her fucking wedding dress! You piece of shit! Why!? I specifically told you that she was off limits! *Why!?*" Tate demanded.

"You don't make all the rules, Tate! You're not in charge of everyone! We're adults, we can fuck if we want to!" he yelled back.

"Sure you can! But hey, here's a thought – if you wanna casually fuck one of my closest friends, maybe *not* tell her that you have a *fucking goddamn special connection! Why would you say that!?*" she shrieked.

"Hey! You're fucking Satan, right? What, I'm not allowed to be the devil sometimes!?" Ang demanded. She gasped.

"Are you fucking serious!? This is because of me!? You're blaming this *on me!?*" she shouted.

"You're goddamn right I am! You fucking threw me over for some asshole because he's a good fuck, which is a really shitty move! *Fuck you,* Tate, I fucking hope you —,"

It all went downhill from there. She began screaming obscenities into the phone. He shouted them right back at her. When she was red in the face and gasping for air between rants, Jameson ripped the phone out of her hand. He handed it over to Sanders, who put it to his ear and walked out of the room. Tate let out another shriek, slapping her hands against Jameson's chest before falling against him, pressing her face into his shoulder.

"What the fuck is going on!?" he demanded.

"Ang. Slept with. Rus," she managed to pant out. Jameson went very still.

"You're this upset over him sleeping with someone else?" he asked. She gave him a violent shove.

"Jesus christ, none of you want to actually be with me, but all of you are jealous of every single fucking move I make!" she snapped. He put his hands on either side of her face, forced her to look straight at him.

"You wanna take your anger out on me, fine. Let's do this," he offered. She glared at him for a second longer, then her bottom lip began to tremble. Her eyes filled up with tears.

"I'm *upset* because he promised he wouldn't. Rus isn't like us, she really *is* a nice, normal girl. She's always had a crush on Ang. He doesn't care about her. He made her all these promises, said all these sweet things to her, and then he just walked out. Dined and dashed. She thinks they're soulmates. He just did it to get back at me," Tate explained.

"Get back at you for what?" Jameson asked. Her eyes slid away from him. He shook her gently. "Talk to me. Get back at you for what?"

She sighed and leaned into him, wrapping her arms around his middle. She could feel his surprise – while a very sexual person, Tate wasn't the most affectionate person. She wasn't prone to hugs; except with Sanders. But she squeezed Jameson tightly and decided it was now or never.

I just don't care anymore.

"He's getting back at me ... for falling for *you* instead of him," she whispered.

14

THE TENSION BETWEEN THEM GREW to be almost unbareable. Tatum hadn't thought that Jameson would take her confession so hard. She hadn't said she was in love with him. She hadn't asked for marriage or babies or anything – she knew what was going on between them, knew it was mostly one sided. She was okay with that, or at least that's what she told herself. And she told him, too, right after he had let go of her and stepped away, his face hard and pale.

She spent the whole next week telling him it was okay, but it didn't seem to matter. Conversation didn't flow between them the way it used to. He became prone to sitting in silence behind his desk, and when she would look up, it was often to find him staring at her. Frowning.

Not a good sign.

She asked Sanders if anything had been said to him, but nothing had – Jameson was keeping silent on his thoughts. She began counting the days, waiting for him to tell her it was over. She would wait till he said something, she wouldn't throw in the towel. She would finally win one of their games.

Strangely, though, it didn't effect their sex life. If anything, he went harder. The day after her little confession, Tate was coming down the stairs when suddenly he was behind her, a hand in her hair, forcing her against a wall and her shorts down around her ankles. A day later, she was held down on the couch in the library. The nights were the same – sex, sex, and just when she was about to fall alseep, a little more sex.

His mouth was filthy and his hand heavy. It was like she had opened a flood gate. She couldn't tell whether she was being punished for her confession, or rewarded. She certainly wasn't complaining. She encouraged him, pushed him to – and *over* – the edge as often as she could; wanted to make it all as good for him as possible.

*I want him to remember me. I want every woman after me to be compared, and found lacking. He **will** rememeber me.*

At the end of the week, as she was bent over his desk, trying to catch her breath, he let the hammer drop. Her panties were in a ball on the floor, her skirt a bunched up mess around her waist. Her scalp was stinging, as well as her ass. She was on cloud nine when he backed away, sat in a chair, and sighed.

"I'm leaving," Jameson said in a low voice. She held her breath for a second.

"Where are you going?" she asked, still laying flat against the desk.

"I have to go to Berlin," he replied.

"How long will you be gone?" she pressed. A long pause.

"I don't know."

Tate took a deep breath. Licked her lips. Stood up and put her clothing to rights. She didn't think it was fair. If she had known that would be the last time they were going to have sex, she would've been more assertive. Insisted on facing him, looking into his eyes. He had such amazing eyes. She walked over to the other chair and sat down as well. The fire was roaring, like always, but she didn't mind the heat. Welcomed the sizzle against her skin. Wondered if Sanders had anymore xanax.

"Is this it?" Tate whispered. Neither of them looked at each other.

"Do you want it to be?" Jameson asked.

"Obviously not. But if you do, it's fine. I'll go pack my stuff, and when you come home, you won't even know I was ever here," she tried to joke.

"Tate."

"We'll have to work out a custody schedule for Sandy, though," she laughed. "He's half mine now. I want to —,"

"*Tatum.*"

"What?" she asked, finally looking at him. The wing of the chair hid his face.

"This isn't a joke," he told her. She nodded.

"I know that, I'm just trying to make you comfortable. It's okay, Jameson. I promise. I'm okay," she assured him. He sighed.

"Why are you so good to me?" he whispered.

"Because you were so bad to me," she teased.

"Do you want to stay?" he asked, and she could see him turn his head towards her. The bottom of his face became visible. His strong jaw, stern mouth. She shivered.

"I don't want to stay where I'm not welcome," she answered his question sideways.

"You're *always* welcome, Tate. Just … you have to know, I'm not ready for what you want," he told her. She nodded.

"I know that. I'm not asking for one single thing. I never did. Maybe we should just end this, go our separate ways. It's kinda sick, right?" she tried to laugh, but choked on the sound. He suddenly stood up, walked over to her chair, and pulled her up as well.

"I don't think it's sick," Jameson breathed, pulling her into a hug. "I care about you, Tate. I hate you, and you ruined things a little, but

I care about you *so fucking much*. How did you do that to me?"

"I'm special that way," she whispered, a tear slipping down her cheek.

"This was all supposed to be a game. What happened?" he asked. She shook her head.

"I have no idea. Maybe you weren't mean enough," she managed a laugh.

"Maybe I was *too* mean. You are a freak like that," Jameson replied, and she really laughed.

"Shut up."

"I don't know what to do with you. I don't know what I want. But I don't want you to go. Wait for me?" he asked in a soft voice, his lips brushing the top of her head. She took a deep breath.

"I waited for you for seven years. I can wait a little longer," she answered. He chuckled.

"I hope I don't take as long this time. Will you be here when I get back?"

"If you want me to be."

"*I do.*"

"Then I'll be here."

"Why can't you be this compliant in bed?" he asked.

Satan's on a roll tonight.

"It wouldn't be as fun," she replied.

"You have ruined me, Tatum O'Shea," he told her. "Completely wrecked me."

Her breath caught in her throat.

"It's only fair, you ruined me first," she whispered. He finally pulled away from her, held her at arms lengths. His eyes traveled over her form, and she wondered what he saw. What he *really* saw in her.

"I leave early tomorrow morning. You're welcome to stay here at the house, otherwise I'm going to have Sanders close it up," he said, his voice all business as he let her go.

Close it up?

"Sandy isn't going with you?" she asked. He shook his head.

"No. He hates long flights, hates Germany. He'll stay here with you, or at a place in Boston," Jameson explained. She sank into her chair.

"And you have no idea how long you'll be?" she asked. He shrugged.

"Two weeks. Maybe a month," he told her.

Tate let out a sigh of relief. That wasn't so bad. She had been expecting him to say something like six months. She didn't know if she could handle that, but a month wasn't so bad. She could do that, go that long without him.

"I'll stay in my apartment. Or hey, if I get lonely for you I'll just go shack up with Sandy, '*mini-you*,'" she teased. He glared down at her.

"Better not. He tells me everything, you know, and I *will* be coming back at some point," he warned. She took a deep breath.

"So. What are the rules?" she asked.

"Pardon?"

"Rules. We have rules for everything, if you haven't noticed. Do the same rules apply?" she asked. He nodded.

"Sure. You can fuck your way through Boston," he said. She snorted.

"*One guy*. I've slept with one other guy this whole time. You've fucked half the country," Tate pointed out.

"That's why I have to go to another continent. Gotta get more stories for you, gotta keep you turned on," he told her.

"You do that just fine, all on your own, Mr. Kane," she assured him. He smirked and leaned over her, his hands on her arm rests.

"Tell me you'll miss me," he demanded. She nodded.

"I will miss you."

"Tell me you'll think about me, if you fuck anyone else."

"I always do."

"Tell me you won't fall in love with anyone else, while I'm gone."

All her breath flew out of her body.

"Not possible, so not a problem," she whispered.

He kissed her. Didn't touch her anywhere else, just her mouth. Slowly and sweetly, lips brushing over hers, his tongue sweeping its way past her own. She moaned, brought a hand up to the side of his face. *This*. More than anything, she wanted to remember him like this; she loved his biting words and his stinging hand, but his kiss. His kiss gave her hope. He kissed her for several long moments and then pulled away.

"Alright, Tatum. Give me a night that'll have me dreaming about you the whole time I'm gone," he told her.

She smiled and slipped to her knees in front of him.

This, she could do. This, she was very good at.

Love, however, was a completely different story.

15

A MONTH WASN'T SO BAD. She could get a lot done in a month.

Tatum broke the bad news to Rus. Explained to her that Ang just wasn't a relationship kind of guy. Tate didn't play it, but she showed Rus a DVD of one of his movies. The cover was enough to make Rus turn a little green. So prim and proper. There were some tears, and a general cursing of men, but she got over it.

Tate wasn't ready to call Ang yet, though. She was still so mad at him. The things he had said to her, the way he had spoken to her. She would wait till after Jameson got home, then she would talk to Ang. She counted down the days.

One really shocking day was when Nick Castille called her; the baseball player she had screwed in her bar. He had gotten her number from her manager. Totally inappropriate and against the rules, but she was flattered.

Tate was lonely and bored, so she agreed to dinner. They had a good time, but she stared at him when he asked if they could go on a "real" date sometime. Nick was extremely good looking, and several times while they ate, people asked him for his autograph. He was also really nice to her, very respectful. It was a novel experience, and she knew he was a catch. But she politely declined his offer – she was holding out for her lord and savior, Satan. Nick seemed a little sad, but he smiled at her, and said he could settle for being her friend.

And he meant it. He got her box seats to one of his games. They went out to eat often, and even took in a couple shows. They got along surprisingly well, despite being from completely different backgrounds and living completely opposite lives. Tate enjoyed his friendship. But she didn't push it – she never went back to his place, and never brought him back to hers. Jameson had never once slept with the same girl twice during their relationship. It wasn't a rule, really, but Tate didn't want to be the one to test whether or not it should be. She would respect Jameson's wishes and actions. She would wait for him.

She didn't speak with him at all, though. Not once. Early on, he texted her a couple times. Mostly filthy things, to remind her who was boss. A couple to ask after Sanders. A couple to remind her of her promises. One to say he missed her. Tate stared at that one for days on end. But then the texts stopped all together, and she found herself hovering near her phone, constantly checking to see if he had sent anything.

When did I become this girl? I surrendered to him without even realizing it.

But nothing, however, was as shocking as what happened during her third week of waiting.

Tate was puttering around her apartment. Rus was at one of her vet tech classes. Sanders was holed up in his penthouse hotel room, doing some translating work for Jameson. Nick was at an away game. Tate was bored. At first she had been afraid that without Jameson paying for everything, she would starve to death, or worse – have to go back to temping. But of course, he thought of everything, and Sanders had supplied her with a steady flow of money. She felt like she was whoring for both of them, but she didn't mind too much. They were both very important to her, so it was worth it.

She was on her phone, getting ready to dial out for Chinese food, when someone knocked on her door.

"Just a second!" she hollered, sliding into the living room. She peeked through the peep hole, but couldn't tell who it was; it was someone wearing a big, floppy sun hat. A woman, she assumed. Tate yanked open the door. "I have religion, so I don't —,"

Her sister turned around to face her. Ellie was wearing huge sunglasses that weren't doing a very good job of hiding a black eye. Her arm was in a cast. And even though it hadn't been that long, her stomach looked noticeably bigger. They stared at each other for a while, till Ellie started to tremble.

"I didn't know where else to go," she whispered.

"Come in, come in," Tate urged, guiding her sister into her tiny apartment. Ellie looked around, then burst out crying.

After Jameson's little O'Shea family reunion, things had apparently gone downhill for Ellie. A broken jaw didn't slow Robert down at all. There had been more fights. More smacks. She thought she could handle it, but then he had pushed Ellie down a flight of stairs. That was where she drew the line. He could do what he wanted to her, but he couldn't hurt the baby. If he could treat an unborn child like that, how would he treat the child when it was standing right in front of him? She didn't want to find out.

"I'm sorry, I know you hate me. I know I ruined your life, but I just didn't know what else to do," Ellie sobbed. Tate grabbed her hand and dragged her to her bedroom.

"I don't hate you, Ellie. I don't even know you. And you didn't ruin my life. My life is pretty awesome. You saved me," Tate told her as she laid her sister down.

"I wish someone could have saved me," Ellie cried. Tate frowned and laid on the bed next to her, got right up behind her and spooned her.

"I wasn't there. I could've called, I could've checked on you guys. I could've saved you," she whispered.

It took Ellie a while to calm down, but finally her breathing evened out. She fell asleep. Tate crawled out of the bed and called Sanders. Appraised him of the situation. He told her that he was "*on it*", though she wasn't sure what that meant. She *really* wanted to call Ang, but they hadn't made up yet. She hadn't spoken to him at all, so it would be awkward, and worse, she worried it would come off as her using him. She decided to make some tea instead, and carried it into her room.

"I'm awake now," her sister mumbled. Tate smiled and knelt next to the bed. Her sister sat up to take the coffee mug and Tate's eyes wandered down to her belly.

"Have you picked out any names yet?" she asked. Ellie sighed.

"Mathias if it's a boy," she said. Tate had to laugh.

"Good old Daddy probably loves that. What if it's a girl?" she asked. Ellie chewed on her bottom lip.

"I was thinking maybe Tatum," she whispered. Tate's eyebrows shot up.

"You're fucking with me," she spat out. Ellie shook her head.

"I want her to be strong. Stronger than her mother. More like you. I always wished I could be more like you," Ellie explained. Tate felt her eyes fill with tears and she forced out a laugh.

"If this gets any sweeter, *I'm* going to have morning sickness, all over you," she joked, and Ellie laughed as well.

Sanders showed up later in the night. He didn't say anything to anyone, just breezed through the living room, giving his tight lipped smile to Ellie. Even though he'd never been there, he lead the way straight into Tatum's room. Tate followed after him and closed the door behind them.

"What's up?" Tate asked, kind of surprised to see him.

"Mr. Kane sent me. He wanted to know how you were," Sanders answered. She laughed.

"*Mr. Kane* could just call me, himself. Tell him I'm fine," she replied. Sanders didn't laugh, though. If anything, his mouth got tighter.

"We were worried that her husband might come here and try to seek revenge. We both feel it would be best if you went to stay in a hotel," Sanders told her. She laughed even louder.

"How would Robert even know where I lived? He thinks Ellie and I hate each other; she had to steal my address from my mom's contact book. I'm not leaving my home," Tate informed him.

"We would feel much more comfortable if —," he started, but she held up a hand.

"*We?* Let's tell the truth, Sandy. It's you, isn't it. Just you. Did you even talk to him?" she demanded. He nodded.

"Yes, I did. He was very upset," Sanders assured her.

"But did he really say that? That he wanted me to go to a hotel?" she pressed. Sanders was silent for a while.

"If he'd had a chance, I know he would have. I know him very well, I know what he would say in these situations. He was very busy when I called," he explained. Tate started to get a little ticked off.

"Busy, huh. Too busy to talk to you about my '*situation*'. Too busy to talk to *me*. Has he said when he's coming home?" she asked, folding her arms over her chest.

"Yes. The end of this week."

Tate was shocked.

"Wow. Were you planning on telling me?" she demanded. Sanders looked away from her.

Uh oh.

"Yes. He wanted me to let you know, there is going to be a party at the house. Sunday. All the partners will be there, people from his offices in New York and Los Angeles and Berlin; everywhere. Black tie. He gets into town that same day," Sanders said quickly.

"Shit, that's cutting it a little close, isn't it?" she pointed out. He shrugged.

"He has me taking care of everything. If his flight can't make it, the party will just go on without him. He told me to ask you to buy a dress," Sanders told her. She laughed.

"Of course he did. A fancy dress, for a fancy party. Is there something you're not telling me?" Tate demanded. Sanders usually had the best poker face of anyone she knew. But now, there was something off. He was back to not quite meeting her eyes.

"Ms. O'Shea, I … I've enjoyed our time together here in Boston. You are a good friend to me. I am going back to the house tomorrow and will be staying there. Would you like to join me?" he said quickly, his voice almost shy sounding. She was touched.

"Why Sandy, are you inviting me to move in with you?" she teased. He blanched.

"No. But your company would be greatly appreciated, as always," he told her. She laughed and pulled him in for a hug.

"Of course I'll come with you. Help me calm Ellie down, and I'll go anywhere with you," she whispered.

And then shockingly, his arms came around her and Sanders hugged her back.

Something wasn't right. Something most definitely, positively, wasn't right.

Tate could feel it in the air. Jameson's house felt like home to her, and she loved Sanders, but she could just tell; *something was not right*. Sanders wouldn't tell her anything, and she'd had no communication from Jameson. She even figured out the time difference and called him once – the first time she had *ever* called him, in the entire time they'd known each other.

He didn't answer.

By Saturday afternoon, she was a wreck. The house had been turned upside down by event planners. Sanders was running around, helping to get everything ready. Tate hovered in the background. Helped where she was needed, asked Sanders if there was anything she could do, but he had practically become a mime. He wouldn't speak, not if he didn't have to. Finally, she cracked and texted Jameson.

Is this a game?

It was hours before he replied. She was laying in his bed, ready to go to sleep, when her phone dinged.

Yes.

She sat up, turned on a light.

What are the rules?

No more rules.

That sounds dangerous.

I thought you liked danger.

She chewed on her bottom lip, glanced around the room.

What is going on?

But he ignored her question and asked one of his own.

Where are you, right now?

Your room.

In my bed?

Yes.

Good.

What is going on?

See you soon, baby girl.

He wouldn't respond to anymore of her texts. She stayed awake for the rest of the night.

The next evening, some of Jameson's colleagues showed up early for the party, made themselves at home in his library. Tate got ready, wandered around the house. She was coming out of the kitchen, struggling to open a jar of peanut butter, when laughter burst out of the library. She stopped by the door.

"Clever man. Keeping girls on two continents," one was guffawing.

Tate's breathing doubled.

"Which one do you think he likes better?" another voice.

"Well, the girl here seems wilder, more his tastes. I bet she's an animal in the sack."

She nodded to herself. Sounded like her.

"But Pet's more polished, more refined. You can take Pet to parties; you take the other girl to bed."

Tate pressed herself against the library door. Fuck being subtle.

"Yes, but what do you do with both of them at once?"

"Sounds like a hell of a party!"

Bawdy laughter.

"I guess we'll find out, they'll be here tonight."

"What's-her-name is already here."

"Jameson and Pet got in on the six o'clock flight. They should be here any time now."

There was a sharp ringing in her ear and Tate stumbled away from the door. Dropped the peanut butter. When she turned around, Sanders was standing behind her. They stared at each other. Just stared, for about a minute solid.

Traitor.

She took off running up the stairs. Sanders thundered after her, calling out her name. She had never heard him speak in such a loud tone before; any other time, and she would've been in awe. She ran down the hall, almost biting it in her heels once. She skated through Jameson's door just before Sanders and managed to shut it in his face, turning the lock. She dashed out onto a balcony that had been converted into a sun room. Jameson kept his computer out there. She had never bothered with it before, never had a reason to.

Tate knew Sanders had keys to everything and would be in the room in no time, so she acted quickly. Typed Jameson's name into Google. More of the same info came up, so she just immediately went to the images tab.

She was shocked to see a lot more pictures of herself – she had never noticed any photographers anywhere they went. Her and Jameson walking out of his office building; her and Jameson eating lunch; her and Sanders, laughing next to him outside of a movie the-atre; her and Jameson kissing while he held an umbrella over her. She couldn't figure out why at first. Why were there so many all of the sudden? She clicked on one so it would take her to the website of origin, then gasped at the headline.

Who Will Financial Mogul Jameson Kane Choose? A Sexy American or A Danish Beauty?

Tate scrolled down. Several of the photos of them together were in the article. But the other pictures interested her more. There were a couple old ones of him and Pet together, but a couple of very new ones, too. Them entering a hotel together, exiting the same hotel to-gether. Him holding a car door open for her. His arm around her waist as they entered a clothing boutique.

It was a German tabloid. Tate learned that Pet lived part of the time in Berlin, that's why there was a lot of interest. Some small time rag-reporter had noticed that Jameson was tooling around Berlin with Pet, then discovered the photos of Tate and Jameson online. Boom. Story. Sex. Scandal. Intrigue. Hell, even Tate would want to read something like that.

*If it wasn't actually about **me**. At least they called me sexy.*

She was scrolling through another article when Sanders finally opened the door and strode into the room. He reached for the com-puter mouse and she batted his hand away. A minor slapping war ensued for a couple moments before she leapt out of the chair. He reached for her arm, but she pushed him away.

"How could you not tell me!?" Tate demanded, circling him. He looked upset.

"I couldn't. I'm very sorry, Ms. O'Shea," Sanders replied.

"*Fuck you!* We're supposed to be friends! How long have you known about them!?" she shouted.

"For about two weeks. I advised him that it was a poor choice," he told her.

"Oh, you *advised him*, how kind of you. Did you know he was bringing her here tonight?" she asked. His look went from upset to pained.

"Yes," Sanders answered softly. She gasped.

"How could you let me come here? I thought we were friends. How could you do this to me?" Tate whispered.

"*Because I told him to.*"

They both turned to see Jameson standing in the middle of the bedroom. He took off his suit jacket and then rolled up the sleeves of his shirt. Took off his watch and threw it onto the side table. Sanders cleared his throat.

"Sir, I think you owe it to Ms. —,"

"*Leave.*"

Glancing at Tate once, Sanders walked out of the room. Tate struggled to even out her breathing and entered the bedroom proper. Jameson was carrying his suitcase into his closet. There was a clattering of hangers and he walked back out with a new shirt in his hands.

"Why?" Tate whispered. He lifted his eyes to hers. A pair of blue icicles. It felt like it had been longer than a month since she had last seen him. She felt like she was looking at a stranger.

Did I ever know him?

"What's that, baby girl?" Jameson asked, changing into the fresh shirt.

"Don't call me that!" she snapped. He chuckled.

"I call you anything I want."

"Not anymore. Why are you doing this? What did I do to you?" she asked.

"It's all a game, isn't it? I thought you liked games," Jameson said, throwing the worn shirt onto his bed.

"Fuck your games," Tate hissed.

"See, now that sounds more like you. It was a very long flight, baby girl, and I could really use something to relax me. Feel like getting on your knees?" he asked. She guffawed.

"Not fucking likely. Ask your *girlfriend* to do that for you," she told him.

"But I don't have a girlfriend."

"Really? Seems to me there is a five-foot-eleven '*Danish beauty*' who would argue that point," Tate pointed out. He sighed.

"There you go again, making assumptions. Would you like to meet her? You'd probably get along," he offered.

"Why are you doing this!? What happened that made you so mad!? I waited for you! Just like you said! Why did you ask me to wait if you were just going to bring her home!?" Tate yelled at him.

"You don't like seeing my picture in the tabloids, right? Well, I like it even less," he suddenly said. She was lost.

"What?" she asked.

"I don't like being made a fool of, Tate. And that's what I feel like you did," he informed her.

"*What the fuck are you talking about!?*" she shrieked.

"You're upset about pictures of me and Pet online? In the tabloids? How about pictures of *you* and a certain baseball player, in the fucking social pages of the goddamn Boston Globe!? How about seeing those on the fucking internet? You and him together, *everywhere*. Pictures of you and me are already out there, and suddenly I'm hearing from people I hardly know that a girlfriend I don't technically have is *fucking a goddamn Red Sox!*" Jameson yelled at her. Tate started laughing.

"Are you fucking shitting me!? Fuck this, I'm getting the fuck out of here. Fuck your party, fuck your supermodel, and *fuck you*," she swore, stomping past him. He grabbed her arm, his grip like a vice.

"Oh, you're not going anywhere, baby girl. Because it's all a game, and if you walk away now, you lose," he warned her.

"*Fuck your games*. I don't want to play games. You're really upset about that? I can't believe it. *The Great Jameson Kane*, jealous. I can't fucking believe it," Tate snarled at him.

"Watch how you talk to me," he warned her.

"*Fuck you*. He and I were just friends, you asshole. *We're friends*. You go off to fuck the entire country of Germany, and I can't make a new fucking friend? You wanna know the truth? He asked me out. He didn't try to sleep with me. He wanted to see *me*. *Date* me. And I'm a stupid bitch, because I turned him down! I was stupid enough to think I had something better coming home!" Tate yelled.

"I certainly won't argue with the stupid bitch part," Jameson agreed.

"Go fuck yourself, Kane."

"I think that's your job."

"You're jealous! All this elaborate planning, hiding from me, bringing her back here, making a scene. You're like a girl, Kane. *A goddamn pussy*," she snapped at him, disdain dripping from her words.

He roughly dragged her across the room, backed her up and slammed her against the wall by the door. She struggled to free her arm, shoving and pushing at him. He moved his hand to her throat and pinned her in place.

"I told you to watch how you fucking speak to me," Jameson growled, his face near hers.

"Like I give two shits. Was it worth it? Is she still a good fuck? I hope so. I hope she's *so good* that she finally does trick you into marrying her. I hope she fucks you all the way into a horrible fucking marriage, and then takes all your goddamn money. *I hope she's that good of a fuck!*" Tate yelled, pulling at his wrist. His fingers squeezed harder on her neck, but she didn't show any reaction.

"She was never even half as good as you. But maybe we should have Ang fuck her, really do a cross-comparison, get more feedback," Jameson suggested.

"Why stop there? How about we broaden the circle. There's an awful lot of men down there, and I haven't been fucked in a really long time. I'm sure I'll get rave reviews, much better than a psychotic supermodel," Tate said in a quiet voice. He narrowed his eyes.

"If you're fucking anyone at this party, it will be me," he informed her. She laughed.

"That's not going to happen, but maybe we can do the next closest thing. How about I fuck Sanders. I'm sure I could turn his world inside out. Hell, maybe even steal him away from you. Who knows, maybe he'll be a better fuck than you."

The words had barely left her mouth when Jameson put his fist through the wall, right next to her head. Clean through the sheet rock. She was glad he hadn't hit a stud – that would have put a damper on the party, real quick. He stared at her, his eyes blazing, a muscle ticking in his jaw, his fingers continuing to squeeze her neck. She glared right back, not moving a muscle.

"Don't ever fucking talk about him like that again," he whispered.

"You don't get to tell me what to do, Kane. Not anymore. *Not ever again,*" she whispered back. Jameson squeezed her neck tight one last time, then let go, backing away from her.

"We can talk about this later. Go downstairs. People are expecting you to be here. Be cordial. Be fucking polite. And don't say one goddamn word to Sanders," he told her, then yanked open his bedroom door, striding into the hall.

Tate gasped in air and choked on a sob. She brought the back of her wrist to her mouth, trying to hold it all in; it didn't work too well. She wasn't sure what to do. She couldn't go home, not without Sanders to drive her, and she didn't think he'd leave the party. Didn't trust him, anyway. A taxi would take forever to get there, and she didn't have any money. She sucked in another breath of air, held it in, then let it out slowly. She straightened out her dress, wiped underneath her eyes.

You can do this. You're Tatum O'Shea. He didn't break you last time. He won't break you this time.

She went downstairs. She was cordial. She was polite. She got a lot of sympathetic looks from women. A lot of lascivious glances from men. She caught a glimpse of the Danish beauty at one point, but the house was big and Tate knew it well. She fled to another room.

She drank, *a lot.* She flirted with anyone who looked remotely male. Sanders tried to talk to her at one point, but she looked right through him and walked away. She chugged whiskey neat. Snuck the Johnny Walker Blue out of Jameson's personal liquor cabinet and finished it off. She laughed at everything everyone said. Kissed people on the cheek, toasted to good health, gave hugs that were way too intimate to people she didn't really know, though none of the men were complaining.

She actually drank the bar out of Jack Daniel's, so she made her way towards the kitchen in search of more. Jameson usually kept some stocked for her. She wanted to get comfortably numb so she could pass out in the guest house, then hitchhike home in the morning, where she could cry until she died. Sounded like a great plan.

She turned into the kitchen, then backed up so quickly, she rammed into the door jam, ricocheted off, and nearly fell into the hall. She scooted behind the frame, then peeked into the kitchen. Jameson was standing with his back to her, head down, both hands resting flat on the counter. A tall, exceptionally beautiful brunette stood next to him. She was speaking softly in what sounded like German. He shook his head occasionally, murmuring things back in the same language.

I didn't know he spoke German. That could've been hot – dirty talk in another language.

When Pet leaned in close to him, pressed her front to his back and whispered in his ear, Tate couldn't take it anymore. She had imagined Jameson in all sorts of positions with women, but never simple, affectionate ones. It was too much. She choked back a sob and stumbled away.

There was a half drunken bottle of Jack in the library, from their long ago last night together. Tate grabbed it and dragged herself upstairs. She wasn't entirely sure of what her plan was, till she was standing outside Sanders' door. She just wanted the pain to stop. She wanted to be numb.

Xanax.

She walked into his room. It was a huge space, almost bigger than Jameson's room. She headed straight for the bathroom, began yanking open drawers and rummaging through them. She found the pills in a bottom drawer, clearly labeled. It took her a while to get the stupid childproof lid off, but she did it. She chugged some whiskey into her mouth and popped in two pills. She didn't want to overdue it – she didn't have a death wish. She just wanted to feel still. Quiet. She swallowed everything and dropped her head back, sighing. She stood that way for several minutes, letting a calm fall over her.

"I knew you were a good time girl, but I had no idea you were this wild," someone chuckled from the doorway. She didn't lift her head, just rolled it towards the voice. What's-his-name. Dunn. Jameson's partner. Wensle-waddle-whatever Dunn.

"I'm wilder than you can even imagine," Tate whispered at him. He scooted closer so they were both crowded into the bathroom's doorway.

"Sounds like a good time. Would you like to have a good time?" he asked. She laughed.

"Sorry. I think I've had enough good times to last me a lifetime," she answered, finally turning to face him.

"Pity. I think we could be really good together. Jameson told me about you," he said. She lifted an eyebrow.

"Did he now," she replied softly.

"Yeah. Told me how you like things a little crazy. A lot rough. Now that Pet's back in the picture, I thought you might need someone else to, uh … *provide* those things for you," Dunn said.

"He told you that," she whispered.

Tate was offended, but it was slipping away. The xanax was taking control. She didn't really care. Jameson thought she was a whore. Jameson broke his promise. Jameson set up an elaborate plan to cruelly humiliate her. What was one more log on the fire? Jameson told all his friends what a deviant freak she was in bed.

I just don't care.

"So. I think, that, we could have a *really* fun time together, you and I. I might even be better than Jameson," Dunn teased.

No one is better than Jameson.

"Sure," she blurted out. Dunn looked surprised.

"Seriously?" he checked.

"I just got dumped tonight, right? Very publicly. What could be better than a revenge fuck? Sounds like a plan, let's suit up," Tate laughed. Dunn's hands went to his belt buckle, started pulling it apart.

Her stomach dipped to the right and she wondered if she would vomit. Hoped she vomited on Dunn. She felt like she was standing outside of herself. She swayed back and forth, wondered if that would help her find her ghost.

I want Ang. Where's Ang?

"So just how rough do you like it, baby?" the guy growled at her, working his pants down his hips. Tate laughed again. It was hollow sounding. Alien. She glanced around. Who was laughing?

"Hit me with your best shot," she chuckled.

He backhanded her so hard that she spun around and her head crashed into the mirror, breaking it.

That's definitely gonna leave a mark.

She groaned, not even sure what the fuck was going on, when he grabbed the back of her dress and slammed her flat against the granite sink top. She let out a cry as her jaw smacked down hard.

*Okay, there's rough, and then there's **rough**. I may not be boss-bitch enough for this.*

"You're so fucking hot. I knew the first time I saw you, I had to fuck you. *So fucking hot,*" Dunn groaned, clawing at her underwear and dragging it down her legs.

Maybe this isn't a really super good idea.

"Wait, wait," she mumbled. Her tongue felt heavy and thick.

"You're gonna love this, I promise," he grunted, pushing her dress out of the way. She tried to push away from the counter, but her movements were slow and clumsy.

"Wait, I don't want —,"

Tate cried out as he pushed inside of her. She wasn't exactly pre-pared for sex, and Mr. Dunn apparently wasn't interested in foreplay. It was rough, and it hurt. She gripped onto the edge of the sink and bit down on her tongue so hard, she tasted blood. She wanted to say stop, but every time she opened her mouth, only a sob came out. A piece of mirror was biting into her cheek and she ground her face down harder, welcoming the pain. But then, suddenly, she was being pulled backwards.

"*No no no no no no,*" she chanted, trying to grip onto the sink so she could break away. But she couldn't really flex her fingers and she slid backwards, falling to the floor and landing on her butt. She fell back against the door and then forward, winding up in a heap halfway in the bedroom and halfway in the bathroom. She tried to focus, but the room was so dark and she was so drunk, she couldn't figure out what was going on at first.

Wrestling. Two people were wrestling. She started to laugh. Jameson was wrestling with Mr. Dunn. They were shouting, but she couldn't tell what they were saying. Jameson sounded *very* angry. She glanced down at herself, realized what a fright she must look. Managed to wiggle her underwear back on, push her dress back down, all while still folded up on the floor.

When she looked back up, the wrestling was over. Mr. Dunn had disappeared. Jameson was slowly walking towards her. She could only see his legs from her position, so she tilted her head back. Back. *Waaaay* back, taking him all in. He was such an imposing man, a person needed outstanding vision to see him. She blinked up at him.

"I fell down," Tate whispered.

"Yes. Yes you did, baby girl," Jameson whispered back. She hiccuped.

"Did you win?" she asked. He sighed and squatted down in front of her.

"For once, I did not. You dealt the last hand. Had all the chips. Did you invite him in here?" Jameson asked in a gentle voice. Tate shook her head and nearly threw up.

"No. He came after," she replied.

"After what?"

"Afterrrrr ..."

"Did you want him to do that?"

"I thought I did."

"You asked him to have sex with you?" Jameson questioned her. Questions. So many questions. Q. What a strange letter.

"No. He asked me. I can't feel my lips," she told him.

"And you said yes," Jameson whispered. She nodded.

"Yes. You have a Danish beauty. I'd like a financier of my own," she laughed. Jameson smiled down at her.

"Wait right here, please," he requested, then he left the room.

She laid back down on the floor. Curled up into the fetal position. She was pretty sure she was crying. What had she done? *What had she done!?* Something horrible, terrible. Jameson was Satan, but she was worse. He hurt other people, which was bad. She hurt herself, which was *so much* worse.

All I have is me.

Jameson came back into the room. Tate managed to push herself upright again, but had to keep her hands planted on the floor to keep from swaying. He squatted down again, and she looked up at him. Narrowed her eyes. He had something in his arms, bundles of something. He began dropping them on the ground, all in front of her. She looked down, tried to focus.

Oh my, that is a lot of money.

When there were no more bundles, she looked back up at him. He had his hands clasped together.

"Eight weeks. $4,000 a week. Your services are no longer required, Ms. O'Shea. Please get the fuck out of my house," he said, oh-so-politely.

Tate held her tears in check until he left the room. Then she sobbed. Climbed to her feet. Stared at the money. She stumbled back into the bathroom. Tried not to look at the broken mirror or the blood on the counter. She grabbed the bottle of Jack from off the floor, then swiped the bottle of pills as well. Then, on her way out of the bathroom, she grabbed a set of keys off a hook by the door. When she left the room, she kicked the piles of money out of the way.

Tate didn't want to see anybody, didn't want anyone to see her. She took a set of back stairs, previously service stairs. Had to go out a back door and cut around the side of the house to get to the driveway. No small feat, while borderline black out drunk and wearing five inch heels. When she got to the line of cars, she pushed the car lock button till she saw the Bentley's lights blink.

"Thank *God*," she groaned, shambling towards it. She had her hand on the door handle when there was a crunching sound.

"What are you doing!?" a voice yelled from behind her, and then she was being yanked in a circle. Sanders was holding her arms.

"Sandy!" she cried out, falling to the side. He wrapped an arm around her waist, pulled her upright and then leaned her against the car.

"Oh my god, what happened?" he asked, holding her face towards the light. She pulled away.

"Oh Sandy, didn't he tell you? I won! I finally, finally won. Chalk one up to the little guy. I'm going home now, I don't know if I'll ever see you again," Tate told him, moving and yanking open the car door.

"I don't think that's such a good idea," Sanders said quickly, grabbing her arm again.

"Oh, I really do. *Mr. Kane* personally asked me to leave. He's a very sore loser. Please keep intouch," she asked, trying to drop into the seat. Sanders pulled her up again.

"Please. I'm begging you. Just stay here," he asked. She pushed him away.

"I wouldn't stay here another minute, not even if you paid me," she informed him. He gripped her arms hard.

"Tatum," he said her name sharply. That got her attention. Sanders had never, ever said her first name before; she wanted to cry again. "*Don't do this.*"

"I have to do this," she replied, then shoved him as hard as she could. He stumbled over the loose pebbles and she slipped into the car, locking the doors. Sanders pounded on the roof but she ignored him and started up the car. Wiggled her fingers at him as she drove off.

See. This isn't hard. Way easier than playing with Jameson Kane.

16

"*YOU HAVE TO STOP HER.*"

Jameson looked up. Sanders had just burst into the library. He looked like a ghost.

"Excuse me?" Jameson asked, leaning back in his office chair.

"Tatum. She just left," Sanders explained. Jameson chuckled.

"I think that's probably for the best," he replied. Sanders shook his head.

"No. She's drunk, Jameson," he stressed. Jameson frowned.

"She'll be fine."

"She's not fine! She just to—,"

Jameson slammed his hand down on the top of his desk.

"Don't fucking talk about her again! I don't want to hear her name, *anything*. Don't even reference her!" he yelled. Sanders stared at him for a minute.

"You don't mean any of this. You need her. What you did was *wrong*. Go find her, and apologize," he said in an even voice. Jameson was shocked.

"I'm not apologizing for shit. Yeah, I did a shitty thing. She fucked my friend, Sanders. *My business partner*, in *my own home*. In *your* bathroom! I gave her money, she's gone. It's done, it's over. Drop it," he snapped. Sanders took a deep breath.

"Are you saying you will not go after her? Not even, at the very least, to ensure her safety?" he asked. Jameson glared at him.

"Your are skating perilously close to the edge," he hissed. Sanders stood up straighter.

"Then consider this my notice, sir," he stated.

The shocking just did not stop.

"You can't mean that," Jameson actually laughed. Sanders refused to look at him.

"Effective immediately. I will clean out my stuff and be gone within the hour," he said. Jameson jumped up.

"I am practically family! You barely know her! You've known me for ... *for forever!*" he shouted.

"I do not wish to be employed by a man of your caliber, sir. I find it beneath me," Sanders replied.

She really got to him.

"If you really feel that way, Sanders, then fine. Go. I wish you all the best. This job will not be waiting for you," Jameson attempted to call his bluff.

"Pardon me, sir, but *I* will not be waiting for *it*," Sanders said, then hurried from the room. Jameson blinked after him, then picked up a heavy crystal tumbler. Threw it at the wall as hard as he could. Watched it explode everywhere.

Well goddamn, no one knows how to fuck something up quite like I do ...

17

TATUM WASN'T SURE HOW SHE did it, but she made it all the way back to Boston without crashing, and without getting arrested.

She couldn't figure out why she was so upset. She had drunken enough to knock out a sailor. The two xanax had been no help, either. She struggled to open the pill bottle while she drove, swerving all over the road. She knocked five more pills into her mouth, then chugged some more whiskey. When she looked into the bottle and saw that there were only four pills left, she figured what the hell. Anything to make the pain stop. The empty bottle went out the window. Then when she was right outside the city limits, she picked up her phone. Called the only person she could think of; the only person she wanted to talk to, ever again.

"I'm so glad you called, sweetie. I'm sorry for everything I said —," Ang began gushing the minute he answered the phone. She let out a loud sob and he stopped.

"I can't, Ang. I just can't. I need you so much," Tate cried.

"What's wrong? Where are you?" he demanded.

"I don't know, I don't know where I am. What am I doing!? He was so horrible, Ang. So horrible. And she was so beautiful," she sobbed, coughing and hiccuping.

"Jesus, you sound really drunk, Tate. How much have you had?" he asked.

"Oh, no no no, not enough. Not nearly enough," she said, her breath hitching.

"Where are you, right now?" he asked again.

"I'm such a horrible person, Ang. I did the worst thing," she whispered, her words starting to slur. The road was definitely getting blurrier.

"Oh god, what did you do?" he gasped.

"I didn't want to do it. I just wanted him to bleed a little. I don't think he has any blood. Does Satan bleed?" she asked, her mind starting to settle. Like a fog. She swerved across a lane and a car honked at her. She jerked the wheel back.

"Jesus christ, Tate, are you *driving!?*" Ang shouted at her. She hummed into the phone.

"*I'm flying,*" she whispered.

"*Shit.* Pull over, *right now,* I'm coming to get you. Tell me where you are," he demanded. She shook her head.

"Don't waste your time on me. I don't have a watch," she laughed.

"What the fuck are you going on about!? You're scaring me right now, stop it. *Stop the car!*" he ordered. She shook her head violently back and forth, then saw two of everything.

"I can't. I'm so dirty. He made me filthy. I have to wash him away. I have to get clean. I'm gonna go get clean. Clean, clean, clean, clean," she began to sing softly, then she dropped the phone. It hit the edge of the door and skittered out the open window, carrying Ang's screaming voice out onto the road.

A long time ago, on one of their jaunts through the city, she and Ang had discovered a swimming pool. In a nicer neighborhood, Olympic sized. Beautiful. But expensive entrance fees. Fuck that.

They had found a basement window that would open if someone wiggled it the right way. All Tate could focus on was getting to that pool. She parked the car – or at least she was pretty sure she parked it – and managed to get the window open, no problem. Dropping down was another issue. She was pretty sure her ankle was sprained.

She hobbled to the pool. Large windows lined the top of the building, flooding the room with light from the parking lot. Everything had an eerie, silver glow to it. She walked around the tiled edge, taking off pieces of clothing. When she was down to her bra and underwear, she stepped down into the shallow end. Waded deeper, and then laid on her back. Floated off into outer space, the bottle of Jack Daniel's still in one hand, floating along next to her. She stared at the ceiling.

See? This is nice. Still and quiet. That's all I ever wanted.

18

ANG STOLE HIS ROOMMATE'S CAR to get to Beacon Hill. He couldn't be positive where she was, but she had babbled on and on about wanting to get clean, so he had an idea. When he saw a Bentley parked sideways on a grass meridian, he knew he had guessed right. He leapt out of his car, not even bothering to shut it off. Banged on the front doors of the building, hoping to rattle a security guard. Nothing.

He ran around to the back, didn't even bother with wiggling the window. He kicked it completely in and then dropped into the basement. He ran through the room, then up two flights of stairs. Found a high heel at the top. Barreled into the dividing areas between the locker rooms. Found another high heel. He rushed through the female locker room first, praying she was in there, just passed out or puking. No such luck. He burst into the main pool area.

There was a trail of stockings and a belt and a dress leading to the side of the pool. He ran along the edge and then didn't even think about it, just jumped. She wasn't in very deep water, it only came up to his chest. Tate was floating on her back, her arms stretched out to the sides, legs dipping down a little into the water. A Jack Daniel's bottle floated nearby. Ang pushed his way over to her, grabbed her under her arms. She was only wearing a bra and panties, and her skin was freezing to the touch. The water wasn't heated at night.

"God, Tate, what did you do!?" he shouted, cupping one hand under her jaw and looking down at her. Her chocolate eyes rolled towards him. Didn't quite focus. Looked over his shoulder. Around the room. At the ceiling. Her pupils were *huge*, swallowing her irises. She looked possessed.

Goddamn Satan.

"I'm good," she mumbled. He began dragging her towards the edge.

"You are so not good. This is so, so, *so not good,*" he groaned. She sighed and her eyes fluttered close.

"I'm good, Ang. I'm good," she whispered.

He lifted her out of the pool and then climbed out after her. Whipped his jacket off and shoved it under her head, propping her up. He called her name, but she didn't open her eyes. He slapped her across the face. Still no reaction. He really started to panic.

Without a second thought, Ang opened her mouth and shoved two of his fingers down her throat. It didn't work the first time, but the second time he really jammed them down there. She heaved forward, rolling to the side as she vomited all over his hand and the floor.

"God, thank god, that's it. Get it all up," Ang urged, rubbing her back. She sobbed and puked again. It was all liquid. Copious amounts of amber liquid.

Christ, how much did she drink!?

She finally fell back against him, crying. Her makeup was everywhere, streaming down her face. She was shivering, her whole body trembling. He looked down at her, wiping her hair off of her face. He had never seen Tate like that before, so broken down. It hurt his heart.

"I'm sorry," she sobbed, reaching one hand up and grabbing onto his shirt. "I'm so sorry. I'm sorry I'm such a waste. Such a waste of time. I'm so sorry."

"Stop it! Stop saying that! You are worth every minute I have ever spent with you! *More* than that!" he yelled back at her. Her eyes finally found his and she smiled. Actually smiled at him.

"*Ang.* Why couldn't it have been you?" she whispered, her hand coming up to rest on his cheek.

"I don't know, baby. I wish it had," he whispered back.

Tate nodded and closed her eyes. Her hand fell away. It looked like she was sleeping. Even soaking wet and covered in makeup, she was still beautiful. She had a beautiful soul, it shined through everything she did – he just wished she could see it.

Her shivering cranked up, grew more violent. Ang decided it was maybe time to take her somewhere warmer, and he attempted to pick her up. But her shivering turned into something else. Her whole body was shaking; he couldn't quite get a hold on her.

When he looked back at her face, her eyelids were fluttering up and down. All he could see were the whites of her eyes. Liquid was streaming out of her mouth. She was having a seizure, thrashing around so violently, he thought she was going to break her arm, or leg. *Or neck.* He started screaming, gripping onto her shoulders as tight as he could.

"*SOMEBODY HELP US!*"

Acknowledgements

So to be 100% honest, this story started out as a joke. No, literally. I wrote several stories before this one, and had read a lot of romance novels, and I follow a lot of book blogs, and I started noticing some trends. I told a friend of mine, "to write these stories, there are a couple key ingredients – and one thing you obviously need is a certain kind of Alpha name."

I prattled off some very well known Alphas from the literary world, and we noticed that a lot of these gentlemen had very distinct, usually unique, usually long, first names, and then very short, concise last names. I don't wanna name names, but for example, *Christopher Prey*, kinda encapsulates what we had noticed.

"So what name would you pick?" I was asked. I'm not sure where it came from, I work around liquor, so maybe Jameson just leapt out at me – thus, Jameson Kane was born. Fits the above formula to a T.

We kinda laughed about it, and I didn't think about it much, till the same friend one day went "what would Jameson's story be?" And I kinda joked that every Alpha needs that spunky, sassy, female lead, who should also have a funky name, usually kinda androgynous. Hello, Tatum! I laughed that she would be sexy and crazy, he would be dark and sensual, they would compliment each other, and complete each other.

The story exploded after that, just came together like it had been sitting in my brain, completely written, waiting to be noticed. I wrote it in a frenzy. Couldn't sleep, didn't eat much, barely left the computer. It just would not stop, it demanded to be released. I put other stories on hold to let it out. So thanks have to go to my close friends for letting me joke about romance novels with them.

DEGRADATION

I have never written a story like this – the language, the sex, the aggression, it all kinda scared me. I am not very much like either Jameson or Tatum in real life. But it just felt natural. I found myself getting nervous and changing sentences, rearranging scenes, and then I came upon this awesome meme that read — "Write in a Way That Scares You a Little".

Well, the scariest thing to me is the idea of someone reading my work and going "ew, that's weird!", so I decided FUCK IT. I'm gonna write it EXACTLY how it comes out of my brain, EXACTLY how it comes out of Jameson's mouth, and if people don't like it, then they don't have to read it. It was the best decision I have ever made, writing this story was such a catharsis, such a joy. It sounds cheesy, but it's the truth. So thanks internet!

And a special thanks to all the authors out there writing dark, taboo, misunderstood stories. It is my firm belief that if it exists in the world, then it should be written about, regardless of "subject matter". As Real Sex on HBO taught me (does that show my age!?), if someone can be into something, then there is an audience for it! So read what you want, write what's in you to write, and fuck anyone who gives you crap about it. I can't imagine a bigger waste of time than criticizing someone's work just because it scares me.

And to my beta readers – I really lucked out with some excellent ones! They are from all over, the U.S. to the U.K., and I have never met any of them in real life, but they were wonderful throughout this whole process. Your feedback and constructive criticism were all appreciated beyond words. Thank you all so much. Some of these lovely ladies are: Cassie Fite – thanks for taking a chance on a "dark read", I honestly didn't know it was dark when I wrote it! Erin Winer – my bestie convinced you to read it, and thanks for doing so. Viveca Benoir, another indie author I found along the way, your help was amazing, you introduced me to my cover designer, and told me about Draft 2 Digital. Everyone, check her out at: http://vivecabenoir.com

Special shout-out to author L.A. Cotton – we met via a beta reading forum. She was looking for a beta reader, and was willing to trade (that's right! You never know who is beta reading for you – I keep hoping I'll submit a book to a beta reader and it'll be like CJ Roberts or something … seriously, I love you CJ Roberts, if you have secretly read my work, please tell me! Just let me love you!).

So Mrs. Cotton and I swapped stories. She is from the U.K., I'm from the U.S., and we had two very different stories, and two very different writing styles. Her book was softer, new adult, all romance and slow burn and *"will they? won't they?"* goodness. I worried that my book wasn't exactly up her alley, seeing as how Erotica and New Adult Romance are pretty far apart on the spectrum, but her feedback and advice were invaluable, her turn around time fast. She has continued to support me and promote me, and I can only hope to adequately return the favor some day. Thanks for all your help!

Too many blogs to name. From the beginning – for both of us! — Watz Teasers and Trailers was BEYOND supportive. Thank you to Cover To Cover Book Blog, Triple B's Badass Book Boyfriends, Intellectual Vixens, Through the Booking Glass, Fallen for Books, Trina and Taylor's Bedtime Stories – all willing to take a chance on a new indie author, and most of you holding her hand along the way.

To Najla Qamber, www.najlaqamberdesigns.com, the wonderful woman who designed my book cover. To be honest, I pretty much fan-girled every time you e-mailed me. I ran around for days going "do you see this!?!? All the cool book covers that I already love!?!? That chick is doing MY cover!" There was a huge time difference between us, and I'm pretty sure I sent you like three e-mails for every one you sent me, but you were so easy to work with, you got my vision and concept right away, and did an amazing job. Thank you so much.

Of course there are a million other people. Thanks to my husband, for being very understanding about me working 8 hours a day, then coming home and sitting behind a computer for another 6+ hours. Thanks to all my friends – none of you are into romance novels, but some of you offered to read it anyway, and all of you listened to me blabber on about it endlessly. Thanks to my real life job, for tolerating my daydreaming, sneaking into dark corners to read, and stretching my lunches well past their time limits so I could write more. Thanks to everyone who has already read it, is going to read it, or plans to eventually read it.

But mostly, thanks to anyone who has read this far and plans on reading the rest of Jameson and Tate's story.

About the Author

Crazy woman living in an undisclosed location in Alaska (where the need for a creative mind is a necessity!), I have been writing since …, forever? Yeah, that sounds about right. I have been told that I remind people of Lucille Ball — I also see shades of Jennifer Saunders, and Denis Leary. So basically, I laugh a lot, I'm clumsy a lot, and I say the F-word A LOT.

I like dogs more than I like most people, and I don't trust anyone who doesn't drink. No, I do not live in an igloo, and no, the sun does not set for six months out of the year, there's your Alaska lesson for the day. I have mermaid hair - both a curse and a blessing - and most of the time I talk so fast, even I can't understand me.

Yeah. I think that about sums me up.